THE
OUTLAW
NOBLE SALT

A Novel

AMY HARMON

LAKE UNION
PUBLISHING

Published by Lake Union Publishing, Seattle

www.apub.com

Amazon, the Amazon logo, and Lake Union Publishing are trademarks of Amazon. com, Inc., or its affiliates.

ISBN-13: 9781662514456 (paperback)
ISBN-13: 9781662514449 (digital)

Cover design by Caroline Teagle Johnson

Cover image: © Stephen Mulcahey, Wayne Greer / Arcangel;
©MagicPics, Vlad Georgescu / Getty

Printed in the United States of America

This is the tall tale
Of the outlaw Noble Salt
And Butch Cassidy

November 1908

At half past seven, Augustus Toussaint unfolded the newspaper carefully, just like he did every morning, organizing the sections into most favorite and least favorite. The ink was so fresh the scent made his head hurt, and the edge of the page nicked his finger, drawing a dot of blood that marked his progress as he first scanned the headlines, checked the market the way Noble had taught him to do, and finally bounced through the obituaries. He wasn't interested in death so much as the stories that filled the macabre squares. People were fascinating.

He turned to the Society section next, another favorite page, though he wouldn't admit it out loud. He'd met a few of the people regularly discussed, and he liked to read the impressions of the columnists. At the top of the section, he found a glowing review of his mother's performance at Saltair. The comparisons of his maman to Jenny Lind were typical, though the writer preferred Jane Toussaint and her "less theatrical style."

His favorite paragraph was this: "Having heard Miss Toussaint many years ago at Carnegie Hall, I find her truly remarkable voice has become only more impressive with time, but it was the deep feeling and musical expression in her performance that was the most notable improvement. The little songbird has become a soprano of the first water, and her rendition of 'Waly, Waly' brought this critic to tears."

Maman would like that part too, though she would insist that no one was as good as Jenny Lind.

The article that stopped his heart was just below the fold on page ten. Not front-page news. Not even second. It took up a section no bigger than the palm of his hand. He'd missed it on his initial perusal; that section of the paper was often his last look before tossing it aside. But the headline was all in caps:

AMERICAN OUTLAWS KILLED IN BOLIVIAN SHOOT-OUT

His eyes raced and then slowed, reading the words in disjointed, haphazard denial before he made himself go from the top and start again.

> *San Vicente*—Bolivian authorities near San Vicente are reporting that on November 6, 1908, they engaged in a shoot-out with two men thought to be famed outlaws Butch Cassidy, born Robert LeRoy Parker, and Harry Alonzo Longabaugh, also known as the Sundance Kid.

> The fugitives are believed to be responsible for the armed robbery of a mining company's payroll courier and were seen in possession of the courier's mule. Local authorities contacted a small unit of the Bolivian cavalry stationed nearby who rapidly moved in and surrounded the adobe hut where the two men were staying. Sustained gunfire was exchanged, and after a period of quiet and repeated unanswered demands for surrender, authorities moved in and found the two men deceased.

> Longabaugh sustained several bullet wounds in his arms and one to his head. Cassidy was found in the

adjoining room, dead from a shot to his temple, a revolver still in his hand. The wound was believed to be
self-inflicted.

The Pinkerton National Detective Agency had been
tracking the two wanted men, charged with a decade's
worth of bank holdups and train robberies throughout
the West, for many years.

A recent tip convinced Pinkerton agents to distribute
the outlaws' photos and criminal histories throughout
Bolivia. Officials are convinced they have successfully brought two armed and dangerous men to justice.
Pinkerton president Robert Pinkerton issued this statement with the agency's report:

"Cassidy was the shrewdest, most daring outlaw of the
present age, and I am relieved to have this era brought
to an end. These were not good men. They were not
heroes. They plundered, terrorized, and killed, and this
country, and every other country, will be better off
now that they are gone. They will not be mourned."

Augustus stood, crumpling the paper to his chest so he wouldn't
have to read it again. His chair clattered behind him, and when he
moved away from the table, his vision blurred and swam, making him
trip and fall to his knees. He would hide the article before his mother
saw it. He would burn it, and she would never know. Or at least . . .
she wouldn't know today.

"Augustus?" His mother spoke from the door. "Did you hurt
yourself?"

He wiped at his nose with his sleeve and blinked the tears from
his eyes, clearing his vision, but they kept falling. He stood, and with

hurried steps and shaking hands, opened the door on the kitchen stove and shoved the newspaper inside.

They *would* be mourned. They would be mourned terribly.

"Augustus?" Maman's voice had taken on a note of alarm, but he could not reassure her. He could do nothing but watch the flame consume the page and ache to be the Augustus Toussaint of half past seven.

The world would not be
Better now that they were gone
Not better at all

1

Do you know my name?
Perhaps you should forget it
I'm a wanted man

September 1900

Orlando Powers had an unexpected visitor Thursday morning. He was alone in his office in Salt Lake City, sitting by the window that gave him a view of the Mormon temple at the city center. Weston Woodruff, his earnest clerk, had just stepped out on an errand, and the lingering summer heat had already coaxed the judge out of his coat and loosened his buttons, though it was barely ten o'clock.

He heard the door open and someone step across the threshold into the foyer, but his office door was closed, and he considered pretending he wasn't there. No appointment was scheduled, and he had afternoon court to prepare for.

The outer door closed and locks were engaged, and Orlando rose, suddenly afraid, suddenly cold. He yanked his coat from the hook and nervously made sure the buttons were secured. Most of his clients were of the harmless variety, but he'd represented his share of the dangerous and despicable.

"Mr. Powers? I'd like a moment of your time," a voice said beyond the door, a voice that brooked no doubt that Powers was inside, scrambling. With a deep breath, Powers bade the man enter, but he kept a hand on his loaded gun. Times were changing, but the West was still wild.

Afterward, Orlando would conclude that the outlaw had been watching the building, waiting for an opportunity to slip inside the establishment unannounced and unobserved, but he was immaculate in his gray summer suit and charcoal hat. No dust or sweat marred his handsome face or clung to his expensive clothes. If he'd been waiting long, he didn't look it. With a jolt, the judge realized who he was looking at.

"Do you know who I am, Mr. Powers?" The question was not issued as a threat or posed with any arrogance. The judge sensed the man wanted to avoid introducing himself if at all possible.

"Are you Butch Cassidy?" Orlando had seen the circular the Pinkertons had sent out and posted in every public establishment in the city, and though they'd never met, he'd represented a few of Cassidy's associates. According to those clients, all the bills had been paid by the man in front of him.

Orlando stuck out his hand to indicate the chair across his desk, and the man, who hadn't confirmed or denied he was the outlaw in question, removed his hat. Not a slicked-back hair was out of place, but it was a little long and sun-streaked at the tips, the first indication he might not be a man of business or leisure. Still, his cheeks were clean-shaven, and there was no dirt under his carefully buffed nails. He'd obviously prepared for the visit, and the judge spent a brief moment contemplating where he was staying. Salt Lake City was thick with tattletales and Goody Two-Shoes.

"I heard they made you a judge," Cassidy said.

"That's right. I was sworn in a month ago."

"Does that mean you don't take cases anymore?"

"I have an associate. He'll help where there's a conflict of interest. But all my old cases and clients are still mine. I'm still an attorney."

"I might want to retain you," Cassidy said, still standing.

"For what?" Powers didn't want to agree to anything yet.

"I won't know until we talk. But it won't take us more than half an hour. Do you have time, Mr. Powers?"

"I do."

Cassidy took five dollars from his billfold. "Will that cover a confidential conversation?"

"It will."

"You don't need me to sign anything?"

"We're just talking."

"Confidentially."

"That's right," Powers agreed. The outlaw sat down, and for the first time, the judge removed his hand from his holster.

Cassidy didn't dance around the truth or linger on small talk. He'd clearly thought about what he was going to say, and he did so succinctly.

"I want to turn myself in."

Powers felt his jaw drop, and Cassidy waited for him to collect himself, not adding to his surprising statement, not rushing to elucidate.

"Wh-why?" Powers stammered.

"I'm tired. I want to be left alone, and I'd like to have a different life than the one I've lived. It's a new century. 'When I was a child, I spoke as a child, I understood as a child, I thought as a child. Now that I have become an adult, I have put away childish things.'"

Orlando Powers felt his jaw go slack again. Plenty of folks quoted scripture in Utah. Religion built the state, after all. But Butch Cassidy quoting Corinthians was almost as surprising as him wanting to turn himself in.

"You find Jesus, Mr. Cassidy?"

"No, sir. But I haven't been lookin' very hard."

"So you want to turn yourself in. You don't need a lawyer for that. You can just walk into the sheriff's office—it isn't far—and tell them who you are. They'll take it from there . . . though I wouldn't recommend that. Your life won't just be different. It'll be over."

"That's where you come in," Cassidy explained. "I want to see their evidence. I want to make them prove their case against me. I don't think they can. I haven't hurt anyone; I've protected more folks than I've stolen from. I've taken from the big moneymen at the top, who can afford to spread the offering a little thicker but never do. I take from the companies with insurance and protections, from the folks who get paid whether the train gets robbed or not."

"That is your reputation," Powers agreed. "But only the regular folks are admirers of Robin Hood. The rich, not so much. You've cost them, and you've inspired other men to do the same. You're famous. You're in the dimes. Did you know that? I caught my son reading a whole stack of them just last week. He runs down the street with a kerchief wrapped around his face, waving a stick like it's a rifle. He wants me to call him Kid Powers."

"The dimes?" Butch Cassidy's face was blank.

"Yeah. You know. Dime novels. The cheap paper books they sell with the frontier dailies at every general store in the country. *The Adventures of Billy the Kid, Wyatt Earp and the Cowboys, Annie Oakley and Buffalo Bill.*"

"I don't read much anymore," Cassidy said quietly, like he hadn't just quoted the Bible, but a deep red stain was crawling up his neck. He cleared his throat and took a small book from his vest pocket. He opened it carefully, placing it on the desk between them. "I don't write much either, but these are the things I'm accused of, far as I can tell. I've made a list. Maybe you could inquire whether there's more. I've put a mark by the ones I know nothing about."

He slid the book toward Powers. The writing was neat, the letters all in caps, and the list stretched down both pages and onto the next. A small check was placed next to most of the lines. Powers studied it for a moment. A few things jumped out at him, train robberies he'd heard about and bank holdups from Winnemucca to Santa Fe. Cassidy had written places and dates on some of them. On others there were no details at all.

"And the lines without a check mark?" he asked the outlaw.

"I might know something about those."

"You served time in the penitentiary for stealing a horse in Wyoming, didn't you? That isn't on here."

"Eighteen months. But I didn't steal that horse."

"What happened?"

"The range wars happened. The big cattlemen in Wyoming want all the homesteaders and the smaller outfits gone. I worked for a rancher they didn't like, got pulled into something I wanted no part of. I got in the way, and they said I was in possession of a stolen horse even though I bought him fair and square. They paid people off, and I went to jail."

"And Telluride . . . that was your first bank job, wasn't it? Even before you stole the horse—"

"I didn't steal that horse."

"Authorities say you got away with twenty thousand dollars from the San Miguel Valley Bank."

"That line doesn't have a check mark beside it, Mr. Powers." Cassidy tapped the paper.

"So that much is true?"

Butch Cassidy met his gaze, unflinching, but didn't answer his question. It was a good thing the wanted circulars weren't in color, because the blue of his eyes was undisguisable.

"Like I said, Mr. Powers, I don't think they can prove it. Or anything else. Most of the things I've been accused of I didn't do. Everything is being blamed on Butch Cassidy and the Wild Bunch, but I sure as hell haven't received a cut of the spoils, and the Wild Bunch is no longer a . . . bunch."

"Ellsworth 'Elzy' Lay killed a sheriff in Folsom after robbing a train. He was one of yours, wasn't he?"

"I had no part in that."

"That sheriff left behind a wife and two young children. Mr. Lay is in jail for the rest of his life."

Cassidy flinched, though Powers wasn't sure if his compassion was for the widow or his imprisoned compadre. Maybe it was both.

"I had no part in that," Cassidy repeated, and Orlando Powers found he believed him, though it made no difference.

"It doesn't matter, Mr. Cassidy," he said, grim but apologetic.

Butch Cassidy cocked his head, waiting for him to continue.

"It doesn't matter what you did or didn't do. You could be as innocent as Jesus Christ himself, and it wouldn't matter. The railroad will make you pay. Just like those cattlemen did."

"Why?" Cassidy asked. The lawyer judged him to be in his early thirties, but that single, plaintive word made him sound like a boy.

"To make an example of you. You're thought to be the brains of the operation. The leader. They'll take you down to discourage anyone else from doing the things you've done. To take away that outlaw, dime-novel shine. You don't rob the trains or the mines or the banks and get away with it. You'll go down. It'll be just like the trial in Wyoming for a five-dollar horse. They'll find someone—lots of someones—who will say they saw you with Elzy Lay in New Mexico, robbing that train and shooting at that sheriff. There was a robbery on the line near the promontory yesterday. The entire passenger train was stripped of their valuables, and I've already heard accounts that it was you and the Sundance Kid."

"It wasn't."

"No?"

"Not my style. And I wouldn't be here now, would I?"

"It doesn't matter," Powers said again. "If you turn yourself in and try to make your case, they'll create whatever evidence they need. And there will be nothing I can do to save you."

Butch Cassidy was quiet for a long time, staring at the wall, processing, and Powers was again struck by his eyes. Deep set and wide, they turned down into his cheekbones at the edges, like half-moons over distant hills. Dark lashes, thick and spiked, created a dramatic fringe above them. His square face was tanned, making his eyes all the brighter and his teeth, when he spoke, all the whiter. He would have to change his appearance or go somewhere far away to have any chance of staying out of prison or avoiding the end of a rope.

Finally Cassidy nodded. There was no anger and no apparent bitterness, though his shoulders slumped slightly as if the weight of his years had just become significantly greater.

"You'll keep on my brother's case? He's too young for the time they gave him. He's been locked up long enough."

"I will. I'll get Van out. I've been working on it, but staying out will be up to him."

"You did good work for Matt Warner," Cassidy said, nodding. "I appreciate that."

"Matt Warner is a no-good, two-bit, wife-beating lowlife. Van isn't any better. I represented him to the best of my ability because you paid me and it's my job, but he deserved the time he got, and you'd be wise to stay away from him or any of his ilk."

"I *am* his ilk."

"No, Mr. Cassidy. I don't think you are. But like I said, it doesn't really matter. They will take you down if you give them the chance, whether you deserve it or not."

"You could take my money, defend me, and if I go down, it's no skin off your hide. Why not do that?"

"I'm telling you what will happen. I'm giving it to you as straight as I can. I'm a lawyer, but I try not to be a liar."

Butch Cassidy smiled at that, surprising Powers again. "And I'm an outlaw, but I try not to be a crook."

"Fine lines we're both walking."

"Yes, sir. And I appreciate you saying it straight." Cassidy sat quietly for a moment, subdued, thoughtful, and then he raised his gaze. "I guess I won't be turning myself in then."

"I think that's best." The attorney slid the little book back toward Cassidy, and the man tucked it inside his breast pocket.

"You won't tell anyone I was here?" Cassidy asked, voice still soft.

"I won't tell anyone you were here," he agreed. "You made sure I was well compensated for the Warner case and for every other case you've sent my way. You came here in good faith, and as your lawyer—even in this brief capacity—you are entitled to my complete discretion."

Cassidy stared at him for a long moment, as if assessing the veracity of his claim, and strangely, Orlando Powers fought the urge to squirm. Cassidy was rumored to be clever and charismatic, planning every heist to the last detail, but his quiet dignity was a surprise. He was not simply the broad-faced, friendly farm boy with nine lives he was often made out to be.

"If you were me . . . what would you do, Mr. Powers?"

"You've got plenty of money?"

"I've got plenty of money. But I'd like more."

"If I were you, I'd go. Far away. See the world. Shake the West from your boots. You run too long with bad men, you become one, no matter how much scripture you quote or how much good you try to do. You've been running with bad men for too long, Mr. Cassidy, and it's going to catch up to you. Leave, and don't come back. And stop robbing banks and trains."

Butch Cassidy stared at him for several excruciating heartbeats and then said slowly, "There's one more thing."

"What's that?"

"Mr. E. H. Harriman wants to meet me. Wants to offer me a job protecting his trains. He sent word through a friend of mine, an attorney, Doug Preston. He represented me in Wyoming, and he knows I want out."

"Harriman?" Powers gasped. "Why didn't you tell me that, first thing?"

"I figured they were two different matters. I got your opinion on the one. Now I'd like it on the other."

Orlando Powers fell back in his chair and steepled his hands beneath his slack jaw. He had no idea what to make of this new revelation. Edward Harriman, a New York railroad magnate, owned the

Union Pacific and the Southern Pacific railroads, and his control of all the lines out West had begun to cause rumblings in government circles about breaking up his monopoly.

"Why would Harriman want to hire me?" Butch Cassidy asked softly. "He's got more money and power than almost any man in America. I'm guessing it's a trap, but I'm intrigued, all the same."

Powers nodded, but his wheels were turning. "Maybe he figures paying you is cheaper than hiring a dozen Pinkertons to bring you down. Harriman isn't a fool, and right now he's got his own problems with the powers that be."

"Mr. Harriman isn't the law. He can't give me amnesty . . . can he?"

"It's like I told you. They can do whatever they want. They're his trains you're wanted for robbing. I suppose he can drop charges. He and Governor Wells are good friends."

Cassidy remained a moment more, his eyes on his boots, his hands on his knees. Then he stood. He wasn't overly tall, but he was powerfully built with a flat torso and thick legs wrapped in a well-cut suit vest and slim-fitting trousers. He was not a man one would ignore, which made him all the more conspicuous. Powers wondered again where he'd come from and where he would go.

"Can you talk to Governor Wells? See if it's even possible? I need to know that much before I proceed."

"I'll do my best. How will I contact you when I know?"

"I'll be back." Cassidy put on his hat, a neat little derby that made him look like a businessman instead of a cowboy. Then he walked from the room, hands in his pockets, and Orlando Powers hoped for Butch Cassidy's sake that he would never see him again.

2

Tick tock, damn it all
I don't want to die today
Why am I still here?

Butch waited all day at the location he'd been given. He trusted
Orlando Powers as well as he trusted anyone. The man had always
done exactly what he said he'd do, but it was dangerous to trust.
People were flawed, but mostly they were just . . . torn. Nobody really
knew what was right or wrong in these matters. The wrestle between
what was fair and what was lawful, what was merciful and what was
good was a universal one. He couldn't unravel it himself half the
time. He'd been blinded by outrage and shocked awake by shame
more times than he could count. Sometimes in the same moment.
Men were greedy and guilty and so selfish he was embarrassed by
his own humanity. Everything made sense and nothing made sense.
Everything was clear and nothing was clear, but it was becoming
clearer by the second that he'd been set up.

He'd left home in '85 convinced that if he was ever going to have
anything in this life, he was just going to have to take it. Oh, he'd ratio-
nalized the taking. He'd told himself that he'd share, and he'd ease the
burdens of those who deserved more but were too intimidated to take
it themselves. Now here he was, thirty-four years old, with nothing to

show for his life but a ticking clock. He snapped open his timepiece and shut it again for the umpteenth time.

He'd come a day early to scope the place out. That was his way. It was always better to see what was coming than to be observed. Still, his skin had crawled since arriving at the abandoned stagecoach station. His senses were jumping, and it had been all he could do to just wait, circling the forlorn shack, searching the terrain for signs of Harriman's approach.

He'd left his affairs in order. Sundance and Ethel had their tickets and plenty of money—the bills would be untraceable out of the country. Most people didn't care anyway; it was safer not to ask. Nobody checked the serial numbers except the banks, and half the time they didn't check them either. They didn't want to know, they just wanted the money, but the boys had never deposited their loot.

Van was on his way home. Powers had secured his release. Butch could do nothing for the rest of the gang, though Powers had promised to keep an eye on Elzy's situation. Once Butch had made up his mind, he'd ridden from Salt Lake to Circleville with his saddlebags full of money.

He'd hobbled his horse half a mile from the homestead and let her graze and rest, and he'd walked the rest of the way in the moonlight, the money over his shoulder and tears on his cheeks. If he tried to give it to them directly, they'd have to refuse it. They knew how he made his money. But maybe they'd take his offering if it came indirectly, if he just left it where they could find it, no explanations. He wanted them to have it, especially his mother. She deserved a comfortable home with a porch to rock away her sorrows. A place where she could look out over the valley they both loved and sing her favorite song.

> *O waly, waly, love be bonnie,*
> *And bright as a jewel while it is new.*
> *But when 'tis auld, it waxeth cold,*
> *And fades away like morning dew.*

He knew all the verses, the ship that sank and the oak that broke, and the love that "me forsook." Ma said the words were so old they'd been rearranged by every singer in every generation, but it helped her remember the people she'd come from and the journey she'd made across the water and the plains.

"You come from strong, good stock, Robert LeRoy Parker," she'd always said, trying to convince them both. "Those blue eyes are not yours. They're my eyes, and my daddy's eyes, and his daddy's eyes. They're Gillies eyes. All the way back to the beginning, whenever that might have been. Don't let those blue eyes fade away like morning dew."

That was her way of telling him to find a good girl and settle down and have children. He hadn't done that. Ma's blue eyes would continue, but not with him. Ann Campbell Gillies Parker had twelve other children who could give her grandbabies.

He'd allowed himself a few deep breaths of sage and mountain air, left a bag full of the cash in the barn where his dad wouldn't miss it, and hid a roll of bills in Ma's watering can, inside her soiled gloves. Ma would take the money.

Then he'd walked back to his hobbled horse, never announcing his visit, and headed north. It was better that way. His presence would only bring them harm and cause them grief.

Ma's song had followed him every step of the way. *O waly, waly. Love be bonnie.*

"What's 'waly, waly,' Ma?" he'd asked her, long ago.

"Wailing, wailing," she answered. "Wailing is what you do when grief and regret are so big, tears are not enough."

"Like the wailing and gnashing of teeth in the Bible?"

"I suppose. But 'waly, waly' is more about hurt than wickedness. About loving and being let down."

He'd learned the song on his harmonica and played it for Ma on her birthday the year he left home. She'd cried and asked for him to do it again, over and over, until Pa had threatened to ban "Waly, Waly" forever.

"I hate that song too," Van had said. "I never understood it. Wailing, wailing, wailing. All the damn day."

The fact that Van didn't understand it was telling.

Butch whistled it now, though he shouldn't, and the words played along in his head.

When cockleshells turn into silvery bells
Then will my love
Return to me.
When roses grow in the wintry snow
Then will my love
Return to me.

The first sign of approach came halfway through the day, but the rider came from the wrong direction, and he was alone. The knot in Butch's stomach formed a noose, and his anticipation became awful dread.

"Oh no. No, no, no," he groaned. He knew the rider, and he knew what his presence meant.

"Hey oh! Brother . . . I'm comin' in." Van put his hands in the air, bouncing in the saddle like they did when they were boys, arms wide open, holding on with their thighs.

Panicked, Butch swept his field glass in a circle, searching for any signs of Harriman and Preston, and anyone else they might bring along. It was a day's ride from Salt Lake, and the rains had caused some flooding, mucking up the roads. It was the only reason he'd waited as long as he had. He'd all but given up on them, and now he fervently hoped they would stay away.

A bit of movement smudged the eastern horizon and he watched it, his mind scrambling.

It would be them, and it would be now. He allowed himself to wallow in the wave of anger and disappointment for the length of time it took Van to amble up on a horse only fit for the plow.

Van swung to the ground and clapped him up in a hearty embrace that, at one time, Butch would have returned. It would have immediately descended into wrestling each other to the ground. More often than not, Butch had let Van pin him, unconcerned with proving himself or besting his brother. For him it had been about fun and affection. For Van it had always been about something else.

They weren't boys anymore, and they hadn't been boys for decades.

"You don't look very happy to see me, Robert LeRoy. It's been at least ten years, and you don't look happy to see me!"

"I'm not, Van." He kept his voice kind, but honesty was the only good thing he'd ever given his brother, and he wouldn't start lying to him now.

"I've been following you for days. You went home and didn't even go inside. I saw you creeping in, but you didn't see me, did ya?" Van laughed merrily. He had aged, but he hadn't grown up at all.

"You were at the house?"

"I was up in the barn loft. Been staying there since I got out. I watched you put the bag of money in the straw. I took a little. I knew you wouldn't mind. Pa will know it's from you. So he'll know it's dirty. Probably won't spend any of it. Figured I might as well use it. I left some. Don't worry."

"You left some . . . or you took some? Which is it?"

"Both. I took some, and I left some."

"You took enough to get you started somewhere? Pay your rent, get some work?"

"Took more'n that."

Butch nodded, refusing to be goaded. Van had probably taken it all. Good thing he'd hidden another stash for his mother. It would do him no good to ask if Van had taken that too. If Van thought it would upset him, he'd tell him he had.

"I need you to go, Van. I've got a meetin' that you can't be a part of. I'm sorry. If you ride back toward town, I'll meet you there in a few hours, and we'll have dinner and some time for catching up."

"No, you won't. You'll cut out on me. Like you've always done. I told myself, now that I got him in my sights, he's not shaking me loose. Never again."

"I can't take care of you anymore."

"You never did, Butch."

He didn't bother to argue. Van had always loved and loathed him, no matter what he did or didn't do. It did no good to defend himself.

"Why are you here?" Van kicked at the side of the ramshackle station, and it bawled like a hungry cow. A plume of dust rose up, and for a moment, Butch thought the whole thing was going down. Van swore and danced away. "I figured the gang was all meetin' up, but you're alone. I want in, Butch, whatever yer doin'. And I'm not taking no for an answer. You look out for everyone else . . . but you never looked out for me."

"There's no gang, Van. Not anymore. Everyone's locked up or dead. Or they soon will be."

"You hit that train in Winnemucca. I heard about that. Knew it had to be you. Uncoupled the cars. Blew a hole in the express car. I said to myself . . . that's got to be Robert LeRoy, gettin' away clean with more money than he can spend. Who helped? Was Matt with you? McBride too?"

"Nah. Matt's trying to stay out of prison. McBride's dead."

"So you really need me now," Van crowed.

"You did your time. You're free. You can do anything you want to do. No running. No hiding. I've got men hunting me and will have until the day I die. You don't want to be anywhere near me."

"You need me. I followed you from Circleville. Two hundred miles I been following you, Robert LeRoy!"

"You always were good at finding me, little brother. Doing what nobody else could."

"So what are you doin' here, Butch?" he pressed again, looking around at the scrubby trees and the abandoned station.

"I'm trying to make a fresh start." In the barest of terms, he explained the job offer from Harriman.

"You can't be this stupid," Van groaned. "Not the great Butch Cassidy, the brains of the operation. The man who plans. The wiliest coyote in the West."

Butch didn't respond.

"You really think they aren't going to have US Marshals stretched out just over the next rise, sights set on you, waiting to take you in? Or maybe it'll be the Pinks. They don't feel the need to stick as close to the law as the marshals. They'll just kill you."

"Harriman signed an agreement. It was also signed by Governor Wells. Signed by Judge Powers too."

"And did you see this agreement?"

"That's what today's about. I'll see it. Read the agreement. And if it looks good—Orlando Powers said he'd advise me—then I'll sign it."

"And you'll be a lawman?" Van spit like the word tasted bad.

"No. I'll be a guard. On the trains. I'll work for Harriman directly."

"If he secured the amnesty, he'll own you. Heart and soul. You'll be his hired killer. His yes-man."

"But I'll be free. Like you are right now. And that's what I want."

Van shook his head in disgust. "Free to do what? Ride trains for the rest of your life? What'll you do when one of the Bunch, or maybe some of the boys from the old Hole-in-the-Wall Gang, decide they want to hit the train you're protecting? You gonna shoot your friends?"

"All my friends are dead or in jail, Van. You aren't listening."

"Well, I'm not dead or in jail. Maybe I'll hit one of your trains. You gonna kill your own flesh and blood?"

Butch was silent, studying the smudge that had now separated into distinct sections. Two buggies and half a dozen horses and riders approached.

"That'll be them, Van. If they see you here . . . they might get spooked. I said I'd come alone."

"Nah. I can't let you do it, Butch."

"Can't let me do what?"

Van was loading his rifle, smiling sadly like a parent telling a child, *This hurts me more than it hurts you*, when they were about to administer a walloping.

"This isn't your decision, Van. This isn't your call. I need you to get on that horse and head back the way you came."

"They're gonna kill you, Butch. And you here all alone." He shook his head. "I'm not going anywhere."

"Van. Look at me. I want this to work. I want to do this. It's my only way out. And if it's a double cross"—he shrugged—"well, then they saved me years of running."

"Shit. You're pathetic, brother," Van said, incredulous. "What's happened to you?"

"Remember how Mike Cassidy taught us how the Shoshone used to separate an animal from the herd and just run it in circles until it was begging to be put out of its misery? That's how this ends. I didn't understand that in the beginning. I let myself believe I could get away with it if I kept the scales balanced. If I did more good than harm. If I helped more than I hurt. But I don't think any of us get away with anything. Fate settles the score, and karma catches up."

"You and your scales. Ain't any angels at the pearly gates keeping track, Robert LeRoy. We've never been big church people. Isn't that what you told me? Churches are just about controlling people with the fear of God. If there is a God, I'd guess he's not too happy with all the assholes down here claiming to speak for him and declaring themselves prophets. I think you taught me that too. When did you get religious?"

"I'm not religious; I'm realistic."

"You're slippery. You always land on your feet. Look at you still. You haven't changed a bit, but you're talking like an old man. We're young."

Butch studied his brother's lined, sunburned face. His hair was dirty, his clothes worn, and his hat tipped back on his head like a stiff wind had caught it but, on second thought, decided to leave the cowboy alone.

Van didn't look good. He didn't look young, and Butch recognized himself in the deep-set blue eyes and unhappy gaze. Van had always been good-looking; the girls liked him until they realized his surliness wasn't a cover for anything sweet. He could be funny, but it was always at someone else's expense. He could be smart, but he used his wit for sarcasm. He could be loyal, but only when he didn't have a better offer, and Van never had a better offer. He'd used Butch's name both to threaten and ingratiate, until he'd ruined both their reputations. But he was Butch's brother, and there was no getting around it or beyond it. They'd grown up as thick as thieves. Butch had always feared they'd go down that way too.

He made out Orlando Powers and Governor Wells in the lead buggy. Harriman and another man were behind them, and several men on horses, their rifles drawn and bodies tense, ringed them.

"Why'd they pick all the way out here?" Van asked, making no attempt whatsoever to conceal his presence.

"I picked the spot. I know the terrain better than they do. I'll just disappear if something feels off."

"Yeah. You're good at that."

Butch let the insult bounce off his back, but acceptance had begun to settle on his shoulders. This wasn't going to happen.

Van snatched up his field glasses and studied the approaching group. "Which one's Harriman?"

"Round glasses. Teddy Roosevelt mustache."

"And the others?"

"Powers is the one who got you out of jail. Looks a little like a hound dog. I like him. He's real. No bullshit. You know Preston. He's on a horse. I don't know the man with Harriman. The man riding with Powers is Governor Wells."

Van whistled. "Fancy. You must think you're something special, Robert LeRoy." He was silent for a moment, studying, before he lowered the glass and pointed toward the approaching party.

"Go on then. Go out and meet your new friends, if that's what you're gonna do. I'll watch your back." He had a look on his face that Butch recognized well. The hair on Butch's arms stood upright, and the pit in his stomach had opened up to the gates of hell.

"I'll be up there. Go on," Van urged, a smirk around his mouth.

"Give me your rifle, Van."

"Now why would I do that?"

"No matter what happens, you aren't going to shoot. So you don't need a rifle. If you're nervous about protecting yourself, you head out as fast and far as you can."

"You think I'm gonna let them shoot you like a dog? You may not care about me, but I care about you. I'll be right there." He pointed to the small ledge that overlooked the stagehouse and the winding, mud-caked road.

"No. You stay right here. Where they can see you, and I can see you."

The party had slowed and stopped, and Orlando Powers stepped down from the buggy, handing the man beside him the reins. He waved both of his arms, and even from thirty yards, Butch could see the strain in his face.

"Put your rifle down, Van," Butch commanded. "Put it down at your feet real slow and careful. Intentional, so they know you can get it but aren't planning on using it."

Van sighed but did as he was told.

"And the one in your holster."

"You first, Robert LeRoy."

"I'm walking out there. I'll be taking mine."

Van shrugged off his duster and lifted the Colt .45 with the nickel handle, almost identical to Butch's, from the holster beneath his left arm. He made to set it down but stayed crouched over it, fingering it.

"Which one of those bastards—Harriman or Wells—is going to die today?" he mused, scratching at his cheek.

"That ain't funny, Van."

"Yes, it is."

"You're scaring them. Stand up," Butch hissed.

Van stood, chuckling, and pushed his hat back even farther on his head, if that was possible.

"Keep your hands up, nice and high, brother," Butch insisted.

"Go to hell," Van spat, his mirth gone. He folded his arms. Butch considered making him walk out with him, but abandoned the plan. He needed to speak freely.

"You gonna start something, Van?" he asked softly.

"Maybe I am."

Butch nodded, mentally flipping through his options. Orlando Powers supplied the best one.

"I'm coming to you, Mr. Cassidy," Powers called. Harriman and Wells hadn't even disembarked. That was good. The riders around them shifted in fear, hands on their weapons.

"I'll meet you halfway," Butch called back. "I'm armed, just like they are, but I'll keep my hands where you can see 'em."

"You're a fool, Robert LeRoy," Van muttered, but Butch started walking, more afraid of the man behind him than the men in front of him.

He *was* a fool. He was a fool for thinking he could shake free of his past. Any of it.

"This isn't going to work, Judge," he said when he reached Orlando Powers.

"Who is that?" Powers asked, jutting his chin toward Van. "Harriman's not happy. Wells is sweating and praying."

"That's my brother Van."

"Ah hell." Powers spat. "We just got him out. He's a dadgum loose cannon."

"Yes, sir. He is. You tell those men they aren't safe, and you all get headed back the way you came, just as quick as you can go."

"But the offer . . . I think this will be the last one you get."

"I know. What was it you said about running with bad men too long?"

"Yeah. That's what I thought." Powers sighed. "It's a damn shame too. Are you sure?"

"I'm sure. And thank you kindly for your trouble."

Orlando Powers shook his head, dumbfounded. "Son of a bitch," he groaned softly.

"Go on now. You earned every cent that I paid you. Thank Mr. Harriman and Governor Wells. I'm sorry to have wasted their time." It was a day's ride from Salt Lake City. They wouldn't be happy to have made it for nothing.

Orlando Powers turned, still shaking his head, and began picking his way back to his party. Butch didn't dare move. He kept his palms out, stance wide, and waited for Powers to climb back into the buggy and for the message to be relayed.

"Watch out, Butch!" Van yelled. "Get down. Get down!"

Butch didn't react.

He didn't even flinch.

If he pulled out his weapon, it was over, and they could say whatever the hell they wanted. If they were going to kill him, they weren't going to be able to say it was justified.

Someone swore, and Orlando Powers threw himself into the buggy as Wells snapped the reins, alarmed by the warning. The riders around the governor had drawn their weapons, and their horses were high-stepping, but they too held their fire.

Van began to laugh, hooting at the terror he'd caused, and both buggies shot forward, the party retreating mere minutes after they'd arrived. The riders followed in their wake, glancing back toward Butch until they were well out of range. Only then did Butch lower his hands and turn away. Van was standing where he'd left him, smiling at the rapid retreat.

"Well . . . that was fun." Van threw his head back and laughed again, and for a moment he looked like the boy he'd been, fearless and fun, just wanting to tag along, and Butch felt that same old tug of love and despair he'd always felt around his brother. Maybe it was because Van always came after him, and no one else had ever bothered. It was a twisted way of looking at it, Butch knew, but Van had always been strangely proud of him even when he was making his life miserable.

His dad had come to visit him once when Butch was in jail in Wyoming, but he'd come on Van's behalf. Van had tried to rob a federal mail coach. It hadn't gone well, and Butch had stared at his dad, hurt and bewildered.

"That's why you came all this way? I've got my own troubles, Dad. I can't save Van. I can't even save myself."

"I don't worry about you, Robert LeRoy. You'll handle what life throws at ya. But Van . . . he's not you. He likes to think he is . . . but he's the unluckiest kid I've ever met."

That's when Max Parker started to cry. Butch had never seen his father cry. Not ever. *"I tried to warn you both."*

"I know you did. I'll do what I can to help him when I get out."

"He wanted to be just like you. Always. They all do."

"I'm sorry, Dad. I'm so sorry. I would fix it if I could."

"There ain't a lot of mercy in the world. And even fewer second chances."

"The man riding with Harriman," Van said, yanking him back to the present. "He had a camera, a big camera strapped in that thing. He took a picture, brother, and it made a popping sound. I thought it was a weapon, I swear. But they weren't ever serious, were they?" Van said.

Yep. Van was unlucky. Pure bad luck.

"They were going to double-cross you. I told you they would. You should be glad I was here."

"They didn't double-cross me, Van. They were spooked. Same as you."

"I wasn't spooked. I was just having a little fun. You'll thank me one day, brother. This isn't your destiny. No sirree. The Parker boys are built for better things."

Van didn't see it coming, and his head was still thrown back in laughter. It was a sucker punch right to the face, but Butch didn't know what else to do, and his brother went down, the blow to his jaw making him quiet for the first time since he'd rambled up an hour before.

"Damn you, Van," Butch whispered, shaking out his fist and blinking the wet from his eyes. Mike Cassidy had taught him that trick, exactly where to hit and how hard, but his hand was going to be sore.

He pulled the saddle from his father's tired plow horse and checked the bags for some rope. He found some, along with the money Van had taken. Fine. He could have it. Then Butch tied Van's hands to his feet. Nothing permanent. Nothing too tight or too difficult to loose, but enough that if Van woke sooner than later, he couldn't follow immediately.

Butch made sure that the horse was hobbled at the old stage trough, full from the rain, and that Van's canteen was within reach, though he'd have to untie himself first. He had a pulse and his jaw was already swelling, but he'd survive. Butch propped Van's head on his saddle and put his soiled hat beneath his lifeless arm.

Then Butch rode away, turning only once to see if his brother still lay where he'd left him. He'd be coming around soon, and he'd be mad. He'd be ugly and sore. But Butch would be gone.

He was going east, as far as he could go, and beyond that, to the only freedom still available to him.

3

Sing sweet nightingale
Angel voice and broken wings
None of us are free

February 1901

"Well, I'll be damned," Butch whispered, shaken. He didn't know the name of the song or the language in which it was being sung, but it didn't matter at all. The woman's voice was so clear and high it rang like a bell in his head and reverberated in his chest. The pain was both excruciating and exquisite.

"She looks like Ethel," Harry mumbled in his ear when Jane Toussaint finished her first number, his tone accusatory. "That's why you like her."

Sundance had always been suspicious of him and Ethel, though Butch loved Ethel like a sister, and Ethel was devoted to Harry "Sundance" Longabaugh even though he didn't deserve her loyalty.

The woman on the stage did look like Ethel. They were about the same age and the same size, and both had a wealth of dark hair and fine features. But that wasn't why Butch liked her.

He liked that she made him feel something other than anxious. And tired. Her voice brought to mind everything beautiful and pure.

Everything holy and sweet. The valley he would never see again. The people he'd left behind. The love he'd been given and hadn't returned.

Jane Toussaint, billed as the Parisian Songbird, sang and bowed, sang and bowed, but she didn't interact with the crowd or speak at all. She simply sang, her voice captivating the enormous audience and her dark beauty enough to hold every eye, but Butch closed his every time she took the stage.

Oddly enough, he didn't want to look at her, and he sat, wishing he could see his mother instead, wishing she could sit beside him in the enormous hall, where every sound was perfectly amplified and the people were fine and upstanding and dressed like they all owned the world, or at least a solid chunk of it.

Ann Parker would love it, and she'd be proud that he loved it too.

Jane Toussaint wasn't the only performer, but she was the draw— for him and the rest of the audience—and for three nights straight, he managed to secure a ticket, once on the balcony, once on the floor, and once—illicitly—in the dark recesses of the stage because his front-row seat was surrounded on every side by what appeared to be politicians and tycoons. Mr. Edward Harriman himself was in a box with the Vanderbilts.

Harriman had seemingly sponsored the whole thing. They'd announced that Miss Jane Toussaint and company would be traveling all along the East Coast on Union Pacific trains, giving concerts at every major hub.

A big banner that read *Union Pacific Welcomes Jane Toussaint* was strung across the grand entrance to the concert venue Andrew Carnegie had built not far from Central Park.

Everything about the six-storied music hall screamed opulence and status, from the Italian-style arched windows and pale stone to the flags that snapped in the salty Manhattan air.

Butch had been drawn to the flapping red banner like a moth to a flame . . . or an outlaw to a train. Harriman was celebrating yet another conquest, a southern railroad that he bought and brought into the fold.

"Union Pacific. That's Harriman's outfit, isn't it?" Sundance asked, like they were talking about a rancher's brand instead of the largest network of railroads in the whole United States. "What's he got to do with this? And what's he doing here?"

"I suppose he'd ask us the same thing," Butch said, tying his scarf up over his ears and neck to protect himself from more than just the cold. He'd pulled a kerchief over his face to disguise his identity more times than he could count, yet there he was, in New York City, thousands of miles from home, still feeling exposed. "Harriman's a New Yorker. This is his world. Not ours."

He and Sundance and Ethel had skated in the park and then waited for the trolley to take them back downtown, standing beneath the banner that snapped and whistled like a faraway train in the February afternoon. He wondered if somehow Harriman had orchestrated that too.

"We should come back tomorrow evening and see her," Ethel had said wistfully. "I read about her in the paper. They say she's the next Jenny Lind, only more beautiful. Can you imagine singing in front of so many important people? She's so young."

"Who's Jenny Lind?" Butch asked.

"The opera singer? The Swedish Nightingale? She was very famous. Toured all over the world. Surely you've heard of her. P. T. Barnum—"

"The circus man?" Harry interrupted. "Barnum and Bailey's?"

"Yes . . . he was best known for his circus. He was a promoter of all sorts of things. He brought Jenny Lind to the States for a huge tour. It was a long time ago, but my grandmother heard her sing. She said I sounded a little like her."

Ethel had a decent voice. She'd sung in Miss Fannie Porter's drawing room before bringing the gentlemen that came to see her upstairs. Miss Fannie had all the classiest girls in San Antonio, and Ethel was top dollar, but apparently Ethel had a different dream. The naked longing in her face as she studied the hall was impossible to miss, though Sundance didn't seem to notice.

"Let's get tickets. Why not, Ethel?" Butch said, looking for the sales window.

Sundance scowled at him. His nose was red and his teeth were chattering. New York had been fun for the first few weeks, but it was February, and the city wasn't just cold, it was filthy and wet. They were all ready to leave, though the SS *Herminius* would undoubtedly be worse.

"Sure. Let's get tickets. Let's parade right beneath Harriman's nose," Sundance grumbled.

"Nobody will recognize you. We're a long way from Texas, Harry," Ethel argued.

The picture the Pinkerton Detective Agency had gotten their hands on had been taken in Fort Worth. Will Carver and Ben Kilpatrick had wanted a shot of the gang—what a stupid idea—and Butch had let them twist his arm. He was always letting someone twist his arm.

"You're much handsomer now," Ethel continued. "And Butch's hair is longer and darker than it was in the picture, and his mustache is thicker."

"That's true. You look like you've got squirrel tails growing out of your nose, Cassidy. Two of them," Harry said. He'd used the line more than once, and Butch ignored him.

Butch had been towheaded as a boy, with hair like an angel. It turned a honey-colored gold when his voice dropped, and by the time he robbed his first bank, it was coming in dirty brown. Every winter it got a shade darker, just like his heart. He no longer resembled the boy he'd been when he'd left home at eighteen. He was a long way from eighteen now, and a long way from the Beaver River Valley.

They purchased tickets to see Jane Toussaint for that evening and fattened the coffers of Union Pacific for a change. The next night, Sundance and Ethel went to visit Harry's sister in New Jersey, and Butch went back to Carnegie Hall alone. Funny, he'd thought Harry was an orphan up until about a month ago. Most of the gang were—that or they just didn't talk about the people they'd left behind or let down. But Sundance had a family, and he wanted Ethel to meet them.

Harry didn't invite Butch, and Butch didn't really want to go. He didn't need to feel accountable to Harry's people. He already felt responsible for Harry's lady. Better to keep his distance from kin. If they were anything like Harry, one of them would get a whiff of who he was and try to collect on the reward.

Butch didn't think a solitary, gilded soul in the crowded hall in New York City would look at him twice, even if he sat among them all night. But he didn't want to risk it, not when he was so close to leaving for good. So on the third night, he stood by the door marked "Stage Entrance" until a man walked out, intent upon the cigar he was lighting, and Butch grabbed the door before it swung closed. He almost tripped over a huge bag of salt in the walkway—the Noble Salt Company, all the way from the Great Salt Lake, just like Butch—but sidestepped it and kept going with the easy saunter he'd perfected in his sordid career.

A man could go almost anywhere with a cheerful smile, a soft-spoken command, and a plan. Open a door. Stride into the room with a purpose, take what you'd come for, get out. Few people would get in your way if you looked formidable—or friendly— enough. It was the way he'd robbed banks and trains without getting caught and without an innocent getting killed. *Plenty of innocents got killed,* his conscience argued.

"Not by me," he argued back. *Everyone gets caught. You will too,* it retorted. That part he believed, and he swatted the thought away and focused on Jane Toussaint. Backstage was not the best view in the house, but there was a stool to sit on, probably for the curtain guy, though he was nowhere in sight. He borrowed that and moved deep into the dusty folds at the back of the stage, found a spot for the stool, and watched through a break in the curtain, hands on his knees, heels on the rung. Like he'd told Harry, he didn't need to see her. He just wanted to *hear* her, though he could see her too, a long sliver of her back.

Her hair was piled high, and feathers and jewels were woven into the coils, catching the light when she turned her head. Her dress was a fiery red, the bodice fitted, and the skirt had just enough swish to move with her steps.

This time he heard the applause the way she would have heard it, facing it, the swell and the surge of sound almost as new to him as her voice had been the first night. The curtains were lowered with an audible squeal—curtain guy must have come back—even amid the now muted approval still sounding, and Jane Toussaint walked off the stage, her steps quick, her skirts gathered in her hands.

"You will sing 'Waly, Waly' for the encore. It has been requested by Mr. Carnegie." A tidy old man in a suit with long tails and a shirt so white it gleamed, even in the shadows of backstage, was waiting in the wings as she exited. He wore a monocle and the chain glimmered from his brow to his breast pocket. His head was as smooth as his cheeks, the only hair on his face a pair of winged brows.

"Not tonight, Oliver. No encore tonight. Augustus is ill."

Huh. She didn't sound French. More English, like his mother. The thought made his insides churn with another homesick twist.

"He is fine, Jane," the bald man insisted. "The curtain is rising. Now go. The orchestra has been informed of the change."

Her resistance was palpable and futile. The bald man pushed her back onto the stage, and Butch was guiltily grateful he would hear her once more, even though it appeared she was unwilling. In the morning he would board a ship, along with Sundance and Ethel, and he had no plan to ever return. Saint Jane—he realized he'd twisted her name and thought it apt—would only be a memory.

She sang his mother's song in a way he'd never heard it before. The wailing, wailing was almost more than he could bear, and his throat ached with the irony of it all. He couldn't escape that song, no matter how far he traveled.

"Damn song," he whispered. He was getting soft. That was what Sundance said. Not Sundance . . . Harry. He had to remember to call him Harry.

Butch didn't fight the description or even bristle at it. Soft and yellow weren't the same thing. He wasn't a coward or a hothead. He just didn't like hurting people and wasn't afraid to admit it.

Sundance—Harry—was the orneriest son of a bitch Butch Cassidy had ever befriended, and that was saying something. The truth was, Butch was the only one of their acquaintances who was unruffled by the gunman, and Sundance—Harry—had been the only one smart enough in the whole damn bunch not to get himself killed or caught.

William Ellsworth "Elzy" Lay, Butch's best friend, was serving a life sentence for killing a deputy. He'd been aiming to scare him off, but Elzy wasn't a great shot, and he'd drilled the man right in the heart. There had been no mercy for Elzy, and no argument either. He hadn't meant to do it, but such things didn't matter when you were robbing a train. That they didn't hang him was probably more mercy than he deserved, and Butch knew it.

Elzy and Ben Kilpatrick were in prison. Will "News" Carver was dead. And Harvey "Kid Curry" Logan had gone stone-cold bad, killing anyone and everyone who crossed him. Sundance and Butch were leaving with their lives and not much else, though if Sundance wised up, he might be able to cobble together a happy future with Ethel.

Butch was pretty certain Harry would never wise up.

Good sense had not been in rich supply among the Wild Bunch. Butch should shake Harry and Ethel loose—hell, they should shake *him* loose—but Butch didn't want to go to Bolivia alone, unable to speak the language, with no one to take care of or look out for.

He'd grown up with his siblings trailing him like ducks, depending on him. He'd resented the responsibility then, but when he'd left home, restless and guilty, searching for a different world, he'd become the leader once more. Someone had to do it. But the members of the

Wild Bunch hadn't trailed him like his siblings had. They didn't listen, and they sure as hell didn't think. They did what they wanted, whether it was part of the plan he carefully plotted or not.

Some days it had all worked out. Some days it hadn't. The days it hadn't, men got killed and men got caught, and Butch refused to do either of those things—kill or be caught—and he was leaving while he still could.

> *When roses grow in the wintry snow*
> *Then will my love*
> *Return to me.*

The woman's voice made everything inside him settle, and for the first time in as long as he could remember, he was able to sit still and enjoy. It was the reason he'd come back again instead of seeking out a game of cards or poking at the underbelly of a very beguiling city. He figured Jane Toussaint had saved him a good deal of money. He liked to play cards, and he was good at it, but he always felt bad about cleaning people out. Sundance said he lost on purpose. Sometimes he did.

He was so enraptured by his own thoughts and her angelic sound, he didn't hear the approach of his visitor, and the tap on his knee had him shooting to his feet, his hand moving immediately to the holster beneath his arm.

A very small boy dressed in short pants, a matching jacket, and a little peaked hat peered up at him, his face shadowed but his eyes gleaming. For a moment, Butch could only stare, the incongruence of the child's presence in the dark bowels of the stage robbing his speech.

"I want Maman," he said matter-of-factly. "Can you get her, please?"

"Wh-where is she?" he stammered.

"Out there. She's singing. She's singing so long, and I came to find her." The boy began to wheeze, the sound high and harsh, his thin shoulders shaking, and he sat down in a heap at Butch's feet, gasping for air.

Butch reached for him, trying to draw him up, and was alarmed by the heat coming off the child's skin, but the boy drooped and refused to stand.

Applause rose again, signaling the end of the encore, and Butch panicked, scooping the child up in his arms. He couldn't just leave him.

"What's your name, son?"

"I'm not son. I'm Augustus," he said, making the *son* sound like "thun," and *Augustus* sound like "Au-guth-tuth." It was cute, but it was too much name. But then the boy started to cry, resting his head against Butch's shoulder.

"Try not to cry, now. It will only make it harder to breathe," he said softly.

The boy stopped immediately and lifted his head. The right side of his face was alarmingly red and puffy, though his opposite cheek was almost as flushed. The boy tried to pull in enough air to converse.

"I want Maman."

"All right, Augustus," he said, trapped. "I'll take you to her."

Jane Toussaint didn't continue to stand for the applause after she sang the last note. She simply nodded her head in regal thanks and left the stage. She didn't slow when the bald man attempted to talk with her, and when Butch moved directly into her path, the boy in his arms, she balked and then jerked Augustus from his outstretched hands.

"I want to go home, Maman," Augustus said, and Butch sank back, determined to leave the way he'd come.

"He is burning up, Oliver. Burning up. Worse than before. And he can hardly breathe with all the croup in his chest." On cue, the boy started to cough, the sound painful and unproductive.

"Are you Dr. Salt?" Oliver snapped. "I sent for you hours ago. Where have you been, sir? Come! See to this child."

Butch couldn't very well use his own name or explain his presence, and he let the presumption slide. He never said he was a doctor, but he moved to stand beside the woman, peered down into the little boy's eyes, and laid his knuckles against his crimson cheek.

"Does your throat hurt, Augustus?"

"This doctor will stay with the boy, Jane," Oliver interjected, trying to wrest the child from his mother's arms. "You must come upstairs with me to the reception. We cannot keep your guests waiting. The Harrimans are here. The Carnegies and Astors too."

Jane turned furious eyes on Oliver, and the man had the presence of mind to take a step back and release the child, but he persisted in his argument. "I sent for him. Dr. Salt comes highly recommended. The boy will be fine in his care for an hour or two."

Butch wasn't sure if the man was lying or if at any moment, a doctor named Salt was going to bustle up, bag in hand, and step in. No skin off his back either way, but he couldn't imagine the woman was going to turn her child over to a man she'd met only moments before.

"You will go and tell our guests that I have a child who is ill," she instructed Oliver. "They will understand. You will *make* them understand, Oliver! I am going back to the hotel with Augustus."

"You will change and return, Jane," Oliver warned. "We have a room full of benefactors upstairs and donors waiting to meet you. The tour is dependent on their largesse."

"I'm not leaving Augustus."

The people backstage were beginning to turn and shift; the distress in the woman's voice was making her shrill, and the man named Oliver clearly had different priorities for her than the child lying limply in her arms, his curly head and flushed cheek tucked into her neck.

"If he doesn't improve, there will be no more tour," she added.

"Are you threatening me, Jane?" The old man drew himself up in outrage.

"I'm threatening the tour, Oliver. I cannot continue this way, and I will not continue if Augustus does not have the care he needs. Please." The little boy began to cough, and the coughing became a retching that sprayed the woman's fine red dress with mucus and phlegm.

Oliver swore, people scattered, and the woman soothed the child, who was crying again. She shook her head, weary, and turned to Butch.

"Will you come with me, Doctor . . . I'm sorry, what was your name again?"

"Salt. Noble Salt," he answered smoothly. It was the name written on the large bag of salt he'd tripped over, the one by the back door, and the only *salt* he could think of. He almost laughed, it seemed such an obvious borrow, but no one blinked or raised a brow. The best fake names were the ones that sounded like rich kids and Englishmen.

"The dressing rooms are cold. He needs a bed. The hotel is just around the corner, and I can have the kitchen make him a compress." The boy started to wheeze again, trying to cough and breathe and doing neither very well. Instead of arguing about the erroneous title he'd been given, Butch scooped the child from her arms and instructed her to lead the way. She ran for her cloak and the boy's while Oliver sputtered and the stage crew dispersed. The woman who'd apparently been charged with sitting with the child was nowhere to be found.

Somehow he'd become a man named Noble Salt and a medical doctor in one fell swoop, and he decided that was just fine. He didn't owe anyone the truth in this situation. He could help, and he would, and then he would be on his way.

4

*I'll hold a vigil
Until the night surrenders
Then I'll sail away*

One winter, every single one of Butch's younger siblings—there were only six at the time—got the croup so bad, it was touch and go for days in the Parker house. He and his mom and dad had worked around the clock monitoring fevers and administering the syrup that made the kids throw up, the only way to remove the thick mucus from their clogged throats. The doctor, when he finally made his way to the Parker homestead, said they'd done well—as much as he could have done—and had let Butch listen through his stethoscope and made him an honorary doc. Butch had considered it for a while; maybe being a doctor would fill the hole in his gut that nothing seemed to touch. But he was working full time on Morten's dairy farm at thirteen, and doctoring quickly became an unlikely dream.

Butch ended up carrying Augustus Toussaint, his mother hurrying alongside him, to the hotel, an establishment a hundred feet from the hall where she headlined.

"Do you have your bag, sir?" she asked him.

He stared at her blankly.

"Your doctor's bag?"

"No, ma'am," he answered. "But we'll send a runner for some ipecac syrup. It won't be pleasant, but the best thing you can do for his breathing is to keep his chest from filling up."

"Nooo," the little boy moaned. "I don't want medicine."

"I have some," Jane said. "But he's hardly eaten in three days. I'm afraid to give it to him. He's so weak already, and he can hardly swallow."

"I need some water," the boy groaned again.

He spoke English well, though he had a French tinge to his words. Butch had heard a French accent plenty. The West was filled with accents. In the last half century, people had come from everywhere to find a bit of gold or stake their claim on the seemingly endless range. His own parents hadn't lost the British flavor from their tongues.

The hotel was clean and the rooms were large, but he was surprised by her accommodations. She seemed a star, a member of the upper crust, an entertainer of the highest order, but the establishment was more a boardinghouse than a luxury hotel.

"Lay Augustus there," she instructed, turning down the blankets on the bed. The room was warm enough, but the boy was trembling, and she drew the covers up over his small body.

"Has something happened to his face?" Butch asked, staring down at the little boy. His cheek was scarlet, but it was not the flush of fever. It looked more like a terrible burn, one that had singed the right side of his face from the tip of his chin to his brow. His white forehead and a strip of unblemished skin at his jaw made the mark all the more glaring.

Jane glanced up, startled, and then looked down at her sleeping son as if seeing him anew. The boy rolled onto his right side, hiding the mark, and she laid her hand against his unblemished cheek as if to shield it too.

"Nothing happened to his face." Her voice was stiff, her posture too, but she kept her gaze on her son.

"Something happened." He didn't know why he cared. It made no difference to him. But he was a curious man, always had been, and he wanted to know.

"He was born this way. Nothing happened," she insisted again. "He has had the mark since birth. The doctors call it a vascular malformation. Have you not seen one before?" she challenged, and Butch nodded and let it go. His baby sister had been born with a birthmark like a strawberry on her brow. It had gone away by the time she was two or three.

He went looking for a porter for water, a bucket, and some fodder for the fire. He would do exactly what he'd seen his mother and his old friend Margaret Simpson do every time someone fell sick.

When he returned with the items and a sleepy porter, Jane Toussaint had changed into a cotton dress of faded blue that did nothing for her dark eyes and hair and porcelain skin, but he still wanted to stare. She didn't need the feathers and jewels or even color to be beautiful. In fact, it was this girl, this weary mother, that made him nervous and quiet and wonder how in the world he always found himself in impossible situations.

You'll never learn, Robert LeRoy Parker. You're so smart, but you never think.

His father's voice was always the one in his head.

The porter started a fire, all the while mumbling that it was warm enough without one, but he cheered up some when Butch slipped him a gold piece and a smile.

"Bring us some dinner—soup would be best for the boy—and I'll make sure you're well taken care of," he promised.

"Yessir, Doc. We've got bread and soup from supper. Cheese and pie too. I'll bring up enough for all of you."

"Where are you from, Dr. Salt?" Jane asked when the porter had bustled away. She stood over Augustus, who had fallen into a restless sleep after a dose of the ipecac and an unpleasant emptying of his phlegm-filled belly. His mother had washed him and was trying to keep him comfortable.

Butch sighed. He wanted to correct her. He really did. He didn't like that she didn't even know his name, though that didn't mean much. He hadn't used his real one in over a decade.

"You certainly aren't from around here," she said.

"How can you tell?"

"You sound very American."

"Last I checked that's where we are." He smiled to take the insolence out of his words, but she didn't smile back. She was so weary she swayed.

"You need to rest too."

She sat down on the end of the bed abruptly, as if she would fall if she didn't.

"Augustus has been sick for days, and I've had performances every night. He has gotten worse, not better."

The inside of the boy's mouth was a grayish white, like mold on cheese, and Butch feared Augustus had more than just the common croup. He'd seen one man die from it in prison. They called it diphtheria or the strangler. Far as he knew, the prison doc hadn't used ipecac to treat it, but Margaret Simpson had. She said it helped expel the white mucus that slowly strangled its victims, and she had doctored everyone in the Wind River Valley.

"Sleep now. I'll keep an eye on him. If he starts to struggle for breath, I'll sit him up and give him another dose. I won't let anything happen to him. Or you. I promise."

She stared at him balefully and then closed her eyes, her dark lashes sweeping her pale cheeks like she was praying or searching for strength.

"I have nothing that you can steal. Oliver—my husband—controls all the money and pays all the bills. All I have are my gowns—I doubt they'd fit you—and my son. And if you wanted to hurt us, you would have done so already."

He laughed at her weary jest but wondered who had made her so suspicious.

"I don't steal dresses or children," he said.

She climbed into the bed behind the little boy and closed her eyes. She was instantly asleep, so worn and lovely his compassion welled. He'd assumed the bald man was a manager of sorts. The husband part surprised him. Jane didn't appear to have help of any kind, and there was no male presence in the space, no room for a man in the narrow bed the woman and her child appeared to share.

Butch pulled the armchair next to the bed and sat down, determined to do exactly what he'd promised, though he didn't know why. He took out the new double-eagle-sized timepiece that he'd purchased at Tiffany's the day after he'd arrived in New York and stared down at it, determining the time he had left, the hours he had to give to the songbird and her son. The ship sailed at five, and his bags were packed. He could spend the whole night with Jane Toussaint if he wanted to.

"Whath your name?" a little voice asked.

The little boy was staring up at him, unafraid.

Damn it all. He didn't like lying to the little boy. So he didn't.

"I've got a lot of names."

"You do?"

"I do."

"I have a lot of names too." The struggle with the *s*'s was very endearing.

"Oh yeah? Tell me all your names."

"Augustus Maximilian Toussaint."

"Maximilian is my daddy's name," Butch said, surprised. He'd always wondered why he hadn't been named Maximilian too. Maybe if he'd been a Maximilian instead of a Robert LeRoy, he would have turned out differently.

"Augustus Maximilian Toussaint is a big name. Can I call you Gus?" he asked.

The boy started to answer, but the yes became a wheeze, and Butch sat him up.

Poor Jane sat up too, her hand on the child's back, but she let Butch lead, gratefully surrendering the boy's care into his hands.

"I have to give you more of the syrup, Gus. I know you don't want it. I know it's hard. But we gotta open up your throat."

The little boy's lower lip trembled, and Butch handed him the watch in his hand. "Do you know how to tell time?"

Augustus shook his head. "No."

"Can you count?"

The boy nodded.

"If you hold the pocket watch really tight, you'll feel the time," he promised.

Augustus pressed the watch between his palms.

"Feel that?"

The boy nodded, and Butch said, "You count the clicks, and before you get to ten, it'll be over."

"Okay," the boy said, so brave, then he opened his mouth to the spoon Butch filled with ipecac, no tears and no argument, though moments later he was gagging and shaking, throwing up into the bucket Jane held beneath his chin.

"That's it. I'm sorry, kiddo. I'm sorry," Butch said.

The third round of vomiting seemed to help, and an hour and two dozen questions later—little Augustus Toussaint liked to talk—the boy managed to gulp down a glass of water and followed it with two pieces of bread Jane had soaked with soup. He fell asleep with the timepiece pressed against his purple cheek, his mother curled up beside him. No one checked on them.

Well after dawn, Jane woke with a jolt and a cry, and Butch, dozing in the chair, his book of verses in his lap, jerked to attention.

"Augustus?" she whimpered, rising up on her elbow and smoothing back the boy's hair so she could see his small face.

"Shh, shh, shh," Butch reassured her softly, rubbing his tired eyes. "He's fine. Just fine. He's sleeping good now."

She sank back down, hands over heart, breathing in little panicked spurts. "I am so sorry. How long have I slept?"

He reached for his pocket watch and realized it was still clutched in the little boy's hands. That was fine. Butch could get another. He tucked his book inside his vest and stretched his aching back. Sitting for hours in a chair was harder than sitting in the saddle.

"Not too long," he lied. "I must have closed my eyes for a bit too. Where is Mr. Toussaint?" he asked.

She shrugged and shook her head. "We have two rooms. Oliver demands his privacy. I am sure he is asleep."

44

"He won't be concerned about his son?"

"Augustus is not his son."

He gaped, and she flinched, but she didn't expound or take the words back.

"He won't be concerned about you?" he pressed.

She ignored that. "If you will leave your card and tell me your fee, I will see that he sends payment," she said instead.

He had no card and expected no fee, so he simply nodded his head, agreeing to something he had no intention of doing. She was so young—most likely a decade younger than he was—but her voice and her brown eyes were ancient.

"You don't really sound French," he said softly.

"I can if I want to," she argued, and suddenly she did, the accent so succulent and sweet, he may as well have been eating pastries in a Parisian café.

"Is it real?" he asked. He wanted to know everything about her, and he knew so little.

"Nothing is real," she murmured.

He cocked his head at that, considering. "No, I guess not."

"You're not even real," she accused, and he froze, caught, but she continued wearily. "Men like you aren't real."

"How do you figure?"

"You stayed all night and have asked nothing in return." She said nothing about his phony medical status, and he didn't correct her, even though he could have. Even though he should have. She was right about one thing. He wouldn't ask for anything in return.

The little boy sighed suddenly but did not wheeze or wake. Good. That was good. He'd turned a corner.

"Thank you for your assistance. I will manage now." She was reassuring herself, and so tired that Butch thought she might drift off again. She eased herself from the bed instead, moving gingerly so she didn't jostle the child, and poured herself a glass of water.

"Go back to sleep, Jane." He shouldn't call her by her given name. It was a liberty she hadn't granted, but he didn't care. She was right; nothing felt real in the little room, and he was not himself. He watched her, unabashed, as she straightened her hair and clothes.

"I can't go back to sleep. I'm afraid Augustus will need me, and I'm so tired, I don't trust myself to hear him when you go. I have slept for hours and heard nothing. What kind of mother does that make me?"

He was not a stupid man. He got the message. She wanted him to leave now. He stood and picked up his coat and hat. "A tired one. You slept because there was nothing to hear. He's breathing just fine, and his fever broke."

She smiled like he'd just told her she'd inherited a diamond mine, and then her brow wrinkled and she wrung her hands and cleared her throat. "How . . . how can I thank you?"

"I heard you sing three nights in a row, and I can still hear you when I close my eyes. You paid me well," he reassured her.

"You are very kind," she said. It seemed to stun her, that kindness. Suspicion lurked beneath her words, but he nodded. Kindness had never been his problem, but *kind* and *good* weren't always the same thing. He straightened his tie, put on his coat—it smelled like soot and ipecac—and dropped his hat on his head.

"Will we see you again?" she asked, and his heart skipped at her interest. Then he realized a doctor would probably return to check on a patient. Time to set her straight.

"No. Probably not. I'm leaving town today."

"You do not live in New York City," she confirmed, though she'd already guessed as much.

"No."

She stood and walked to him, her brown eyes ringed in fatigue but her jaw set. She was a little on the small side, especially in her stocking feet, though her voice gave the impression of a bird with a puffed-up breast and plenty of power.

He was not a tall man or a short man. His face was too square and his neck was too thick to look like anything other than what he was, which was common. He was average in every way, except for maybe the color of his eyes. They were a vivid, true blue, and they'd given him away more than once. But she didn't know Butch Cassidy. She thought he was a doctor, a *noble salt* of a man.

"You are very kind," she said again. Indecision flickered across her face, and she bit her lip. Then she rose up on her toes and touched her mouth to his.

Had she drawn a belt across his face, he couldn't have been more surprised, but he was a quick draw, and he took her face in his hands and turned her little peck into something more substantial. He didn't care that she had a husband. At thirty-four years old, he had nothing to show for his life but regrets, and kissing her was well worth the weight of one more. She didn't slap his face or pull away like a lady should, especially a married lady, but he didn't judge her any more than he judged himself.

Later, he would think about the softness of her face in his hands, her scent and her beauty. He would compose a dozen verses trying to capture it all, but in that moment, he could think only of her mouth. Every girl he'd ever kissed was more experienced than he was, and they—and he—were too aware of the cost and the choreography that must occur in the twenty-minute session. He'd known a few ladies who scheduled men every ten minutes to maximize profits. The kisses weren't languorous or long, and he could sometimes taste the men who'd been there before him. It was not like that with Jane.

She was pliant in his arms, but she didn't return his ardor, and he realized, belatedly, that she was holding her breath and clenching her fists as if preparing to do battle. He suddenly understood. She was suffering him because she thought she owed him and knew it was what most men wanted.

She wasn't wrong. He did want it, but he wouldn't take it, nor did he expect it. Instinctively, he knew others had done just that, and stepped back, dropping his hands and holstering his enthusiasm. He turned to go, bidding her sleep once more.

"You're really going to go?" she asked, doubtful. Hopeful.

"Would you like me to stay?"

She hesitated, and he felt only compassion for her indecision. It wasn't her fault he'd fallen a little in love with her. He'd done it gleefully and without her consent or encouragement because he was leaving and, like she said, it wasn't real.

Her husband should have been there. He wasn't. Not Butch's problem. But yes. He was going to go. In fact, if he didn't leave now, he was going to have a dickens of a time boarding that ship.

"Goodbye, Saint Jane," he said, proud of himself for meaning it.

Her brow furrowed at the nickname. "Goodbye . . . Dr. Salt." She sounded relieved, and he sighed, sad that it was over. He was a no-good son of a bitch, and he'd just given her the best he could, which wasn't a whole helluva lot, but he didn't want it to be a lie.

With the doorknob in his hand, he confessed. "I'm not a doctor, Jane."

"What?"

"I'm not a doctor. And I never said I was," he said, meeting her wide, dark eyes. "Mr. Toussaint did. I'm just a fella who knows a little about croup and ipecac and diphtheria, which I'm guessing poor Gus has. But he's on the mend. I've seen a whole lot worse. So when Mr. Toussaint decides to check on the two of you, tell him to get a real doctor. Tell him Gus has diphtheria—he'll be fine, I promise—and don't go any further, no more traveling, until he's all better."

He stepped from the room and closed the door behind him without looking back. He touched his lips and tried not to wonder what she thought about him now. He was accustomed to people's fear and disappointment, but when he left the hotel he actually felt noble, maybe for the first time in his life. And he liked the feeling.

5

I am a stranger
That's what all the people say
No way I can hide

July 1, 1907

The bearded man noticed his mother immediately. She wore a simple
white dress with brown buttons and a big brown silk hat with no adorn-
ment, though the size itself would have turned heads had that not been
the fashion. But it was, and her hat was no bigger than any of the other
women on the Paris streets. But she was different. She was beautiful.
Not a blemish, not a spot, not a hair out of place or an unfortunate
feature. From the top of her head to the tip of her toes she was well-
formed and flawless, but she'd given birth to him. It was a surprise to
all who knew her. It was a surprise to Augustus and a secret source of
angst. It might have been easier to be ugly had she been ugly too. He
knew it was not her fault, but he blamed her a little, just as he knew
she blamed herself. He was marked, and his mark in turn marked her.

She'd tried to fashion hoods for him, ones with holes for his eyes
and his mouth and nose, but that drew more eyes than his uncovered face, and the hoods were uncomfortable and frightening, both to
him and those around him; people wondered what disease he might be

hiding. Better to let them see that his face was a misfortune and not a plague. That was what the housekeeper, Madame Blanc, had said—"'Tis a misfortune, not a plague"—when interviewing governesses. He was grateful there would be no more governesses. Mother said she could handle his education herself. He had his books too, though he had to leave most of them behind.

"There will be books in America, Augustus. We will get more."

He had a satchel full of his favorites selected, mostly dime novels with paper covers and rough pages, but if he was to go west, he needed to know everything about the cowboys and the rustlers, the lawmen and the outlaws. Maman said those days were over. The Wild West had been tamed. He hoped not. He thought he might find a place among the bandits and the outcasts. He could grow a beard like the strange man, one that would cover his lower face and half of the big purple mark that had only deepened and thickened over the years.

He didn't think about his face much until he left the flat on the Rue Lamartine. Then people stared and he remembered, but soon they were going on a journey, an adventure, and he wasn't going to think about his deformity or the flat or the books he was leaving behind. He was going to think about the future. And freedom. For him and his mother both.

"It will be a new life, Augustus," she'd promised. "There are all kinds of people in America, remember? And so many different places. We will see them all."

But the bearded man did not stare at him. He stared at his mother, and that was almost as bad. There was admiration there, but there was something else too, recognition, and it made Augustus's nerves jangle and his heart jump. Most men and women looked, but polite society demanded they be somewhat discreet about it. This man was not discreet. He was wearing a fine suit of charcoal gray and a black hat a few shades darker than his beard. He stared openly, his blue eyes unwavering, a stillness in his posture that made Augustus think of the American gunslingers in his books. That's what his books called the cowboys who could shoot fast—gunslingers.

Augustus tried to imagine the bearded man wearing a cowboy hat and a gun belt with spurs about his boots and a shiny gold star over his heart. He could picture it, though the man was in a suit that rivaled any of the fancy men his mother sang for. But he had no softness about his waist or in his hands, no softness anywhere, but for some reason that made Augustus relax a little, and he didn't question why. Mother said his instincts were good.

The man stared at his mother like he'd seen her somewhere before. Like he knew her. And there was something about him, something familiar and almost . . . dear.

"Maman, do we know that man?" he asked.

His mother stilled, the only movement the tightening in her hand around his. Maman had too many secrets, even from him. "Which one?"

"The man there. He was inside the clinic. The man Madame Moreau was yelling at. He is staring at you."

Maman was suddenly trembling, though she looked down at him and smiled. Maman only smiled for him. Everyone else was treated to stony stares and steady eyes when she looked at them at all. Madame Blanc said his mother was *hautaine*. Haughty.

The man had paused just outside the clinic, the doctor's wife still scolding him, but he stepped forward and removed his hat, as men often did when they approached his mother. The doctor's wife grew more incensed and apologized to Maman before berating the man again, though he didn't appear to understand a word she was saying.

"Monsieur Santiago, for your sake and for the sake of all who visit this place, you need to enter through ze alley and wait until I let you in. We do not enter and exit in the same place, remember? I am sorry, madame. He is a stupid American."

"It is fine, Madame Moreau," Maman said. "We are . . . old friends."

Maman didn't have any friends, and Augustus gaped up at his mother as Madame Moreau retreated with another hiss for the bearded man.

"Noble Salt . . . is that you?" Maman asked.

"Jane Toussaint," the American said, and all at once Augustus recognized him too.

"You're Noble Salt. Maman, it is Noble Salt!" Augustus cried.

"Yes," his mother whispered. "It is."

The man extended his hand toward Augustus, his eyes lingering on his cheek the way all eyes did, but then his gaze landed and caught, direct and warm.

"You've grown into a fine young man, Augustus Maximilian Toussaint."

"You remember us!" Augustus crowed, grasping the man's hand. It was large and rough like a cat's tongue, and it swallowed his.

"I do. You've lost your lisp."

Augustus wrinkled his nose, not understanding the English word. His mother explained in rapid French.

"Yes. I've lost my lisp!" He laughed. "But I still have your watch." Augustus dropped the man's hand, pulled the watch from his vest pocket, and unwound the chain from his button.

"See?" He even wore it when he slept, holding it between his palms and counting the clicks as he drifted off.

"You made quite an impression on Augustus, Mr. Salt," his mother said. Her voice was soft and shaky, so different from her regular tone. "He recovered beautifully, with no lingering maladies, but you were right. He did have diphtheria."

Augustus had never seen his mother be kind to a gentleman. She'd not been kind to Oliver. She was not kind to the men who paid her to sing or the men who took care of their home and carriage or sold papers or swept the streets. She was not nice to the banker or the butcher or even Georg, who made wonderful pastries. She was not cruel or unfair. She was simply *cold*. She did not smile at them or make conversation. She did not answer their questions beyond the business at hand. No small talk, the housekeeper said. All business.

"Of all the places in the world and all the doctors in Paris . . . why are you here? Are you seeing Dr. Moreau? Are you ill?" she asked Noble Salt.

Gus could only stare at his mother, slack-jawed. She sounded interested and concerned.

"Not ill. No. Dr. Moreau is a . . . colleague of mine," Noble said. "And as you may have heard, I am not welcome back. I went in the wrong entrance, which is why I saw you and Augustus in the first place."

"Dr. Moreau gives people new faces. But he can't give me one," Augustus explained.

His mother winced, and Noble Salt said nothing. He'd placed his hat back on his head, and Augustus felt a sudden flash of fear that he would simply walk away, and they would never see him again.

"We've been . . . consulting him . . . for a wh-while," Maman stammered. "He's tried ice and different ointments and even grafts. The treatments have only served to make my purse lighter and Augustus more uncomfortable, physically and emotionally. I went to him because he had the reputation of being . . . innovative and . . . unconventional. We will not be going back."

"We're going to America!" Augustus whispered, unable to help himself. Surely it was all right to tell Noble Salt—and Luc, their driver, didn't speak any English at all.

His mother didn't reprimand him, but he felt a tightening in her hand. Luc was still waiting to help her step into the auto, watching the interaction with great interest.

His mother turned to Luc and, in French, instructed him to come back in an hour. She told him she was going to consult with another doctor—a colleague of Dr. Moreau—and would need more time.

Luc frowned and then shrugged. He was accustomed to the appointments and did not seem overly suspicious.

He climbed back up into the car and, with a bounce and a chuff, eased out into the Paris street without a look back.

"There is a lovely park just around the corner, Mr. Salt, and a shop at the entrance that sells the most wonderful treats. Could we have a few moments of your time? I never properly thanked you, and to see you like this feels quite providential."

"Really, Maman? Can he really join us?" Augustus could hardly believe his ears.

Noble Salt was hesitant. His eyes followed the car and the man at the helm.

"Monsieur Salt?" Augustus added his petition to his mother's invitation. "Won't you please?"

"All right." He nodded. "Lead the way, Augustus."

Augustus tried to walk, but he skipped instead, bouncing at Noble Salt's side.

"Where are you staying, Mr. Salt?" Maman's question was rushed and stilted, and Noble Salt hesitated the way Augustus did when he didn't want to cooperate.

"Do you still have a gun in your boot?" Augustus blurted, unable to help himself.

"Yes," the man answered, and he sounded relieved that he'd been saved from Maman's inquiry. His honesty made Augustus laugh.

"Can I see it?" Augustus asked.

"No."

"Augustus," Maman warned. "Be courteous."

"Why do you need a gun, monsieur?" Augustus asked, trying to speak more softly, more *courteously*. "You are a doctor. You cannot shoot people."

"I'm not a doctor."

"Of course you are. And a very good one. But you are also a cowboy, yes?" He'd never forgotten the picture in Mr. Harriman's big house.

"Augustus," his mother chided again. They walked into the patisserie, and Augustus forgot the gun momentarily, distracted by the rows of lovely treats.

"What will you have, Monsieur Salt?" Augustus asked, hoping his mother would let him have a bite of everything. He rarely tried anything new because he was afraid of missing out on something he knew he loved for something he might not love as much. Sweets made everything better.

"You choose for me, Gus," Mr. Salt said.

"You remembered that too!" he cried. He didn't even care that the patrons were staring at him. The owner of the shop knew Augustus and his mother and was used to the way Augustus looked, but there were always those who gaped or grimaced or even left the shop.

Once, at one of the finest restaurants in all of Paris, he and Maman had been asked to leave. Someone had not liked his face. Maman had asked who, precisely, had complained. When the waiter would not tell her, she stood and with a lovely, dimpled smile, sang an aria for the entire restaurant, announcing when she was done, amid boisterous clapping, that she was Jane Toussaint and would be performing at Versailles all month, but sadly would not be patronizing the restaurant again because someone had complained about her son's birthmark. The people had squirmed and looked down at their tables, and the waiter, red-faced and apologetic, tried to take back his earlier request. Maman had simply finished her meal and made Augustus finish his, and the two of them had walked out, hand in hand.

Maman was that way, championing him even when he would rather not be championed. "We cannot slink off, Augustus, just because someone thinks they are better than we are. I sing so they know that *no one* is better than me, therefore no one could possibly be better than you. I rub it in their nasty little faces that they have just offended the greatest soprano in Paris, and I will never forget or forgive."

By this time, the patisserie owner's daughter, a girl the same age as Augustus, was there and she waved at him as he pressed his nose to the glass.

"Bonjour, Augustus."

"Bonjour, Monique."

She had always been nice to him, asking easy questions about his face that, once answered, never came up again.

"You must come back and see my new kitten. He has the cutest black spot that covers his right cheek, a spot just like yours, so I named him after you. I've been hoping you would come in today, knowing Mondays are the day you see Dr. Moreau."

"Monique, take Augustus into the back, but don't let the kitten in the kitchen."

Augustus followed Monique without hesitation. Maman would know what to get him, but just in case she was amenable to something extra, he turned to add a lemon tart to his order. Maman and Mr. Salt were still staring down at the rows of éclairs and cakes and tarts, but Maman was speaking intently, standing closer to him than was proper, and he was listening just as keenly, his hands clasped at his back, his bowed head almost touching hers. Maman was almost as passionate about sweets as Augustus, but he did not think they were talking about what they would choose.

"Augustus, come on," Monique urged, impatient, and he followed her around the displays, unwilling to disappoint one of his only friends, even for the novelty that was Noble Salt.

Butch had been scolded for coming in the front door, but if he'd been instructed to come in a different way, he'd missed it. The doctor prided himself on his English, but his French accent was so thick, it took Butch hanging on every word and decoding him every step of the way. The Spanish he'd picked up in Bolivia was of no help, though he was much more accustomed to speaking in hand gestures and body language. Everyone understood the language of a gun, sadly, and he'd reverted to waving one a time or two, just to get his point across.

The French doctor's wife spoke better English than her husband, but she came at him like one of the chickens he'd grown up fighting,

It made sense, but it was too late now. She tried to shove him back the way he'd come.

"Go out. I will let you in through ze back."

A woman was being ushered out of the doctor's office—a place he'd had his own confusing consult the week before. She was holding the hand of a boy of nine or ten. The right side of the boy's face was a deep purply black that split his image right down the center, leaving half of his brow, nose, and lips unmarred and the other half swollen and completely discolored.

Butch found himself staring for a moment, the way one does when faced with an oddity. The boy swiveled his head so his unblemished left side was all Butch could see. A flood of pity washed over him before he froze in shocked recognition.

"Get out!" the doctor's wife shooed, but Butch ignored her, sweeping his hat from his head. The doctor had followed the woman and the boy from the examination room, still speaking, and it was clear he was apologizing.

The woman nodded, her shoulders stiff, and she squeezed her son's hand.

"Let's go, Augustus." She addressed the boy in English but thanked the doctor in French, and at long last turned her eyes on him.

He'd dreamed of her, romantic fool that he'd always been, but nothing flickered in her eyes or across her face when her gaze swept over him. She didn't slow or even study him beyond a passing glance. She was eager to leave.

"Step aside, sir," the doctor's wife insisted. "You have broken our rules. Do not come back again. We will not serve you."

He shrugged and followed the woman and the boy from the building, relieved he wouldn't have to make the decision after all. He hadn't much liked the thought of a broken jaw and a busted nose and reconstructed cheekbones. The doctor had promised him a new face and a new life, but he thought he could probably get someone to break his nose for free, change his hair and keep his beard, and no one would recognize the old Butch Cassidy.

His beard was thick, and it disguised the very square jaw that would make him more identifiable. He'd never worn a beard in his younger days, never could stand the itch and prickle and the way it caught every crumb when he ate and every creeping thing when he slept. His hair was longer too, though he slicked it back from his broad forehead and kept it short on the sides and on his neck. It had grown darker too, though not as dark as his beard, and he'd thought about making both black just to give him an added layer of disguise.

The woman was marking the approach of a shiny new motorcar bouncing down the street amid horse carriages and pedestrians, and the boy was staring back at him. Surely Augustus didn't recognize him. He'd been maybe four years old—a precocious four, no doubt, but four—in a different city on a different continent.

The birthmark on the boy's face had thickened considerably, making his right cheek droop a little and his eyelid hang. His smile was lopsided from the weight, but he smiled all the same. He was sharply dressed in short pants and a coat and vest, a hat sitting angled to the right, as if to shade his marked side.

He pulled on his mother's sleeve, but she was already looking back.

He saw the moment she knew him, and his heart and his stomach did a dangerous dance. He should turn and walk away, quickly, but he stood still instead, waiting to see what she would do. It should have discouraged him that she and the boy saw through his paltry disguise. It should have, but it didn't. Something in him rejoiced.

He would later blame his loneliness; he was very lonely. He would blame the miles he'd traveled and the heartache he'd seen; he'd seen so much. He would even blame Mrs. Moreau for making a scene. She spat and threatened, giving him a little shove, and then she turned to Jane Toussaint, apology in her voice. She called him a stupid American. He understood that much.

He *was* stupid. But he could not make himself walk away.

Whatever Jane said to Mrs. Moreau reassured her, and she walked back inside and shut the door and turned the little sign in the window.

"Noble Salt . . . is that you?" Jane said.

It had been more than six long years since he'd set foot in the States, and he'd only been Noble Salt for a day, but he stepped forward, hat in his hand, and assumed the role.

They had gone to Dr. Moreau for the same reason he had. A new face. Apparently Dr. Moreau's talents stopped at noses and chins, and Augustus, with his scarlet, burgeoning cheek was out of luck.

Butch didn't want to say he was sorry. Augustus had a nice face. It just wasn't going to ever be the kind of face that made for an easy way or a quiet existence.

They asked him to walk with them—a visit to a pastry shop and a stroll in the park—and he found himself moving on wooden legs, caught in a dream, taking shallow breaths so he wouldn't wake up. *He'd been so alone.*

Then Augustus slipped away, just for a moment, and Jane started speaking rapidly in dulcet tones. Her English was more accented than it had been years before—or maybe she was simply out of practice. The sense of the surreal continued, and he could hardly focus on what she said because he had not yet adjusted to the fact that *she* was saying it. Jane Toussaint stood beside him while the tinkling bell above the shop door warned him to wake.

"I would like to hire you, sir."

"For what?"

"For protection."

He could only stare at her blankly.

"I am going to do another American tour . . . like the one I was doing when I met you."

"I'm not going back to America," he said, and the words, spoken out loud, even softly, almost made him weep. He was homesick. So damn lonesome and homesick.

"Are you a good man, Mr. Salt? Noble, like your name?" she pressed, not even looking at the assortment they were supposed to be considering. She was flushed, and her eyes were so bright he wondered if she was well.

"No, ma'am."

Her eyebrows shot up along with the corners of her mouth—he'd surprised her too—and a deep dimple creased her right cheek. He stared at the divot, entranced.

"You are not good?" she pressed again, though she had certainly heard him the first time.

"I am not good."

"But . . . can I trust you?"

"With what, ma'am?"

"With my son and with my . . . self."

"I don't make it a habit of hurting women and children, if that's what you mean."

"You don't make a *habit* of it?" she repeated flatly.

"I have never mistreated a woman or a child."

"And what about other men? Do you make a habit of hurting men? Are you dangerous?" She sounded so hopeful that it eased the stiffness in his spine and tempted him to smile.

"I don't like hurting anyone. But I have. And I would . . . if the need arose."

"Do you know how to shoot?"

"Are you asking me to kill someone, Miss Toussaint?"

"No! *Mon dieu*, no. I need security. A personal guard. And you're American. I need an American."

He couldn't go back. *He wanted desperately to go back.* He started shaking his head, and her whisper turned into a torrent of hushed words.

"It's all arranged. But I find myself in need of security." She didn't seem to know what word to use.

"A bodyguard?"

"Yes. A . . . bodyguard."

"And you want to hire me?" The urge to laugh was almost overwhelming. So little was funny anymore. So little was sweet.

"You just said you still wear a gun strapped to your boot. If I recall, it had a big wooden handle. A Colt .45, I think it's called."

That stopped the laugh that bubbled behind his teeth. "Well, I'll be damned."

"Have you killed before?"

He stared down at her, stunned.

Jane Toussaint's color was high, her anxiety zinging like bullets overhead.

"I am performing at the Palais Garnier this evening at seven o'clock. The opera *La Bohème*. A seat will be reserved for you . . . in the front row. Will you come?"

His head was spinning, but one question took precedence above all the others. "Where is your husband?"

"I do not have a husband."

He frowned. That was one thing he remembered quite clearly. Jane Toussaint had a husband. "His name was Oliver, as I recall. He was old enough to be your grandfather, and he sent you off with a complete stranger and never checked to see if your boy survived the night."

"He thought you were a doctor—an impression you reinforced, I might add—and it turns out he was right to trust you, though I've never been able to figure out what on earth inspired you to do such a thing."

He couldn't explain it himself, so he didn't try. He'd done thousands of impulsive, stupid things in his life and couldn't explain any of them. A verse rose in his head, and he made a note so he could jot it down later.

Tumbleweed tumble
Always bouncing with the wind
Headed for the cliff

"Oliver is dead," she said, plunging onward. She was a bit like a tumbleweed herself. "The tour is scheduled. The travel arranged. Dates set. I need someone to accompany me. Us. Augustus and me." She cleared her throat and straightened her shoulders, meeting his gaze and squaring her jaw.

"I will pay you well," she added.

"And you don't have a manager," he said. "No boss breathing down my neck or telling me what to do."

"I have a tour promoter, an orchestra in every city, and a conductor, but no manager . . . and no husband. I am managing myself, and I will breathe down your neck and tell you what to do. In fact, doing what I say will be your primary job."

For some reason the idea did not bother him in the slightest, and he was fairly certain she had no idea how suggestive she sounded.

She was afraid he would tell her no. He could see it in every rigid line of her body, in the way she hardly breathed. Jane Toussaint was desperate.

"I would prefer not to discuss this in front of my son. Will you come tonight?" she pleaded.

He nodded, dazed, and Augustus returned just in time to save him from Jane—or save Jane from him—and ordered for them all.

6

Noble is the man
Who gives his life for others
Sadly, I'm not he

It was a month after she met the doctor who was not a doctor that Jane Toussaint came face to face with a "wanted" handbill for one Butch Cassidy. Noble Salt stared back at her, his eyes solemn, a bit of a smile around his lips. He had no mustache in the picture, which took years from his face. But she recognized him instantly and stopped to stare, reading quickly, incredulously. She tore the flyer from the wall of the train car where it was posted.

"What are you doing?" Oliver had asked, waving a porter forward to take their luggage.

"It is Dr. Salt," she said, staring down into his deep-set gaze. There was no color in the photograph, of course, but she knew those eyes were a bold, guileless blue.

"Who?"

"The doctor who attended to Augustus . . . It's him."

"It is not," Oliver snorted. He had indeed sent for a doctor when Augustus was ill. The man was Edward Harriman's wife's cousin, a sallow-faced, hollow-eyed man named Virgil Salt. Dr. Virgil Salt had reported to the hotel not long after the first Dr. Salt departed, apologizing wearily for not coming the night before and blaming an outbreak of diphtheria in the city. He also confirmed that he'd never heard of Noble Salt.

"My brother is Jasper, and my son is Alonzo. My father is Teddy, and I am Virgil. I have a cousin named Norman. All are doctors, but none are Noble." He'd laughed at his tired joke and, with a quick look at Augustus's throat and a brush of his hand over his cool forehead, declared him out of the woods. He left a hefty bill, a "curing ointment for the boy's face," and a baffled Jane in his wake. The ointment proved as useless as her inquiries, and Oliver presented Mr. Harriman with the bill the day they left for a new city on one of his trains.

Oliver had not been present for any of it. He'd had shoulders to rub and palms to grease. Oliver was a social climber, a poor relation to nobility, and her success was his success. Her future was his future. He'd undoubtedly fallen into bed in the wee hours of the morning having done all he could for the Parisian Songbird and the Toussaint Conservatory, and she did not fault him for it. They had an arrangement, and she would not have wanted him there.

She'd said nothing to him about the long, strange night, not knowing at all what to make of it. What to make of Noble Salt. What to make of herself.

She didn't know why she'd kissed him. It was not like her. The thought forced a rueful laugh. No, not like her at all. She could blame it on her gratitude, on the wash of overwhelming relief she'd felt at seeing Augustus resting peacefully beside her, his skin damp and cool, his hands curled around the watch Noble Salt had given him.

But it wasn't that. Not entirely.

She'd made it clear she wanted him to go, and he'd immediately risen to leave, courteous and kind, like he hadn't just sat up all night in an uncomfortable chair watching over them. His eyes had lingered on her face and form, and his admiration—*Three nights in a row he'd heard her sing!*—was apparent.

She'd panicked, but it was not the typical panic she felt around men. Instead, she'd become inexplicably afraid that she would never see him again, and the thought had produced a sharp, unexpected pang. She had never fancied a man before, and certainly never admired one. He was so handsome and gentle. And so she kissed him. Then she'd panicked again, because he'd kissed her back, the way a man kisses a woman he wants.

Noble Salt knew what he was doing.

She did not.

And she had never had a *real* kiss. A nice kiss.

But all she'd been able to taste was her own terror. He'd tasted it too, for he immediately stepped back, apology in his face. She'd almost tried again, aghast that she'd wasted her surprising moment of courage on an unmemorable goodbye.

The man on the poster *was* Noble Salt. Jane was certain of it, but Oliver urged her to hurry. They had a dozen cities left in Harriman's tour, and Oliver was more concerned about their trunks and the accommodations than a faded notice in the private car. Augustus was pulling at her skirts too, eager to move.

She'd rolled the stiff page and stuck it in her reticule.

The handbill called him Butch Cassidy.

Butch. What a terrible name. It was almost as unfortunate as her own, and she wondered how he had come by it. Such names always had a story. It didn't suit, and no matter how she tried, he remained Noble Salt in her thoughts.

It made no sense. *He* made no sense. The handbill proclaimed him armed and dangerous, wanted for robberies spreading from coast to coast. The notice was clearly an attempt to give passengers a good look before they boarded trains that might be carrying the outlaws, for it wasn't only Noble Salt/Butch Cassidy they wanted to apprehend. Another man, Harry Longabaugh, called the Sundance Kid, was a known cohort, and the two were thought to be together.

She began to look for Noble Salt in every audience, and half expected him to step out from behind the curtains backstage. She thought perhaps she might have imagined the whole thing, but he'd left his timepiece—an expensive one—and Augustus talked endlessly of Dr. Salt.

"He left without saying goodbye, Maman. I want to see him again. He had a revolver. Remember the gun in his boot?"

She did indeed, but it *was* America, and she'd been so weary and Augustus was so ill. And it wasn't like he'd taken it out or let the boy hold it. He'd simply responded with a calm "It's just for protection. I don't always know who I'm dealing with." Then he'd eased the cuff of his pants down over the black handle strapped to his boot, and Augustus had been too distracted by his own misery to investigate as he normally would have done.

At the end of her American tour, she and Augustus and Oliver had returned to New York before they set sail for Paris. Mr. Harriman and his wife had hosted them for three days at their home in Arden, where she sang again for their prestigious guests and roamed the grounds with Augustus, grateful for a small respite before boarding the ship for home.

Harriman was a small man with quick eyes and movements and round glasses that sat on a big nose, made all the more prominent by his enormous, shaggy mustache. It hung from beneath his nose like the grill on the front of a train, hiding his mouth and brushing his small chin. He did not seem at all interested in her or her music, but he was intent on impressing the Carnegies, who had built the music hall where she'd opened her tour.

He left the Toussaints to his wife, Mary, for the entirety of their stay. She was gracious and accommodating and patient with Augustus—she'd lost a little boy in '88 when he was Augustus's age—though she brought her cousin, Dr. Virgil Salt, back for another look at his face.

"Surely there is something that can be done," she said, tutting and pressing her fingers to his cheek. "What a shame, poor dear."

Mr. Harriman introduced her performance with a stiff little bow and a reminder to his guests that he, too, was a great lover of "musical philanthropy."

Oliver accompanied her for several numbers on the piano, his eyes skipping from her to Andrew Carnegie and his wife, Louise, sitting off to the side. Oliver had been told they were ardent fans.

Carnegie, the railroad tycoon and steel magnate, was a small, dignified man as well, with a white beard and a curious gaze. He requested she sing "Waly, Waly" like she'd done the night she'd walked backstage and met Noble Salt. Mr. Carnegie clapped happily when she sang both the traditional words and the newer variations, all terribly sad, and all very Scottish.

> *O waly, waly, love be bonnie,*
> *And bright as a jewel while it is new.*
> *But when 'tis auld, it waxeth cold,*
> *And fades away like morning dew.*

Mr. Carnegie's eyes had grown wet, and he asked her to sing it again, without accompaniment, "like you are standing in the Highlands looking out over the sea," and he'd praised her and Mr. Harriman for a "most pleasant afternoon" when she finished.

Carnegie, a Scottish immigrant, reportedly had an organ built in the lower hall of his Manhattan home, and Oliver, ever the promoter, suggested that he might like to have Jane come sing for him there at some future date. He said he would like that very much, but thankfully, Oliver did not press the matter.

When the conversation turned to business—Mr. Carnegie had recently sold his company to JP Morgan for $480 million—she was forgotten. Augustus was warily included by the children playing a game of croquet on the vast south lawn, and Oliver was lurking at the fringes of manly conversation, looking for an opening. Her talent alone was not enough to fuel all of Oliver's ambitions, though it had gotten them far.

"Jane is convinced she saw him at Carnegie Hall," she heard Oliver say, raising his voice to be heard.

"Who, dear?" Mary Harriman asked, pausing in her own conversation with a small group of ladies nearby.

Jane shook her head, feigning ignorance, but Oliver had succeeded in hooking Mr. Harriman and Mr. Carnegie both. He had their undivided attention.

"Butch Cassidy . . . the outlaw . . . isn't that right, Jane? She was quite adamant, and Jane is not one for flights of imagination. She saw the circular on the train and recognized him."

Mr. Harriman was suddenly regarding her with more interest and intensity than he'd shown in any of their previous interactions. He began striding toward her, Carnegie at his heels, Oliver following behind, triumph in his smile. She wanted to slap him. She'd reacted to the circular, and he'd dismissed her. That was all, and she'd kept the rest to herself. Now he acted as if it was all a thrilling coup that he had been a part of.

"We thought he was Dr. Salt. We'd been waiting for him to come take a look at the boy," he prattled, keeping himself in the conversation.

"What did he say his name was, Jane?" Oliver called.

"He didn't," she lied. "As you said, we just assumed he was Dr. Salt. Oliver is convinced I was mistaken," she said serenely, pinning him with her gaze. "I fear many Americans look the same to me."

"But why was this man backstage?" Carnegie asked.

"And why would he let you assume a status he did not have?" Harriman chimed in.

"We thought you had sent him," Oliver said. "And he did not correct the assumption. He accompanied Jane and the boy back to our quarters to administer to the boy."

The women gasped, and Harriman's jaw dropped.

"Good heavens, man!" Carnegie frowned. "Mrs. Toussaint is lucky to be alive. The boy too."

"Perhaps the man wanted to kidnap them for ransom. It is something I fear greatly." Mrs. Harriman shuddered.

"But he didn't do any of those things," Jane interjected. "He was very helpful and knowledgeable. He attended to Augustus and went on his way. I'm sure he simply bore a resemblance to this train robber. It's very exciting to imagine it, but he was a perfect gentleman. I'm sorry to disappoint you all."

She wondered what they would think if they knew she'd been a proficient pickpocket once. At Arden, there were only blue skies and green grass, crystal goblets and fine china, and ever since arriving, she had fought the urge to steal something. Anything. A fork or spoon, to slip it into her shoe or up her sleeve. She hadn't taken anything in so long, and she wouldn't take anything now . . . but she *wanted* to, if only to balance the scales.

"You must come with me," Mr. Harriman insisted, taking her firmly by the arm, and she jumped guiltily. "I will show you the real Butch Cassidy."

"We will all go and see Edward's collection. It really is quite fascinating," Mary Harriman cried, waving her hands and drawing her guests together. The children were still being supervised by a governess and a nanny, and Augustus did not even look up from their game. She allowed herself to be drawn into the house at Edward Harriman's side, leading the party like they were off to confront a rival gang on the docks in their silks and suits.

Harriman's collection was in a room he called his study. An entire wall was plastered with maps showing the lines where his trains ran. Pins were stuck at various spots, and stories were framed above the pins to explain the robberies that had occurred there. On the adjacent side of the room, articles detailing the story of Harriman's rise as a railroad tycoon and dozens of other interesting pictures were displayed in gallery style, but it was the most recent photo—a new one, from the placement—that captured her gaze.

She tried to look away so she would not be too obvious in her perusal and asked a question she already knew the answer to.

"Is that him?"

"Yes. That is the outlaw known as Butch Cassidy. A man who has made my life miserable for the last few years, in particular. He's a train robber, and he's good at it. But I have reason to believe he's left the States behind."

"And where did you get that photograph?" Carnegie asked, saving her from the same question. "It hardly looks real. How did you get the man to pose for such a shot?"

Harriman chuckled, pleased with himself. "That picture made the entire frustrating episode worth it. We were to talk of a truce. I thought Cassidy could work for me as a consultant on the trains. He knew where they were vulnerable and where they would most likely be hit. He also knows the tricks of the trade, ones we could protect against. That picture was taken the day we met up. He was holding still enough, waiting for his lawyer to approach, and my photographer got a great shot. Really captured him, I think."

"I do see a resemblance, Jane, but it can't be the same man," Oliver said, studying the image of the man in a weathered western hat, standing against a hilly backdrop, his hands slightly flared at his sides, waiting for something she could not see. It was a striking picture, something that could be displayed in a museum. She supposed Harriman's house *was* a museum of sorts.

The man they'd seen at Carnegie Hall bore very little obvious resemblance to the dusty cowhand in the picture. The clothes were markedly different. The landscape too. But Oliver was wrong. It *was* the same man.

She moved closer, pretending to examine his face, though she didn't need to. Noble Salt's eyes met hers, sad acceptance in his gaze, and she looked away, shaken. She immediately looked back.

"You're right. It can't be him," she said lightly. She was an accomplished actress when she needed to be. "Where was this picture taken?"

"Near the Idaho-Utah border. An abandoned stagecoach station. A world away. A world away," Harriman repeated, sighing as though he almost missed it.

"It is not just a world away, it's another world entirely," she said, still staring at the outlaw.

"Indeed," Harriman said, nodding.

Jane had never had any trouble believing in God. After all, there were a million worlds just in London. A million more in Paris and in New York. And they rarely intersected. She supposed heaven was no different, just another world that was beyond reach. The man in the photograph existed in yet another dimension.

She could not look away from the picture, and Harriman continued with his story, seemingly thrilled to have a rapt audience in the centerpiece of his collection.

"He's a fascinating character," Harriman said, but Carnegie drifted away, and Mary Harriman was already leading several people out of the room. They were not as interested in the outlaw as she was.

"For him to be at Carnegie Hall . . . it would make no sense at all," Harriman mused. "But he's very unpredictable. Our last attempt at a meeting was disastrous . . . but perhaps . . ." He tugged at his billowy mustache, and his eyes strayed back to his map. "Will you tell me if you see the man again? Don't be fooled. He's not what he seems. He's crafty. And elusive. You cannot trust him."

"Of course," she said, though she heartily disagreed. She was quite convinced she could trust him. Implicitly. "Of course I will tell you. But it was not the same man."

Later that night, when the whole house was asleep, she'd tiptoed down to the room where Harriman's collection was kept. They were leaving the next day, returning to Paris on a steamer, and she wanted one last look at the picture and the rest of the collection without being observed.

She expected the door to be locked, but when she closed her eyes, so hopeful it was almost a prayer, and turned the knob, the door sprang open, not locked at all. A few glowing coals remained on the grate, and she thought surely the Harrimans were done for the night. She lit a lamp and, in the quiet, pored over the articles Edward Harriman had framed, connecting the news to a place on his map with a string and a pushpin. Each article described a robbery. She read them all, taking in every word before studying the spot on the map where each heist had taken place.

She could not reconcile the man who had helped her with the man who blew holes in the sides of trains with dynamite and emptied bank vaults. He liked dynamite.

"Maman?"

She jolted, screeching softly, and her arm came up in a defensive swing, knocking the picture of Butch Cassidy from the wall. It slid to the floor with a bump and a crack.

Augustus was standing in the doorway, his little legs trembling beneath his nightshirt, his dark eyes wide. Tears gleamed from his disparate cheeks.

"You left me! You left me, and you didn't come back."

"I'm sorry, my darling," she breathed, and crouched beside the fallen photograph to assess the damage. "Stay there. There might be glass, and you've no shoes on." Augustus tiptoed forward, ignoring her instructions. The glass over the picture had cracked and the frame had come apart at the corner, revealing the small finish nails that kept it together.

She picked up the frame, turning it carefully upright so the pieces wouldn't fall. Augustus leaned against her shoulder and peered at the picture, his upset forgotten.

"Maman . . . it's Noble Salt!" Augustus crowed. "He's a cowboy!"

"Shh, Augustus," she begged. There was nothing to be done now, and surely someone had heard the commotion. "You'll wake the whole house."

She laid the picture on the floor where it had fallen. Hopefully Mr. Harriman would think it had fallen without her help. Scooping up her son, she lowered the lamp, then fled from the room and up the stairs, leaving Noble Salt to his fate.

No one said anything about the accident. Mr. Harriman was not at home when a servant collected their trunks and prepared to take them to the steamer, but he'd seen the damage. The picture had been removed from the frame and was lying on his desk.

It was wrong. She knew it was, but it belonged to her. *He* belonged to her.

Before she even made a conscious decision, she was rolling the picture into a tight scroll. She slid it up her narrow sleeve, just like she'd imagined herself doing with the silver, and buttoned her cuff so it couldn't slide out. Then she marched from the room and out into the foyer where Oliver and Augustus were waiting.

They would be sailing for Paris before Edward Harriman even knew it was gone.

When she'd arrived back in Paris, she'd begun to collect every account she could find, not just about him, but about the Wild West in general, searching for his name among the storylines, most of which featured people and events from several decades past. According to the storytellers, Butch Cassidy seemed to be "the last of a breed."

She'd scoured every newspaper she could get her hands on, searching the pages for glimpses of him and his escapades, and found nothing but a brief mention in a story about a heist on a train heading to San Francisco. The apprehended robber, a man named Van Parker, was thought to be an associate of Butch Cassidy and was cooperating with authorities.

She'd found three dime novels about Butch Cassidy and the Wild Bunch, each caper more outlandish than the next. The only tale that sounded remotely like the man she'd met described a winter that was so cold that most of the livestock died—they called it the great "die off"—and the animals weren't the only ones. Diphtheria, of all things, had spread across the frozen West. Butch Cassidy traveled back and forth from the Simpson Ranch, where he worked as a cowhand, bringing the medicines Mrs. Margaret Simpson had brewed and bottled to sick children across the state and into several others, saving lives and raising his stature in his community. If it was true, he deserved a reward and not a noose, which was what he would get if he were apprehended.

He was an enigma, robbing banks and stealing the payroll from miners, but he always managed to get away with minimal chaos, and he hadn't been charged with killing anyone, though that was little comfort. The books were written for thrills, not facts, so it was hard to know what the man had truly done and what was just a good story written to sell the cheap yarns.

Sometimes she would take out the stolen picture and the circular and study his face and replay every moment of the night they'd met. She'd been aided by an outlaw. Kissed by an outlaw. What a story she could tell! They were offering a reward for information that led to his capture. She could send her statement to the Pinkerton Detective Agency, listed on the bottom of the notice, or even sell her story to the papers. But she never did.

She'd placed the items beneath glass on her vanity table—like specimens in a laboratory—and then covered both with a thick piece of lace and a vase filled with silk flowers.

As the years had gone by, the dime novels became Augustus's, and more were added to his shelves. He was as fascinated by the stories as she, though she'd never told him about the connection between Butch Cassidy and their Noble Salt. For that was what he was—theirs—and Augustus talked about him like he'd given him life and not just a gold pocket watch and a steady presence through a miserable night.

To see him standing there outside the clinic, so different yet so familiar, like he'd finally heard her prayers and come to save her, was too much to take in. She'd stumbled with her words and shaken and stuttered. Even Augustus had noticed her discomfiture. But she had so little time, and miraculously . . . he had come.

7

When roses bloom in
The wintry snow then will my
Love return to me

It was not at all uncommon for the cast to request and reserve seats for friends or family, but it was unheard of for Jane. She worried about drawing attention or raising eyebrows, but when she spoke to the stage manager, he did not question her.

He simply said he would see to it and reported back shortly before curtain call that the gentleman was seated, as requested, at the end of the front row. The stage manager was not friendly or warm, nor was she. The cast and crew kept their distance. It was better that way, Oliver had always said. "It adds mystery. You are a beautiful, mysterious woman with a voice that makes your listeners weep. That is all they need to know about you."

Oliver was a cousin of the late Lord Aubrey Toussaint, Earl of Werthog, and he used the Toussaint name at every turn. It was Lord Aubrey's wife who heard Jane sing and plucked her from the obscurity of a London orphanage and placed her into the skilled hands of Oliver Toussaint, who had been training and fostering singers and musicians for decades in his Paris conservatory.

The first time Oliver heard her sing, he wept and praised God, as if twelve-year-old Jane had been sent directly to him, a reward for all his labors. "You will change everything for me," he'd whispered. "And I will change everything for you."

From that day, she'd been molded into Jane Toussaint, the Parisian Songbird, and she had quietly—even gratefully—let them do their worst. They'd taken a scalpel—and sometimes a battering ram—to everything that made her undesirable. Her cockney accent was stamped out and her posture, poise, and manners were drilled in. She had no say—and wanted no say—in any of it. She simply opened her mouth and sang when she was told to sing, studied when she was told to study, and fell into an exhausted stupor when she was allowed to sleep.

She was well acquainted with hunger, loneliness, and fear, and nothing they threw at her was as frightening or as difficult as being indistinguishable from every other street rat in London with no home and no hope. She knew she was not just lucky. She'd been saved, and from age twelve to sixteen she worked with unflagging focus toward becoming a songstress of the highest order, simply to earn her keep.

She'd done more than earn her keep. She'd exceeded every goal and smashed through every barrier. She'd been unstoppable, and Oliver had been ecstatic. His considerable investment had paid off.

At seventeen, she landed her first big part as the understudy for Musetta in the Paris Opera's *La Bohème*, and when the lead had gotten sick, she stepped in and finished out the three-week run. She was never an understudy again.

Tonight, more than a dozen years and hundreds of performances later, the opera was *La Bohème* once more. Jane preferred the feistier Musetta and her musical numbers, but she'd been cast as Mimi. Perhaps that, too, was fortuitous. It would be better for Noble Salt to see her as a Mimi—vulnerable, gentle, and desperately in need. She was *so desperately* in need.

She'd thought he wouldn't come. *Why* had he come? Thinking back over her impassioned plea at the patisserie, she had determined he could not have been greatly impressed. Everything about their interaction—both today and six years ago—would not inspire trust between them. Yet their first meeting had included sickness and sorrow and several revelations on her part, and she had never been the same.

Noble Salt—Butch Cassidy—had made an indelible mark.

That they had met again, in almost as strange a circumstance, had her acting anew, though this time the curtain would not close, and if she was lucky, he would not leave.

She sang, wept, and died just for him in the space of three acts, and thought it might be the best she'd ever performed. The conductor praised her highly, and the rest of the cast looked at her askance. That was her own fault. She had never allowed anyone to get close, and they all thought her a terrible prima donna.

But when she finally stepped out into the balmy evening, Noble Salt was waiting for her. He wore the same suit he'd worn that morning, and he was right where she'd asked him to be. She had a fur stole, but she didn't need it. Though a nip was in the air, she was nervous and warm, flushed from singing and the anticipation of a meeting, and she was suddenly terrified. She had not thought this through.

"I don't have a motorcar . . . or a carriage. But I have a reservation there." He nodded toward a popular restaurant that served the late-night opera crowd. "I walked."

"From your home?"

"It's hardly a home. It's a room in a hovel. And temporary. I haven't been in Paris long." He had the flavor of places she couldn't even imagine in his voice. A land of long stretches, tall mountains, and blazing suns, but she had no time now to bask in its warmth. They stood on the busy street, and Paris had eyes. Luc waited for her in the long queue of cars, about half a block down. She would need to be quick and impersonal.

"I can't dine. I have a housekeeper who sits with Augustus, but she is old, and Augustus is a worrier. He will wait until I'm home before he sleeps."

"He's the man of the house."

"Yes."

"How far is your place?" he asked. "Can we walk?"

"Not far at all. But Luc—my driver—is waiting."

He rocked forward on his feet and then back again, his stance wide, his hands in his pockets, looking at her steadily. "Tell me what you want to do," he said softly.

She hesitated. That Noble Salt had done everything she'd asked was a hopeful sign, but it was better that Luc not see them. He would remember the man from the afternoon, and he would report back.

"I need to tell Luc," she said in a rush. "He's a terrible snoop, and I would rather he not see us together again today."

Noble Salt pulled a little book from his pocket and opened it to the last page.

"Here. Write a message. Tell him to go home. He can't argue with a bit of paper."

She took the small pencil from his fingers and did as he instructed, her hand shaking slightly, her breath short.

He ripped the page from the book, folded it, and looked around. A boy of about twelve was selling programs a few feet away. Noble Salt took a bill from his pocket and handed her the message and the money.

"I don't speak French, so I can't do it. Go tell that boy to deliver the note to your driver. I'll be waiting there." He pointed to the opposite side of the street. "And if you change your mind, just keep walking. We'll forget all about it."

She took the bill and the folded note and did as he said, telling the boy to wait to deliver it until Luc was first in the queue. The boy agreed, taking the money so fast, the paper sliced her finger, and she thought it possible that Luc would not receive the message at all.

So be it. She did not answer to Luc. Soon, she would answer to no one. Then she walked across the street toward the man she was about to entrust her whole world to.

~ ∞ ~

"I will not ask the address; though . . . under the circumstances, I suppose we should learn to trust each other," Noble said as he matched his gait to hers. She didn't answer him. She didn't want to talk yet. She was walking too fast, not looking right or left, though the crush of the Paris street, even at the late hour, did not allow her to move as fast as she'd like.

He swerved to miss a bicyclist and hissed as a basket of cabbages rolled off the back of a lorry, the heads bouncing merrily down the street. He kicked at one, and she stumbled on another.

"Jane," he said, a note of censure in her name. She darted a look at him. He offered his arm, and she hesitated a moment before looping her gloved hand around his elbow. It would be less conspicuous than the alternative.

"Slow down," he murmured. "You're acting like you've got a burr under your saddle."

She nodded, her fingers flexing uncomfortably. He wrapped his hand around hers and slowed to a stroll. "We're just walking."

"We're just walking," she repeated, and tried to match her breaths to his. His arm was warm, his presence reassuring, and she let herself be soothed, though she was anything but calm.

A block later, the traffic thinned as the commercial district merged into residences, and she pointed down a narrow side street that was a less direct route home. Luc would take the other way. It was then that she remembered what he'd said.

"'Under the circumstances'?" she asked. "What does that mean?"

"If I am to be your bodyguard, you should feel safe with me."

"You will take the position?" She stopped walking and her hand on his arm became a clamp. He urged her forward again, his hand returning to hers with a slight squeeze. She eased her grip and made herself breathe.

"I haven't decided. I've got a few questions."

"I might not have answers," she said, her nerves whistling once more.

"Where are we going, Jane?" he said gently, and she didn't protest his use of her name. It would be odd to do so now. She'd jumped into immediate intimacy with him and could hardly fault him for being familiar.

She pointed the way, directing him until they were on her street. They passed her house—a light burned from Augustus's window—and she said nothing. At the corner, she pointed toward the bench by the paper stand where people stopped to read the dailies.

"Stop here. I'll walk the rest of the way."

His mustache frowned, but he didn't argue. He sat obediently, leaving half the bench for her.

"Your questions?" she asked, perched on the very edge.

He sighed. "How many do I get?"

"I have ten minutes. Then I must go."

"What happened to Oliver?"

"He'd been feeling poorly for a while. He had a stroke at a gentleman's club and did not wake up from it."

"How long ago was this?"

"Almost a year."

"Plenty of time to find a bodyguard. Why me?"

She squirmed. It was not an easy question to answer. "I do not trust many people. I do not *know* many people. I had all but decided I would hire a man when I reached the States. One of those Pinkertons I've read so much about."

She was purposely poking at him, but if he stiffened, he hid it well. She continued, "Then you appeared this morning out of nowhere, an American I actually knew, and it seemed fortuitous."

"Hmm. Fortuitous. So why are you so skittish? You're a bundle of nerves."

"I am not skittish," she began to argue, and then stopped. She didn't have time for bickering. "Mostly I don't want to be seen with any gentleman. I am a celebrity in this city, and a bit of a recluse as well, when I'm not performing. I don't attend galas and parties, especially now that Oliver is gone. It would invite interest and speculation, which I would think is something you would like to avoid."

"Oh?" he asked. "And why's that?"

She made herself meet his gaze, unblinking. He was colorless in the darkness, no vivid blue or golden brown. Just gray and quiet, waiting for her to speak. She was afraid, just like he said, but she found she was less afraid of him than she was of everyone and everything else. He'd proven himself an ally once. She needed to believe he would be again.

"Because you are a bit of a celebrity yourself," she whispered.

Silence. She made herself wait.

"Who exactly do you think I am?" he asked, and a shiver shimmied across her shoulders and took root in her stomach. Maybe it was better to pretend she didn't know.

"Jane?" His voice was no louder than hers had been, but she heard his fear too, and it made her bold.

"I saw a handbill for two wanted men six years ago, not long after you helped me. I recognized you. The circular identified you as a man named Butch Cassidy, a fugitive from the law, according to the Pinkerton Detective Agency."

He didn't move. Didn't blink. But neither did she. She simply stared at him and he at her, and a small eternity formed around them. It popped a moment later, the sudden barking of a dog and the returning yowl of a cat jolting them both into the here and now. He sighed and she inhaled, a shift in the air and their expectations.

"And yet . . . you still want to hire me," he said. It was not a question, nor was it a denial.

"I do."

"Why?" The word was flat and hard.

"You helped me once and asked for nothing. I need help again, but this time I will make it worth your while."

He began to shake his head. Her desperation rose, and her pride sank.

"Please, Mr. Cassidy."

"That is not my name."

"Should I call you Mr. Parker? That is your real name, isn't it? Robert LeRoy Parker?"

The head shaking grew more adamant, though she wasn't sure if he was telling her no or warning her away.

"Then what shall I call you?" she pressed.

He ignored her question. "I am not a good man, Mrs. Toussaint. And you seem to know it. You're afraid someone will recognize me . . . in Paris . . . and you don't want to be seen with me. Yet you want me to accompany you and your son across an ocean and a *continent*. That doesn't make sense."

She was Mrs. Toussaint again. That was not an encouraging sign. "Don't you want to go home?"

Ah. She had him there. The naked longing that shuddered over his face was brief, but it was marked, and she saw it. He closed his eyes as if willing it back.

"You look quite different now and far different from the handbill," she continued. "It's been six years. I read the American papers. There's been no mention of you at all. I've looked, believe me. It was quite a shocking discovery for me, as you might imagine. And as for my reasons . . . If I was going to Ireland, I'd want an Irishman. If I was going to Africa, I'd want an African. But I'm going to America, and here you are. We can help each other."

He shook his head again, though this time much less adamantly.

"I have read everything I can find about you and your Wild Bunch. I would not describe you as a good man, that is true—good men don't rob banks—but you aren't the kind of bad man I try to avoid."

She'd surprised him, and he turned his head, studying her face. It was all she could do not to sink back. He was too close.

"What kind do you try to avoid?" he asked softly.

"The kind that hurt women and children. You assured me you don't. I believe you." She dug in her handbag, using her movement as an excuse to increase the distance between them, and fished out Oliver's ticket. She'd brought it to the opera house in hopes he would come, in hopes she could convince him. "Here. Take it. It's yours. Regardless of what you decide."

He didn't take it.

She placed it in his lap.

"It is a first-class ticket on the *Adriatic*, a world-class ocean liner. It would have been Oliver's room. Augustus and I will be right next door. There will be times when you will join us for meals both in the first-class dining hall and in our quarters—when I go out, you must go out—but for the most part, you will stay in your room, and we will stay in ours. It's not a terribly long voyage. Eight days is all."

She was almost begging, and she clenched her teeth, bidding herself to slow.

Noble Salt sat looking straight forward, his hands on his knees, deliberating. But he hadn't said no.

"I will be performing the first and final nights of the voyage in the ballroom in exchange for our fare. Oliver was very good at negotiating such things. The tour opens in New York City at Carnegie Hall, just like before. But then we will take the train across the country and work our way back to the East Coast, city by city. We have a full week of performances in Utah. That is where you're from . . . isn't it?" She took a breath and barreled on, not waiting for an answer. "I'm singing at Saltair. Do you know Saltair?"

"Everybody knows Saltair. It's the Coney Island of the West. Augustus will love it."

"Yes, well. When the tour is over, you will go your way, and we will go ours."

He took his hands off his knees and picked up the ticket. Then he turned his gaze on her. "There hasn't been a single person in my life I haven't disappointed," he warned.

His honesty left her momentarily stunned. It rang in the air, a solemn guarantee. A quiet confession. And in that moment of humble candor, she almost loved him.

He didn't amend his statement, and for a moment they sat, side by side, letting reality settle.

"I'm not hiring you to make me happy, Noble Salt. Can I call you Noble Salt?"

He nodded.

"I'm not hiring you to make me happy," she repeated. "I'm hiring you to keep me safe and to aid my travel. If I make it to the end of my tour with my son, my money, and fifty performances behind me, I will be the happiest woman on earth."

"And you'll come back here?"

She considered not answering that question. She did not want to open new avenues of discussion and query now, and she didn't want to tell him more than she had to.

"I'm not coming back. No. But I will pay for your passage to return, if that is what you wish to do."

His brows disappeared into the shadow of his hat, and she surged ahead, giving him a skeleton of an explanation. Better a glossing than a full interrogation.

"The house and everything in it will be sold and the servants—there are only three—paid a small severance, and the rest will go to the conservatory. I have enough of my own money in jewels and cash to finance the balance on the tour, including your pay, so you needn't be worried that you will not be well compensated. What I make on the tour should give me enough to settle somewhere. I am hoping I will be able to do appearances frequently enough to provide for myself and Augustus in America, long term."

"This ticket is for the day after tomorrow," he said in sudden realization.

"Yes."

Air whooshed between his lips. "You don't waste any time."

"I was leaving with or without you, but I don't mind telling you how much I hope . . . that it will be with."

She stood and smoothed her skirt. A light had appeared in the sitting room window. Luc had arrived home and would be waiting. She was out of time.

"I will pay five dollars a day and all your expenses, but I won't pay you until we're done. That ticket is a deposit. A . . . bonus."

He moved to stand as well.

"My flat is on the corner. I do not need an escort, Mr. Salt."

He sank back obediently.

"The ship sails at five o'clock from Cherbourg. Boarding time is three. You will need to take a train, of course. It's a six-hour ride, so go early. The trains from Paris aren't always reliable, so leave yourself plenty of time."

He was silent, but he hadn't released or relinquished the ticket.

"Augustus and I will meet you there."

Jane could not sleep. Her mind spun and whirred with all that could go wrong, and she was not safe in her own home. She hadn't been safe for so many years, but it had only gotten worse since Oliver died.

In the beginning, when she was a very young soprano making her debut, Oliver had dangled her like ripe fruit in front of anyone he thought could further her career, but he had only dangled. He would whisk her away after every performance except for those rare times when she was brought in, like a bird in a cage, for people to gawk at. Occasionally, if they were very rich donors to the Paris Opera, or possible benefactors to Oliver's conservatory, they were allowed to kiss her hand or talk with her for a moment.

And then Lord Ashley Toussaint, the new Earl of Werthog, took an interest in her.

Lord Ashley called her *cousin* when he greeted her, as though her enrollment at Toussaint Conservatory made her family property. He also attended every performance of *La Bohème* and promised a donation in her name to the Paris Opera and an increased endowment to the conservatory if he could only spend an "afternoon in her presence."

Oliver readily agreed, thrilled with what it would mean for her to have such an influential admirer. "He is family, Jane, and the conservatory needs his support more than ever. His mother, your benefactress, will one day give him full control. I am the director, but I do not have the funds to keep us afloat—to keep your career afloat."

He sent her off with Lord Ashley with a fatherly warning and a wink.

"Take care of her, my boy," he said, though Lord Ashley was nearing thirty. "She is the future of the Toussaint Conservatory and the Paris Opera, mark my words."

They went in a carriage to the park and on a picnic in the pretty gazebo on his family's Parisian estate, not far from Versailles. He'd then rolled atop her, tied her wrists over her head, and covered her mouth so she couldn't scream. He didn't try to woo or seduce her. He seemed to enjoy the tears that streamed from her eyes and the blood that trickled from her body. He pinched and bit, enjoying the bruises and the breaking of her skin.

When he was finished, he stood over her, drew a bottle of champagne from the basket, and toasted her. "To you, cousin, and your maiden voyage." He'd broken the bottle, the way they did when a vessel first set sail, and approached her with the jagged, dripping edge. He pulled the bindings from her mouth and dribbled the champagne over her lips and down her breasts that he'd bared and bitten. When he pressed the edge of the bottle to her throat, a tender smile on his lips, and told her he didn't want to see her again, she said her very first prayer of thanks.

"Clean yourself up now. I'll take you home," he said blithely. "You and I don't suit, I don't think. You are beautiful, and your voice is otherworldly. You will be a big star, I have no doubt, but from here on out, we will just be friends. Cousins. How does that sound?"

She'd been so afraid she'd simply nodded, unable to control the tears that kept coming and the cold that was creeping up her limbs and numbing her thoughts. She just needed to get away from him. She'd buttoned her clothes and tidied her hair while he chatted about the beauty of the woods and a game of cricket later that afternoon, popping blueberries into his mouth and nibbling at the cheese she hadn't eaten.

He'd taken her back to the school, just as he said he would, and Oliver's precious conservatory had received their increased endowment, as promised. Oliver had been so pleased, especially considering the young lord had moved on and set his sights elsewhere. "We don't want him to fall in love with you. Marriage would stunt your career. But that was the easiest increase the school has ever received. And not an unpleasant afternoon for you either, my dear, I'm sure."

She never told Oliver what had transpired, and he never let on that he knew. Maybe, like Jane, he'd simply hoped that would be the end of it. Lord Ashley had said they did not suit.

But it was not to be. That day had marked the first of many unpleasant afternoons. Unpleasant evenings. Unpleasant years. And she'd endured it.

Now Oliver was gone, and Lord Ashley controlled everything. She had no one to appeal to. No one to act as a buffer or a barrier, though Oliver hadn't been much of one. Lord Ashley had begun to make insinuations about taking "his son," though she was convinced he only did it to terrify her.

He'd never married, though he'd strung several young ladies along. Something in his mother's will—she'd passed nine months after Oliver— had enraged him, and he'd come to Jane's door drunk and demanding, insisting that they wed. She'd rung the police, and they'd simply escorted him to his residence. He'd been back the next night after Augustus was in bed, whispering threats in her ears and making her bleed.

Tears gathered behind her eyes but she did not let them fall. She needed all her tears. All her strength. And all her considerable rage. She was leaving Paris, with or without a hired gun, so help her God.

8

You think you know me
But you haven't got a clue
I don't know myself

There was no decision to make, yet he sat in the dark, pretending to make it. Stewing and worrying, as if he wasn't going to be there, on the gangplank where Saint Jane had asked him to be, day after tomorrow.

It was not at all what he had planned, though to call kicking around Paris trying to get the nerve to change his face a "plan" was probably giving himself too much credit. How would it be to just float around the States for a while before he went back home, saw his father, and put some flowers on his mother's grave?

Ann Gillies Parker had slipped quietly away with no fuss and no warning on May 1, 1905. Van had brought word of her death himself, triumphant that he'd finally tracked his brother down and sobbing into Butch's chest as he shared the terrible news. It was a calculated move. Butch didn't have the heart to send him away.

Butch hadn't been the same since. For the last two years he'd thought of little else but his mother and the valley where she'd been laid to rest. He needed to go home one more time.

Playing bodyguard to Madame Toussaint wouldn't be a bad cover either. With a woman who looked like Jane and a boy who looked like

Gus, nobody would glance at him twice. It was a job and a first-class ticket, and he was going to take it.

Jane knew who he was. It relieved him, oddly. And absolved him. He could take the job with a clear conscience. Whatever hell his identity inadvertently brought down on her and her boy was hell she'd courted.

He'd always told himself that doing bad things didn't make him a bad man. But he'd come to believe that doing bad things was the only measure that mattered. Doing good things didn't make you good, he supposed, but if good was done, what was the difference?

His parents had believed in the way—the Bible, their church leaders, the promises of wide-open spaces and the American dream.

He'd never seen two people work so hard and have so little to show for it. Thirteen kids, hot summers and bitter winters, never enough to eat. Never enough. He wasn't sure why his parents' dream was lost on him. Maybe because they'd traveled so far. Across the Atlantic from England to America in a boat, and then another three thousand miles from the East Coast to the land of the Great Salt Lake in a covered wagon. They were both youngsters when they set out, but once they married and were settled in their valley, they didn't ever want to leave again.

It'd never been like that for him.

He had wanted to go and never stop going, never slow. Just go and go, and see what life had to offer. He wasn't greedy. He wasn't mean. He didn't have any habits that could really derail a life. He didn't drink too much or dabble with other men's wives. He was honest—more honest than most, he figured—and he often found himself in charge, even though he'd rather not be. It was the role he'd always played. Big brother to twelve siblings will do that to a fella. He'd tried to shake that off too, his tendency to lead, but it was like shaking off your skin, or your eye color, or the way you walked. Some things you couldn't escape.

"I know who you are," she'd said.

He hadn't confirmed or denied Jane's assertion. He hadn't given her excuses or assurances, hadn't told her anything about himself. But she seemed to know the salient points. He supposed if she wanted, once they arrived in the States, she could turn him in and collect a fairly sizable reward. That had to be considered. He thought about it for all of five seconds and shrugged. Whatever Jane Toussaint wasn't telling him—and it was a lot—she wasn't trying to collar a fugitive.

Stupid American, the doctor's wife had called him. *Stupid American.* And he was the stupidest, because he was going to board that ship back to America with Jane Toussaint and her boy.

"Robert LeRoy Parker, you never learn," he said to the palms of his hands. They were big and rough, but he'd kept them clean for a long time.

"And I'll keep them clean now too," he argued. He turned them over and took out his little book, but he didn't feel like composing a verse. Instead, he wrote down the worst that could happen.

Maybe I'll get caught.
Put in chains and hauled away.
I don't give a damn.

He'd written his thoughts in the same five-seven-five meter he always used, and it made him laugh. Old habits die hard. When it all came down to it, if he got caught and hauled away, he'd ask Powers to represent him if he was willing and if there was any money left in the retainer. If not, so be it. Butch had done fine in the pen the first time. He'd always handled work and discomfort well, and he could sleep anywhere. It was easy for him to make friends. He'd be fine.

"I don't give a damn," he said again. And he didn't. "I can help her. I'll do a good job," he said to the empty chair across his empty table. "I'll get her through her tour as smoothly as possible, as far as possible, everything organized and the details thought out." He nodded, encouraging himself. He was good with that stuff, good with the little things. He could be good for Jane too, manager and muscle, and a Colt .45 to make sure everyone behaved themselves.

Van might get wind that he'd gone back. Van always found him eventually. He was a better bloodhound than a bank robber. The problem was, Van always left a trail, and then Butch had to cut and run again.

Van materialized across from him, shoveling beans into his mouth, his hat pushed back on his golden-brown head, firelight turning his face into a hellscape.

"I can always find you 'cause I know how you think, brother. You lie low and stay on the straight and narrow, working for a dollar a day from sunup to sundown, but pretty soon you get wind of someone else getting screwed over by the big men. And you just can't help yourself. You gotta rob a bank, or a train, or hit the mine on payroll day for some fast, big money."

"I haven't hit a bank or a train in years," Butch said to Van's mirage, but Van never listened to him. The mirage kept on jabbering.

"Then you give most of it away. It's the deal you made with the devil. It's the reason you never get caught." He licked his ghostly fingers. *"You think your generosity wipes your sins clean."*

"What do you want from me, Van?"

"I want some of your famous generosity, Robert LeRoy! You keep running out on me. Me! Your kin."

Butch stood and turned down the lamp, and Van disappeared, gone but always creeping around.

"I'm just trying to save you, brother," he whispered.

The RMS *Adriatic* was the newest vessel in the White Star Line, and Maman said it was the finest ocean liner on the water. It had set out from Southampton to Cherbourg, across the English Channel, earlier that day. Now it sat out a ways from shore, a floating fortress in the outer harbor, and passengers were ferried to it on tender ships.

Augustus loved ships and tall buildings and trains and automobiles; anything that one could build he wanted to ride or climb or explore. He remembered the voyage from Paris to New York and back again when he was four. Maman had gotten sick, but he had loved the motion and the movement of the ship on the sea. Oliver had taken him up to the top deck because Mother was bedridden. Oliver had sat on a deck chair and read the paper while Augustus watched the waves and the endless water all around. It didn't scare him; he'd never been scared of things like that. Not the big things.

Maman said they weren't going back to Paris. She was going to be an American opera singer from now on.

She was nervous again, her eyes darting this way and that. The quay at Cherbourg did not have a train station. Two rows of tracks ran along the wharf, but it was an easy walk to board the tender ships, and Maman had not wanted to arrange yet another carriage from the station across town. Their trunks were unloaded right beside the tracks, along with a hundred other passengers. Noble Salt had not been on the train, and Maman was as brittle as the square of chocolate Augustus had eaten after lunch. His stomach twisted in compassion. He wished he had a little more chocolate, and he hoped Noble Salt would not disappoint them.

They stood next to their trunks until a steward with a rolling cart made his way to them. Two simple canopies had been erected to handle luggage checks and customs, but the sailors were sharp in their White Star Line uniforms and jaunty caps, and it was a second mate from the *Adriatic* named Simon who took their tickets and tagged their trunks.

"I am Jane Toussaint. My . . . security, Mr. Noble Salt, has he arrived yet, sir?" she asked the man.

His eyes flared in recognition, and his spine straightened. "Madame Toussaint. We are honored to have you. Captain Smith himself asked me to tell you that he is looking forward to your performances and has asked that you sit at his table this evening . . . with Mr. Toussaint, of course."

"Mr. Toussaint passed away last year. I will be traveling with my son and my security. Has he boarded yet?" she asked again.

"Oh dear. My condolences, madame." The man looked down his list and back up again. "What was the name again, please?"

"Noble Salt." Maman said his name with a note of doubt, as if she worried he'd used another.

"I see no one by that name on our manifest. What class, ma'am?"

"First. The stateroom next to mine."

"Do you know the ticket number?"

Maman gave him the digits, and he looked again. "*Non*, madame. I show that ticket has not yet been presented. We will tell him you have already gone aboard when he arrives." He hesitated then and looked pained as he asked, "The boy's face, Mrs. Toussaint. It is not contagious, is it? There are rules about bringing illness about the ship, you understand."

"It is not contagious, sir. It is a birthmark. Like that unfortunate mole on the end of your nose. No more, no less."

His eyes crossed slightly as he tried to see the nonexistent mole on his nose, and then he scrubbed at it, sheepish.

"Oh. It was just a bit of something. You've got it now," Maman said easily, and the dimple in her creamy cheek peeked out as her lashes fluttered.

The man blushed and apologized. "Just company policy. You understand."

"Of course," Maman purred, but Augustus knew behind the warm answer was a row of bared teeth.

"Keep your tickets, madame. And please board. We will ferry the first- and second-class passengers over on the *Nomadic*—the gangplank is straight ahead—and steerage and luggage after that. As soon as your man arrives, we will send him your way."

"Don't worry, Maman. He will come," Augustus said. She smiled wanly.

"Of course he will," she agreed. "But we will manage if he doesn't."

Augustus palmed his watch and flicked the cover open.

"Four o'clock, and all is well," he said, reassuring them both. They were early. Maman had left instructions and a fat envelope with Luc's name written across it, sitting on the kitchen table. A carriage had come for them and their trunks just after breakfast and taken them to the train. Maman had been unable to eat, and Augustus ate too much.

Luc and Madame Blanc had gone for the day, Luc to the races and Madame Blanc to her sister's. Maman had made certain of it. She didn't want anyone to know where they'd gone or where they were going, but Maman was worried about the close connections. The train left at 9:00 a.m. Six hours to Cherbourg meant a three o'clock arrival if everything went smoothly. Boarding the tender ships began at five, and the *Adriatic* would depart at seven. It didn't leave much room for error, but it also didn't allow time to be detained. Augustus knew all of this because his mother talked to herself when she was nervous, working it all out beneath her breath while arranging and rearranging his trunk.

Maman did not tell him everything, but Augustus paid attention. He didn't know why they had to be so secretive, but Maman's answer was always the same: "They will try to stop me. They won't like that I'm going alone. And of course . . . it will be a shock for them that we are not returning. I do not want any messy goodbyes."

Maman did not like messes, Augustus knew that, but he couldn't imagine Luc or Madame Blanc would shed any tears for them. He knew for certain his mother wouldn't cry. His mother was an expensive vase, beautiful and hard, or so Oliver always said.

It had been so hard not to slip and say something wrong. But he'd managed. Madame Blanc never listened to him anyway, and Luc only paid attention to Maman. Augustus had told Monique day before yesterday—sworn her to secrecy—and whispered the secret into her new kitten's soft fur. He'd been bursting with the news.

"Will you send me a letter?" Monique had asked, a frown on her friendly mouth.

"*Oui.* I will send you postcards from all over America and sign them Gus." He didn't tell her about Noble Salt. He hadn't known. Maman had kept that from him too, up until they'd boarded the train he was supposed to be on. Now he wished she hadn't told him at all.

The tender was a small steamer that ran between the dock and the massive liners in the outer harbor, and it was not equipped for comfort. The passengers, all of them first class, all of them dressed in their very best, clung to the rails and were liberally doused with sea spray as they bounced across the choppy waters. Maman's lips were white and her forehead dotted in sweat when they arrived at the *Adriatic* a mere twenty minutes later. An enormous door on the side of the ship had been opened, a floating staircase lowered, and the tender ship sidled up to it and latched on, and the first-class passengers were assisted up the swaying gangplank with reassurances all the way that the *Adriatic* was "the finest ship in the world."

He and Maman were greeted by an English-speaking steward who would escort them to their stateroom, but Maman asked for a moment on deck.

"My personal security was delayed. I am worried he will not arrive in time. I'd like to watch for him on the upper deck. If you will just give me the key and see that the trunks are delivered to the right room, we can get settled later and ring you then."

It was Augustus who saw him first, looking down on the undulating circles, hats of every size and color, crushed together on the decks of the final ferry. Noble Salt walked with one hand pocketed and one hand swinging a case that looked brand new, and a rucksack, not so different from Augustus's, was slung over his shoulder. He had on the same gray suit he'd worn before, and when he looked up to survey the gleaming ship, he wore the same wary expression beneath the brim of his bulbous hat.

"It's him, Maman," Augustus said, and oddly felt tears rise in his eyes. "He came."

Maman must have been fighting tears too, for she did not answer or even squeeze his hand. She gripped the rail and said, "Thank you, Noble Salt."

"Do you think he can see us?" he asked.

Augustus began to wave his hands wildly, but his mother kept her hands on the rail, staring down, down, down at Noble Salt's upturned face. Slowly his hand came up, palm flat, a signal that he'd spotted them, and Augustus whooped happily, not even caring that others stared. They always stared; it was hardly new.

"He sees us, Maman. He sees us both."

They watched him board, scrambling up the steps like he already had his sea legs, until he disappeared into the massive hull of the ship that would be their home for the next eight days.

"Goodbye, Paris. I will miss you." Augustus waved, and there were tears on his cheeks. "Goodbye, France. I love you."

"Do you really, *cherie*?" Maman asked, surprised.

"Yes. I do. Won't you miss her?"

"No. It is a wonderful city, but you are the only thing I cannot live without, the only face in this whole world that matters to me."

"But Paris loves you. You are the best soprano in all of France!"

"In all of Europe," she corrected him with a quirk of her lips.

"And soon to be America too."

"Indeed." She said it like it was a foregone conclusion, like she had no doubt it would be so, but there was no enthusiasm in the word.

"Isn't that what you dream of, Maman?" he asked, confused. She worked so hard and with such single-mindedness. It was all she ever did.

"No, my darling. I dream of peace."

The first mate gave him a key and summoned a steward to escort him to his quarters. His legs were shaking and his breath was still coming harder than it should. He'd run all the way. The sway of the gangplank had almost bucked him off into the water. Had it not been for the sailor behind him, reaching out to steady him—*Mon dieu!*—they would have been fishing him out of the harbor.

"You're in first class, Mr. Toussaint; you should have come over on the first boat," the porter said, taking his new suitcase and reaching for his sack. The man's cockney English was a relief to hear, but Butch didn't correct him. His name would be up to Jane, and he had no idea what story she was telling.

"That would have been nice, but I almost missed the second." He'd gotten off at the wrong station, the one all the way across town, and no one understood him when he'd asked for help. One woman seemed to understand his dilemma, but answered in a stream of French, gesturing west. He thought she said five kilometers. He'd started walking toward the sea, frantic, and made it to the tender ship as the final passengers were boarding. His ticket said Mr. Toussaint, but no one had questioned him. The first-class passage helped, he was sure.

"I'm sure Mrs. Toussaint will be very happy you are here, sir. We have delivered her trunks to your rooms, and I believe she is up top. We will be casting off soon if you want to go join her. It's always exciting to hear the whistle blow."

He knew where she was. He'd seen her there in a white dress, clinging to her enormous hat; hats and ocean breezes did not mix. He'd almost lost his on the way over. Augustus had flapped his arms in greeting, and for a moment, little Bobby Parker, the boy he'd been, had the urge to wave back in the same frantic motion, waving at Augustus Toussaint with all the enthusiasm suddenly surging in his breast. He was going home. God help him. And God help Jane for signing on with an outlaw. He'd do his best to look out for her, but he was going home, come hell or high water.

"Hell or high water," he repeated, and the porter in front of him turned.

"Pardon me, sir?"

"Nothing." He was going to have to stop talking to himself. It'd become a habit over the last six years. Jane and Augustus would think he was crazy. He'd thought so himself, a time or two.

"I want to wash up and change my shirt. I'll find my way to the upper deck when I'm done."

"Very good, sir." The steward took out his key and opened a door that was coupled with another at the end of the corridor. "This is my favorite of all the staterooms." He stepped aside and ushered Butch forward. The room was decorated in blue and gold with deep wood paneling and heavy furniture, and Butch had never felt like more of an impostor in his whole sorry life. The steward bustled around, opening this door and that, lighting the lamp and lowering the flame, fluffing the pillows, and turning down the bed though night had not yet fallen.

"Your things were unpacked and your tails pressed, as instructed by Mrs. Toussaint. We have taken the liberty of removing the trunk to the storage, but should you need anything else from the contents, it is accessible." He swept open the ornate wardrobe. It was full of clothes Butch had never seen before. "I can also take your wash, monsieur."

Butch stared at him. "My wash?" His tails?

"You said you wanted to change your shirt. I can have the one you're wearing laundered and pressed, sir. I can do that now, or you can leave it there." He pointed to the wardrobe he'd flamboyantly opened. "I will be your valet for the duration of the journey."

"Well, I'll be damned," Butch whispered, and then bit his tongue. He'd never had a valet before and had no clue where the clothes had come from. Plus, the Mr. Toussaint business was getting out of hand.

"I'll leave my shirt there." He indicated the wardrobe with a jerk of his head. "Thank you. And I'm not Mr. Toussaint. I know that's what the ticket said. But I am Mrs. Toussaint's personal security. You can call me Mr. Salt. Please." Noble Salt might not be his name, but it was a hundred times more comfortable than Mr. Toussaint.

The steward bobbed, folding his hands. "I see. Yes. An American. Very good. I will check back later, Mr. Salt. And there is always the bell." He indicated the tasseled pull that led to parts unknown and bobbed again, excusing himself at last.

Butch collapsed into a chair but stood almost immediately. If he rested, he'd never get up again, and he really wasn't sure he was in the right room. A few minutes later, freshly washed and changed—from his own luggage—he shrugged on his suit coat and placed his hat firmly on his head, but not before tugging on the tassel and putting his soiled shirt in the designated spot.

He'd never liked being dirty. But life was dirty business. He'd always kept himself as clean as he could, as clean as he was able. The boys teased him about it, the way he brushed his clothes and kept his face cleanly shaven, even when a beard would have hidden his face. He wasn't sure when he'd made the shift from filthy boy to fastidious man. Maybe it was when Mr. Woodard called him a thief at twelve. He'd taken a pair of dungarees from the man's store, yes, but that was because it was closed and he needed some pants, and he couldn't miss half a day of work coming back the next day for them.

He'd left a note and signed his name, promising to pay for them when he came for supplies the following week. And pay for them he had, though Pa had walloped him first, even though he'd explained what he'd done. Mr. Woodard pressed charges too, and the sheriff and his deputies had shown up at the Parker homestead and arrested him in front of his younger siblings and his mother like he'd gone on a killing spree. A judge had eventually dropped the charges, but it had soured him on every authority figure from that point on.

He would never forget the displeasure in Pa's eyes half a dozen years later when he couldn't stay put. Or the tears his mother had cried when he'd saddled up his horse and rode away, knowing if he didn't, he would always be poor and filthy, a disappointment to himself and everyone who looked up to him, the sorriest excuse for a big brother in the whole valley.

It was a pretty valley, ringed by purple mountains on every side and sprawling fields dotted in flowers and streams. Besides his mother, it was the thing he missed most. He missed it even more than his dad and his brothers and sisters. Its silence always soothed him and eased the ever-present ache to wander.

It was a pity you couldn't take places with you.

You could take people. You could take things. But not places. If you wanted to love the land, you had to stay put. And he hadn't been able to stay put, even for a valley that stole his breath and kissed his face with sweet breezes.

But he would see it again.

When he stepped out onto the uppermost deck, the sea air and sunshine embraced him, and his euphoria surged again, swelling his chest and burning in his throat. Words rose in his mind like a snippet of prayer, but he didn't pull out his book. Soon the horn would sound, and he wanted to be standing at the rail.

9

Take me home again
Never thought I'd see the day
O waly, waly

It took him a minute to circle, striding along, trying to get his bearings. The ship was enormous and far more luxurious, in every way, than anything he'd ever been on. It smelled new—wood and plaster and paint. The voyage to Bolivia had been on an ancient vessel, and he'd been in steerage, where he'd shared a bunk with Sundance, who slept more than his share and left Butch to wander the deck. Ethel had the other bunk, and more than once, they'd locked him out.

When he spotted Jane and Gus, he paused, struck by the moment all over again. Their backs were to him, mother and son, both in white, though the color wasn't at all practical for travel. He didn't know if Augustus was big for his age or small, but from the back he was every other well-dressed little gentleman. No one stood next to them at the rail. A six-foot gap stretched between Augustus and the next waving passenger. They were a true odd couple, a woman of extraordinary beauty—even though her hat was so big it resembled a toadstool—and a boy with a face that would cause him a lifetime of pain. It was a bit of a shock, Gus's face, and Butch wondered if he would feel the same tremor every time he looked at him or if he would stop seeing it as they grew more accustomed, the way he'd stopped seeing his mom or his dad, or even his own reflection.

Then Augustus turned as though he felt the attention, and a lopsided grin lifted his scarlet cheek.

"Mr. Salt!"

The swells and coils of Jane's hair were almost covered by the chocolate satin of her hat. The hat matched the sash beneath her breasts. Both the sash and the hat were the color of her eyes, eyes she aimed at him with a mixture of hope and censure.

"Ma'am," he said, closing the distance. He inclined his head and touched his brim. "Augustus."

Augustus surged forward and wrapped his arms around Butch's waist and pressed his face to his chest. "Mr. Salt. I knew you would come. Maman wasn't sure, but I knew you would come."

Butch patted the boy's back, moved by his greeting, and Gus blinked up at him with a tremulous smile. At that moment, the ship's horn began to blow, a shuddering giant's belch that rumbled up from its belly and out over the water. The behemoth moved, and the wind split, whipping around their heads in a sudden irritated gust, a ruffled owl startled from its perch, and Jane's big hat went with it.

She shrieked a little, grabbing at it, but the wind howled and sent it spinning away. She teetered, extended too far over the rail, and Butch lunged for her, the boy still clinging to his waist. Her arms pinwheeled, and he caught the fabric of her dress at the cuff of her neck, yanking her back and sandwiching poor Augustus between them.

With his hand still clutching the back of her dress, she righted herself, both hands now firmly on the rail. Augustus squirmed between them, and Butch stepped back, releasing her.

The three of them watched as the hat spun and dipped like a kite, end over end, and finally landed on the swells.

"I liked that hat," Jane mourned.

"You almost fell in, Maman!" Augustus scolded.

"Yes. Well. Mr. Salt has already earned his keep," she said, her color high. "Thank you, Mr. Salt." She bobbed her head toward him, not meeting his gaze. His heart was still quaking; he imagined hers was too.

"I'm not a very good swimmer," he warned, his tone wry. "If you fall in, I'll come after you, but we'll likely both drown, and it's a long way down."

"I shall keep that in mind, sir."

The style in which so many women wore their hair reminded him of the hot water bottles Ma used to put on their heads when they had an earache or a sore tooth. The sides puffed out from the knot on top, but the wind that had taken her hat had loosened her pins, and the knot began sliding down her back. Brown-black tendrils whirled about her face, but she didn't release the rail to smooth them. Instead, she turned her face into the gust and closed her eyes.

"Perhaps a dolphin will find your hat," Gus said, holding on to his own with a hand clamped to the crown.

"Yes . . . and be the envy of every fish in the sea," Jane quipped, her eyes still closed.

Butch chuckled. "I don't know about that."

"Didn't you like Maman's hat?" Augustus asked.

"Not particularly," he answered, frank. He liked her hair uncovered much better.

Jane opened one eye and looked at him, a quirk to her lips. Jane Toussaint was already unlike any woman he'd ever known. It was his honesty, not his praise, that she seemed to appreciate.

"You are the most peculiar man I've ever met, Noble Salt," she said, but it sounded like a compliment.

"When's dinner, Maman? I'm hungry." Butch was famished himself, and silently thanked the boy for asking the question foremost on his mind.

"We will send for dinner from our rooms. I have a rehearsal, and Mr. Salt has a fitting, so we'd better go down so I can tidy my hair."

"A fitting?"

"Yes, Mr. Salt."

"Does this have something to do with the clothing in my room?"

"It does. They are yours now, if you want them. I think they'll fit well enough. Oliver was trim and about your height, if you remember."

"I saw the man once, and I wasn't very impressed."

"No. But he had excellent taste. Expensive taste. And he can't use the clothes anymore."

"And what if I hadn't come? I didn't say I was coming."

"I chose to believe you would. And if you hadn't, then the steward and all of his friends would have enjoyed the spoils. There is a coat with tails— two of them. You will need it for dinner on the nights we dine in the hall."

"Am I your husband or your bodyguard?"

She blanched, and he explained.

"I was addressed as Mr. Toussaint multiple times. I corrected the . . . valet"—he tripped over the English pronunciation—"after the fifth or sixth time. I hope I didn't step in something."

"We can't pretend you're Oliver. He was very French . . . You are very . . . not. And though it's not likely, we might see someone who knew him. Lies catch up with you, and so do false identities."

"People think you are Oliver?" Augustus asked, hanging on every word. The boy missed nothing, and Butch would do well to remember that. "You said you have many names . . . Is that what they are, Mr. Salt? False identities?" His eyes were wide and his voice squeaky.

"Oliver's name is on the ticket, Augustus. That is what we're talking about. Mr. Salt is . . . Mr. Salt. And that is what we will call him."

Augustus frowned, unconvinced, but Jane turned back to Butch, addressing him.

"I will introduce you as Mr. Salt, my security, and you will go where Augustus and I go."

"Everywhere?" Augustus interjected. Jane had evidently not filled him in on much.

"Yes, darling. Now, Mr. Salt, all the alterations can be done before we disembark if they're minor enough. We should return now; the tailor might be waiting. I have a rehearsal in an hour with the musicians. You may accompany me, but once I'm there, you and Augustus can explore—Augustus is dying to explore—while I practice. We have a valet and a lady's maid assigned to our rooms, though I'm sure we share them with others in our corridor."

"Maman, you are talking so fast!" Augustus sighed. "Are you nervous? Does Mr. Salt scare you? You aren't scary, are you, Mr. Salt? And can I call you Noble?"

Butch tried not to smile. Neither of them would get away with anything with Augustus around. To Jane's credit, she took a deep breath and took Augustus's hand.

"I do not do well on ships . . . of any kind, Mr. Salt. I get seasick. I am dreading the voyage. I must sing at nine this evening for a small group in the captain's salon, and on our final night I will perform in the ballroom for the first- and second-class passengers. I am hoping that I will have adjusted to the motion by that time."

"This ship is long and deep and heavy. If the wind blows, we won't even feel it," Butch reassured her.

"One can hope," she said, and took another deep breath. "Shall we go?"

"You look very smart, Mr. Salt," Augustus said. He was standing in the door between the two staterooms, too curious to stay away for long. The tailor, who was waiting for them just as Jane predicted, had performed a double take upon seeing his purple cheek, and Augustus had kept a distance he otherwise wouldn't have. Jane stepped up behind him, curious herself.

"I feel like a peacock," Butch said, eyeing the assortment of ties and suspenders—yellow and red and purple and striped. The suit he wore was a royal blue that made his eyes glow in his brown face.

"The colors suit you. Not a peacock at all," Jane reassured. "Oliver loved color, but there are plenty of blues and grays and browns to choose from. Leave the bright ascots and bold vests if you don't like them," she offered. "But you look good in them."

The tailor tucked a bit here and there, sniffing and squinting.

"The clothes fit as well as any I've ever worn," Butch admitted, an indication that he thought the fussing tailor was unnecessary.

"The length of the sleeve is fine," the tailor mused. "The shoulders are a bit tight, and the body a little loose, but the trousers and vests have buckles in back to loosen or cinch, and suspenders will keep them high on your hips. It won't take much, monsieur," he added, his tone sour. He had clearly hoped for a bigger paycheck as well. "I will have these ready in three days. You can wear the tails tonight. I could make the suit look better, but . . ." He shrugged. "It will do."

It was odd to see Oliver's clothes on Noble Salt. Her mind tried to change his name to Butch Cassidy and immediately spat it back out. For his sake and for her own, it was better not to think of him that way. But Oliver's clothes took on an entirely new aura, and Noble Salt looked very noble indeed.

She was holding on thus far. It was likely the air up on the deck—the longer she could avoid the close air and the close spaces, the better off she would be. Hopefully, the worst would hold off awhile longer. She knew from experience that she wouldn't make it through the first night, but still she hoped.

Augustus peppered Mr. Salt with questions all the way up to the salon where she would rehearse and was still firing away as they turned to go, leaving her to her practice. Noble Salt was handling it with aplomb, though he'd stumbled and called Augustus *Van*, a fact Augustus immediately pounced on.

"You called me Van."

"I did, didn't I?"

"Who's Van?"

"He's my brother. One of 'em."

"How many do you have?"

"A bunch."

"You're the oldest of thirteen kids," Augustus rattled off.

"I'll be damned. You remember that?"

"I remember everything. Does he look like you?"

"Who?"

"Van. Your brother."

"Yeah. He does. A lot."

"I wish I had a brother. Do you like him?"

"Not particularly."

Ah, there it was. The candor that she liked so much. She smiled even though she knew she needed to intervene, especially with the cursing. She didn't want Augustus popping off a *hell* or a *damn* in polite company.

"Why don't you like your brother?" Augustus asked, perplexed.

"Augustus?" Jane intervened.

"Yes, Maman?" Augustus ripped his gaze from Noble Salt.

"Be courteous."

"Of course, Maman." Augustus looked insulted.

"Some questions are too personal. Some confidences come with time. I'm sorry, Mr. Salt. You don't owe Augustus an answer simply because he asks. You are entitled to your privacy."

"Don't be sorry. I was the same way. I drove my dad crazy."

"Your dad was Maximilian . . . right? Like me?" Augustus asked, proving that he did indeed remember everything.

Jane was caught in sudden indecision, almost envious of the time they would spend together, the conversation they would have. She wanted to go with them, and she didn't like watching Augustus walk away.

"Go on, Jane. He'll be fine. I promise. We'll be back in an hour, just like you said," Noble Salt said, his voice gentle, reading her like a book.

Emotion welled in her chest. That would not do. She needed to sing.

"All right," she said, tamping it down, trusting him. It was a brand-new feeling, trust. She wasn't sure she liked it. She watched them walk away, Noble in Oliver's deep blue suit, Augustus bouncing along beside him, chattering like a little bird, his first time out of the nest.

"Will you miss Paris?" Augustus asked as they wandered through corridors, climbed winding stairs, and worked their way through the maze of the enormous ship. Others seemed to have the same idea, clogging the lower halls, and Butch and the boy found themselves back on the first-class deck staring down into the water. The land had disappeared, and the sun was setting, a fat orange tabby on a windowsill.

"I don't have anyone in Paris to miss," Butch confessed.

"Nobody?"

"Nobody."

"Then why were you there?"

"I went to see Dr. Moreau."

"Did he help you?" Augustus asked.

"No. But I didn't give him much of a chance."

"He didn't help me either. Maman was not impressed with our options. She was afraid he'd make it worse. I think she likes my face exactly the way it is but doesn't want me to suffer."

A lump formed in Butch's throat. "I guess we're stuck with the faces we've got, huh?"

"I guess so," Augustus agreed. "But why do you want to change yours?"

He'd walked right into that one. The boy had disarmed him with his quick-fire questions, and he'd been alone so much in the last year he'd gotten rusty at conversation.

He didn't answer immediately, but Augustus didn't move on. He just waited, his face tipped to the side, his hands looped over the railing.

"Well . . . the thing is, Gus, I've done some things I shouldn't have done. And I made a lot of powerful people mad. I thought maybe if I got a new face, I could start over. But I've got my mama's eyes and my daddy's nose. My grandfather—my mom's dad—had the same square jaw as I do. My brothers look like me. My sisters too. I guess I want to keep the family resemblance." It was as much of the truth as he could give the boy. He also wondered what Jane had told her son. Did Augustus know he was Butch Cassidy? The cowboy comment on the Paris street indicated he might. Damn, he hoped not.

"I don't have any family," Augustus said. "I don't know what my grandfather looked like. And I didn't look anything like Oliver."

Butch didn't know what to say to that, but there was no need. Augustus kept on prattling about this and that, his energy for conversation boundless. He talked all the way back to the room where Jane was still practicing, and when they found a bench and sat to wait for her to finish, he apologized for the steady verbal stream.

"I don't get to talk to people very much."

"No?"

"Only Maman and Madame Blanc. And Luc. It's nice to talk to someone new."

"Yeah. It is. You don't go to school?"

"I have—I had—private tutors. Oliver wanted to send me to school. Maman would not hear of it. She did not speak to Oliver for a month. She is very stubborn. And she loves me very much."

"Noted."

"I am surprised she trusts you. Maman doesn't trust anyone."

"You think she trusts me?"

"You are here," Augustus said, his palms turned upward, sounding very much like a Frenchman.

Noble Salt nodded again. "Why do you think that is?"

"I don't know. But I'm glad. I need a man in my life. How can Maman teach me to be a man if she is not a man?" He seemed very troubled by this fact.

"Lots of good women raise good men. All by themselves."

"Maman loves me very much," he repeated, sorrowful.

Butch laughed and scratched at his beard. "Why do you look so sad? That's a good thing, isn't it?"

"It is. Yes. But some love doesn't make us strong."

Butch gaped at him, and for once Augustus was quiet, thoughtful.

"You're a smart kid, Gus. You know that?"

Augustus nodded, solemn. "Yes. I know that."

"Did you want to go to school?"

"Yes. Even though . . . even though I know some people would not be kind."

"I know you love me," Butch murmured, counting syllables again. "But some love won't make me strong. That's why I can't stay."

"What?" Augustus asked.

"Nah. Nothing. Just something I do sometimes. A little poetry game I play."

"I like games."

"This is a word game."

"I like word games too. How do you play?"

Butch explained the rules, describing the five-seven-five pattern of the lines. He repeated the verse he'd just crafted, counting the syllables as he did, and Augustus got the hang of it with no trouble at all.

"This ship is so big." Augustus counted five syllables on his fingers. "Four decks and a thousand doors. That's seven." He held up both his hands. "A floating hotel. Five more."

Butch grinned. "That's it, Gus. You're a natural. I think that one deserves to be written down." He pulled his book and a pencil from his inner coat pocket.

"Is that a storybook?" Augustus asked, scooting close.

"Nah." He turned a few pages until he found one that was blank. "It's a journal. Kinda. I jot things down. Mostly a line here and there. Nothing lengthy."

"I have a journal. But I don't have anything to say."

"You don't?" Butch chuckled. "You ask a lot of questions for a kid that has nothing to say."

"Well, a book can't answer. I want to talk. Not write."

"Remember when Mrs. Moreau called me a stupid American?" Butch asked.

"You heard that?"

"Yeah. *Stupid American* in French doesn't sound much different than *stupid American* in English."

"You aren't stupid."

"I am . . . a little. I can't write pages and pages. But I can write verses. I wrote one about your mother's hat. The one that blew away. Now I won't forget it." He tapped the verse he'd recorded while the tailor was pinning his trousers.

"The one you didn't like?" Augustus snickered.

"Yep. And now I'm going to write yours here. I'll put your name beside it and give you credit." He wrote the lines, the date, and put the initials *AMT* beneath it.

Augustus stared down at the words with pride and read them aloud again.

"You two look like you're plotting something," Jane said, her eyes on the book in Butch's hands. Neither of them had heard her approach or realized her rehearsal had ended.

"It's a game, Maman," Augustus exclaimed. "A word game." He explained—quite succinctly, Butch thought—the pattern of the lines.

"It's hokku," she said.

"Yeah. It is," Butch admitted. "I learned it from a Japanese man who worked in a mine with me near a place called Telluride. A long time ago. It's stuck with me."

"Can you read us some of yours?" Gus asked him, eager and sweet. "The one about Maman's hat?"

Butch felt his neck heat and was grateful for his beard.

"Nah. That one isn't very good." He closed the book and stood, tucking it back inside his pocket with the pencil beside it. Jane stepped back, and Augustus rose too, slipping his hand into Butch's as if he feared Butch might bolt.

"Maybe we can make up a new one on the way back to our rooms," Augustus suggested.

Jane was smiling slightly. "Maybe we can. Perhaps one about Mr. Salt's hat this time."

Jane took Butch's offered arm after the barest hesitation, and they walked back to their staterooms, Gus counting syllables all the way.

> *We're crossing the sea*
> *Sailing to America*
> *To buy a new hat*

10

Don't dare look at you
Don't know how to talk to you
We'll just sit awhile

Jane wore a black evening gown that bared her lovely shoulders and hung in a straight sheath below the gathers at her breasts. The dress had a small cap sleeve that hugged her upper arms, but she wore long black gloves that left very little skin exposed. Her dark hair was piled high in the swoops and whorls of the current fashion, and she wore diamonds at her ears and around her neck, as well as an impressive diamond ring on her finger. He assumed it was a wedding ring, a nod to her late husband, but the black gloves made a dramatic foil for the rock.

She was pale, far paler than he thought natural, but she'd rouged her cheeks and lips and lined her eyes with kohl the way she'd done when he'd seen her perform years before. She was every inch the opera singer and not simply a woman dressed for a formal dinner. It was her costume, and though she was lovely in it, it was a boundary of sorts, a warning: Do not approach.

Butch wore tails, as he'd been instructed to do. Augustus did as well, though none of them ate at the captain's table. Jane claimed she could not eat before she sang, so they had service brought to their rooms before they left for the captain's salon, and saved Jane some supper for when she was through.

It was late, and they were all dragging, especially Augustus, but he didn't want to be left behind, and Jane needed an escort through the ship. She drew eyes and excitement when she was out, and the word had already spread about her presence on board. A framed picture of her was hung by the ballroom doors beneath a gold plaque that said, *Jane Toussaint, The Parisian Songbird.*

It was a stunning portrait, and Butch had never wanted to steal something so badly in all his life. He would wait until they arrived in New York, and he wouldn't steal the frame . . . just the picture. Surely no one would mind, once Jane Toussaint was no longer performing. He needed a memento. Something to remember her by when the tour was done and they went their separate ways.

Jane sang for half an hour—all songs he didn't know—and then excused herself with gracious smiles and curtsies, and let the band continue entertaining the captain's guests. She was wonderful—even better than she'd been six years ago at Carnegie Hall—and Butch was rattled by the emotion she stirred in him. It brought him back to those final days, the days where hope still glimmered and a future still seemed possible.

He and Augustus sat at a small corner table where he could reach Jane if someone decided to approach the stage in a suspicious manner. Augustus was composing hokku verses on a piece of paper, but his eyes were drooping before his mother even started, and he put his head down on his arms and went to sleep, leaving Butch to hold vigil by himself.

By the time Jane was done and they were heading back to their quarters, he was spent. Augustus had gotten just enough of a nap to feel refreshed, and babbled all the way back to the staterooms, Jane and Butch following wearily behind.

And what quarters they were. He had a big bed to himself. Crisp, sweet-smelling sheets and down pillows. A sitting area and a table to eat, and a washbasin almost big enough to sit in, though he was too tired to do much washing tonight. Baths were available too—seawater was brought in—and he looked forward to that come morning.

Jane and Augustus were on the other side of a door that connected their rooms, and Gus opened it the moment they arrived.

"You don't mind, do you, Noble?" The *Mr. Salt* had been abandoned after their afternoon of exploring. They were friends now.

"I don't mind. But your mother might."

"We will close the doors when it's time to go to bed," she said. "That's only proper."

"Maman says I snore," Augustus confessed. "She's used to it, but you might be bothered. My one nostril is half-closed, see?" He wrinkled his nose and tipped his head up so Butch could look down his snout. The weight of his face on the one side did indeed restrict his airflow.

Butch took off his suit and donned a pair of Oliver Toussaint's silk pajamas, laughing at himself as he did. He'd never worn anything but his drawers or a nightshirt when he slept in a bed. But with Jane and Gus right next door, he needed to be dressed. He stretched out across the bed, registering the clean scent of the pillows and the comfort of the mattress, but that was all. His sleep was as deep as the Atlantic they were sailing across, his worries paused on opposite shores, waiting to wrap their arms around him when he docked. But for now, there was nothing but fine food, fine lodgings, and fine company, and all three made for excellent sleep.

It was nearing dawn when he felt a tug on his arm and a pat on his cheek. He slept on his stomach, one arm and a few toes hanging off the side. He'd never had a big bed of his own—rarely had a little one either, and he didn't take up too much space, even when the space was there.

"Mr. Salt?"

"Yeah, Gus," he rumbled, trying to make his lids unfurl.

"Maman is sick. She's been sick all night. She needs fresh air, but she's too sick to walk by herself. And it's probably not safe for her to be by herself, no matter what. Someone might try and take her. Steal her for ransom."

Butch was already rolling to a sitting position, feet on the floor, eyes wide, his lethargy gone.

"What kind of sick . . . ya mean seasick?"

"Yes. I think so."

"Augustus," she called. "Are you in there disturbing Mr. Salt?"

"Am I disturbing you, Mr. Salt?"

"No."

"He says I'm not, Maman."

They both heard her laugh, though it quickly became a moan followed by painful retching.

"You can have my bed, Gus." The boy was swaying on his feet.

"We can share," Augustus said, crawling up onto the bed behind him.

Butch stood, pulling the blankets up over the child. "Nah. I'm done sleeping. It's all yours."

He lit the lamp and held his watch up to the glow. Four a.m. He'd slept six hours, at least. By the time he'd abandoned the silk pajamas, yanked his pants on over his drawers, and snapped his suspenders into place, Augustus was already asleep, his chin tucked into his shoulder, his purple profile bathed in the mellow lamplight.

Butch knocked on the doorframe, warning Jane of his presence, but she didn't warn him back or welcome him. She was crumpled on the floor near the chamber pot.

"Do you get seasick, Mr. Salt?" she asked feebly.

"Not usually."

"I do. Always." She moaned and whimpered, and he turned away to give her the privacy she required. When she collapsed back onto the floor, he moved beside her.

"Come on. You need to get up."

"I can't. I am a mess."

"You can. If you don't get some fresh air and your legs underneath you, you're going to be on your back with a bucket for the whole trip."

"Don't touch me!" she squawked, and he immediately stepped back, his hands in the air like she'd threatened him with a gun.

"I'll just help you stand, and then I'll hold your arm. Just so you don't fall. You're weak and dizzy. I don't want you to fall."

"We can't leave Augustus."

"He's sleeping like a bear. We'll lock the door behind us. He'll be fine. It's you who won't be fine. Come on. Up you go." He propped her up and sat her on the bed.

"Oh no, please, Mr. Salt."

"Jane. You gotta get your sea legs. You need air."

"But I'm in my nightgown." Her hair was a mass of dark waves down her back, and she tried to comb it with her fingers.

"Where's your coat?"

She pointed feebly at the long black fur coat she'd worn to the reception the night before, and he bundled her in it, one arm at a time, and pushed a pair of kid boots on her feet.

"No . . . not those. If it's wet up top, they'll be ruined."

He patiently trundled his way through her closet until she gave her approval, though she stopped midsentence to heave into the little bucket by her bed.

Butch didn't ask her permission, he simply shoved the acceptable shoes on her feet and hoisted her up, a tankard of water swinging from his left hand while he supported her with his right.

"Let's go, honey."

The air, cold and clear, was an immediate balm, even to him, and the sense of being rocked was diminished by the unending sky and the abundance of space. Jane pulled in a deep lungful of air, and he kept her propped up, waiting for her to be strong enough for more.

"Are you okay to walk, or should we stand at the rail for a bit?"

"I don't want to be seen," she moaned. "People know who I am."

"It's four thirty in the morning. Not many people will be out and about. And those who are probably suffer from the same malady. We won't chat or even make eye contact. We'll just walk or stand looking out at the water until you are feeling restored. But hold on to me, for God's sake. No tumbling overboard."

"I don't like to be touched," she muttered.

"I'm not touching you. I'm aiding you."

She let herself be drawn forward but needed more than his arm to stay upright. When he scooped her up in his arms, she didn't have the strength to argue. She laid her head against his chest and let him carry her to a deck chair, where he laid her down and tucked her coat around her legs.

He sat down in the chair beside her and made her take a few careful sips from the tankard of water. Then he sat back and awaited her instructions.

"I don't mind if you talk to me," she said after several quiet minutes. Her voice already sounded stronger.

He held the water to her mouth and urged her to take another drink. She was pale and her hair riotous, but she was still so beautiful that he kept his eyes on the tankard and avoided looking directly at her face. She would see his admiration, and it was clearly not what she wanted.

"Don't dare look at you. Don't know how to talk to you. We'll just sit awhile," he muttered.

"You're writing verses again, aren't you?"

He frowned and counted syllables. "Yeah. I guess I am." He hadn't done it on purpose. He hadn't even meant to speak out loud. It'd become a bad habit.

"Why don't you dare look at me?"

He breathed in deeply and then exhaled in a whoosh, letting the truth come with it. "The first time I saw you on that stage at Carnegie Hall, I had to close my eyes. It was all too much to take in. The sound. The beauty. The emotion. It was overwhelming to me."

"But you came back all three nights."

"I did."

"Why?"

"I came back the second time 'cause I wanted to see what you looked like."

She glowered at him, confused. Then her lips twitched. "And the third?"

"I was ready for the full experience."

"Behind the curtain?"

"Yeah. Behind the curtain."

"But you're back to not looking at me again."

"You are a beautiful, prickly woman. I like looking at you, but I know better than to get close. You're like a cholla. Look, but don't touch."

"A cholla?"

"A cactus."

"I have never seen a cactus before."

"You're not missing much. They have all these sharp little barbs."

"Thorns?"

"Not so obvious. A cholla doesn't look like it'd hurt you, but you get close, and you'll be picking out nettles for a week, if it doesn't kill you first."

She was silent for a moment, breathing deeply, and he wondered if she was fighting off another round of sick.

"You okay, honey?"

"Yes. I'm okay. Much better now. Thank you." She didn't protest his endearment, and he relaxed slightly. It just kept slipping out.

"A woman has no cholla defenses, Mr. Salt. Unfortunately. It is a pity that we don't."

"You have barbs."

"Yes. I've had to grow a prickly skin. It doesn't deter all men, but it helps."

"It only deters the good ones."

"I haven't met many of those."

"Nah. Me neither," he said.

The sky had begun to lighten in lavender wisps, and they both sat with their eyes forward, hands in their pockets, feet crossed. The entire deck was empty, and the whoosh of the water against the hull created the illusion of privacy and peace. A floating confessional. Every word would be whisked away, every spot wiped clean.

"I don't think it is—or was—in my nature to be so thorny," Jane said. "I think I would have liked to be held and kissed and patted for good behavior. But I never was . . . and any attention and kindness always had painful strings attached. So I stopped trusting it. Now I simply don't know how to be any other way."

"You aren't that way with Gus."

"You cannot seem to say his full name."

"You're changing the subject. And I like his name. I just like it in all its variations."

"He is my child. I've never had to guard myself with him. And I did not want to do to him what was done to me."

"What was done to you, Jane?" he asked softly.

He was being bold, and she might bristle up and burn him down, but he had nothing to lose. She was stuck with him for a while, and he wanted to know. He wanted to know everything about her.

"I was brought to an orphanage in London when I was a day old. I was raised in the orphanage until I was twelve. A wealthy relation of Oliver's—the wife of an earl also named Toussaint—who was a patron of the orphanage heard me sing." She sounded detached, like she was reading him a bedtime tale that had no bearing on her own life.

"I'll be damned," he marveled. "That's quite the story."

"Yes. I suppose it is," she said, wooden. "I am . . . fortunate. I know that."

She did not continue but left her lifeless acknowledgment sitting between them like a closed door. He immediately pushed it open.

"So you sang and this woman took you from the orphanage?" he prodded. He wanted her to keep going.

"She . . . adopted me. Unofficially. And dropped me into a French music school run by Oliver Toussaint. Lessons all day long, every day. And I became Jane Toussaint—the name of the conservatory—the Parisian Angel. Oliver became my manager when I was sixteen and my husband when I was nineteen."

"Why?"

"Why what?" Her head swiveled and her eyes met his.

"Why did you marry him?"

Her eyes widened, and her jaw dropped slightly. Then she looked away. "It was convenient."

"For you or for him?"

She breathed in deeply and let it go. "For both of us. I do not want to talk about my late husband, please, Mr. Salt. You are being very rude. I am in mourning."

He almost scoffed. He didn't believe her. And she had dropped his identity on him like an avalanche at the first opportunity. Mourning was just her excuse to button up like a clam.

"Who were you before you became Jane Toussaint? What was your name?" he pressed. When she didn't answer, he shook his head. "Turnabout is fair play, madam."

She was quiet for several long seconds, and then she answered, her voice revealing the first true signs of strain. "I was Jane Boot."

Jane Boot. He was stunned she'd even told him, and wondered how many people knew that little detail.

Incredibly, she continued. "That's how they found me. Stuffed in a man's boot. Not a basket or a blanket. A boot. So that became my surname."

"And Jane? Who chose Jane?"

"I don't know." Her gaze was back, and she'd collected herself. "Aren't all the unknowns called Jane or John? I suppose I should be grateful. I could have been named Old Boot or Smelly Boot or something equally descriptive. Jane Boot is a little better."

He grinned at her, grateful for her humor, even dry as it was.

She did not smile back, but she arched a brow, an acknowledgment of her jest.

"So when Augustus came along . . . ," he began.

"I gave him the grandest name in all the world," she finished. "A big, powerful name that he could be proud of."

"When did Augustus make his entrance?" He knew Oliver was not Gus's father. She'd confessed that truth the night they met, though now he wondered why.

"March 29, 1897." She tipped her chin up to the blue-black sky, a little point atop the length of her pale neck, and closed her dark eyes, shutting him out. It was not what he meant, but he let it alone.

"Your turn, Mr. Salt," she said. "Tell me all your secrets."

"You know enough about me to get me strung up," he reminded her softly.

"Strung up?" she asked, startled. "Do they really do that in America? Still? I thought that was just in the dime novels."

"The West is so big and wild that 'law and order' is more like 'kill or be killed.' It's what makes it wonderful . . . and terrible too."

"It's wonderful?"

"And terrible."

"Like you?"

"Nah. I'm not wonderful."

"You are not terrible either."

He didn't argue with her, though he wasn't sure he agreed.

"And wild? Are you wild?"

"Not wild. No. Just . . . reckless."

"Still?"

"I'm here with you, aren't I?"

She frowned slightly, though his tone was light. For a moment she was silent, contemplative. "And you're worried that I will tell your secrets to your enemies, like Samson and Delilah?"

"It's entered my mind."

"There *is* a reward for your capture."

"Is that what's happenin' here?" he asked, voice mild. "You're luring me to America with new suits and fancy rooms, and you'll have a gang of Pinkertons waiting to arrest me?"

"I say, that is a very good plan, Butch Cassidy. I can have the captain send a telegram. It will all be in order, and they will drag you away, leaving me in exactly the same pickle I was in when I hired you," she huffed. "I don't need a reward. I need a man."

His brows waggled, and she rolled her eyes, but her weariness was evident. He made her drink a little more water, and this time she held the tankard herself. He took it from her and corked it, sitting back.

"I am very alone in the world, Mr. Salt. I always have been. And I need security. Just like I told you. It's really quite simple."

"Well . . . I guess that's where we're different. I've never been alone enough."

She didn't press him on that and remained quiet for several deep breaths.

"Why did you do it?" she blurted.

"Do what?"

"Rob banks. Rob trains. You had no mouths to feed. No gun at your head. Why?"

He watched the last stars begin to disappear, trying to formulate a response. He didn't want to excuse himself or point the finger of blame. But it wasn't an easy question, and he really didn't want to talk about it.

"Because I'm a tumbleweed," he answered finally. "You're a cholla . . . and I'm a tumbleweed."

"What does that mean?"

"A tumbleweed goes wherever the wind takes it. It doesn't put up any resistance. That's how I was. Naive. Young. Idealistic. I got swept up and then . . . I didn't know how to get out. It wasn't until my brother wanted to do the same things I was doing that I woke up. I felt responsible—still do—but he wouldn't listen. None of them would. So I made rules for myself, and tried to make rules for them, so nobody would get hurt, but it was like herding cats."

"'Herding cats'?" They spoke the same language, but they didn't. All his colloquialisms wrinkled her brow.

"Cats do what they damn well please. Just like cowboys. We all just want to roam. Never grow up. Never settle down. Our fathers all did it hard. We wanted easy. But easy has a venomous bite, and it's a long, painful death. Not one of the boys I rode with came out ahead. Not one."

"Tell me about your father."

"Not now, honey. Not now. Morning's here. That's a conversation for the dark."

"That bad?"

"No. Not bad at all. He was a good man. I've got no excuses for how I turned out. None whatsoever." He rolled to his feet. "You ready to take a lap? Walking will be good for you. Then we'll head down below and see if you can get some sleep. You've got to be tired."

She rose gingerly and didn't flinch when he looped her hand through his arm.

"I can't figure you out, Butch Cassidy."

"Not much to figure. And you can't call me that, Jane Boot. Not if you truly need the man and not the reward."

She grimaced at his use of her name, but his point was made. He let her set the pace, and it was painfully slow.

"You kissed me once, Mr. Salt," she muttered. Her head was down, and he wasn't sure he'd heard right.

He cocked his head. "Actually, you kissed me, Mrs. Toussaint."

"Yes. But. Not . . . I mean, I realize I . . . may have given you the indication that I wanted the kiss . . . but I didn't. And I don't. I mean . . . that is not the kind of arrangement I am proposing. It is a business relationship, and possibly . . . a friendship, if we are fortunate. But I have no intention of ever marrying again. I do not like men. At all."

"You don't like men," he repeated.

"No."

"But you have a son."

"Yes. And when he is a man, I am sure I will still like him. But since he is just a boy, I don't have to worry about that yet." She was almost hanging from his arm, and he stopped and made her drink again, holding the tankard to her lips.

"So no kissing," he said when she had finished.

"That's right. No kissing," she said, ducking her head and wiping her mouth.

He patted her hand. "All right, honey."

Together they walked the deck like two old folks, out for their early-morning constitutional. And they watched the sun rise.

11

In the Wild West
Every man is an outlaw
Or he wants to be

From the moment Augustus was born, Jane had ceased to exist. She became Jane the mother. Jane the protector. Jane Toussaint, someone's whole world. It was transformative and obliterating. She ceased sleeping deeply. Ceased thinking singly. Ceased dreaming for herself first and became a wholly fragmented being.

She had worried that she would not be able to love because she had never been loved. The closest thing to love she'd ever experienced was the swell of appreciation she felt when people heard her sing. The indrawn breaths, the rapidly clapping hands, the hush and then the marvel. That feeling had kept her from wilting and withering like a flower in a vase, but her petals had started to fall and her head had begun to droop before Augustus came along.

She'd named him Augustus because he would be great. Her little Caesar. And she'd loved him instinctively, exactly the way she sang, as if her soul knew how and she had only to let it save her, lead her, rescue her.

He was not Lord Ashley's son. He was hers and hers alone, and she'd loved him well, even perfectly. But a perfect love does not a perfect life make, and she had not slept well in the decade since his birth. She listened in her sleep. Hovered. Tensed. Cried. And woke each day with Augustus foremost in her mind.

Now she woke slowly, blissfully, and heard Augustus giggling from the other room. It took too much energy to smile, so she just listened and let herself marvel at the state she found herself in.

Somehow she trusted Noble Salt. Six years ago, he'd elevated himself above every man—every person—she'd ever known. In two days, he'd only reinforced everything she'd seen then. He was Noble Salt, the very epitome of those two words, good to his bones, honest to his core—impossibly so—and such a godsend that she'd had to reconsider her limp and often lifeless belief in the Almighty.

From the sound of it, Noble was teaching Augustus to throw a lasso. Everything in the room was secured against stormy seas, but the bedposts were perfect stand-ins, or so Noble Salt claimed. They were trying to be quiet, bless them, but she'd been in bed for two days, and rain on the second day had kept them from going up on the deck. She'd managed to keep her sickness in check by sleeping, something she'd been afraid to do every time she'd sailed before. A mother could not enter oblivion. But she had. Complete and utter oblivion. And Noble, perhaps sensing her need to know they were near so she could truly rest, had kept Augustus occupied hour upon hour.

They'd tied knots, lassoed bedposts, and composed verses, and after a steward delivered their lunch, tidied their rooms, and brought water for a bath, she went right back to sleep and Noble Salt story time began. She'd drifted in and out of it, wanting to hear but so filled with contentment and relief, she'd floated beyond it, and the outlaw's voice became part of her dreams, complete with narration and moving images.

"If I ask you some questions, will you tell me the truth?" Augustus was wheedling. She knew that voice.

"It depends. Will the truth hurt you?" Noble asked.

"Hurt me?"

"Yeah. Sometimes knowing the truth ain't good for us. We're not ready for it. We gotta grow into it, I think. We're not ready for some stories."

"I've been reading for a long time. Since I was six. And Maman lets me read whatever I want. She bought these for me."

For a moment there was a cessation of speech, and Jane drifted away again, the whisper of pages being turned the only sound in the room. She wasn't sure how much time had passed when Noble spoke again.

"That ain't how it was. They got all kinds of things wrong. Where was this published? Ha. New York City. Well . . . that explains it."

"How do you know that's not how it was?"

Silence again. "'Cause I knew him."

"You knew Wyatt Earp?"

"Yeah. Not well. But well enough to know he wasn't a saint like this story makes him out to be. He and his brothers were tough, and they didn't worry about killing all that much."

"But he was a lawman!"

"Yeah. But in the West, most of the lawmen are just outlaws with badges."

"Were you ever a lawman?"

"No. Never was."

"Were you an outlaw?"

"Tell you what. You ask me your questions, and I'll tell you if I can. But if I think it might be something your mama doesn't want us talking about, then you can save your breath."

"You were born in Utah."

"Yes. You know that."

"You're a cowboy."

"We called them cowhands. But yeah. I started working on a ranch when I wasn't much older than you. I've had lots of jobs."

"You said you had lots of names too. Can you tell me some of them?"

"No, Augustus. I can't."

"Why? Are you angry? You sound angry when you call me Augustus."

"I'm not angry. Just bein' firm."

"What's your favorite book in the whole world?" Augustus switched tracks suddenly.

"Hmm. I don't know. I haven't read all of 'em. So it seems kind of unfair to pick a favorite."

His voice was so kind, so calm, and she allowed herself to surface, letting it lap against her like warm water on sand beaches.

"I can't pick a favorite either. But I like this one. It's called *The Outlaw Butch Cassidy*. Have you ever heard of him?"

Oh no. Augustus was up to something. She forgot sometimes how smart he was, how observant.

"Let me see that," Butch said. The calm had become incredulity, and she sat up, knowing it was time to intervene. The room spun and she collapsed back down, moaning softly. Damn every ship in the sea.

"You can read it, if you like. Or I can just tell you about it," Augustus offered. It didn't sound like he'd surrendered his book. "Butch Cassidy was born in Utah. Like you. And his dad is Maximilian. Like you too. When is your birthday?"

"I'd like to see that book, if you don't mind, Gus," Noble insisted again. Strain was starting to show through.

When she heard the whisper of turning pages, she rolled to the side and eased herself slowly. The room cooperated. She rose, shakily, and walked to the mirror. She looked like she'd escaped from Bedlam, and she reached for her brush and began taming her hair, horrified by the matted lengths. Noble Salt was going to have to fend for himself a little longer. She braided it quickly, pulling it over her shoulder, and then brushed her teeth, dabbed a bit of rose oil on her tired skin, and put her robe over her nightgown. She needed to dress but wasn't quite that confident yet. Plus, Noble needed rescuing.

"What was your favorite job you ever had?" Augustus asked. They were squared off over the table, a stack of dime novels between them. Noble Salt was turning slowly through the pages of his life . . . or the life that had been written about him.

"The job I've got now is a pretty good one." He shut the book and pushed it away. He'd likely seen enough. "Working for your mom and for you . . . I like this job best of all." His voice rang with sincerity, but Augustus wrinkled his nose like it couldn't possibly be true.

"Are you just being nice?"

"No. Nice is good; honest is better. I've never had a better job than this. Beautiful ship. Good company. Work I can be proud of. I even like wearing tails and being fancy."

"You're right. Honest is better," Augustus said, and Jane could see his play a mile away. Her brilliant boy was closing in for the kill. "And I hope you'll be honest with me, Mr. Salt."

Noble didn't say anything. He just waited, his blue eyes steady on Augustus.

Augustus took a deep breath and blurted, "I know what your real name is. I know who you really are. You don't have to pretend with me. But maybe we should shut the door so Maman doesn't hear."

"Too late," she said from the doorway. Her voice was scratchy from underuse, but she was standing. "By all means, don't stop on my account."

Both of them jumped.

"Maman!" Augustus cried, startled. He bounded up and grabbed at a bit of rope. "Noble calls this a lariat. Do you know that he owns a railroad? And a copper mine?"

"I don't own them outright. I'm just an investor. I own stock."

"He says when we get to New York, we'll go to the exchange, and I can buy some stock too. He'll show me how. And lots of the stories in the dimes aren't true. Did you know that, Maman?"

"I suspected."

130

"Can you eat, honey?" Noble asked quietly, his eyes surveying her pale face. She knew she didn't look good, but she was much better.

"You need to call me Jane . . . or Mrs. Toussaint," she reminded, though Augustus didn't appear to be bothered by Noble's endearment. Augustus was worrying his lips and tying a knot, but the deep groove between his brows indicated trouble on his mind. Noble was wearing the same look. He smoothed the two sides of his mustache with his thumb and his forefinger, stroking down into his beard, a habit she'd noted when he was trying not to say something he thought he should.

"I asked them to bring soup and bread for supper. It's here. We were going to eat but got sidetracked with Gus's books."

Night had fallen, and soon it would be time to sleep again. Three days into the journey, and she'd hardly moved from her bed.

"Noble has met Wyatt Earp and Doc Holliday. And Bill Cody and Annie Oakley," Augustus said, his voice sober.

"My goodness," she said, though she wasn't terribly interested in any of those people. Augustus was gearing up again; she could see it. He was going to tell her all about Butch Cassidy, and she was going to have to confess she knew all along.

Noble cleared the books and moved the food from the rolling tray the steward had delivered supper on. "France has music and artists and culture . . . and what've we got? Traveling Wild West shows," he muttered.

Augustus set the table and pulled out a chair for Jane and waited until she was sitting before he took his own. Noble was the last to sit, but he bowed his head, clasped his hands, and said a quick prayer.

"Father in heaven. Thank you for this food we'll eat. Jesus' name, amen."

"You even pray in hokku, Mr. Salt," Jane said.

Noble cocked his head, counting, and nodded. "I guess I do."

A few minutes later they were sipping at the lukewarm soup and spreading butter on their bread, but Augustus was not at all interested in his supper, a first for him. He set his spoon down and folded his cloth napkin once, twice, and then again. Then he stood.

"Maman . . . you need to know something. I don't want to tell you because I don't want you to worry. But Noble is not . . . really . . . Noble Salt. I'm sorry, Mr. Salt. But I have to protect my mother, you understand?" His voice was pained, and his hands were shaking around the cloth.

"Of course I understand, Gus," Noble said, eating like nothing at all was amiss. He caught Jane's gaze and let it go with a slight nod that seemed to say, *Tell him.*

"Sit down and eat, darling. I'm not going anywhere. Mr. Salt is not going anywhere. And you can say all the things you need to say."

Augustus collapsed back into the chair, but a frown was forming between the two sides of his face.

"You know?" Augustus accused her.

"Yes. I do."

"Everything?"

"I know enough."

"And you hired him to . . . protect us?" The question squeaked a bit on the end.

Noble choked a little, and his mustache quivered with a smile. "That's what I said, Gus."

"Do you trust me, Augustus?" Jane asked.

"Yes." His answer was immediate.

"Do I love you more than anything in the world?"

Augustus looked at Noble, and something passed between them, some private conversation she had not been a part of.

"Yes. You do," Augustus said, somber.

"Then you must know that I would never do anything to hurt you or put you in danger. I believe in Mr. Salt—"

"Do we have to call him Noble Salt? We all know his real name."

"Truth be told, Butch Cassidy is as made up as Noble Salt—" Noble interjected.

"And calling him Butch Cassidy will get him killed," Jane finished. "So we will call him Noble Salt. Always. Do you understand, Augustus?"

Her voice was sharp, and Augustus's eyes were wide. It was not a game they were playing.

"It says in one of those books that you got your name working in a butcher shop in Colorado," Augustus said slowly, gauging whether the conversation could continue. Noble answered without hesitation.

"Nah. My brother Van is the one who started calling me Butch."

"Why?"

"I was watching the kids—always. My mom and dad both hired out on other spreads. We were running wild at home, up until I was thirteen or so, and big enough to do ranch work.

"My sisters thought it would be a great idea to decorate all the little ones' hair with burrs, kinda like wildflowers. But burrs, once they get stuck, don't come out. I ended up cutting out more than a hundred burrs from a bunch of little blond heads. It probably would have been okay, but some of them were caught real close to the scalp, and when we cut them out, there was long hair in some places, short hair in others, with complete bald spots in between. When Ma got home she cried, and the only way to fix it was to go short all over—sisters, brothers all.

"I didn't have any burrs in my hair, but I was supposed to be watching them, and I felt bad. So I let her cut my hair too. It was half an inch long all over my head, if that. After that mess, my younger brother Van started calling me Butch, letting everyone in the valley know it was my fault the Parker kids no longer had any hair. Of course, he still had all *his* hair."

"You said you didn't like Van."

"No . . . but I loved—love—him. Other than my mom, I probably loved him most of all. We were only a year apart, so he wasn't just my brother, he was my friend. My only friend. Wasn't anyone else for miles. We did everything together up until I left home. He wanted to come, but I was tired of looking out for everyone but myself. I wanted to be on my own, live a little, and I didn't want to worry about being a bad example."

"Where did the Cassidy come from?" Jane asked. If he was talking, she had some questions of her own, and she'd told him about Boot. She'd never told anyone about Boot except for Augustus, and he knew not to speak of it.

"There was a man named Mike Cassidy who worked on the ranch I rode for. He had the reputation of a gunfighter. And he was nice looking and friendly. Happy to show the younger cowboys how to tie a better slipknot or how to pick a good saddle. He quickly became well liked and emulated by the whole bunkhouse. And he took a liking to me. Taught me some things. Gave me some encouragement. Made me believe that I was good for something, that I had skills and talents. My pa was a good man. I think even better than I gave him credit for, but he wasn't good with praise, and I needed it."

"Is it dark enough?" Jane asked. He hadn't wanted to talk about his father before.

"I'll tell you about my dad if you tell me about yours, Noble," Augustus said, petting his arm.

Noble shot Jane a look. "That might be something you'll have to get permission to do, son."

Jane schooled her face into a blank slate, and Noble cleared his throat.

"My dad was a good man," he repeated, firm. "But he wasn't good at encouragement or praise. He never apologized when he was wrong or angry. He never said 'I love you,' not to any of us. Not even to my mother, though maybe he just waited until they were alone. Life was hard, and they weren't happy. Or maybe it just didn't seem like happy to me. I knew for damn sure that if I was going to have a life different from the life my parents led, I was going to have to do different things."

"Noble . . . you probably shouldn't swear around me," Augustus scolded.

"I'll try not to, Gus."

Augustus nodded solemnly, as if Noble promised more than an improvement in his language. Then turned his tragic brown eyes on her. His hound dog face with his spotted cheek was crowned by two severe cowlicks that made the hair stick straight up at his temples like little horns above his tortured face.

"He'll try not to swear, Maman."

"Yes, my love. I heard."

Augustus turned back to Noble Salt. "And you won't rob any more trains or banks . . . or ships, will you? There's probably all kinds of treasure in the storage hull."

Noble stroked his beard, as if thinking long and hard about resisting something so tempting.

"Please, Noble?"

"Tell you what, kid. I'll give up my thieving ways while we're together if you promise me one thing in return."

"Is it a good thing? Because I don't want to make a bad promise."

Noble rested his hand on Augustus's cheek for a moment and then patted it and pulled away, continuing. "You're a good boy, Augustus Maximilian Toussaint. And there's nothing better in the whole world than a good boy."

"What about a good girl?"

Noble's lips twitched, and he stroked down his mustache again, wiping off his smile. "I kinda like the mean ones," he said.

"Noble Salt!" Jane warned.

"What's my promise, Noble?" Augustus jumped in, playing the peacemaker between his new favorite people. Jane sighed. Her boy was going to get his heart broken.

Noble leaned in and got nose to nose with Augustus. "Hear this, Augustus Maximilian Toussaint. Butch Cassidy was not a hero. He wasn't even a good man. Those books are just stories where no one gets hurt. They aren't real life. I'm going to try my best to be good for you and your mom, but don't ever think, not for one minute, that Butch Cassidy is someone you want to be like. Okay?"

"Okay," Augustus said, blinking like it was all too much to take in, and Butch sat back, patting his cheek again.

"I'd take one Gus Toussaint over a thousand Robert LeRoy Parkers."

"Mr. Salt? Are you still awake?" she called out hours later. Augustus was asleep beside her. She'd bathed after dinner and was feeling quite restored. Unfortunately, it was nearing midnight, and she was alone with herself. The doors between the staterooms had been left ajar—Augustus's doing—and she listened, trying to hear whether Noble slept. She could hear nothing but the distant sound of parting waters.

"Noble?" she said again, not expecting an answer but enjoying his name on her tongue.

"Yeah, honey? You need something?"

"No," she snapped, startled that he'd heard.

"You feeling sick again? You need to go up top?"

"No. I've just been sleeping all day. I'm wide awake."

"You've been sleeping for *two* days."

"Hmm. Yes. I'm sorry about that."

"Nothing to be sorry about. Gus and I had a good time."

Amazingly, she believed him.

"Thank you," she said, her voice awkwardly loud. She grimaced, but Augustus didn't stir.

"Thank me?"

"Yes. Thank you. You took such good care of Augustus. He's fallen in love with you, you know. He's smitten. It broke his heart to tattle on you."

"Yeah. I know. But I was so proud of him."

She laughed out loud but then had to blink away the sudden moisture that rushed to her eyes. "I was too. So proud."

"Not an easy conversation."

"No. He's asked me about things over the years. I'm not sure when he figured it out . . . but I suppose we both wanted to protect each other. You were our rescuer. Our savior. And we let you be exactly what you were to us that night. But . . ."

"But Butch Cassidy is an outlaw," he finished for her. Final. Unapologetic. "And Augustus Toussaint is the real Noble Salt," he added. "As noble as they come."

She sighed, knowing she should let the man sleep. He'd been on duty too long. She looked over at her son, the perfection of his profile making her reach out and trace the dark line that was almost obscured by his pillow. She missed the part she couldn't see.

"As noble as they come," she whispered. She rose over him and pressed a kiss to his crown.

"Mr. Salt?"

"Yeah, honey?" He didn't sound tired either, and she knew she needed to put an end to his tendency toward endearments, but she liked them too much.

"Tell me about Mike Cassidy."

12

Oh to hell you ride
And home dissolves behind you
A paradise lost

"Mike Cassidy has never had anyone to look after but Mike Cassidy," Maximilian Parker said, shoveling food into his mouth. They'd stopped for supper, but sundown was a long ways off, and there was work to be done. Always work to be done.

"You don't even know him, Pa," Butch answered, rolling his sleeves and digging into his own pile of mashed potatoes.

Pa snorted. "I know his kind."

That didn't sit well with Butch. "What kind is that?"

"The kind that bounces from one ranch to the next, never stays too long, and never settles. If he has a woman, he leaves her fending for herself more often than not. He likes to gamble. Likes to impress folks with his gunslinging. Feels entitled to what he didn't earn. Wherever he goes, he leaves things worse than the way he found 'em. He's a small-time crook, but he thinks that makes him a big man. Yeah. I know his kind."

Butch couldn't have been more insulted had his father been talking about him, and for a moment he sat, smarting at the scathing assessment, collecting his thoughts.

"He isn't a bad man, Pa. He taught me how to hold my gun and plant my feet, and I'm already shooting straighter and faster. He said I'm a natural. He says he's never seen someone with a better touch with horses either. Animals like me."

"That's 'cause you are one, Butch," Van quipped. *"They feel right at home with you."*

Butch ignored him. Van liked to poke at him, and Butch had learned that what really bothered Van was no reaction at all. So he didn't give him one. He wondered suddenly if his father employed the same method with him. He already seemed to have forgotten Butch had spoken.

"He's not a bad man," Butch repeated, firm. Loud. Pa looked up at him with his faded blue eyes and sunburned face and finished chewing the food in his mouth.

"He's not a good man neither," he pronounced, and went back to his supper as if that was the final word on the matter. Butch's temper flared.

"What's a good man, Pa? I know what the church folk say around here. The good man is the guy that looks all shiny sitting at church services every week, repeating the doctrines and saying all the right things. He's a good man, right? Even if he's cheatin' on his wife and beatin' on his kids. But we won't talk about that."

"Go ahead. Cast your stones, since you're so perfect, Robert LeRoy," Pa muttered, his eyes still on his plate.

"That's not what I'm saying, Pa. I'm asking, what is good? You're telling me one man isn't and one man is, but one's a damn hypocrite. You're telling me good is the one who goes to church on Sunday. You don't go to church . . . so are you a good man?"

His siblings were listening. Ma was too, and Butch felt a surge of power at cornering his father.

"No. I'm not," Pa said. *"I'm not a good man. I'm as flawed as the next. And no, church doesn't make the man—one way or the other—and I never said it did. But neither does skill with a gun or a fast horse or smooth talk. Don't put Mike Cassidy on a pedestal, son. And don't follow in his footsteps. He'll lead you straight to hell."*

Butch groaned. "I don't believe in hell. I thought you didn't either, Pa."

"I believe in it. But it's not just a place we go when we die. It's a place we create for ourselves right here. Right now." Max Parker tapped his plate with his knife to emphasize his point. "We make our own hell, and we make hell for the people we love with our poor choices."

The table grew silent for all of three seconds, and then the baby spilled her milk and someone else got wet. Ma was up, scrambling to soothe the upset, and the conversation was forgotten by everyone but Butch.

"Mike Cassidy is nice to me," he said softly. "He's shown me a few things, and he doesn't mind having me around. When he leaves outta here . . . I'm going with him."

If anyone heard him, they let it slide. But true to his word, he was gone by the end of summer.

"Where did you go?" Jane asked, transfixed.

"I went to Telluride—a straight shot east—in Colorado. It wasn't even that far in the scheme of things. Three hundred fifty miles, thereabouts. But it might as well have been the moon."

"Telluride," Jane murmured.

"To hell you ride."

"You got a girl, Butch Parker?" Mike Cassidy asked. "Mormon girls are pretty. Must be all that clean living."

"No. The only girls I knew back home were all related to me."

The man laughed, throwing back his head and slapping at his dusty thigh. "Well, that won't be a problem in Telluride. You're never going to want to leave."

"I don't know about that. A day or two here will be fun . . . but I gotta find work."

"*Work will always be there,*" *Mike said.* "*You need to enjoy yourself a little.*"

The woman behind the bar might have been pretty once, but that day had passed, and in the place of pretty was a dull-eyed doll with yarn-red hair and painted lips that grimaced every time the volume got too loud. Butch guessed the volume was too loud all the time. Mike Cassidy bought him a drink, the first drink he'd ever had, and he tossed it back expecting nectar and got ear wax instead.

"*That's terrible,*" *he choked.*

"*Tastes bad, feels good.*"

Butch coughed a little, eyes watering.

"*When does it feel good?*" *He didn't know if he could wait that long.*

"*When you get to the bottom.*"

Butch drained it, slammed it down, and said a word that made his own ears turn red.

"*One more for the kid,*" *Mike Cassidy called to the bartend.*

"*I'm not a kid, Mike,*" *he said. And he meant it. Those days were done.*

"*Not after tonight you won't be, Butch Parker. And definitely not after tomorrow. Tomorrow we're going to stop the train between Grand Junction and Telluride. I've got it all mapped out. All planned. If you do what I tell you, we'll be a whole lot richer.*"

"*I don't want to do that.*" *But he did want to do it; he wanted it so bad he'd been dreaming about it, making his own plans and calculations, and he was ashamed of himself.*

"*You aren't hurting anyone,*" *Mike said softly, sipping at his drink. Butch was sipping too, and it didn't taste so bad anymore.*

"*How do you figure? I'm guessing it'll hurt the folks who get robbed.*"

"*The conductor—it's not his money. The steward, even the guy in the vault. Not theirs either. These big moneymen come in—some from other countries—and they buy up the land. They buy up the cattle too, and they don't even live here. They control all the big herds, and the small homesteads, the small ranchers, can't compete and they get bought out . . . or beat out.*"

"Railroads are the same. There are three big companies—three companies run by three men—who own all the railroads. And if you control the railroad, you control supply and you control demand. So when we rob this train—and we are going to rob the train, Butch Parker—you have to remember that all that money we're taking is not hurting anyone, not even the big moneymen at the top. What's a dollar when you've got a million of them? It won't change their lives one iota. It won't take food from their children's mouths, but it'll make a huge difference to us. And if you choose to spread it around a bit, to make yourself feel better, it'll improve a few more lives. Think of it as spreading the wealth a little."

Butch nodded slowly. "I can see that. But . . . don't call me Butch Parker."

"Isn't that what your family calls you?"

"Yeah. That's what my family calls me." And Mike Cassidy wasn't family. Mike Cassidy was a whole different world, and in his heart of hearts, Butch didn't want the Parkers tainted by the things he was about to do. Butch owed them that.

"Cuttin' ties, huh?" Mike said.

"Yep." O waly, waly . . .

"You can use my name if you want to. Butch Cassidy has a ring." Mike Cassidy was smiling at him, almost proud, and for a minute Butch forgot about the pain and reveled in that unfamiliar feeling.

"Yeah. I guess it does."

"How old were you then?" Jane asked, afraid he would stop talking.

"When I left home?"

"Yes."

"Eighteen."

"Did you ever go back?"

He was so quiet she sat up in bed, afraid he'd fallen asleep and left her alone in the dark with all her questions.

"I did. But not for a long time. And I never saw my mother again."

It was her turn for silence. She didn't know how to talk about such things, and he didn't elucidate. Maybe he needed her to ask, and her throat ached with a thousand questions. But she simply waited, hardly breathing.

"You sang a song my mom loved the night I met you at Carnegie Hall. The encore. Oliver sent you back out onstage. It was a change in the program."

"'Waly, Waly.'"

"Yeah. That's the one. It felt like you were singing it just for me."

"It's such a sad song."

"Well . . . I've lived a pretty sad life."

"Ladies and gentlemen, we don't want you to be afraid, and we surely want to get you on your way. But there is a large amount of money on this train, and we have a terrible need."

A woman shrieked and a child began crying, chaos and panic burbling up just like he'd feared.

People started pulling their wallets from their vest pockets and bills from their purses. "No, no, no," Butch said, waving his gun in the air. "Put all that away. That money is yours. We're not taking your money. Put it back. I just need your weapons."

An old man with feeble hands and peering eyes looked up at Butch, and returned his money to the billfold in his lap.

"That's right. Put it back. If you all just sit quietly for a few minutes, we'll let you get on your way."

Another man looked as if he was considering a takedown, so Butch put his back to the door between the people in the car and the goings-on in the safe.

"I'd be very sad if I had to use this, and I have no intention to, unless somebody in a gray derby with a twitchy hand gets jumpy."

The man jerked.

"Yes, sir. I'm talking to you. Just sit still, now. I know it's hard. I never could sit still myself, but I'm not taking anything from you or the rest of these fine people. So your job, even though you want to fight, is to keep everybody safe."

"I own this railroad," the man in the derby said. "I can't let you do this without a fight."

"Well, congratulations!" Butch said. "That's something to be proud of. And just think. You'll be a hero when we're done here, if all goes well. People will say, 'His train was robbed, but Mr. Railroad Baron the third kept everyone calm, and none of his passengers lost a dime. Nobody was hurt. Train just got in a little late, is all.'"

Butch swung his Colt toward another man getting twitchy. "Put your hands on your head, curly. Yes, you. You trying to get someone killed? There are kids in here. Women too. I'm not taking anything from you. Just hold tight."

He turned back to the railroad man.

"The safety and trust of your passengers is your highest priority, right? And you're going to keep everyone safe by sitting right there and being calm."

The man ground his teeth and folded his arms, his eyes wide behind his glasses. Butch knew the look. He was plotting, so Butch kept an eye on him while visiting easily with everyone else.

A boom, crash, shudder, and a settling, littered with screams, was Butch's signal to go.

"Now, if you would please hand me your weapons," he demanded.

"I thought you weren't taking our things?" one woman protested.

"I'm not. I just don't want anyone getting hurt. Not you. Not me." He took her husband's revolver. The man seemed almost relieved to be free of it. No weapon, no reason to be a tough guy.

"So if you'll just lay your weapons here in this box, I'll tuck them away in this here compartment, until you reach your destination."

He moved down the rows. "Show me your shins, mister. Hold those pant legs up. Your jacket too. Waistband's clean. Well done," he said, nodding and continued down the line, directing the collection with his new .45. He felt like a kid wearing new shoes. He could hardly keep his eyes from the pretty nickel barrel.

When it was done, he thanked the folks for their cooperation, locked the box into a compartment, and took the key that dangled from the door. He was sure there was another one somewhere. If not . . . they'd have to wait to get to the station. Even better.

He stepped out, slid the connecting door closed, and climbed out the singed hole that had just been blasted in the wall of the safe compartment.

"Let's go!" Mike Cassidy yelled, climbing up onto the horse being held for him. The palomino shimmied under his weight. The leather bags he'd so carefully constructed were bulging. Butch relieved him of one of them, swung up onto his own horse, and away they all went, thundering over the rise before they changed direction about a mile behind the train and rendezvoused at the cave where they'd spent the previous night.

Nobody followed. Nobody could. The train had been stopped in the middle of nowhere, and it would be some time before it was moving again.

"What did you get from the passengers? They looked like a wealthy bunch," Mike asked him, panting and smiling as he threw down the bags and crouched beside them to divvy up the take.

"I didn't take anything from the passengers," Butch said.

The silence in the cave was deafening. The men who'd helped him move all the passengers into one car squirmed. They'd stood at either end with their weapons drawn, but they hadn't intervened. They'd just been told to keep the passengers from interfering.

"What did you think you were doing, Butch?" the burly man Mike called Boggs bellowed right in his face.

"I was guarding them. Mike never told me I had to steal from the people."

"You didn't take anything?" Mike asked, dumbfounded.

"I didn't take anything."

"What about their guns?"

"*Their guns are all in a locked compartment in the engine room.*" *He held out the key. "It'll be a while before they get them back."*

"*They're going to be coming after us!*" *Boggs shoved Butch against the rock wall, knocking his head against a protrusion that took blood and hair and a good bit of his self-control.*

"*Come after us with what?*" *he cried. "They don't have horses. Those people are going to want to get to Denver. They're not coming after us, and since we didn't take anything from them, they're not going to be hounding the railroad to recover their personal property."*

Boggs stuck his face close, his fear-laced breath tickling Butch's cheek. "That was your portion. Guess you won't be getting anything, kid. Live and learn."

Mike Cassidy sighed and shoved his hat back on his head. "Nah. He gets a cut like the rest of us. He did his part. It went smooth, smoother than any job I've been on. Maybe that was smart, not riling up the regular folks. But next time . . . for hell's sake, send the collection box through the passenger cars, Butch. You left a pretty penny back there."

Boggs let him go. Butch didn't reach to check the back of his head. It was bleeding, but he would heal. He nodded once, agreeable like always, but he knew the next time—if there was a next time—he would be the boss.

"You were the brains of the operation. That's what the papers all said."

"If you knew the rest of the guys . . . you'd realize that's not saying much," Noble muttered.

"How many trains?"

"Twenty years' worth. I robbed banks too, though not near as many. First one was in Telluride in '89. The San Miguel Valley Bank. Telluride wasn't good for me. That's when Van found me, and I let him be a lookout on the job and gave him a cut. That was the worst thing I coulda done. And I'll be paying for it for the rest of my life."

"Why was it the worst thing?"

"It was too easy. When you grow up with nothing, the way we did, to have that much money, so fast and so damn easy, it's hard to go back to working for a dollar a day. I ruined my little brother."

Again she waited.

⌒

"*Go home, Van.*"

"*You can't tell me what to do, Robert LeRoy. I'm a man, same as you. I got to make my own way, same as you.*"

"*Stealing isn't making your own way.*"

"*I'm not going back.*"

"*Well, you're not coming with me. You're too slow and too stupid for this kind of business. You'll just get caught or killed. Or you'll get other fellas caught or killed. Here's your money. It's more than you could make being a cowhand in a year. Go find work you can be proud of. Work that Ma and Pa will be proud of. I won't take you with me, Van. I won't. You follow me, I'll disappear. You keep trying, I'll run you off.*"

⌒

"I gave him his cut and sent him home. He wouldn't go. So I got mean with him. I wanted to scare him away. He ran off, half-cocked and wanting to show me I was wrong."

"Were you wrong?"

"He wasn't any slower or stupider than the rest of us."

"Were you wrong about him being killed or caught?"

"No. He eventually robbed a stagecoach carrying the US Mail, and a federal marshal was there to meet him. Mom always said he was my spittin' image. Thirteen kids, you're going to get a couple that look alike. He tried to say it was me who robbed the coach—gave them my name and everything. Fortunately, or unfortunately, depending on

147

who's telling the story, one of his coconspirators told the authorities who he really was. He got locked up for a long time."

"Where is he now?"

She heard him sigh, but he didn't answer.

"Noble?"

"Damn, I hate that name. Every time you say it, I think you're laughing at me."

"Why?"

"Because I'm not noble at all."

"What should I call you then?"

"It's fine . . . I just can't abide it anymore tonight. I'm going to go to sleep now, honey."

She felt stung. Of all the things he'd freely imparted—his candor astounded her—it was talk of his brother that had shut him down. Or maybe it was the use of his made-up name.

"We can't very well have men robbing trains and holding up banks," she blurted, suddenly so angry with him—or for him—that the words tumbled over themselves to get out. "And don't think I excuse that. But more than the crimes themselves, it's the fact that you ruined any chance you might have at a different life. That circular I saw said DEAD OR ALIVE. That's the part I can't abide, Butch Cassidy. And don't call me honey."

"I'll try not to," he said softly. A few minutes later, the door between their rooms closed.

She fumed in the darkness for a long time. If Butch Cassidy tossed and turned or slept like a baby, she couldn't hear him. And somehow that made her even angrier.

13

*I'll give you the moon
If you give me the morning
A world we will make*

Augustus knew he was talking too much, but he couldn't stop. He had too many thoughts, and Noble Salt didn't seem to mind hearing them all. Noble never seemed to get tired. Or angry. Or bored. And he listened better than anyone Augustus had ever met. Of course, Augustus hadn't met many people, but in his experience, most were not good listeners.

Maman was practicing for her performance in the dining hall while an army of men in uniforms prepared the tables for supper; the clangor and clamor were not ideal, and she had a little V forming between her brows. The cellist seemed to know what he was doing and the fellow on the piano was sweating profusely—Maman had that effect on people—but he kept up too. Maman sang through her set, stopping here and there to direct her accompanists.

Mr. Salt liked listening to Maman too . . . Augustus could tell by the way he got really still, and his eyes got dreamy, like he needed a nap. Augustus loved his mother, but he was not nearly as entranced by her singing. She was just Maman, and he was accustomed to her voice.

It was their last full day on the ship—one more sleep too—and he was teaching Noble how to play chess. He wanted to be up on deck, but Noble insisted they stay with Maman.

"Why don't you speak French, Gus?" Noble asked, moving his pawn.

Augustus swiped it up with a grin. "You should have moved there," he instructed. "I would still have been able to take it, but it would have been a better move, long term."

"Hmm." Butch studied the board.

"I don't speak French because you don't speak French. Do you? And I want to talk to you," Augustus answered.

"No . . . I mean, how come you speak such good English?"

"Maman is English. She only ever speaks to me in English. I learned French from the city—from my governess, from Oliver. Oliver always spoke French."

"He was good to you . . . Oliver?"

Augustus shrugged. "I suppose. It embarrassed him when people stared at me. I think that's why I always called him Oliver. It is uncomfortable for the people who love me."

"He loved you?"

"I think so. He *was* my dad." He wrinkled his nose, considering that. "He loved Maman more. But Maman did not love him. Maman hated him."

Butch shifted and looked at his mother, who was singing a note so high and clear, Augustus was surprised the pieces on the board didn't vibrate.

"He wasn't around much. But he liked me well enough, I guess. He wasn't cruel. He mostly handled Maman's career."

"Yeah. She told me that."

"I cried at his wake, but Maman didn't. Maman doesn't cry as much as I do. I cry when things make me happy sometimes too. Not all tears are sad. I cried when I saw you walking up the gangplank. I was so excited." He grinned.

"I almost cried when you waved at me," Noble confessed easily.

"You did?"

"I did. Van used to tease me about my tears. Harry too."

"Harry?" Augustus asked. "You've never talked about Harry."

"I called him Contrary Harry. His nickname was Sundance. Didn't fit him at all."

"The Sundance Kid?" Augustus squeaked in disbelief.

"Yeah. That's what people called him. He in those dime novels of yours?"

"He's on the handbill Maman has. She doesn't think I know. But I know lots of things. She has another picture of you too. One with a cowboy hat and mountains in the background. She stole it from Mr. Harriman's house."

"Did she now?" Noble's eyes were wide.

"Yes. She used to keep it under glass on the table where she brushed her hair."

Noble seemed dumbfounded by that.

"How did Sundance get his name?" Augustus asked. Noble shook his head, as if trying to clear it.

"He stole a horse in a place called Sundance . . . or maybe the horse was named Sundance. I don't remember. But it didn't really fit him, either way. Contrary would have been a better fit. He had a lot of names . . . like us."

"What does 'contrary' mean?"

"Always arguing about something. He was sour."

"I'm not contrary."

"No. You aren't. That's good. You're easy. You're No-Fuss Gus."

"Is the West green, Noble?"

"Here and there. But no . . . I wouldn't say the West was green. Parts of Colorado look like the moon."

"The moon?"

"Yeah. Nothing but white dust and craters. Dry. Flat. No mountains or rivers or trees. Ugly. But then, you get to parts that take your breath away. Life is like that, I think. Beautiful and ugly, right next to each other. But when I think of the West, I think of red and gold and pink, mostly, with so much blue sky it makes the mountains looks purple."

"Purple?"

"Yeah. And you've never seen mountains until you've seen Utah."

"We're going to see Utah. Maman said. Tell me more," Augustus demanded, taking Noble's king. "Checkmate."

"The West is hot and cold and not a whole lot in between. The West is desert red and snow white."

"Red and white make pink."

"Yeah . . . maybe that's why the sky's the color it is in the winter. The red sun reflecting off all that white snow. In the West you can see for miles in every direction."

"Don't the mountains get in the way?"

"Sure . . . eventually . . . but the mountains ring huge valleys, and there aren't many houses and hardly any trees. My eyes never got bored."

"My eyes are bored today," Augustus declared, sitting back, the game won.

"Yeah. Not much to see on a boat," Noble agreed.

"There is a lot to see! But we're stuck here," Augustus grumbled.

"There isn't a place on earth I'd rather be," Butch said, and he bowed his head a moment, listening as Maman sang about a place called Shenandoah. Augustus hadn't heard that one before and turned in his chair.

"Across the wide Missouri," Butch whispered the words as Maman sang them. "Damn, that's pretty."

And Augustus looked at his mother anew.

⁓

Augustus liked his suit with the little black tie and tails. He felt like a penguin . . . or a dolphin, and immediately had an image of one wearing Maman's hat, circling the big ship and chattering with his dolphin friends.

They were dining at the captain's table on this final night of the voyage. Captain Smith had insisted, and Maman said she couldn't put it off any longer. Noble wasn't dining with them. He said he was the help, not a guest, and Maman didn't press the issue.

"Don't you want to meet the captain, Noble?" Augustus asked.

"I'll meet him."

"Are you afraid someone will recognize you?"

"Nah. I'm afraid of eating with the wrong fork, Gus."

"I would help you."

"I know." Noble straightened his tie. "And I'll be there. Close by. Gotta make sure nobody messes with Saint Jane."

Augustus wanted to meet the captain and sit at his table, but he was worried too. The people would not like that he was present. They would try not to stare, and their determined avoidance was more obvious than a frank inspection, which he preferred, though that was hard too.

"Does your face ever hurt?" Noble asked him as they shared the mirror—Noble above, Augustus below—combing their hair. Noble seemed as nervous as he.

"No. It itches sometimes. And I get headaches. My bloody noses are bad too. Dr. Moreau says it's because my skin has a lot more capillaries. It's the overproduction of capillaries that makes the skin red and puffy. Like an extra juicy grape. Or a mosquito after he's taken a big bite and filled his belly full. Have you ever slapped a mosquito while he's still attached?"

"More times than I can count."

"You look nice, Noble," Augustus said. "Don't worry. Everybody will think you're one of the good guys."

Noble chuckled. "Thank you, Gus. You look nice too."

"I look like a bad guy."

"You don't look like a bad guy."

"I look like a monster," he said. He'd meant to be easy—No-Fuss Gus—when he said it, but it came out a little bit shaky, and he took a deep breath, avoiding Noble's eyes in the mirror.

"See, the thing about monsters is, Gus . . . most of the time, they don't look like monsters."

Augustus frowned, confused.

"A monster is someone who makes people miserable, just because they can. A monster is someone who likes inflicting pain and suffering on everyone around him. That doesn't sound like Augustus Toussaint to me."

"People are afraid of me," he whispered.

"That's okay. That ain't a bad thing."

"It's not?"

"No. People respect what they fear."

"Maman says it's my secret weapon. The good folks will look past it, and the bad ones will steer clear."

"Smart lady."

"Shall we go, gentlemen?" Maman called from the other room, and he and Noble Salt headed obediently for the door.

Maman wore red, and everyone turned or paused in their conversation when she entered the enormous dining hall.

"See? No one's looking at you, Gus," Noble said, putting a hand on his shoulder.

He and Noble fell back as they approached the captain's table.

Captain Smith was a distinguished-looking fellow with a neatly groomed white beard and a matching white cap of closely cropped hair. He was stout but not portly, grave but not grim. He shook hands with Augustus and offered him a sailor's cap, and didn't seem alarmed or disgusted by his face. The captain then introduced them to his wife and two other guests, the only other occupants at the table for eight.

"I'm sure you know the earl, Madame Toussaint. And this is Mrs. Judith Morgan, my sister and the wife of my first mate, who is on duty this evening," he said, gesturing to the two others at the table. They were not old and not young—Augustus found he had no sense for the age of adults—though they were handsome enough in a wealthy, well-groomed sort of way.

The earl looked familiar, and Augustus frowned, trying to place him. The man had risen, and he inclined his head, a small smile playing around his lips.

"Madame Toussaint and I know each other well, Captain Smith," he said. "Her late husband was a relation. We are practically cousins, aren't we, Jane? Or at least that is our little joke."

Maman would not like that. No one called Maman Jane in public. She was Madame Toussaint, and even Oliver had learned to refer to her that way among guests. But Maman said nothing.

Noble pulled out her chair, the one beside the captain, and as she sank into it, she jostled the table, rattling the saucers and upending a wineglass.

Everyone at the table scrambled, and Augustus slid into his own chair amid the fuss. Maman reached for him, clasping his hand beneath the table. She was shaking, and when he looked up into her face, she was gray beneath the powder and lipstick she wore to perform, and her eyes were glassy and fixed.

"Are you ill, Mrs. Toussaint?" the captain asked, judicious.

"No. Please. Forgive me. I'm fine. This is my son, Augustus, and my security guard, Mr. Noble Salt. He will be joining us this evening as well. Please have a seat, Mr. Salt. Captain, thank you for the invitation." Maman had still not acknowledged the lord or the first mate's wife, Mrs. Morgan. The woman's eyes flitted to Augustus before she let them settle on Noble, who still stood behind Maman's chair. She seemed to like his face and let her eyes rest there a little longer.

Noble hesitated, clearly torn between his desire to remove himself and Maman's direct order. Three empty seats remained at the table, and Noble slipped into the one beside Augustus.

"Mr. Salt," the captain said. "With a name like that, and a beard like that"—he pointed his fork at Noble—"I would think you were a sailor."

"I prefer the mountains over the sea but have been lucky enough to enjoy both," Noble said agreeably.

"You're an American?"

"Yes, sir."

"What part?"

"I've lived in several western states and South America as well."

The captain asked him a question in very accented Spanish. Noble answered him in kind. Then they both smiled politely, their language skills exhausted, and turned to their suppers.

Augustus ate with his eyes on his plate, taking small bites so he could savor each one. Food was ruined by people's stares, so he did his best to ignore them, but a pulse began behind his bloodstained eye, and he stopped caring about savoring and quickened his pace.

The wake.

He'd seen Lord Ashley at Oliver's wake. An older woman had been with him. She'd embraced Maman, though Maman had not returned the gesture, standing stiffly in the old woman's arms.

When he'd asked her about it afterward, she'd been dazed and distracted, and claimed she didn't know which old woman he was referring to.

"Her name was Toussaint too," he said. "At least . . . I think it was."

Her countenance cleared. "That was Madame Toussaint. Her late husband and Oliver were cousins. She was the one who discovered me and sent me to the conservatory. I didn't see her much after that, though she was, in many ways, my benefactress. She lived in London, and the conservatory was in France."

"She seemed very nice . . . and very rich."

Maman smiled wanly. "Yes . . . well. She is rich, that's for sure."

"She talked to me. I was playing chess by myself in Oliver's study. She came in looking for a book she wanted . . . something he'd borrowed but never returned."

"What did she say?"

"She was curious about my face . . . but that's to be expected." He shrugged. "But then she asked me to turn my face so she could just see my good side. She asked nicely, and I didn't want to be disrespectful to an old woman. So I turned my face like she asked. She stared at me for a long time."

Maman had grown slightly pale.

"Why does your face look like that, Maman?"

"Like what?"

"You look scared and trembly. Like you're going to faint. Don't faint, Maman. You'll fall and I won't know what to do."

"Did she say anything else?"

"Just that I look very much like my father. Do I really look like Oliver?"

Maman silently picked at her dinner, even though Augustus knew she didn't taste it. She would be ravenous after her performance with nothing to eat. Maybe he would tell Noble Salt to have the kitchen send some trays to their room, and maybe an extra piece of cake for him to eat before bed.

Butch ate very little on his own plate, though he had to be hungry. His stomach had growled relentlessly while the valet had made him try on all his newly altered clothes, and he'd apologized, pleading hunger.

"I am ready to go back to the cabin, Maman," he said softly, trying not to be discourteous. The captain's wife had prattled nonstop to Judith Morgan, who'd barely been able to respond with a "yes," a "hmm," or a "you don't say?"

"Will you excuse us, please, Captain Smith?" Noble inserted. "Mrs. Toussaint needs a few moments to prepare for her performance."

"Of course," Captain Smith said, setting down his silver and rising as Maman stood. Lord Ashley rose as well.

"The boy should stay, though. We have the best seats in the room," he said, his eyes flitting over Augustus. "We'll take good care of him."

It was a perfectly reasonable—and even gracious—suggestion, but Augustus shrank inside, wishing desperately for his berth and a bit of chocolate.

Maman hesitated, and her hand flexed against his collar, as if she wanted to draw him back, the way Noble Salt had done when she lunged for her hat.

"Mr. Salt can remain with him," the captain's wife chirruped, sipping at her wine and looking at Maman with raised brows.

Maman looked at Noble and down at Augustus, and her lips trembled.

"Very well," she said softly. "Please excuse me."

Augustus sat back down, his eyes on his empty plate, and tried not to be contrary, like the Sundance Kid. Noble returned to his seat as well, though he did not seem at all happy about it. He watched Maman walk toward the dais, where the pianist had already taken his place and was softly playing dinner music.

"She does not seem stable, Mr. Salt," the earl murmured. "I do hope she will still be able to serenade us. I have been so looking forward to it."

"As have I, Lord Ashley," the captain's wife cooed.

"I have been looking forward to meeting you as well, Augustus," Lord Ashley said, leaning toward him. "Your mother keeps you locked away in your tower, doesn't she?"

"My tower, sir?"

"She's very protective of you."

"Yes, sir."

"I thought it high time we meet."

"I'm sorry, sir. I didn't know Maman had any cousins."

The man chuckled and winked at Augustus, like it was their little joke. Augustus just felt confused, and Noble shifted beside him and rested his hand on his shoulder. Augustus wanted to press his face into Noble's wide palm and hide for a minute, but instead he turned toward the musicians, giving the folks at the table his good side, and worried about Maman. He had never seen her so rattled before a performance. Maman didn't get nervous, but something was definitely wrong.

Butch shouldn't have worried.

Jane was magnificent. She sang with so much intensity, Mrs. Morgan shivered and put her hands over her ears at one point like it was unpleasant. Butch skewered her with a look of such disdain, she immediately dropped her hands.

"I prefer sweeter tones," she babbled.

He had also not missed the earl's insinuation that Jane was unstable.

She sang a half hour set—that was what she called it—accompanied by a piano and a cello. She didn't need more. When she sang, the room grew very quiet, no whispering or giggles, no treating her like background entertainment. They wanted to hear her, it was plain, and she commanded every eye and trained every ear. A true star in their midst.

He didn't know many of the songs, and certainly didn't understand the language she was singing in, but when she finished with "Shenandoah," something in his heart eased and he exhaled in appreciation. He loved that song, loved it deep, and when she was done, he wished she'd sing it again, but he guessed she could probably sing anything and make him feel it in his bones. Hell, she could make him love "Clementine," a song he'd hated whenever someone sang all umpteen verses around the fire or wanted him to play it on his harmonica. It would sound different with Jane's crystal tones and trained vibrato, and he knew she could make him beg to hear it again.

The captain proposed a toast in her honor, and she sang one more song, something French and happy, and Augustus declared it his favorite.

The moment she was done, she left the dais and strode toward the captain's table, smiling lightly, looking this way and that, a regal nod here and an upraised hand there at the standing ovation around her, but she was trembling and her eyes were desperate. Butch met her halfway.

"Let's go then, Mrs. Toussaint," he said, wrapping his hand around her elbow and taking her weight into him. She stiffened and then curled into his side, eyes closed, not breathing.

"You gonna be sick, honey?"

"Yes." She was speaking through her clenched teeth. "If I close my eyes and don't move, I will be just fine."

"Well, we gotta move. Otherwise your adoring audience is going to want autographs and conversation. If you can get beyond that door, I can carry you. I'm guessing you don't want them to see me carrying you."

"I can walk."

And she did, just long enough to get through the doors of the dining hall. Then she broke away from him, and ran, careening toward the bridge. He found her emptying out every morsel she'd managed to keep down over the railing.

He'd thought she'd adjusted to the ship and the sea in the last few days, but apparently not. He pulled his handkerchief from his pocket and handed it to her.

"Tell me what you need," he said.

"Please go back and get my son, Noble. He's alone in there with him," she groaned, dabbing at her mouth. "Please just get Augustus."

"I'm here, Maman. Don't worry," Augustus said behind them, making them both turn.

"You were wonderful. Everyone thought so. I thanked the captain and excused myself. I was courteous. But I don't like Lord Ashley."

Jane threw herself toward her son, clutching him to her and stroking his hair. Augustus embraced her in return, though he seemed as clueless as Butch.

"He is not to get near me or my son, do you understand, Noble Salt?" Jane said, voice shaking, dark eyes huge. "He is not my cousin. He is nothing to me. He thinks because he is a Toussaint, he should have special access to me. Oliver would never tell him no. But Oliver is dead, and I don't ever want to see Lord Ashley again."

"So why is he here?" Butch asked softly, not understanding.

"I don't know. I don't know."

Then Jane Toussaint began to cry.

14

*I am never full
There's a hole in my stomach
And one in my chest*

"Maman?" Augustus looked up at her, baffled as she crumpled around him.
"Jane?"

She straightened immediately, smoothing her hands down her dress. She gave Augustus a smile, blinking the tears from her eyes and pressing her hands to her cheeks. She avoided Noble's gaze, but threw a smile in his direction as well.

"Let's go, shall we? I'm not feeling well, and I've let that terrible man upset me."

Augustus needed no convincing, and he turned for the door. "I'm still hungry, and after your stomach settles, Maman, you'll want something too," he said, sounding like the Nurse Nana he was. She'd taken him to see *Peter Pan; or, the Boy Who Wouldn't Grow Up* at the Duke of York's Theatre in London, and they'd both loved it. He'd begged for a big, shaggy companion ever since, and she'd promised him that when they finally settled in America, they would get a dog, any dog he wanted.

Noble Salt walked behind them, saying nothing, his gait slow. She felt his gaze on her neck and brushing the side of her flushed face.

He deserved an explanation, though she had no intention of giving him one.

He did not press or question when they returned, but retreated to his quarters, leaving the door open and letting Augustus buzz between the two rooms. She retreated into the small washroom to collect herself, brushed her teeth and her hair, and changed from the red dress that made her waist so small and her breasts so round. It also chaffed and dug, and her skin looked like latticework when she peeled it from her body. It was a wonder she could sing in such clothes.

She was distracting herself, she knew, keeping up a mental babble to avoid the panic that wanted to break free. Her vision swam, and her heart screamed, but she mechanically prepared for bed, smoothing cream over her cheeks and down her throat, and called to Augustus that it was time to sleep.

He didn't answer, and she assumed he'd gone next door to visit with Noble. When she finally stepped out from the washroom, she found him tucked beneath the covers, already dressed in his nightshirt, a dime novel creating a steep roofline over his face. His little snores ruffled the pages. She took the book, rolled him to his side, and sat beside him, wondering how she was going to get through the night ahead.

A soft knock sounded on her stateroom door. It was far too late for the valet. Far too late for a courtesy call.

Noble was suddenly standing in the doorway, his coat and his collar had been removed, his top button undone, but he was otherwise dressed.

The knock came again.

"I'll get that."

"All right," she agreed, dread numbing her hands. But she stood and followed him to the small entryway, remaining behind the divider that gave privacy to the occupants of the room.

"Forgive me, sir, for the late interruption. This basket is for Madame Toussaint and her young son. Compliments of Captain Smith."

Jane relaxed. It was only a delivery, ill-timed though it seemed. But then the steward continued.

"I also have a message from Lord Ashley. He, too, sends his compliments for Madame Toussaint's performance and wishes to walk with her on the upper deck at half past the hour."

"Madame Toussaint is unwell. She will not be able to join Lord Ashley. Please send her apologies," Noble responded without hesitation.

"He was most adamant, sir. He told me not to accept no for an answer."

"Oh, did he?" Noble's voice sharpened. His displeasure was evident, and the steward spoke faster. She assumed the expression Noble wore was not his usual easy gaze.

"Yes, sir. He says it is a business matter concerning Madame Toussaint's tour."

"And that couldn't wait until the morning?"

"I apologize, sir, I was sent with instructions, and I have delivered them."

"All right." Noble's tone gentled. It was not the steward's fault he'd been sent on an embarrassing errand.

"I can tell him yes, sir? Eleven thirty on the bridge?"

"Eleven thirty on the bridge." Noble shut the door.

Jane was already shaking her head. "I will not speak with him. I will not come when he calls. He has no right."

"I'll go with you," Noble answered softly. "Or . . . I'll go alone. You can stay right here, with Augustus. I'll handle it."

She stared at him, indecision warring, fear churning. She turned away and sank onto the settee.

"He will find out who you are," she worried. "I should not involve you."

"Jane . . . who is this guy?"

"Lord Ashley Charles Toussaint the third. Earl of Werthog."

The name was meaningless to him, clearly, so she continued. "He is a member of the British House of Lords from a very old and powerful family. His father was an earl—and Oliver's cousin—and his mother was my benefactor."

"Cousins."

"We are not cousins. We are not family," she hissed. "I was a student at the conservatory and given the surname to use professionally, even before I married Oliver. I was a protégée . . . but I was not . . . I was never . . . family."

"What does he want?"

"He wants to torment me. That is all." She couldn't give him more. The words were pressed down so deep, boxed up in impenetrable places, and if she began unearthing them, she didn't trust herself to keep going. Especially now, when her freedom seemed so precarious.

"I don't want to talk *about* Lord Ashley. I don't want to talk *to* him."

"How did he know about the tour?"

"I'm sure Oliver told him at some point and gave him a rough itinerary. But why have I not seen him before now?" She took a deep breath, trying to control her panic. "He must have boarded in Southampton. I did not see him at Cherbourg. If I had . . . I would not have boarded. I was so careful . . . but I should have known. I should have known."

"So you stay away from him."

"I cannot believe he would truly think I would voluntarily meet him. Under any circumstances. Neither of us will go. He has no authority over me. But he has the connections and the clout to make my life miserable."

"I'll go. I'll inform him that you will not be meeting with him tonight. If he has concerns about the tour, he can tell me."

"He has no connection with the tour, Noble. I have handled every detail with the help of Mr. Bailey Hugo, who handled the promotion for my last American tour. We will meet Hugo in New York, if all . . . goes well.

"I have not even used Toussaint money . . . money I made, mind you." She thumped her chest, and he reached for her hand. She let him take it, let him pull it to his heart, palm open. Both his hands and his heartbeat were big and steady, not racing or raging, not pounding or pulling, and immediately she felt better.

"This is what you hired me for . . . isn't it? He's been a problem for a long time?"

"Yes," she whispered. She didn't trust herself to say more, and she could not look at him. His words from that first night—*I can't look at you. Don't know how to talk to you. We'll just sit awhile*—echoed in her mind.

"So I'll handle it. And I'll be back in a little while. You get some rest."

Before he left, he hesitated and turned back.

"Let's put you in my room. Both of you. I don't like that he knows where to find you."

He woke Augustus, who stumbled from one bed to the other and was immediately asleep again, no questions asked. His innocence and lack of concern grounded her as much as Noble's heartbeat, and she lay down beside her son, Noble's scent wafting around them. Sudden, grateful tears pricked her eyes, and she buried her face in the pillow, pulling the covers over her shoulders. Noble closed and locked the double doors between the two rooms and then knocked once, softly.

"Don't open the door for anyone, honey," he called. "I've got a key. I'll let myself in."

ॐ

"I thought she might send you." Disdain dripped from Lord Ashley's tongue, but the man was not surprised to see him—or disappointed, and Butch hesitated, searching the darkness around the earl. Butch was armed, but shooting the man—shooting anyone—would cause all kinds of trouble he didn't want.

"I don't have time for this. Take me to her quarters now," Lord Ashley insisted.

"You know where her quarters are . . . so why request a meeting?"

"It was an attempt at courtesy," he snapped.

Ah. No argument. He knew exactly where Jane was.

"Huh," Butch said, still searching the darkness. His neck itched, and his nerves jangled. He didn't like this guy. Not at all. "Mrs. Toussaint is ill. You observed that for yourself. The boy is sleeping. A late-night demand for a meeting is not particularly courteous." His eyes flickered to the patrician profile, and recognition wormed. He'd seen this man before. "She asked me to see what it is you need."

"She knows what I need." Ashley's tone was dry, the studied nonchalance of an Englishman heavy in his throat.

"No, sir. I don't think she does."

Lord Ashley sighed like it was all so tedious to explain, especially to a servant. "Jane Toussaint and I have been lovers for a decade. She knows what I want quite well. But she's being difficult—and she has been since Oliver died. I have made several attempts to see her, even working through the solicitor. I was convinced that now that she is free from her marriage, she would have more time for me. But she has had less."

Butch felt the punch in his chest and the slice in his back, but he didn't flinch. The man had placed each word for maximum impact, and Butch had spent too many years keeping everything hidden to react to the man's calculated attack, regardless of the shock value.

"She's beautiful, isn't she, Mr. Salt? Handfuls of dark hair. Pale pink skin. Deep, sooty eyes. I had to have her."

He'd spoken in perfect hokku.

> *Handfuls of dark hair*
> *Pale pink skin, deep, sooty eyes*
> *I had to have her.*

Butch counted the syllables, blurring the images the words brought forth.

"Augustus is my son. You know that, don't you?" This time, Lord Ashley saw his surprise. "She didn't tell you?" This seemed to please him.

"I'm just a hired man, Mr. Ashley. I don't know you. I don't really know Mrs. Toussaint. I'm just here to relay a message."

"He is my son. And she's kept him from me all these years. Now she's trying to run away. What is a man to do? I can't allow that. Surely you understand."

"That's not my business. Is there something about Mrs. Toussaint's tour you're concerned about?"

Ashley checked his pocket watch and snapped it shut, his demeanor changing.

"Captain Smith received a telegram about an hour ago. The authorities in Paris have opened an investigation into Oliver's death. They have asked Captain Smith to detain Madame Toussaint and return her to France for questioning.

"Of course the captain came to me, as a relative of Mrs. Toussaint's late husband, to ask for my assistance. I thought only to warn Jane that Captain Smith will be visiting her quarters early in the morning. A message will need to be conveyed to the tour company—Mr. Hugo, I believe his name is."

Butch nodded, but he didn't say anything. He remained still, his hands in his pockets, waiting for the earl to reveal whatever he was going to reveal. Nothing felt right, and the man in front of him had gone from suggestive lecher to indignant father, to concerned citizen, all in a manner of minutes. One thing was clear: he knew Jane's plans, and he had no intention of letting her carry them out.

"This is a very serious matter, Mr. Salt," he added when Butch failed to react.

"I see. Well, I'll tell Mrs. Toussaint."

He scoffed. "You're not very smart, are you, Mr. Salt?" *Stupid American.*

"That's what I've been told."

"And what kind of name is Noble Salt?"

"It's my name. What kind of name is Ashley Charles Werthog the third?"

"I'm an earl," he spat.

"Huh. Well, I'd go by Earl, if I were you. It's so much easier. Warmer too."

"You will tell Jane what I have imparted?"

"I'll tell Madame Toussaint. But she's not likely to agree to go back."

"She will have no choice, you dolt. She's a French citizen."

Butch didn't respond to the insult but kept his tone slow and folksy. "I thought she was English."

"The moment she married Oliver, she became a French citizen," Ashley enunciated, as if explaining to a young child.

"But this is an English ship. Why would Captain Smith agree to detain her?"

"It's an English ship, commissioned and maintained by the Royal Navy, and dependent on French ports. Captain Smith will do what he is told when it comes to extradition. Nobody wants to upset their international partners. My family has powerful allies. I've reassured Captain Smith that we will look after Madame Toussaint."

"I see. Well, in that case, I'll make sure Mrs. Toussaint is informed first thing in the morning. No sense upsetting her tonight."

Lord Ashley checked his watch again.

"You may go, Mr. Salt," he said. He pocketed his watch and pulled a cigar from an inner pocket. He drew it along his nose like he sampled a rose or the nape of a woman's neck. "And watch yourself. The water is cold and dark. No one would even know you were missing should you lose your balance and fall overboard."

The mildly delivered warning, devoid of venom or verve, had the desired effect. Butch returned to his stateroom with weapon drawn, pausing every few feet to assess his surroundings.

When he finally turned down the corridor to the pair of staterooms, his fear had grown wings, a vulture circling overhead.

The door to Jane's stateroom was ajar, and the room had been turned upside down. Drawers were upended, clothes strewn about, and the wardrobe hung open.

"Jane?"

He ran to the connecting door. It, too, was unlocked and thrown wide, and the door on the other side was no longer secured.

"Jane? Gus?"

His bed, where he'd left them, was neatly made, the room in perfect order. And it was empty.

∽

Maman was shaking him, whispering his name, and something about her grasping hands and sharp demand to wake had him sitting up in bleary obedience, blinking in the darkness.

"Listen to me, Augustus. There is someone—not Noble, someone else—in our room. The door between is locked on our side. They will have to come through the main door. When we hear them leave our room, we are going to go through the connecting door."

He thought he understood. When whoever was in the room was finished looking—and he could hear the search—he and Maman would dash from one room to the next.

"Come . . . slip out of bed. I'm going to tidy it, so it doesn't appear we were here," she mouthed into his ear. "Listen by the connecting door and tell me when they leave."

He didn't ask why they were hiding or why someone searched their room. He was not as blind as Maman thought. Maman had hired an outlaw to provide security. Maman had sworn him to secrecy over their trip to America, and earlier that night, Maman had cried in front of him for the first time in his whole life. No, he did not question why they were hiding or whispering or waiting by the door for a cue in their nightclothes.

Maman plumped the pillows and straightened the covers, smoothing them so the bed did not appear slept in. She was not crying now, but moved with haste, her movements sure, her face hard.

The voices next door were discussing the other room where the "bodyguard" was staying. They rattled the locked connecting door—each side had its own bolt—and Maman grabbed him, pulling him back, her hands over his mouth so he wouldn't scream.

They said they didn't want to break the door. They were employees of the *Adriatic*, not gunslingers, and they retreated from the room, agreeing to go around.

"They're gone," Maman said, easing the lock on the connecting door so it released soundlessly in her hand. Behind them, a key scraped in the corridor door. The searchers were coming into Noble's room.

Maman pushed him through and pulled the connecting door closed behind her, latching it from the other side. She then ran to the tall wardrobe, pushed her dresses out of the way, and stepped inside with Augustus, pulling one of the doors closed behind them. The people had already searched once, but if they stuck their heads in again, suspecting the switch, they needed to be out of sight.

"Just until Noble returns," Maman murmured, as if she had no doubt that he would. Her confidence calmed his hammering heart, and he stood, listening, trying not to think of his growling stomach. He'd fallen asleep without eating his cake, but now he wanted a full English breakfast and a chocolate croissant.

The searchers clearly believed Noble Salt had taken them with him and were not trying very hard to keep their voices down. One man seemed concerned that they were in the wrong room altogether, and another insisted that the earl had miscalculated. But even when it seemed they were well and truly gone, Maman made him remain with her in the wardrobe.

"Just a few more minutes. Just until Noble returns," she whispered, but she was worried about Noble too. He could tell, because her little prayers were formed in hokku, like Noble's, as if she didn't know any other way to pray.

"Protect Noble Salt. He's the only one I trust. Please, Lord Jesus, please."

Augustus added his own version. "Please, Lord Jesus, please. Protect Maman, Butch, and me. Keep us safe from harm."

Not long after their feeble prayers, offered up from the darkness of the wardrobe, they heard him come through the door and call their names. He unlatched the connecting doors before he turned back again, his voice loud and scared.

"Jane! Augustus!"

Augustus tumbled out of the wardrobe, trying to be as brave as Maman—she wasn't crying—and failing. Butch kissed the top of his head and squeezed him tight, and then reached for Maman too, bringing her into the fold. Maman was as rigid as a lamp pole, but Butch didn't seem to mind. He squeezed her anyway, and after a few shuddering breaths, she let herself be embraced, wrapping her arms around Augustus as Noble Salt wrapped his arms around them both.

"We've got trouble, Jane, and there are some decisions we need to make," he said, eyeing the mess around them.

"Do you think we could eat a little something?" Gus asked, wiping his nose on his sleeve.

"We should report this to a steward, but I don't know who to trust," Maman said, picking up her clothes and gathering the bedcovers off the floor. Nothing seemed to be missing, but Noble said it wasn't stuff the searchers wanted. They just tried to make it look that way.

"Lord Ashley wanted me out of the room," Noble said. He looked at Augustus and then at Maman. "I think he wanted to grab Gus and expected us to leave the boy sleeping while we met with him up on the deck. That was the play. I guarantee it."

Maman was shaking her head, her eyes so desperate, Augustus reached for Noble's hand to make him stop.

"You're scaring her," he scolded. Noble squeezed his hand, but he kept speaking, his voice gentle but his words blunt.

"Lord Ashley told me Captain Smith received a telegram this evening with an order to detain you and take you back to France on the return voyage. I don't know if it's true. I don't know if it was simply his way of delaying me—it felt that way—but if it's true, and Captain Smith has been ordered to not let you get off this ship when we dock tomorrow, then we've got bigger problems than Warthog."

Augustus laughed. "You called him warthog, Noble. Did you do that on purpose?"

"I did, Gus. I don't like him very much." He gave Gus a small smile, but his eyes were worried, and he turned back to Maman, who had begun to pace.

"What grounds have they to detain me? What is this all about?"

"French authorities have opened an investigation into Oliver's death. You are wanted for questioning."

Maman's legs ceased striding, and she sank onto the bed. She hadn't bound her hair, and it hung in dark waves to her waist. He was not accustomed to this mother, the one who wasn't painted and curled and quietly controlled. Her bare feet stuck out beneath the hem of her nightgown, and he noticed how small her feet were. They were smaller than his. When had that happened?

"If I go back to France, I will be at his mercy, totally and completely."

Augustus jerked back to attention. "Maman? What are you talking about?"

"Jane . . . listen to me," Noble urged, but Maman continued to babble quietly.

"The coroner said he died of natural causes. We buried him. Yet now . . . the very week I leave, a case has been opened, and I must return? This is Lord Ashley's doing."

Noble sat beside her on the bed and pulled Gus down with him, still holding his hand. Maman would not even look at either of them.

Her hands were clasped in her lap and tears had begun dribbling down her face. Maman was crying again.

"If you're an American citizen, Captain Smith can't detain you or send you to France," Noble reasoned.

"But I'm *not* an American citizen," Maman said.

"I know. But I am. And in America—and France—a woman's citizenship is directly tied to her husband's. The minute you marry me, you're an American. The French will have no grounds to extradite you."

Maman gaped at Noble, her cheeks wet and her chin trembling.

"I'll be damned," Augustus breathed, borrowing a phrase from Noble. "You want to marry Maman?"

"Yeah, Gus. I do. If she'll have me."

Augustus leaped onto the bed, unable to contain himself. He jumped and spun and hooted before collapsing beside Noble Salt once more.

"Say yes, Maman. Please say yes."

15

*I will say I do
And mean it from the bottom
Of my crooked heart*

Noble retreated to the adjoining room, giving her a minute to compose herself, but he returned a minute later carrying a battered leather document holder and sat beside her once more. "I have everything we might need, right here. I even have a birth record for Noble Salt."

Augustus moved to the table and celebrated the marriage proposal with the goodies from the basket the steward had delivered. It was filled with crackers and cheese and bread and apricot preserves. He ate all the chocolate-covered cherries before guiltily asking if anyone else would like one, and mulled over changing his name to Augustus Salt.

"It sounds like a cowboy, doesn't it, Maman? Augustus Salt." He licked his fingers and went to wash, still mumbling the name to himself.

"Jane, it doesn't have to mean anything at all," Noble said softly, eyes steady. "Noble Salt's not my real name, which would probably make the marriage invalid." He smoothed his mustache. "What I'm trying to say is, I'm not going to pretend it means anything. I'm not going to make demands or act any different than I do now. I know who I am to you and what my job is. I know why I'm here. That won't change. When this is all said and done . . . I'll go my way and leave you be, just like you want. No kissing."

For whatever reason, that made her laugh, though the chuckle became a wet hiccup. She was being held together by a song and a prayer, and the outlaw who had just confessed to having half a dozen birth records in his valise thought she was worried about kissing.

"Why in the world do you have a birth record for Noble Salt?"

"When you're a fugitive from the law, it's not a bad idea to have a few sets of papers. I've spent the last six years opening and closing bank accounts in different names, and I've got papers for all of 'em. Figured it couldn't hurt if I ever wanted to use the name again. It made me smile when I thought about it, one of the few names I can say that about."

He opened the leather pouch and handed the document to her. "Born on the day I met you—different year, of course—February 21, 1866. Made Virgil my daddy—wasn't he the name of the real Dr. Salt?—and kept my mom's name, Ann Parker. It's real . . . I mean . . . a real document. Only the writing is fake."

"What do you want from me, Butch Cassidy?" she whispered. "You've known me for mere days. Surely there's something you want. And I'm in no position to barter."

"I've known you for six years. And I don't want a damn thing, honey. Not from you. And that's my solemn promise. I wouldn't mind hearing you sing again. I could listen to you sing for the rest of my life and never grow tired of it, but this ain't a trick or a trap. I can help you. And that's what I intend to do."

When he called her honey like that, so soft, so kind, like he would take it all on his broad shoulders and all would be well, it did something to her heart, and she couldn't afford to trust him or his soothing voice.

She nodded once, but didn't concede or refuse. If the morning came and they were able to disembark without incident, they would forget about the marriage proposal, and her answer would be unnecessary.

They readied themselves and packed their trunks so they could go ashore at the first possible opportunity. Then they went to bed fully clothed, waiting. She could not believe that Lord Ashley would slink off, thwarted, but the remainder of the night, long and restless though it was, was uneventful.

But just as Noble had predicted, Captain Smith knocked on her stateroom door just after dawn, the circles under his eyes indicating a sleepless night and a troubled mind.

He told Jane he had received an order from his superiors at White Star Line as well as a telegram from French authorities. He was to detain her—under lock and key—and bring her to Cherbourg when the ship made its return voyage. There was no warrant for her arrest. She was only wanted for questioning, but members of the peerage were applying pressure in the investigation, and the captain was fit to be tied.

"White Star Line sails out of Cherbourg. We try to accommodate extradition requests with our partners. White Star Line must operate according to the rules and whims of many international governments, and in this case, I have been instructed to do exactly as the French police are requesting."

"What if she were an American citizen?" Noble interjected quietly.

"Pardon me?" The captain frowned.

"If Mrs. Toussaint were to marry an American citizen, she would immediately become an American citizen herself, as would her fatherless child."

"That is the law as I understand it, yes."

"I'd like to marry Mrs. Toussaint, Captain Smith. Can you officiate?"

Captain Smith's jaw dropped, and Jane's stomach followed. He'd done it. Noble Salt could not be accused of idle speaking.

"It would solve your problem," Noble explained. "You would have no reason through treaty or even professional courtesy to send an American citizen to France based only on a request for her return."

"So you will marry her—"

"Yes. Right now."

"But will she marry you?"

They turned in tandem and looked at Jane, who observed it all in a weary fog. Nothing felt real, so nothing felt wrong, and she nodded her head. "Yes, Captain Smith. I will."

Captain Smith folded his hands across his lap and cocked his head, stewing for several seconds before he nodded and released a sigh that fluttered his mustache.

"I can give permission for the marriage to take place, but I do not have the authority to perform the legalities. A chaplain would have to do that, and I have just the man. He's returning to New York and has the required credentials." He meditated a moment more.

"Do you have some documentation showing your American citizenship, Mr. Salt? Your birth record is all that matters. Madame Toussaint's citizenship will be attached to yours."

Noble took out the birth record for Noble Salt and handed it to the captain.

"Very good," the captain grunted. "Come with me."

The chaplain, a man named Stephen Landsem, asked them a few questions. He seemed pleased and surprised when he discovered they'd known each other for over six years. Captain Smith appeared relieved at that as well, and within the hour a small group had assembled in the captain's office.

It was over in less than three minutes, signatures, vows, and an awkward, prickly peck on the lips that embarrassed everyone and prompted a sincere apology from Noble when they were alone. The captain recorded the action in his log: Mrs. Jane Toussaint of France married Mr. Noble Salt, an American citizen, on July 11, 1907. Marriage officiated by US Navy Chaplain Stephen Landsem. Witnesses, Augustus Toussaint, the bride's son; Mrs. Sarah Smith, wife of Captain Edward Smith; and First Officer William Murdoch.

Jane wore no veil, Noble did not loop a sprig through his buttonhole, and Augustus's stomach growled incessantly, though he was overjoyed at the turn of events and clapped when they were pronounced man and wife. The captain patted Jane's hand, and the chaplain beamed at her and asked for an autograph for his mother.

"She will not believe I met you, Madame Toussaint. She heard you years ago. She has raved about it ever since. After your performance last night, I know why. You are magical. Magical."

"The first tender ship will depart for the New York harbor at 0800 carrying some of the sailors and the harbor master," Captain Smith instructed. "You three will be on that boat. I have made the arrangements, and a steward is on his way. It will get you off the *Adriatic*—and out of my jurisdiction—as soon as possible."

"I will be forever grateful for your help, Captain Smith," Jane said, clasping his hand. She had no doubt he would have a fire to put out when it was discovered that she and Augustus had disembarked.

"Some call me 'the millionaire's captain.' I'm not fond of the title. I don't like uppity lords interfering with people's lives, Madame Toussaint, or telling me what I can and can't do on my ship. You've given me a way out, and I appreciate it. Best of luck on your tour."

"Thank you, Captain." She was flushing and tearing up at once, a wretched combination.

"And you can sail with me anytime, as long as you are willing to sing."

"It would be my great pleasure, sir."

"Mr. Salt . . . consider this a wedding gift," he said, turning to Noble. His wife brought forward the framed picture of Jane that had hung in the corridor leading to the first-class dining hall. "Augustus informed me that you wanted it. You can even keep the frame."

"I told him you only needed the picture," Augustus volunteered, "but Captain Smith was worried it would get damaged."

"Thank you, sir," Noble gasped, and his eyes met Jane's before dancing away.

"I have a present for you too, Noble," Augustus said as they were escorted from the captain's quarters. "I've written a new verse."

Mister Noble Salt
Blue eyes, strong hands, gentle voice
Can I call you Dad?

☙

The sun bounced off the water, blinding them, but the air was brisk and pulled at their clothes. Even Jane, pale and perspiring, survived the choppy ride from the *Adriatic* to the shore with a smile on her face.

"We are almost there, Augustus. I can't believe we are almost there," she said, hugging her son to her side.

Gus was giddy with excitement, but Butch grew more and more anxious as they neared the shore. He'd loved the days at sea and was none too eager to face a new journey, one in which he was both the stranger and the protector, navigating a theater world he was not at all accustomed to.

They needed to leave the docks as soon as possible, and all Jane's plans would have to be redrawn. He wasn't sure she'd faced the truth of that yet. Captain Smith was no fool, and he'd given them a head start, but Werthog would be coming ashore. They hadn't seen the last of him. Of that, Butch was certain.

Arriving in New York wasn't the same as the departure in Cherbourg. The enthusiasm was different—tempers shorter, crowds bigger. Cherbourg had also been a stopover with a few hundred passengers added to the thousands already on board. In New York, several ships were boarding and unloading, and the rush of stewards and sailors amid people clamoring for their destinations was more than Butch had anticipated. They may have missed the crush of a disembarkation from the *Adriatic*, but the docks were teeming.

The sailors aboard the tender wasted no time unloading their trunks and piling them aboard a lorry that would take them to the street, and Butch, Jane, and Augustus trailed after their luggage, legs wobbling at the feel of dry land beneath their feet, clutching at each other as they swayed.

The clangor and the chaos coexisted with industry and efficiency. It wasn't purple mountains and red cliffs, but it had its own brash appeal, and for all its filth and flavor, all its sunshine and stink, Butch would have liked to sit on the docks and watch life unfold.

But not now. Now he was nervous. He generally felt safer in a crowd, but not with Jane, and certainly not with Augustus. Maybe it was the stress of the last twenty-four hours, no sleep, a new wife— God forgive him—and his feet on solid ground, but he was tired, and he didn't trust himself. He thought he saw Sundance, sitting atop a coach, and Augustus swore he spotted a man who "looked just like you, Noble," and all of his fears bubbled up and spilled over, leaving him paranoid and short-tempered.

Everywhere they walked, everywhere they turned, people gaped. Not at Butch and not even at beautiful Jane, who was wearing another enormous hat decorated with feathers and a bird's nest filled with bright blue robin's eggs. Maybe she wore ridiculous hats to draw attention from her son, because everyone stared at Augustus.

It was exhausting, the swiveling heads and the heavy stares, and Augustus bore it with his eyes forward and his hat tipped at an angle, holding his mother's hand and keeping a half step behind Butch. The boy was starving all the time; maybe it was the energy he expended enduring the unwelcome attention.

"Wait here with the trunks," Butch directed, steering them to a newly abandoned bench. "I'll hire a coach to take us uptown. And, Jane?"

She met his gaze, her face tight and her eyes wary. She was not immune to her child's discomfort. Not at all, and there were other worries there as well. She kept looking back at the *Adriatic*, now anchored in the port. People poured down the gangplank like beetles on dung.

"Where are we staying?" he asked.

"The Plaza. I told no one. But . . . the original tour schedule was created by Oliver. Maybe he informed Ashley. Since his death, I have handled every detail exclusively with Mr. Hugo. We should go directly to Mr. Hugo after we check in."

"Or maybe before, honey." Everything felt fraught with danger, and Butch didn't yet have a feel for the players. "Where are his offices?"

"He said he'd meet me for tea at noon at the Plaza."

"You called Maman 'honey,'" Gus said, grinning. "Is that because she's your wife?"

Butch felt himself flush. "It's just a nickname. Like Gus." He scanned the busy street, looking for a coach that could accommodate three passengers and three trunks.

"Is Maman your sweetheart now?"

"My mom called me honey. She called all of us honey. It's just a name that means you care."

"You hear that, Maman? Noble cares. Do you love him too?"

"Augustus Maximilian Toussaint," Jane scolded softly. "Please stop."

"Just one more thing. I thought of a new hokku. This verse is for you."

If you don't love him
Just remember love can grow
If you start as friends

Butch had created a hokku monster. "Wait here, Jane. Augustus. Don't move. I'll be back."

"Noble?" Jane questioned, but he was already walking away.

It wasn't far, only a few steps to gain a better view of the street, but if he'd just stayed put, just been patient, he and Harry Longabaugh would not have seen each other at all. Instead, fate settled around his shoulders and whispered, *Gotcha.*

"Is that you, Cassidy?" Sundance asked, his hand creeping to his hip though no weapon was holstered there. He sat atop a coach, whip in hand, a cigar between his lips, wearing the hat of a hansom driver and looking like he'd been dropped from the sky, the grim reaper come to collect his dead.

"Goddamn it," Butch whispered. "I thought that was you."

"If I didn't know you so well, I'da looked right past you," Sundance said. "Where did you come from?"

"Paris."

"Paris," Harry repeated, wrapping the reins of the team around the hitch. He studied Butch with the same flat eyes Butch had looked into for too many years. "You don't look much different. Except the fancy clothes. And the beard. You get a new face?"

"No. This your coach?"

"It belonged to my brother-in-law. It's not a train. Or a bank. But it beats ranching. When you cut out . . . I thought maybe it was time I did too. You know about the trouble I had in Chile."

The trouble in Chile had resulted in a shoot-out over a card game, Sundance killing a man, and Butch bribing officials to get him out of jail so they could make a run for it. That hadn't gone over very well, and they'd made it back to Bolivia just in time for Van to show up and make everything worse.

"You with her?" Harry inclined his chin toward the bench where he'd left Jane and Augustus. They had risen, clearly expecting a ride in Harry's coach. "She looks like Ethel."

"Noble . . . we should hurry," Jane called.

"Noble?" Sundance grinned. He was missing one of his incisors, and it marred his handsome face. "That's what she calls you?"

A handful of high-hatted coppers were striding up the pier. Butch scanned for another coach.

"He got some kind of disease? What's wrong with his face? I'm surprised they let him sail."

"Nothing's wrong with his face, Harry Longabaugh. What's wrong with your soul?"

But Sundance wasn't listening to him. He was staring at Jane. "She's that singer. The one who looked like Ethel. The woman we saw at that music hall back in '01. I'll be damned. How did that happen, Butch?"

He wasn't going to talk about Jane or Gus, not if he could help it.

"Noble!" Jane implored. She'd seen the coppers too, and Werthog had joined them.

"You need a ride, Cassidy?" Sundance smirked. "Because I've got a coach for hire. In fact, where's your brother? Van's here too. Somewhere. I'm sure you'll be glad to see him. He's grown a beard just like you. Funny thing is . . . with half his face covered and those Parker blue eyes, he's your spittin' image."

"Son of a bitch," Butch whispered, and straightened his hat. Things just kept getting worse.

An instant later, Van pushed through the throng and swept Butch up in a jolly reunion, though he hissed venom in his ears as he bounced him up and down. Van was half an inch taller and maybe ten pounds heavier, but he liked to pretend he was the burly big brother—stronger, tougher, meaner, smarter. Always in competition. And with his beard and his darkened hair, he looked so much like Butch, they could pull a con.

"I knew eventually you'd turn up. We've been watching the ships come in for weeks. Nice to be back in the old US of A, huh?"

"Butch has found himself another Ethel, Rip," Harry called.

"Ethel? Where?" Van hooted, looking around at the ever-increasing crowd.

"Help me get these trunks loaded," Butch said, striding to the cart and urging Jane and Augustus forward. He assisted them inside the carriage and had just managed to muscle the trunks into place with Van's help before the officers descended, the Earl of Werthog leading the way.

"You there, sir. May I have a moment?" an officer barked, and Van slinked away, putting the coach between him and the authorities. Butch felt the familiar, icy disdain that always accompanied his interaction with lawmen and politicians, but he greeted the men with level eyes and a calm demeanor.

"How can I help you, gentlemen? We've had a long journey, my wife is unwell, and I'd like to be on my way."

"Your wife?" The lead officer frowned.

"Yes. Madame Toussaint is my wife, and I'm assuming this pertains to the issue we addressed aboard the *Adriatic*. Captain Edward Smith received a request for extradition from the French authorities. But my wife is not a French citizen any longer, and Captain Smith determined—quite correctly—that he had no grounds or authority to send an American woman back to France simply to appease this man." He indicated the earl with a nod of his head.

The Earl of Werthog had grown ashen, but his ears were twin flames. "This is a deliberate attempt to evade prosecution. She has married you solely to gain American citizenship."

"Whatever her reasons, I consider myself a very lucky man." Butch smiled at the officers, who were already looking uneasy at the exchange.

"Werthog"—he pointed at the earl—"is obsessed with Madame Toussaint, and he's not happy to see her go. I wouldn't be either. My wife is a rare beauty." The men craned their heads to see inside the coach as Butch continued to spin his tale.

"But involving the police for his own vulgar purposes . . . well, I expect better of an English lord. Don't you, gents?"

The officers shuffled their feet and looked at each other, and the Earl of Werthog began blathering about international agreements and telegrams, demanding that "this woman be detained immediately."

"Are we loaded, sir?" Butch called up to Sundance.

"That we are, *Noble*." He emphasized the word ever so slightly.

"I'll sit up top with you, then," he said cheerfully. "It's a beautiful day for a ride."

He swung up, doffed his hat, and Sundance flicked the reins, almost like old times. Then the back of the coach bounced with the weight of one more, and Butch turned to see his brother grinning at him from the footman's perch.

"Where we goin'?" Sundance asked as the coach lurched forward.

"Take us to the Plaza," Butch answered, keeping his voice low. "You know where that is?"

"Fancy, fancy," Sundance mumbled, but seemed familiar with it, and he eased the coach into the crush of traffic leading away from the waterfront.

The officers made no attempt to stop them, but Butch wasn't sure if he'd escaped yet again or if he'd just been dropped into a pot of hot water.

"Did you hear that, Rip Van Winkle?" Sundance called over his shoulder, using the nickname Butch had bestowed on his brother long ago. "Butch has got him a new family. A wife and a little toad of a son. And they're staying at the Plaza."

If Augustus heard the banter, Butch wasn't sure, but if Sundance hadn't been driving, he'd have been flat on his ass with a bloodied nose.

16

There is no leaving
I travel in a circle
Always returning

Harry Longabaugh was handsome in an even-featured, wild-eyed kind of way, but he was too thin and mean around the edges, like a dog that snarls when you get too close but follows you when you leave. Jane understood that kind of mean—she suspected she was guilty of it too—but when he called Augustus a toad, she took a visceral dislike.

The other man was Noble's brother. The resemblance was unmistakable. Uncanny even. Where they'd come from was a mystery to her, but the coach and the speedy getaway were appreciated.

"Noble called him Harry," Augustus said, subdued. He hadn't missed the comment about a new wife and the toad-faced son. "Contrary Harry. He's the Sundance Kid."

"Yes. I think you're right," she said.

"And the man he called Rip Van Winkle . . . that's Van, Noble's brother."

"The one he doesn't like," she affirmed.

He looked like Noble, but the complexity was absent. He wore his dirty brown hair the same and slicked it back from an identical forehead. His eyes were the same vivid blue, though they were a little too close together. He moved the same, smiled the same, and sounded the same.

But he was not the same.

Jane knew it the moment words left his mouth. This was Van, and Van was volatile.

"Where are we going, Maman?"

The coach was closed but a window on each side gave them a view of the streets. The recent rain had turned it to mud, and she didn't recognize anything. She pulled on the tassel to get Noble's attention, and a few minutes later, the carriage stopped and Noble jumped down and opened the door.

"Are they taking us to the Plaza?" she asked.

"Isn't that what you want?"

She nodded, her stomach twisting sickly. Noble looked as wrung out as she felt, and her head kept spinning like she was still on the boat.

"Who are these men, Noble?" she asked, though she really wanted to know why they were there.

"I told you, Maman."

"Harry Longabaugh—" Noble began.

"The Sundance Kid," Augustus inserted. "And Noble's brother."

Noble nodded. "And my brother. Van Parker."

"Did you know they were going to meet us?" she asked.

"Honey, if I'd known they were in New York, I would have thrown myself overboard and taken my chances with the sharks." He tried to smile, but it was more grimace than anything.

"Are you all right, Noble?" she asked.

He seemed surprised by her query, as if his welfare was not a common concern, but he had to be as overwhelmed as she, reeling from one crisis to the next. And he'd not once lost his calm demeanor. He'd even made her laugh, talking his way right through the officers, up onto the carriage seat, and whisking them all away with no trouble at all.

He had a charm that disarmed his enemies and diffused even the most tense situation. But this last blow—his past popping up out of nowhere—had furrowed his brow and tightened his jaw. His lips were white with strain.

"I'm not happy, I can tell you that much. And, Gus . . . I told you about Sundance, you remember?"

"Contrary Harry?"

"That's right. He's not all bad. He's actually a good man to have around if you need someone to watch your back. He's tough. And he's a helluva fast gun. We've been in some bad scrapes together, and we've always managed to get out. I trust him as well as I trust anyone. I just don't like him very much."

"Yeah. I don't like him either," Augustus muttered.

"And what he said about your face . . . that was not okay with me. So I want you to think real good and hard about what you want to say when he says something like that again. 'Cause he will. I'll help you come up with something just as mean and nasty as he is. And you'll drop it on him so he knows he doesn't mess with Gus Toussaint. But until then . . . don't you worry about it. He had the love of a good, sweet, beautiful woman . . . kind of like your mom. She loved music, and she loved him. And he didn't treat her right. He let her go. And now he hates himself for it, and it's made him even more contrary than he was before, which was pretty damn contrary. So anything he says about you is just pus from his rotten soul. It has nothing to do with you."

"Okay, Noble."

"And . . . as for your verse earlier, if it's all right with your mom, of course you can call me Dad. I'd be honored, just as long as you know it's temporary. I'm still just your mom's bodyguard, trying to get her through this tour, safe and sound, with her pockets jingling."

"All right, Dad."

"All right, Gus."

"I heard what you said about me," Sundance said as Butch climbed back in place beside him.

"Yeah? Good. 'Cause he heard what you said about him, and if you hurt that boy in any way, I'll kill you. His name is Augustus. Augustus, you got that? And you better watch the way you talk to him."

"You ain't as nice as you used to be, Butch."

"And you ain't as pretty."

"Will you two shut up?" Van snapped. "This foot perch isn't the most comfortable place to ride, and I need to take a leak. I'd like to make it home without messing my pants."

"Home. That's what he calls it. Home," Sundance grumbled. "It ain't his house. It's my sister's, but you'd think the whole damn world revolved around him, way she treats him. Dotes on him, she does."

"That's Van for you," Butch conceded.

"I can hear you sons of bitches! Start drivin', Harry. I mean it."

Butch couldn't help himself. He laughed. He laughed! Maybe it was nerves or just exhaustion, or maybe, in some part of his black heart, he was glad to see them. He hated to admit it, but he'd missed them.

Sundance gave a good jerk on the reins, and the carriage lurched forward again, and Van's curse was audible.

"I thought you were going to stay, Harry. That's what you told Ethel. You said you weren't ever comin' back. She gave up on you. But here you are."

"Yeah. Here I am. And here you are. Reunited. Ain't it sweet?"

"Why New York?"

"I've got family here, Butch. Real family." Harry's eyes were flat, the same expression that had made Butch want to shake him off and never look back. Somewhere along the line Harry had stopped being worth it. Loneliness was better than Harry. Jail was better than Harry. Goddamn hell was better than Harry "Sundance" Longabaugh, though he made most every place a hell, Butch could attest.

It had gotten to be too much for Ethel, and she'd gone. Harry had blamed Butch, but that was typical.

"You're too nice to her," Harry said. "Making her think she can make it on her own. She's getting too old to whore, and nobody's gonna want a washed-up prostitute teaching music lessons to their kids."

"Ethel will do just fine."

"Ethel will do just fine," Sundance mocked, and Butch had simply finished his dinner and rolled over and gone to sleep. Van and Harry had stayed up late playing cards and drinking, which was part of his plan. The next morning, while they slept off three bottles, he walked out of the shanty they'd called home for two months and kept on walking. He didn't take anything they would say was theirs or anything they might need. He didn't even take the money they'd taken from the bank in San Rafael, though Van still owed him for a gambling debt Butch had paid.

He hadn't helped them with the operation, and he sure as hell wasn't going to be caught dead with San Rafael loot on his person. But he took his own little stash, the one he'd sewn into the lining of his lambskin coat. Money was easy. He wasn't worried about getting more. He just wanted to get gone.

"You two got a plan?" he asked, scrambling for one of his own. He was out of his element, in unfamiliar territory, and he needed a minute.

"Nah, Butch. You're the man with the plan, remember? Maybe we'll just tag along with your new little family. You don't mind, do ya?"

Butch was quiet, gathering his thoughts, corralling his temper. It never did any good to get angry with Sundance. Harry just didn't care. But he needed to understand, in no uncertain terms, that there would be no tagging along. Never again.

"You know I've never killed a man, Harry."

"Yeah. I know."

"And you know I don't want to. Not ever."

"Yeah. Shame. You're almost as fast as me with that Colt. You still got the Colt in your boot, don't ya?"

"I do."

"Well, good. Because by the looks of that English guy, you're going to need it."

"I'm tired, Harry. And I've got a job. An honest job. You aren't coming. Neither of you. If I'd wanted you with me, I wouldn't have left the way I did. And I'd ask how the hell you found me . . . but I know. Van always could find me."

"I wasn't lookin' for you, Butch Cassidy. I was mindin' my own damn business, if you recall."

"Good. That's good. Because I'm going to need you both to leave me alone—and I mean forever. There's only one thing I want. I want to go home and see my dad and put some flowers on my mom's grave. I want to make amends and ask their forgiveness. After that . . . I don't give a shit. I'll be the old man of the mountain or a dead man in the ground. But I'm not the leader of the Wild Bunch anymore. I never wanted to be. And if you come after me, I will kill you."

"Not if I kill you first."

"Well . . . I suppose there's that."

"You're an asshole, Butch Cassidy," he said, rolling up in front of a hotel that was so new and glistening, with flowers spilling from giant tureens atop pillars and flags snapping in the wind, Butch could only stare, his apprehension growing.

He said it loud enough for passersby to hear, but other than a few offended mothers, hurrying tired children along, no one reacted or seemed to know who Butch Cassidy was.

"I am." Butch nodded.

"This is your stop then, *fine sir*," Sundance spat. "Pay up."

Van jumped off the foot perch and disappeared, most likely to take that leak, but Butch sat, contemplating the columns and the red carpet that led to the undoubtedly fine hotel. His instincts were screaming, and he was so damn tired he didn't trust himself.

"We're not staying here," he said, adamant. He took out his pocket watch and checked the time. Noon was fast approaching, and he'd like to get that meeting out of the way so he knew what they were dealing with, but after that . . . they needed to hunker down somewhere else.

"You're on the clock, Cassidy." Sundance shrugged. "And I'm not cheap, but as long as you pay me, we can sit here all day."

"Jane has a meeting. It's important. But my gut's screaming at me to get the hell out of here."

"Maybe Harry and I can come with you," Van offered, appearing out of nowhere. "Be lookout. You know, like old times."

Butch's chin sank to his chest and his hands covered his eyes. "How in the hell did you find me, Van?"

"I've been watching for you, brother. I knew you'd show up eventually."

"But . . . why?"

"Because we're the Wild Bunch," he scoffed. "We're family."

"There is no Wild Bunch, Van. I've been trying to tell you that for years. Years. But you won't listen."

"There will always be a Wild Bunch, Robert LeRoy. We're going down in history. That shit'll live forever."

"Your lady . . . she's a big deal, ain't she?" Sundance pointed at Jane's name surrounded in bulb lights announcing her opening night at Carnegie Hall in two days, with an exclusive performance at the Plaza for hotel guests.

Butch's gut twisted in pride and horror. He was in so far over his head. "Yeah. She is. And she's in a heap of trouble. I need a place to take her and Augustus for a few days. Not here. Somewhere they will be safe where I can figure out what to do."

"So what you're saying is you need my help now . . . so you'll kill me later."

"What I'm saying is, I've been getting the two of you out of scrapes for the last seven years—hell, even longer than that with Van—and I never asked either of you for anything. And when I tell you to git, to go your way and let me go mine, I'll expect you to honor that too."

Sundance sighed, ever the cantankerous martyr, and relented. "My sister rents out two rooms—they're empty now. She'll feed you, wash your clothes, if you need, and give you a fair deal too. The house has indoor plumbing. No freezing your cheeks off and traipsing to the outhouse in the dark."

"That might work," Butch grunted. And it might be the most foolish thing he'd ever done.

"Gentlemen?" A groomsman had stepped forward. "Are you checking in or making a delivery?"

"We are having lunch." Sundance stepped down and removed his tall hat and his duster, revealing clothes much more suited to lunch at the Plaza. Butch climbed down, weak-kneed and oddly giddy to have a little backup going into a situation he did not understand. At all.

He assisted Jane and Augustus from the coach and dug some notes from his pocket for the groomsman.

"We'll be back in an hour. Two at the most. Leave the horses hitched but give them a little water and feed. And keep an eye on the trunks, if you would."

"Yes, sir, of course." The man handed Harry a claim ticket for the coach, and the five of them walked inside the great front doors, the oddest posse that had ever lived.

Mr. Bailey Hugo descended on them, his arms as wide as his eyes. He was a large man and immaculately dressed, though a lock of dark, straight hair kept falling over his forehead. He was all smiles, all boom and bravado, but he was clearly panicking.

"Madame Toussaint, you are here. Are you ready to sing?" His eyes ran over her navy-blue traveling dress and the feathered hat with bluebird eggs nestled at the crown and a few clumped on the wide brim.

"Sing?"

"Why yes. Mrs. Harriman and Mrs. Louise Carnegie have sponsored this luncheon to welcome you back to New York and to kick off your tour. Their sponsorship is very important, as you must know. The Harrimans have given you carte blanche on their trains for travel, and Mrs. Carnegie has been a donor to the Toussaint Conservatory for many years."

"Of course . . . but I have no musicians and no program prepared, Hugo. I was under the impression that we were to discuss the tour over lunch. I did not know I would be performing."

"I have Mr. Ravel on the piano. He played for you years ago at Carnegie Hall, along with many other musicians of course, but he is familiar with every number from your repertoire. You have only to tell him which numbers you would like to perform."

Butch saw her dismay, but she quickly quashed it and squared her shoulders, ever the professional.

"And who are these gentlemen?" Hugo was looking at the motley crew with equal parts fear and awe.

"This is my son, Augustus, as you might remember." Jane drew Augustus forward and then placed a hand on Butch's arm.

"My goodness! You have grown. Why, you were just a toddler biting at your mother's knees when I saw you last. Now you are almost as tall as madame!"

"And this is Mr. Noble Salt. He is serving as my manager for the time being, and will be involved in every negotiation and step of the tour."

Hugo's mouth dropped open. "Your manager?"

"Yes, Hugo," Jane said, with no inflection or explanation whatsoever. She fluttered a hand toward Van and Harry. "These gentlemen are my security, and will sit with my son while I sing, if you can seat them at a table that won't infringe on the women's luncheon and make sure they are fed. We've come straight from the ship, and we are hungry and tired. As I said, I had not expected to perform today but will endeavor to do my best."

"Of course, madame. Would you need to eat before you sing?" he asked, slightly shaking his head. Judging from the emptied plates and the curious glances, the women were ready to be entertained immediately. Jane took a deep breath and let it out slowly.

"A glass of water, please, Mr. Hugo, is all I need. And a moment to confer with Mr. Ravel, if you'll find my people some seats?"

Hugo clapped a waiter forward, explained his wishes, and hurried the men away from the curious eyes of the dining women.

"Go on, Noble," Jane urged. "Make sure my son is not kidnapped or held for ransom."

He quirked a brow. "Sadly, I wouldn't put it past them. Somehow, I think Gus could win them over, but I better stay with him. You'll be all right?"

"I have no choice." She shrugged. "I will open my mouth and do my best. The rest is beyond my control. I don't know how such a thing was scheduled without my knowing it . . . but it's not the first time I've been thrown into the lion's den and expected to survive the night."

Ten minutes later, she was singing at the front of the room, standing next to a grand piano with hood raised and a man doing his best to keep up. She sang with power but no fear, with passion but no panic, though his own heart was pounding on her behalf. Six songs, each one a crowd-pleaser, and twenty minutes later, she was bowing beautifully and thanking Mr. Ravel like he was an old, dear friend.

And Butch was floored by her once more.

"Are you going to eat your pastry, Noble?" Augustus whispered, staring at the powdered treat.

"Nah. You go ahead, Gus." He'd hardly looked at his plate.

"What about that chicken stuff? You gonna eat that, brother?" Van wheedled.

Butch was starving, but he shoved his plate toward the others and let them fight over what was left. He would eat when Jane ate, though he snagged a piece of bread from the basket to quiet the grumbling in his gut.

"What names should we use, Mr. Toussaint?" Sundance mocked, patting his mouth with his napkin. He knew a little more than Van when it came to manners at a restaurant.

"Harry Long and Van Winkle. How does that sound?" Van suggested, happy as can be.

"Fine with me," Noble grunted. "Augustus, I'm going to retrieve your mother. Are you okay right here?"

"What do you think we're going to do, Noble?" Sundance grumbled. "Hell's bells. I've never hurt a kid in my life."

"You called me a toad. I didn't like that," Augustus said, solemn.

Van reached over and poked at Gus's cheek. "It's kinda scary looking, kid. I'm not going to lie."

"Noble said folks being scared of you isn't all bad. Sometimes they respect you more."

"Noble, huh? Where in the hell did he come up with a name like that?" Sundance asked.

"I'd say it fits pretty good," Van drawled. "Butch has always been a big, fat, noble pain in the ass."

"You should watch your mouth around me, Mr. Van," Augustus warned. "You too, Mr. Sundance. My maman doesn't like it. And she's a lot scarier than me . . . or Noble."

Butch chuckled and turned to go. Gus would be fine.

"Do you guys like word games?" Augustus asked. "Noble—I mean my dad—taught me one. Only smart people can do it."

"Well, then Van can't play," Sundance muttered.

"What's it called?" Van was always game for something fun. "And do you have some cards, Harry? We could teach Gus to play poker, show him how smart we really are."

Sundance just kept eating, but Butch was fairly sure his hokku habit would be spreading.

Jane was speaking politely to a woman she addressed as Mrs. Harriman. Butch bowed deeply and kissed the woman's hand like she was Queen Victoria herself.

"Mrs. Harriman, this is my manager, Noble Salt, no relation to your family, I'm quite sure."

"Any connection to the Noble Salt Company out of Salt Lake City?" Mrs. Harriman asked.

"Yes, ma'am. Those are my people," he lied easily.

"Well, how lovely. You will have to speak with Edward, my husband. He owns a significant share in Noble Salt."

"Yes . . . he does. I have modeled many of my investments over the years from your husband's example. His is a very impressive story. You should be proud."

"I am, Mr. Salt. I am. Thank you." She smiled politely and inclined her head but was quickly swept up in other conversations.

"Hiding in plain sight might just be the way to go," Jane murmured, as he took her hand. "I was afraid she might recognize you. Her husband was quite obsessed. He has a whole room in his house dedicated to you and your escapades."

"Ahh. That explains it."

"Explains what?"

"The picture you stole. Augustus told me all about it. I'd like to see it sometime."

"Augustus?" Jane searched the room.

"Augustus is fine. Harry and Van might be teaching him how to play cards, but knowing Gus, he'll clean them out."

She giggled, but he was too tense to join in. He wanted out of the Plaza as soon as possible. The walls were closing in.

17

Tell me you love me
Even if it's not the truth
I'll cherish the lie

Harry's sister Emma Harvey did indeed have a big, lovely house on the Jersey Shore with rooms she rented out, but she'd just filled one with a doctor from Connecticut in town for a medical lecture, and Van and Harry shared another, which left one room for Butch, Jane, and Augustus. "It's a big room, and the boy can sleep on the sofa quite comfortably. There's a private bath and everything, and I'll feed you three squares and wash your clothes too."

Noble and Jane would be in the same bed, but they were both too tired to care or to quibble. The close quarters on the ship had made them comfortable with one another, and they *were* married. It made sense, and they readied for bed, climbed in on their respective sides, and gave each other their backs.

Augustus chattered for a few minutes from the sofa, excited by the new surroundings, especially with Noble so close, but he yawned in the middle of composing a verse about Contrary Harry and Rip Van Winkle, and drifted off without finishing it. Minutes later, his snores began rumbling the crystals from the chandelier and bouncing off the walls.

Jane rose from the bed and rolled him to his side, and the growling became a soft *grrr.*

When she climbed back in, she made the mistake of making eye contact with the man in her bed before she scrambled under the blankets.

"How is it that your eyes are still blue in the dark?" she murmured.

"What color would they be?"

"Gray or black or white, like everything else."

"My mom always made a big fuss about my blue eyes. I think they reminded her of her family, the one she had before she made all of us."

"What happened to her?"

"She passed away in '05. Died in her sleep. They think her heart gave out on her."

"Do you miss her?"

"Every day. Like an open wound."

She sighed heavily. "How nice."

"Yeah. Open wounds are sure my favorite," he drawled.

She rolled to look at him. "That's not what I meant. I have never loved someone enough to miss them when they're gone. How nice that you loved her that much."

"You're a funny kid, Jane Boot."

"I'm not a kid. And I'm definitely not funny. I'm a sourpuss. Like Sundance. I understand that man completely, and did the moment he opened his mouth. We are not going to get along, I regret to inform you. We are too much alike. I'm guessing I won't get along with Van either. He's used to charming his way through life, and I have no use for farce. I've lived in a world of carefully orchestrated appearances and very little substance for too long. It's why I like you so much."

"You like me?" He sounded so pleased.

She liked his face. She liked his hands and his scent. She liked the way he moved, purposeful but patient, as if he had time but didn't want to waste it. His brown hair was darker but shot with silver, and his beard was peppered too, though not nearly as much, and she liked that too.

She was accustomed to the admiration of others, but she could think of so few people who'd impressed her. She had admired voices. Admired talent. Admired a beautiful dress or a clever response, but she had so little regard for the opposite sex and almost none for her own.

It had been her sad experience that most men and women, especially those who appeared one way, were not at all what they seemed or what they wanted the world to see.

Butch Cassidy was the exact opposite, and he had been from the first. His sins were laid out on the table for her to examine, and instead of being repulsed, she found herself intrigued. Instead of fear, she had the sensation of a deep exhale, a settling in her soul. She did not tire of his presence or yearn for solitude.

He was easy and exhilarating at the same time, and his patience and good humor were a well that never ran dry. Augustus hung on his every word, though he talked far more than he listened, and Butch—Noble—seemed fine with that too. His eyes didn't skitter to the side in impatience, his voice didn't sharpen, and his weight didn't shift. He listened and smiled. Nodded and noticed. And they were both completely besotted by him.

She had never been besotted. She found herself poking at him like one does to a strange object, intrigued but fearful, trying to assess the danger, and she had yet to find anything she *didn't* like.

But she didn't tell him all that.

"Yes. I like you," she said instead. "And you know I do. Your honesty astounds me. It's my favorite thing about you. It also scares me to death."

"Why?"

"Because you're going to get yourself caught, and I need you, Noble Salt, Butch Cassidy, Robert LeRoy Parker. I need you. I don't know what I would have done without you—from the moment I met you, you've been indispensable. And the tour hasn't even begun."

Thoughts of the tour had them lapsing into pensive silence.

"Hugo will do whatever Werthog tells him to do. You realize that, don't you?" Noble murmured.

"Yes. I know." The meeting that afternoon had made that abundantly clear.

Mr. Hugo promised it was all "well in hand," and that every detail had been arranged. Jane had only to follow the schedule, sing like an angel, and he would handle the rest, starting with her first performance, day after tomorrow, at Carnegie Hall.

"We need a new way to finance the tour so that Werthog can't interfere," Noble mused. "I think I can come up with something. I'll know more tomorrow."

Thinking about it induced a panic that would take her legs out from underneath her if she let it. So she simply wouldn't think about it.

"I don't want to talk about the tour. Or Lord Ashley. Not right now. We will trust Mr. Hugo, and proceed with the schedule."

Noble sighed, but he didn't persist. He was good that way, laying it out and letting it go. But she needed a distraction if she was to sleep at all.

"Tell me about Ethel."

She felt his surprise before she heard it. "Ethel? Why?"

"Because . . . Mr. Sundance compares me to her. And he insinuates that you and she . . . had a connection. He's bitter about it."

"Mr. Sundance." He laughed softly. "That makes him sound fancy. He'd like that. But it's like I told you and Gus. He had something good. And Harry Longabaugh is an asshole, but he's not a liar. He knows what he's done."

"Where is she?"

"San Francisco, last I heard. She was a beautiful girl who didn't have much going for her beyond a pretty face and a decent voice. She could sing, but nothing like you. Sundance met her at Miss Fanny's—a whorehouse in San Antonio. She fell hard for him. Don't know why. I guess that's the way it works."

"Did you love her?"

He lifted his head and looked down at her, a small smile around his lips. "Sure I did. I spent a lot of years with that little gal. Tried to look out for her, keep her safe. But it wasn't me she wanted. It was Sundance. And he loved her. Madly. He loved her madly . . . but he loved her badly too. Damn fool."

"Were you *in love* with her?"

He laid his head back down and was quiet, his eyes on the ceiling as if he were composing a careful answer.

"I want to answer honestly, but I don't want to scare you off."

"Why would I care?" she asked, cold. Prickly, like the cholla he'd accused her of being. "It has nothing to do with me."

"It has everything to do with you. And I don't want you to run."

"Me? Run? Where would I go, Noble Salt? Where in the world would I go? Haven't you noticed that running is futile for me? And you're still not answering my question."

"Sometimes . . . you fall in love with someone. And it doesn't matter if it makes sense. It doesn't matter what they look like or what they've done. They get their hooks in you, and there's no getting loose."

"She was like that for you?" The pang became more intense.

"Nah. Sundance was like that for Ethel. She loved him hard. And he loved her easy. He loved her when he felt like it. But even with all that, she would have kept on loving him."

"She stopped?"

"She got scared. She got a premonition that he was going to die, that she was going to have to *watch him die*. And she couldn't bear it. I think her fear for him pushed her over the edge."

"And she just . . . left?" Jane's admiration for the woman rose and her jealousy slipped away like the last note of a song. "How brave. How incredibly . . . brave," she whispered.

Noble cleared his throat. "Have you ever loved someone so much that whether they love you or not is completely irrelevant? It doesn't change anything? They could walk away, and you'd just follow? You'd walk over hot coals, gladly, to spare them a moment's anguish?"

"That's exactly the way I feel about Augustus."

He nodded, and for a moment she thought he would cry. His brow furrowed and his pale eyes grew impossibly bright. "That's the way Ethel felt about Sundance. And I ain't your mama, Jane Toussaint. But that's the way I feel about you. Like I swallowed a star or something. A bolt of light. And I'm all lit up inside."

She gasped, and for a moment the light he described blinded her. Stunned her. And she could only stare at him.

"Noble Salt. You stop this right now," she said, her voice barely a whisper.

"I don't know when it happened. Maybe it was the moment you walked out onstage and opened your mouth. Maybe it was that old blue dress you put on when Augustus was sick. Or the way you wrapped yourself around him even though you were so tired you couldn't stand. Maybe it was that kiss that you gave me. It didn't take much. Which is funny in a way. I'd gone my whole life without feeling that pull, and then the moment you got close, it snapped me into place. You've been in my thoughts ever since."

"Ever since?" she squeaked.

"You've been a little dream. A little bright spot I would visit when the mess of my life overwhelmed me."

She shook her head, incredulous. "I don't believe you." She didn't *dare* believe him.

"You don't have to believe me. But it's true."

"You always call me honey . . . as if I'm sweet. And I am not," she warned. "Not at all, and I will not have you thinking I am."

"You are. Deep down, you're the sweetest little Jane Boot there ever was. But that's not why I call you honey."

"No?"

"No. I call you honey because that's the way you make me feel. Soft and warm and golden."

She felt the flush rise up from her belly, but her eyes stayed steady on his. "I don't want to be kissed," she reminded him, though at that moment there was nothing she wanted more.

"I'm not asking for anything. Not one thing. I told you that, and I meant it."

She bowed her head to hide the lie in her words and the hope in her heart, but she inched closer. He didn't know who she really was. What she really was. She'd been as honest with him as she knew how to be. More honest than she'd been with anyone in her life, but kisses were promises. And she couldn't make promises.

"Would you hold me, please?" she whispered. "Just . . . hold me. I want to be close to you, but . . . I don't want anything more."

He didn't laugh or tease. He didn't even smile. He just held out his arms, and she laid down on his chest and let him wrap her loosely in his embrace.

For several minutes they remained that way, not speaking, listening to each other breathe, sinking into a new silence. And then he made her a promise of his own:

"This is what I'm going to do, Jane. I'm going to love you with everything I have left, all the good and the bad. All the rusty and the rarely used. I'm going to love you. I'm going to take care of you and your boy, as long as you need me. And that's all. Okay?"

She squeezed her eyes closed and bore down on the emotion that wanted to flood her eyes and billow from her mouth. It took her several minutes of concerted effort to control the torrent, but he said nothing more and seemed to expect no response.

"You're not real," she whispered, echoing the words she'd said to him so many years before. "You're not real." But she buried her face in the wall of his chest and let herself drift in the fantasy of him, safe and warm. Cherished. And he let her sleep.

Augustus woke first, the hokku about Van and Sundance he'd been trying to craft the night before whirring to life in his rested mind.

He sat up and looked around the new space. The early morning sun caught the crystals from the chandelier and splashed them over the white walls.

Maman and Noble were still asleep, Maman's forehead tucked between Noble's shoulder blades as though she wanted to butt him off the bed, a bighorn sheep against a rock wall. It was odd to see them that way, and not odd at all, and he stared for a moment, wishing he was brave enough to worm his way up from the bottom of the bed and sandwich himself between them. Then his stomach growled, and he forgot about everything but his suddenly mountainous hunger and his very full bladder.

Emma Harvey was nice, a lot nicer than her brother, and her husband was dead and her children grown, so she welcomed him with a plate of hotcakes three inches high and pleasant conversation to go with it. While he ate, he composed a hokku for her:

I like breakfast best
Especially with a friend
Who makes me pancakes

She laughed and gave him another, and Noble joined them smelling fresh and soapy, his hair wet and slicked back and his sleeves rolled.

"Is Maman up?"

"Nah. She's feeling sick again. Maybe just tired. I think we should let her rest today." Noble looked a little tired himself, his shocking blue eyes made bluer by the dark moons beneath them.

Mrs. Harvey studied him like she had something to say but let it go with a shake of her head.

"I thought you could come with me today, Gus. I've got places to go, and I'd like the company."

Augustus wanted nothing more, but his loyalty to his mother wrinkled his brow and had him rubbing at his droopy cheek. Maman had been sick so much since they left France. He wasn't used to that, and it made his stomach knot and his pancakes not taste as good.

"Don't worry, Augustus. I can keep an eye on her," Mrs. Harvey said. "It'll do her good to have a day to herself. I guarantee it. Mothers get tired sometimes. Van and Harry are gone for the day. They've promised me they won't get into any trouble while they're living here."

"Noble promised me the same, didn't you, Noble?" Augustus said. "He didn't even take the picture of Maman from the ship, even though he wanted to really bad. The captain gave it to him as a wedding gift."

"Is that so?" Mrs. Harvey looked at Noble with new suspicion, and Augustus wished he hadn't said anything. He forgot who knew what in this world of outlaws and wild bunches. He'd just assumed Sundance's sister knew it all. Guess not.

Noble ate quickly, grabbed his hat and a small case, like a banker would carry, and they were on their way together, calling a goodbye to Maman through the bathroom door. She told Augustus to be courteous, as she always did, and made him promise to stay close to Noble and mind him well. Her voice sounded odd, like she'd been throwing up again, but Augustus was eager to go, and he chalked it up to the mysteries of being a lady.

"I told you I'd take you to Wall Street, remember?" Noble said. "I've got to visit a man about some money, but we're in no hurry. Anything you want to see or any place you want to stop, you just holler."

They took the ferry from Hoboken—Augustus loved saying Hoboken—to Barclay, standing at the rail amid the crush of passengers, and then jumped aboard a streetcar to Wall Street, stopping at a jeweler to buy Maman a ring.

"She needs something, and I don't know what size or what she likes, so you're going to have to help me, Gus."

Augustus walked carefully through the store, peering at the baubles through the glass and trying to ignore the stares of the jeweler wearing the thick loupe.

"That one," he said, tapping at the glass. "It's the color of honey. She acts like she doesn't like it when you call her that, but she does. It makes her smile. Maman doesn't smile very much, Noble. She worries too much, I think."

"I think you're right, Gus." He whistled at the ring. "You've got good taste, little man. I'll give you that."

They figured Gus's hands were about the same size as Maman's—small and slim—but the jeweler was hesitant about letting Augustus try on the ring. It was the same suspicion that was always present, that somehow he would spread his deformity with his touch, but when the jeweler saw the ring Noble wanted to buy, he became much more friendly and let Augustus slide it on his finger.

"That one is a very good choice indeed. The amber center with the diamond border is very striking and nouveau. A wonderful piece. If for some reason it does not fit, please bring the lady back, and we will size it for free."

Noble bought another ring for himself, just a plain gold band, which he slid on his finger before they even left the store.

They had an appointment on Wall Street with a man named Jakob Hurwitz. Noble said he was a broker, which brought to mind someone who smashed china and windows and all things glass. Jakob Hurwitz was small and sharp-eyed, but he didn't break anything. He made deals, Noble said. Made money.

Gus was very careful just to call Noble *Dad* so he didn't forget what name he was using. The broker called him Roy Cassidy and had a list of stocks he thought Noble should buy. Noble wanted to cash out one of the accounts and had his own list of shares he wanted to trade.

"I wouldn't recommend that, Mr. Cassidy. I wouldn't do that. You're making money—you made money all through the Panic—and you can keep making money if you're aggressive."

Noble finally had to get mean and quiet, demanding that the man do what he say that instant, or he would find someone who would. The man snapped his mouth shut, and by lunchtime, Noble walked out of the bank with twenty-five thousand dollars in the little case he'd brought with him. According to Noble, he still had more money in his other accounts than there had been when he'd opened them in 1901.

"I invested, and my money made me money. Feels kinda like stealing, but nobody gets hurt . . . and it's legal."

They bought two hot dogs apiece from a dog wagon in front of the temple-like columns of the Stock Exchange on Broad and walked, dripping mustard, toward the curb market outside the Blair Building, a place Noble was determined he see.

Augustus thought the hot dog was the best thing he'd ever tasted, and had eaten two and was licking at his lips and wishing for another within half a block. Noble gave him the rest of his second one. "I gotta keep my gun hand free anyway." He winked, and Gus forgot all about his hot dog and started looking for bad guys instead.

"What are you gonna do with all that money?" he whispered, blotting at his cheeks with his handkerchief.

Noble stopped, took it from his hand, and swiped a spot he'd missed.

"I'm going to make sure Jane Toussaint has a tour. Without anybody pulling her strings."

"Like a puppet?"

"That's right. We're going to cut her loose."

"She won't want to take your money."

"Well . . . she married me, so now it's her money too. And if the tour goes well, we'll make it all back, plus some. That's a good investment."

"Is that how it works?"

"That's how it works."

"I better find myself a rich lady, then."

Noble laughed, but then he got serious. "Nah. You make your own. You know Mr. Harriman who owns all the trains?"

"Yes?"

"I hated him for a long time. He owns most of the railroads out West, and I made it my business to rob as many of them as I could. One man shouldn't own everything when so many other people have nothing. President Roosevelt thought so too, I guess. He sued him for creating a monopoly."

Monopoly was another very fun word, and he repeated it softly, matching his steps to the rhythm.

"That's why I robbed his trains. That's why I stole from the banks. I saw things that I thought were unfair, and I didn't know how to fix them. Stealing felt good. It made me feel powerful for a while. It was exciting, and I liked the challenge. But you know what the Hole-in-the-Wall Gang and the Wild Bunch did with all the money they stole?"

"Had fun?"

Noble grinned, but the smile faded as he spoke. "They spent it on women and booze and horse racing. They spent it on land they didn't want to work and animals they didn't want to raise."

"What did you do with yours?"

"I blew some of it too, and bought things I didn't need—I always liked nice clothes. Oliver and I have that in common—but then I started watching guys like Harriman and Carnegie. Harriman is a New Yorker, the son of a minister, and he didn't go to school any longer than I did. He wasn't born with anything better than I had. But he was buying trains . . . and I was robbing them."

"So you didn't hate him anymore?"

"It's convenient to blame Harriman and others like him for how I turned out. But it's not honest. The only thing he was given that I wasn't was maybe an opportunity. But an opportunity . . . that ain't nothing. It might be the biggest something in the whole world, though I'm guessing he's a whole lot smarter too. They say Carnegie worked in a factory for a buck a week putting thread on a spool or some such thing.

"There were no factories where I was from. Just cattle and sheep and poor, dry farmland. We did the work that was available to us. They lured folks west with the thought of land. Wide, open spaces. Fresh air. But the Homestead Act killed more folks than it helped. They said, 'Here's a free slice. Work it, and work yourself right into the ground.' My dad planted seed that blew away three times one year. Then he couldn't afford to buy more."

He sighed and shook his head like he didn't want to think about that anymore.

"Carnegie's folks came from Scotland. Mine came from England. He's about my dad's age, and nobody made it easy for him. But he made something of himself. I decided I wanted to be more like Carnegie and Harriman and less like me. So I gave some of what I stole away—made life better for a few folks. If I saw a need and had the means, I did something about it. But the rest, I invested."

"In what?"

"In trains and automobiles and mining. In weapons and farming equipment and anything that would make life a little easier for the homesteaders out West."

"You own all those things?"

"Not exactly. I spent three months in New York, right around the time I met you and your mom. That's when I learned that game." He pointed toward the shouting, shoving, curb market taking place right on the street in front of them. Officials had cordoned off a section of the street right in front of the Blair Building where orders and purchases were bellowed down from brokerage windows and negotiated on the sidewalk before being tossed back up with shouts and hand gestures.

"What are they doing?" Augustus breathed. It looked like fun. It also looked like a fight was going to break out any second.

"They're trading."

"Is it safe?" Augustus squeaked.

"No. Not at all." Noble laughed. "But I figured it was safer than playing with dynamite, which I've been known to do. And if I lost everything, I could always get more." He shrugged. "I was a thief, after all. But if investing and trading could do for me what I'd seen it do for others, men like Harriman and Carnegie, then I wouldn't have to steal again. I could just do good things. Build music halls and schools and whole industries. All the things rich men can do and poor men can't even dream about."

"Did it work?"

"Yeah. I think so. I mean . . . I'm a wanted man. And I haven't been here to watch it and really work it like those guys do. I had to find a broker." He nodded toward the roar and rabble of the curb market. "But I wasn't here to panic when everyone else did either. My money just sat while everyone else scrambled. And I wasn't invested in the banks that almost went under. Lucky for me, I guess."

"Van told me you're the luckiest son of a bitch he knows, and Sundance says you have nine lives," Augustus inserted.

"Don't say that word in front of Saint Jane, okay?"

"I won't. But are you lucky, Noble?"

"I feel lucky today," he said, and he held his hand with the little gold ring up to the light.

"Do you love my mother?" Augustus asked, shielding his eyes when the sun caught Noble's hand.

"I love your mother."

"I think she loves you too, though it's hard to tell."

Noble laughed. "It's okay if she doesn't. It's probably better if she doesn't."

Augustus would need to think about that.

"Hey, Gus . . . that money you won off Sundance and Van yesterday? Let's stick a little aside, shall we? You keep enough for your sweets. I'll take you to the shop, just like I promised. But let's get you an account that can start growing, and then I'll teach you what I know."

"You'll teach me how to get lucky?"

"Nah." Noble laughed again. "You make your own luck. But if you get rich, and you get powerful, nobody will turn their noses up at Augustus Toussaint, no matter what you look like. And if you take that money and make the world a better place, you'll be a bigger, better man than Butch Cassidy or Wyatt Earp or Jesse James ever thought of being. You can make things. You can build things. You can invent and invest. And you'll be a real hero. Not just the kind in those dime novels."

18

Opportunity
Dances past and laughs at me
Catch me if you can

Butch and Gus walked through the door to Emma's house when the sun was just an orange smudge in an otherwise twilight sky, and Augustus pronounced himself famished and near fainting from want of food. He'd stuffed his cheeks with candied nuts from a vendor after eating three hot dogs, then belched "Frère Jacques" into the wind on the ferry, a talent made possible by the cream soda he'd gulped to wash it all down.

"That was the best day of my life," he said wearily, following Butch into the foyer and hanging up his hat and dapper suit coat. Jane dressed the boy with the best, from his head to his toes, which reminded Butch of the ring in his pocket; he hoped Gus had chosen well.

Mere seconds after they arrived, Van and Sundance rolled in smelling of the docks and horse sweat, and ribbed Augustus for another poker game later on.

"You can play, but no money this time," Butch grunted. "I bought a bag of candy that should last a week." He cast a pointed look at Augustus. "Use the candy instead of cash, gentlemen. You'll thank me for it when you lose again."

"Why do you always think you're the boss, Butch?" Van grumbled. "It's been two days, and you're already throwing your weight around. You can't tell us what to do."

"I always have. Why stop now? And Gus is a kid. He doesn't need to develop a gambling habit at ten years old."

"He's not a kid, he's a card sharp," Sundance complained, but that just made Augustus laugh.

The kitchen smelled of bread and butter, and Butch wandered in to see if there was a slice he could swipe before he headed up to check on Jane. Everyone followed him, led by their own noses, and settled around the table that wasn't yet set for supper, a clear indication that there was time for poker.

Heavy steps on the stairs drew their attention upward as Emma's temporary tenant made his way down. Dr. Laszo had enormous white eyebrows but only three long strands of hair on his head. Butch remembered his name because Augustus had called him Dr. Lasso and written a verse about the doc sacrificing his hair to weave a lariat. The kid was already better with words than Butch was.

"Which one of you three gentlemen is Mrs. Toussaint's husband?" the doctor asked, scribbling on a small white pad in his hand.

Van and Sundance looked at Butch, expectant, and Butch felt himself flush even as he answered, "I am."

"Well, Mr. Toussaint . . ." Butch didn't correct him even though Van snickered. "I am sorry to say your wife has had a miscarriage. It was early days still—maybe twelve weeks—and she will bleed for much of this week, much like a regular menses."

"What in tarnation?" Sundance muttered. Van frowned at Butch, confused, but the doctor went on blithely, the oblivious professional, spilling out his prognosis and treatment plan as if he wasn't talking to a room full of shiftless, fatherless men.

"I've left laudanum if she needs it for pain, but she seems fine now. A miscarriage this early is not much different than menses. The body knows what to do. Some women never even realize they were pregnant.

She should be well enough in no time at all. The worst is over." He patted Butch's arm, absentmindedly, thoroughly unconcerned. "My apologies, chap. It's always a disappointment, and she'll be blue, but she's young enough. There will be other children, I'm sure."

Silence reigned as the doctor made his way back upstairs to the room he rented, leaving the bill for his services in Butch's hand.

Emma came bustling in from the backyard, laundry spilling from a basket, took one look at their bewildered faces and the doctor's bill, and sighed. "Do they not teach these doctors some common sense? Give me a midwife any day, for heaven's sake. I leave the room for one minute!"

Augustus stood abruptly and headed for the stairs, calling for his mother. Sundance snaked out an arm and caught him by the back of his shirttails, showing more presence of mind than Butch had ever given him credit for.

"Augustus, your mother is sleeping. Stop that hollering," Emma said. "She needed a good, long nap, and I'll not have you disturbing her. She'll want to hear all about your day after supper."

Sundance pushed Augustus back into the seat he'd just vacated. "Sit down there, Augustus. I'm ready for that rematch. I'm thinking you're a no-good, yellow-bellied cheat, is what I'm thinking. Van thinks so too."

"I'm not a cheat!" Augustus gasped, expertly distracted. "I'm just lucky. Like my dad."

Butch jerked and Van hooted. "Well then, nephew, prove it."

"Another round. Right now," Sundance grunted. "We got time before supper."

"Not much time," Emma warned. "Dinner is fifteen minutes away. I've made something special for you, Augustus, something that will inspire another verse, I'm sure. And I'd like to speak with you, Mr. Salt, about your rent, if you'll give me a moment. You paid me through the end of the week. Would you like to reserve another?"

Emma breezed out of the room, giving Butch the gimlet eye as she passed him, and he followed her, leaving Augustus in the questionable care of the two outlaws, who were already divvying up cards.

Emma turned to him once she'd reached the foyer and took the doctor's bill from his hand, running her eyes over it and pronouncing it fair. "Dr. Laszo didn't handle that well, but I was glad he was here today. He put my mind at ease, and he doesn't have a bad bedside manner, believe it or not."

"Mrs. Harvey," Butch asked. "Is Jane all right?"

"Your wife was scrubbing the blood from the washroom floor and soaking her white nightdress and the sheets in a tub of cold water— though I doubt either of them can be saved—when I checked on her this morning. I just had a feeling something was off. I sent the doctor in to have a look at her, which he did, hours ago, though he rushed right down here to present his bill as soon as he heard you come in." She shook her head.

"Mrs. Harvey," Butch urged, his concern warring with his patience.

"She's fine, Mr. Salt. She's been resting all afternoon. She's not too happy with me, bringing the doctor in, but I had to make sure she wouldn't keel over in my house."

"She had a miscarriage?" The words felt wrong in his mouth, like he'd intruded where he didn't belong.

"She did. I'm sorry, Mr. Salt. I'll explain to the boy, if you like. But you need to go upstairs and see to your wife. She's not complaining. But she's hurting. And some women—I know because I'm one of them— don't know what they need until it's forced upon them."

Butch began shaking his head. "No, don't do that. Jane should explain to Augustus."

"All right. But she needs you."

He shook his head again. "I don't know about that, Emma. I didn't even know she was . . . pregnant."

She leaned in and lowered her voice, giving him the same flat-eyed stare that Sundance used.

"Mr. Salt. You need to go in and put your arms around your woman. You need to hold her tight and let her cry and hate on everything in her body and her life that has let her down. From what I understand, you haven't been married all that long. Maybe she's feeling some guilt too. I felt guilt every time I lost a baby, and I lost a few. But whatever she's feeling, if you'll just hold her and give her time, she'll let it out, and you'll both be better for it."

"I . . . I . . . ," he stuttered. "Damn it."

"Take all the time she needs. I'll keep the boy occupied and out of earshot if his mother needs to cry. And I'll make sure there's no corrupting happening with that poker game. I'll feed him supper too. That boy likes his food."

❦

Jane was wearing a white nightgown buttoned to her throat, and her hair was braided down her back. She didn't look at him when he walked in the room, but sat, propped against the pillows like she'd been banished there.

"I wouldn't have left you all day had I known," he said.

"There was nothing you could do. I could have handled it myself . . . truthfully. The cramping started this morning again. I had cramps on the ship, but I assumed it was the seasickness."

He didn't know what to say, and they lapsed into silence.

"Emma said—" he began.

"Emma is very nosy and insisted Dr. Laszo give me an examination when she saw all the blood. I told her to mind her own business. She informed me that while I am a boarder in her house, I am her business."

"You told me this morning it was just your time." He treaded slowly.

"I lied," she said, still unable to meet his gaze. "I'm fine. Better than fine. I am relieved."

Each word was delivered with her signature style—unemotional and composed, but she had a tell, and if he ever got the chance to teach her to play cards, he would clue her in on it.

The pulse at her throat thrummed wildly, and her neck was covered in red blotches.

He sat down beside her on the bed, and she jerked her legs to the side like a skittish colt.

"How was your day?" she asked. "Was Augustus any trouble?" The welts on her neck were now touching, the lily pads of red now a solid line.

"We had a real good day," he said softly. "He's a good boy."

"Yes. He is." She cleared her throat. "Emma says he can stay here tomorrow while I'm at the theater. It will be a long day. He'll be happier here."

"You can't sing tomorrow, honey."

Her chin came up, and her eyes flashed. "I can and I will."

"But . . . aren't you bleeding?"

"Women have been bleeding since the beginning of time, Noble Salt. It's never stopped me before, and Dr. Laszo says the worst is over. I don't want to talk about this. I'm fine. Please go away now."

He rose and removed his suspenders and unbuttoned his shirt before retreating to the washroom, where he stripped to his waist and splashed around for several minutes, trying to cool the heat on his skin and the temper in his blood. He trimmed his beard, brushed his teeth, soaped his body from his waist to his temples, and put a clean under-shirt on before returning to the bedroom. Jane hadn't moved, but this time he wasn't as timid when he sat beside her.

He gathered her up in his arms and pulled her across his lap, taking the comforter with her.

"Wh-what are you doing?" she yelped, pushing against his chest and arching her back. He held on tighter, pinning her head between his chin and his shoulder.

"I'm doing what Emma suggested I do. I think it was good advice. I'm going to hold you like I did last night, and I'm going to make you talk, because . . . I can't do my job . . . whatever the hell that is . . . if

I don't know what's going on with you. If I don't know what you're running from or running to."

"You're angry."

"No, I'm not. Got no right to be. Got no call to be. But if I have to get mean to get some honesty, well, honey, I'm going to get mean."

She stopped fighting, but her voice was cold when she spoke. "I'm well acquainted with mean. You don't scare me."

He wilted, his bluff called, and he searched for something to say. Her heart was racing, belying her stiff limbs and insolent response.

"I told you I loved you last night, and I meant it," he murmured, letting the words ruffle her hair. He felt a tremor run through her, but she swallowed and shot him down, her voice even colder.

"Last night you didn't know I was pregnant with someone else's child."

He tightened his arms, and she struck out again.

"I knew when I hired you that I was pregnant."

"All right," he said.

"I let you marry me too." There was loathing now, though he wasn't sure if it was for him or for herself.

"We got married to keep you from being sent back to France. That was understood by both of us. You don't owe me explanations, Jane Boot. But I'd like to hear them anyway. I want to know your troubles so I can fix them."

The tremor multiplied, and when she spoke again, the trembling had settled in her throat.

"He's not going to leave me alone," she said, and he didn't know who she meant.

"Who, honey?"

"Lord Ashley. He's never shown the slightest interest in Augustus. When he saw him for the first time, he was horrified. And I thanked God for giving my son a face only a mother could love." She had started to pant, but instead of breaking down she groaned, low and guttural, like she was warning him away.

Butch had never been an angry man. Never been able to maintain a grudge or a grumble. He just moved on. Made new paths, forged new friendships, but his anger was brewing on her behalf. Jane Toussaint had been plucked from obscurity and sold into slavery. The more he observed, the more likely it was. She'd been used—her gift and her beauty—and abused.

She moaned again, denial and protest rattling in her chest. "He lied. What he told you . . . it was a lie. I was not his lover. Ever."

"He just took."

"Yes. He just took." With those words she became limp, like he'd deflated her with his belief. Then she turned her face into his neck and curled her hands into his shirt, pulling at the hair on his chest and pinching his skin, but he didn't loosen her grip, and he felt her muffled words in his own throat.

"I thought, after the first time, that maybe that would be the end of it. I was seventeen. He said we did not suit, like I'd disappointed him."

Rage tickled his nose and ached in his teeth.

"But a few months later he was back, and my . . . wishes were not taken into account. I told Oliver what he'd done, but Oliver didn't want to believe me, and so . . . he didn't. He allowed it to happen. Repeatedly. It did no good to fight. I had nowhere to go. And my pain was the part he liked best. When I became pregnant with Augustus, I was terrified, but part of me was overjoyed. Because I had proof. Now Oliver would have to face what I'd endured."

"How long?"

"I was nineteen when Augustus was born."

Two years. Two years of hell.

"I told no one. I wasn't sick. I even convinced myself it wasn't true. And I managed to hide it for five months. I'd landed the starring role in *Carmen* with the Paris Opera, and it was everything violent and volatile that I needed. I was a star, and Oliver was overjoyed. The skirts were full and high waisted, and my ribs stayed narrow, but it was only a matter of time. The costumer told Oliver, and Oliver informed Lord Ashley that I was pregnant."

She was quiet, and for a moment he thought that was all he was going to get, that he would have to fill in the blanks as best he could. His hand rose to her hand, knotted in his shirt, and he stroked her fingers, coaxing her to let go. After a moment, she did.

"I don't know what Oliver thought it would accomplish. I would not marry him, and Lord Ashley would certainly not marry me. I'm a street rat. A circus performer. And he laughed and told Oliver it was not his. Oliver convinced me that I should give it up for adoption. But . . . when Augustus was born, it was evident immediately that no one would take him because of his deformity. He would end up like I had, in an orphanage, but it would be worse for him. And I . . . I loved him. He was *mine*."

The panting started again, and he thought she was going to fight free of his arms and bolt. He soothed her the way he would a highstrung horse, chuffing and murmuring and telling her to go easy. "Shhh, we got time, Jane. We got time, honey. That's it."

Her breath quieted, like the worst was past, though it wasn't. Not by a long shot.

"I asked Oliver to marry me—to give Augustus a name and a home. And I promised him I would be the best soprano in the world and the best mother if he would help me. We had an agreement. I sang, and he was able to keep his star performer."

"Didn't Oliver want to marry you? Augustus claims he loved you."

"Oliver was not . . . attracted . . . to me. He was much older than me, and more like a father, though not a very good one. If he loved me, it was not a physical thing. He loved my voice. He loved the access it allowed him. He loved the music."

"And Werthog?"

"He stayed away for a while. Sometimes for years at a time. But he always came back eventually. Every time I performed a new role, he would become fixated again. And Oliver always looked the other way. Right until the very end. I think he told Lady Toussaint about Augustus before he died. He'd been unwell, and his conscience got the better of him. Lady Toussaint had an interaction with Augustus at the wake that makes me think she knew. But I can't be sure. She's gone now too. She died four months ago."

Butch swore, and her fingers became claws once more. He followed his own advice and breathed, keeping himself steady. "Why didn't Oliver protect you?"

"I don't know. Because Ashley is an earl? Because Oliver didn't want to lose his support? The conservatory meant everything to him."

He had no words. Helplessness roared in his ears and tightened his arms, but she kept going, picking up steam.

"I came to expect it and learned to endure it. I had a child to support. And it wasn't very often . . ."

Years. It'd been going on for years.

"After Oliver died, I swore to myself, no more. The tour was planned. Much of it paid for. And Lord Ashley had never been involved with the business of the conservatory. It was Oliver's life's work, though it was owned by the earl's estate. When Oliver died, I thought the conservatory would die too. A large portion of my earnings went into the conservatory, and I felt no qualms at all about the funding that had gone into my tour. I did everything I could think of to prepare. I thought if I got far enough away, Lord Ashley would leave me alone. Let me go. Find a new woman to torture.

"But something in his mother's will greatly upset him, and he turned up again at my home, three months ago, and demanded to speak with me. I changed the locks but Luc would let him in. I fired Luc, but he just ignored me. I stopped paying him, and the earl paid him instead. I endured his advances, simply because Augustus was in the house. I endured it, and he left, and I kept planning."

"You got pregnant. Again."

"Yes. I missed a period. Then another. And I knew. Dr. Moreau confirmed it."

"Dr. Moreau?" he gasped.

"Yes. He is discreet, and he'd been Augustus's doctor for years. I trusted that the word would not get back to Lord Ashley, though Luc reported everything I did. Every person I saw."

He thought of the day they met again, her nerves and her desperation, and all the little pieces fell into place. It felt like a lifetime ago.

"But then you were there. In Paris. Of all places. Hat in hand, looking at me like you'd heard my prayers. And I thought . . . maybe I will survive this too."

"You'll survive this too, honey. I promise." And he committed then and there that he would make it so, no matter the price.

"But he followed me. And he's going to find out who you are, I know it." For the first time, she sounded afraid. "I don't know what to do, Noble. I don't know where to go. We have to hide. But how do you hide a boy like Augustus?"

"How do you hide a boy like Augustus?" his mother wailed, the words muffled but abundantly clear.

Augustus knew he should have knocked, but Emma had been so adamant about him staying downstairs, and he didn't want to get in trouble. He'd lost his winning streak and all his candy in poker, hardly tasted his dinner, and when he announced he was tired and ready for bed, Emma had begun to make him a place to sleep on the sofa in the sitting room. That had set off alarm bells. He was not going to bed without seeing his mother.

He'd marched up the stairs with the excuse of washing and changing into his nightclothes, to which Emma called after him, "Use the bathroom in the corridor, not the bedroom, so you don't disturb your parents."

He was feeling very out of sorts with his *parents*, since no one would tell him what was going on, and they'd left him to worry for the last hour. He'd heard water splashing and Butch moving about earlier—quite loudly in fact—so surely Maman was awake.

He pressed his ear to the door, disregarding everything Emma said, and strained to hear what was going on in the room he'd been banned from.

He didn't hear it all, but he heard enough to understand three things: Lord Ashley was his father. Lord Ashley had hurt his mother repeatedly for many years. Maman needed to hide, but couldn't because of Augustus.

Everywhere he went, people stared at him. People remembered him, and Lord Ashley would find them, eventually. He'd find Noble too. And he would tell the Pinkertons. He would tell the US Marshals. And they would take Noble away from him and Maman. Noble would be strung up. Hanged from the neck until he was dead. That's what the dimes all said would happen.

And it would be his fault, because he couldn't hide.

"Don't be yellow-bellied," he moaned into his hands, trying to control his tears and his growing horror. He stumbled into the washroom and went through the motions of getting ready for bed, but he knew what he had to do.

19

Where have you been, love?
We are almost out of time
And I want to dance

"Where's Augustus?" Butch asked, making his way wearily to the plate of cold food Emma had set aside for him.

Sundance was dozing in his chair, his fingers laced over his middle, his feet crossed. Van was shuffling cards and drinking something strong.

"We thought he was upstairs with you and his mother," Van said, not looking up from his piles.

"No. Emma said she'd keep him here."

"She has bid us all good night and retired to her room for the evening, having 'waited on us hand and foot,'" Van quoted in a high-pitched voice, mocking Emma's last words.

"You said you'd play poker with him," Butch accused, his unease rising. He kicked at the leg of Harry's chair, rousing him.

Sundance peered at him blearily. "I'm not his daddy."

"We played but not for very long," Van admitted. "His heart wasn't in it. He said he was tired, and Emma made him up a bed in the sitting room, but he never came back downstairs. We just figured he'd gone up to see his mother. Can't blame the kid. He was worried about her."

Butch walked back up the stairs and checked every room, even Dr. Laszo's, though the man didn't appreciate being disturbed. Butch wasn't repentant. He searched every room downstairs, informed an irritated Emma, and walked around outside. It was dark, but the full moon was rising, lighting up the rosebushes and outlining the trees where a sulking boy might climb for some alone time.

But no Gus.

He returned to the house, his stride long, his temper spiking. *What a day.*

His valise of cash was still sitting where he'd left it when he'd been gut punched by Dr. Laszo. He was lucky Van hadn't cottoned on to what was in the bag—he would have helped himself—but when Butch opened it, a dent the size of about two hundred dollars was missing from the corner. A little scrap of paper was in its place. Gus had composed an IOU in verse.

> *I will pay you back.*
> *I don't know when, but I will.*
> *Augustus Toussaint*

Gus's hat and suit jacket were gone too, and Emma, who was more worried than the others, claimed a loaf of bread was missing from the bread box. Butch didn't know where Gus was heading, but it was clear that he'd left of his own accord—nobody'd kidnapped him—and he wouldn't starve.

"Gus is gone," Butch announced.

"He'll be back," Sundance said, eyes closed again.

Van snickered and then whooped as he turned over a card he'd apparently been waiting for.

Butch's temper flared, and for one hot moment, he thought about the gun in his boot and imagined whipping it out and drilling them both—*boom, boom*—and ridding the world of the pair of 'em.

Sundance opened one eye.

"He's got no idea where to go. He's not a Jersey boy. The ferry's closed, so even if he thinks he's going there, he'll have to turn back. He's ten years old, Cassidy. And he may be ugly, but he's smart as a whip. He'll be back. Calm your trigger finger. Don't think I can't feel your hate from over here."

"I kinda like his birthmark. He looks like one of those pups with a big dark spot on one side of his face, all droopy and cute," Van said.

He put his hands in the air, triumphant. "Full house."

"Congratulations. You beat yourself," Sundance grumbled. "The candy bag is all yours."

"Jane is asleep." Butch kept his voice level. "It'd be nice if she could stay that way. I'm going to look for him. If he comes back, keep him here . . . and be nice."

"Or you'll kill me. Yeah, yeah. I know." Sundance yawned.

"Hey, Butch . . . I been thinking. How long you known Jane? The kid told us you all just met up again right before settin' sail. I'm thinking she might have another fella, if you know what I mean. That baby couldna been yours." Van tapped his temple like it wasn't hard to figure out. "I know that's not easy to hear, but I'm just lookin' out for you, brother."

Sundance groaned, half laughing. "You are brutal, Rip. Brutal. That or you're the stupidest man I've ever met. I'm leaning toward stupid."

Butch let himself out into the night, shutting the door quietly behind him. He didn't want Jane waking up and discovering Gus was missing.

For a minute he bowed his head and prayed in the only way that ever felt right to him, nothing public or performative, and asked God to help him find Gus.

"And, God, if you don't have any feelings one way or the other, could you take out the two assholes in the kitchen, because I'm about to, and though it'll make me feel good, Lord, it won't solve the issue of finding Gus. Or helping Jane." His voice caught on the last line, and he ground his teeth, swallowed his emotion, and said "Amen" before heading toward Hoboken, where he and Gus had started their day.

☙

"Your dad's out lookin' for you, Aug Dog," Van said, when Augustus tried to slip quietly through the kitchen.

Sundance winced. "Aug Dog?"

"Yeah. It just came to me. I like it. Told ya, he looks like a pup."

"Where you been, kid?" Sundance asked.

Augustus wiped at his face, hoping the two cowboys wouldn't see his tears.

"Just walking around, thinking about things. I was going to turn myself in . . . but the ferry's closed."

"Did you eat that whole loaf of bread?" Van asked.

"No," he said, embarrassed. "There's still a little left." He held up the butt end, and Van laughed.

"What do you mean, turn yourself in?" Sundance asked.

"My real dad's looking for me too. So I figured if I just turned myself in . . . he'd leave Maman and Noble alone."

The two men stared at him, dumbfounded, and Harry straightened slowly, putting his feet on the floor and his hands on his knees.

"You think that'd work?"

"Maman says we can't hide, and Noble is gonna get caught, and . . . and Lord Ashley has been hurting my mom for a long time. He made her pregnant. And he won't leave her alone. Noble—Butch—is trying to help us, but he's a wanted man."

"He damn sure is," Van said, nodding. "Luckiest son of a bitch in the West. Pinks haven't caught up to him after all these years. I don't think they ever will either."

"Shut up, Rip," Sundance said, his gaze never leaving Augustus's face. "Your plan won't work, kid, though it ain't a bad one."

"Why?"

"'Cause your real dad doesn't want you. If he did, he'da taken you from the beginning. He's an English lord. They do what they want, and he doesn't want you. He wants your mother. So don't go running off thinking turning yourself in is going to solve anything. You'll just hurt the people who *do* want you."

Augustus wilted, ashamed, but he was relieved too.

"I ever tell you about the time Butch tried to turn himself in?" Van asked. "I had to swoop in and save him. If it weren't for me . . . they'da shot him like a dog. Instead, I had 'em runnin' away with their tails between their legs."

The door opened behind Augustus, and Noble stepped inside. His shoulders drooped in relief at the sight of Augustus.

"We talked to him, brother. He knows what he did was stupid, don't ya, kid?" Van jumped in.

"Augustus?" Noble asked gently. "Are you all right?"

Augustus nodded, though his lip jutted out, all on its own, and tears started leaking from his eyes even though he blinked harder than he'd ever blinked before.

"I'm fine, but can I go see my mother?"

"Sure you can. I'll take the couch tonight. You go on up."

Augustus turned, thought twice, and walked back to Noble and handed him the money he'd taken. Then he hugged him tight around the middle, resting his tear-streaked face on his chest for half a second and let him go.

"Good night, Dad," he whispered.

"Good night, Gus."

"You want in, Butch?" Sundance asked, indicating the game in progress.

"I'm tired."

"It's hard bein' a daddy," Van said.

Sundance rolled his eyes. "Sit down, Cassidy," he ordered, kicking at a chair. "You aren't going to sleep for a while yet. You're too jumpy. Give us a shot to win that money in your pocket."

Butch relented and collapsed into the chair, accepting the cards that were passed his way.

"Is this what you two do every night?" he asked.

"When we aren't out raping and pillaging," Harry drawled. "You know us."

Van stood and grabbed another glass and filled it with something golden brown. He passed it to his brother. "Drink it. You need it."

Butch studied the amber liquid and thought of the ring in his pocket and twisted the ring on his finger. Then he drank it down in one gulp and prayed for a good night's sleep, because he was about at the end of his rope.

They played in silence for several minutes, saying only what was necessary for the game, and Butch slowly began to relax, knowing that for the moment, he'd done what he could.

"Noble?" a little voice said from the kitchen door.

"Good hell, kid," Sundance moaned. "Don't you ever sleep?"

Butch set down his cards and turned. "Yeah, Gus?"

"Maman is asleep. And it's dark up there. And I'm still feeling pretty sad."

"Deal him in," Sundance barked, pulling up yet another chair. Van did as he was told, and Augustus slid into the chair beside Butch, look-ing like one of Pan's lost boys in his nightshirt and bare feet.

They'd played an entire round before Augustus spoke.

"My father is a bad man," he said, his eyes on his cards.

"Who, Butch?" Van asked, brow wrinkled, confused.

Augustus drew from the middle. "The Earl of Werthog. He's my father, isn't he, Noble?"

"Yeah, Gus. He is."

"Hit me," Sundance inserted, and Van obliged. Moments passed, but Augustus wasn't done.

"He hurt my mother."

"I fold," Sundance said.

"Me too." Butch tossed his cards in.

"What you got, kid?" Van prodded.

"Large straight."

"You've got to be cheatin'," Van howled, but he poured another round and even filled a glass for the boy.

Augustus snatched it up so fast, Butch had no chance to stop him.

"Bleck!" Augustus spat, his eyes watering and his chest wheezing.

"What the hell do you think you're doing, Van?" Butch hissed.

"Just trying to make him feel better. And maybe go back to bed so I can win."

"No more, Augustus. You got that?" Butch snapped. "You know better. That will ruin your life faster than anything else you can do."

"Ease up, Robert LeRoy," Van inserted. "You sound just like Dad. Ain't nothing wrong with one drink. All things in moderation, remember?"

Butch shoved back from the table and turned Augustus toward him, essentially shutting the others out.

"Listen to me, Gus. My dad was a good man. Always worked hard. Always came home. Never drank, never gambled. Never stole. He loved my mother and never raised his voice at her or raised a hand to her."

"He whooped us kids when he had to," Van added. "But we were so wild it was that or sell us to the Gosiutes."

"The Gosiutes?" Augustus asked, eyes wide.

"A local Indian tribe, if you can even call 'em a tribe," Van answered.

Butch tried again, using Van's interruption to further his point. "The Gosiutes were scavengers. They ate bugs and roots and trapped small animals. Their homes weren't much more than a pile of sticks or a crevice in the side of a hill that they could easily abandon, though as soon as they did, another Gosiute would move in. Not much of an existence. We didn't have much either, but we had more than that, and Dad always wanted us to appreciate it. I didn't appreciate what I had."

"Your dad was a good dad," Augustus said. His lower lip jutted out, and tears the size of pebbles began to wet the cards he'd placed on the table. "Not like mine."

"Gus . . . listen to me," Butch soothed, patting the boy's back and mopping his face with his handkerchief. "Even though my dad was good, and my mom was good too, I still turned out the way I am. I still did bad things. Lots of 'em."

"You didn't hurt people."

"Sure I did. We all do. Some worse than others. I made a lot of bad decisions, though I'd been warned by my dad, and I knew better. I wanted a life I didn't know how to get. So I became a thief. I robbed banks. Robbed trains. I wasn't a good man, even though my dad was. Van isn't a good man either."

"I'm not so bad," Van interrupted. "I've done good things."

Butch ignored him. "The way Van and I turned out isn't my dad's fault."

That seemed to make sense to Augustus.

"What your dad does isn't your fault either. Do you understand?"

Augustus was still sniffling, but he nodded.

"Your father makes his choices. You make yours. If you want to be a good man, you will be. It's that simple."

"Didn't you want to be a good man?" Augustus asked, timid.

"No. Not for a long time. I convinced myself there was no such thing. I thought I could balance it all out. Be bad . . . and do good . . . keep score."

"Did it work?"

"Hell yes it did," Van interjected again, and Butch sighed.

"No. No, Gus. It sure as hell didn't."

"Why?"

"Because now I'm a wanted man, and I'll always be a wanted man. I can't fix that. Someday, someone is going to recognize me, even though I've tried hard to change and be better. They're going to see these Butch Cassidy blue eyes, and I'm going to get caught. That's something I have to live with every day. Your mama said you can't hide . . . but I can't hide either."

For a moment, Gus seemed stunned. "We're both stuck with the faces we've got."

"Yeah. Just like I told you on the ship." Butch nodded.

"But Van said you're the luckiest son of a bitch in the world. So nobody's gonna catch up to you."

"Nope. Nobody's gonna," Van predicted, pouring himself another shot.

Butch shot his brother a warning look. He'd already been a terrible influence, and it had only been two days. Then he turned his attention back to the boy. "You gotta quit saying stuff like that, Augustus."

"I won't. Because I want it to be true. And I want you to be my dad for real. Not the Earl of Werthog."

"You don't have to claim him. You don't have to give him that title or any thought at all. He's not part of your life. Never will be, if I can help it. So don't give him any of your tears or your time. He's not your father in any way that matters."

"But . . . do you think he's the reason I look the way I do?"

"What do you mean?"

"Maman called him a monster. That's what people call me too."

"Now that's just plain nasty," Van said, shaking his head. "And you should apologize, Sundance, for calling him a toad. Apologize right now."

"Will you shut up, Rip?" Sundance growled.

"You don't look anything like Werthog," Butch lied, ignoring the bickering. Augustus had the earl's patrician nose, chin, and brow, and were it not for his birthmark, the resemblance would be undeniable. Butch had noticed it from the first, though it took him a minute to realize the reason he recognized Werthog was because of Augustus.

"I've got my mother's eyes . . . just like you do," Augustus conceded.

"Yep, your eyes are Jane Boot brown. My new favorite color."

"I always thought you liked green best," Van contended, but Sundance shoved him, and they were both quiet again, pretending not to listen.

"Maman doesn't like that part of her name."

Butch nodded, acknowledging Gus's warning. "That's because she's private. None of us like sharing all our hurts. The people who love us can know, and that's enough."

"But . . . if I'm not with you, you'll be safe," Augustus argued. "You can both hide."

"If you're not here, your mom would rather be dead. You're the best thing in her life. The best part. Without you, she won't even want to live, Augustus." Butch's voice was sharp, and Gus's eyes filled all over again.

"But she has you now," Augustus cried. "And she loves you too. I know she does."

"She has me now. And I'm going to do everything I can to make things better, Gus. But sacrificing yourself isn't the answer."

Gus's nose was running, and tears glimmered against the crimson of his misshapen cheek. Still, when he showed his cards, he had them all beat.

"Ah, for hell's sake," Sundance snapped, throwing down his hand.

"Love means you stay," Gus said. "That's what Maman told me. Do you think that's true, Noble?"

Love means you stay.

Butch's chest ached, and he couldn't meet his brother's eyes. "I think that's true, Gus. Love means you stay. I've never been very good at that. So we need to figure out how to stay together, okay? We don't want to be apart."

"Okay." Augustus stood and hugged him, laying his head on his shoulder. "I love you, Noble."

"I love you too, kid," Butch answered, no hesitation. "You gonna sleep upstairs?"

Augustus nodded. "But I'll take the couch like last night, so you can have the bed with Maman. It'll make her feel safer to know you're there."

Butch patted his back. "All right. Go on. It's been a long day. And don't tell your mother about the whiskey, please. I don't like Van, but I don't want him dead."

"Thanks a lot, brother," Van muttered.

Augustus turned for the stairs once more, wobbling like an old man.

"Night, Gus," Harry called. "Rematch tomorrow. And you better not hold back."

"Good night, Sundance."

"Good night, Gus," Van added, not to be outdone. "I was thinking we could work on your draw too. You know how to shoot, don't ya?"

"Van," Butch warned.

"Good night, Rip," Gus said, snickering. His laughter continued until he shut the bedroom door.

"Good night, you two," Butch said, standing. He retrieved his valise but left his money on the table. He supposed the assholes had earned it in their own way.

"Good night, Noble Salt," they said in unison, smirking at him and counting the pile.

20

All I prayed for came
After my darkest hour
A son to heal me

Jane woke briefly in the middle of the night when Augustus pressed a wet kiss to her cheek, smelling oddly of whiskey, and then again, not much later, when Noble eased down beside her, trying not to shake the bed or disturb her.

She reached for him, ran her hand along his arm, and held his hand, more grateful than she'd ever been in her whole life, before drifting back to sleep.

In the morning when she woke, a ring had been placed on her finger, an amber stone surrounded by diamonds on a delicate gold band.

Noble was still asleep, his dark head tucked partially beneath the pillow, taking up less space than he should, considering his size. He wore a ring on his left finger too, a simple band that she'd somehow missed in all of yesterday's discontent.

Augustus didn't even stir on the couch as she slipped past him, needing the washroom. Her body ached low and deep, but not like it had before. Dr. Laszo was right. Physically, it felt no different from a difficult menses, if that. The pain was a mere reminder of what was no longer, and she could only rejoice.

"Thank you," she whispered to the silence. "Whoever you are, whatever you are, wherever we go when our spirits fly. Thank you for this pardon."

Oddly, she had not been afraid of the pregnancy. She'd been angry, even enraged, but not afraid. She'd been through it before.

She'd survived worse.

And once upon a time, the worst thing that had ever happened to her produced the best thing that had ever happened to her.

She had no doubt that the same could happen again, and it had given her perspective where once she'd had none. Still, she was not sorry to pass the bitter cup, and felt no sadness for the child who would not be or the cross she would not bear. She'd been given a reprieve, and she would not plumb her relief for new trauma.

She suspected she had some explaining to do, however. She'd waited far too long to tell Augustus things he needed to know. She'd lied to him, letting him believe Oliver was his father, which had produced its own set of problems. Its own brand of pain. She'd left Noble to handle the entire household last night, her son included.

What must they all think? She had no illusions that Dr. Laszo or Emma had been especially discreet.

She heard movement in the room and Augustus blearily wondering aloud what Emma was cooking. Noble told him to use the washroom in the corridor, and he must have done the same because neither of them knocked on the door. She washed herself and left the bathroom to dress before loosening her braid and drawing a brush through the length of her hair.

Noble reentered the room, dressed for the day as well, his hair slicked back and the scent of coffee and bacon clinging to his clothes.

"I had Emma save you some breakfast. If you're determined to perform tonight, you're going to need your strength."

"Thank you," she said, setting the brush aside and centering the stone on her finger. "And thank you . . . for the ring."

"Gus picked it out. He thought you'd like the honey color. I just thought it was beautiful, like you."

His voice was rough with sleep and his eyes were weary, but he smiled at her anyway, and she stood, rose up on her toes to kiss his cheek, and at the last moment, changed course and kissed his mouth.

He froze, and she withdrew and turned back to the mirror. "Thank you," she said again. "I love it. And you're wearing a ring too."

"Jane."

She didn't look at him.

"Jane, honey."

She took a deep breath and pulled down the haughty mask that was second nature. "Yes, Noble?" She met his eyes in the glass.

"Do that again, please."

Augustus was being fed down below, there was no reason not to accommodate the request, but she'd lost her nerve.

"Please," he whispered, tugging her hand to turn her back to him.

He had asked, but he wasn't initiating or forcing. That was up to her. She stepped into him, raised her hands to his cheeks, his beard prickling her palms, and pulled his head toward her so she could touch her lips to his once more.

There she stayed, breathing softly, her eyes closed, her mouth to his mouth, her belly to his belly.

She didn't part her lips or align their faces, but there was a sense of merging, of joining. Warmth spread from her chest to her thighs, and his hands rose to sit on her hips.

"I like that," she marveled, and realized she'd spoken aloud.

She felt his face lift beneath her palms—a smile—and she pressed in again, this time more firmly, and tilted her head to get a better angle.

He let her explore, answering her questions in exactly the same way she'd asked them. A brush, a caress. A breath, a sigh, a taste, a tentative touch. He gave her exactly what she sought. It was kissing. Careful kissing, and it never became more.

When she felt the coiling in his body, the hard heat of his legs, and the pump of his blood, she stepped back and dropped her hands from his face, knowing she'd gone as far as she wanted to go, though her own heart raced and her breasts ached at the tips. He dropped his hands from her hips and placed a kiss on her hair.

"I like it too," he said softly, and walked out of the bedroom.

She was surrounded by a pack of brooding males. The stairs leading up from the kitchen funneled the sound, and she stood at the top, listening to all the things none of them would have said if they knew she could hear.

"This guy isn't going to go away," Sundance was arguing. "She's a hot commodity. You know his type, Butch. He's like the big cattle outfits that took out everything and everyone in their way, or the railroad tycoons that got government contracts to take whatever land they wanted, all in the name of the greater good. They don't know how the rest of the world lives, and they frankly don't give a shit."

"Can we please not discuss assassination in front of the boy?" Butch muttered, but Sundance continued without censoring himself at all.

"The difference between you and me, Butch Cassidy, is I got no problem killing someone who needs killing." He swallowed whatever he was eating. "But you've never listened to me. I don't expect you to start now. You're the straightest damn arrow I've ever seen. Problem is, you don't bring arrows to a gunfight."

Van had his own suggestions. "Seems to me you need security on Jane's shows, good security. Not just you trying to be all things to all people. You know how you used to plan it. A lookout up high. A lookout by the door, a lookout across the street. And that doesn't count the men inside keeping everything cool while another guy fills the bags."

"We're not talking about taking a bank or robbing a train," Butch argued.

"No . . . we're talking about keeping your woman safe. Sundance and I are going to help you. Maybe Harry can work his way back to San Francisco and win Ethel back."

Sundance snorted. "I don't want Ethel back."

"You're getting way ahead of yourself, Van," Butch cautioned. "Let's just see how today goes. Maybe the son of a bitch has played all his cards."

"How come you can say son of a bitch, Noble, and I can't?" Augustus whined. The late night and events of the previous day were evident in his voice, though he too spoke between bites.

"Come on, brother," Van wheedled. "It'll be fun. Sundance and I will be your backup for the whole shebang."

"I didn't volunteer for that, Van," Sundance protested. "I've said what I think. I'll kill the warthog to save the little toad."

Amazingly enough, Augustus laughed, and Sundance, the surly outlaw who set her teeth on edge, chuckled with him.

"We could be the new Wild Bunch if you guys wanted to come along," Augustus suggested, suddenly cheerful.

"That's the spirit, kid," Van hooted. "We got Salty over there." She guessed he was talking about Noble. "I'm Rip, but Sundance needs a new name. We probably shouldn't call him Sundance since that's what the circulars say."

"Noble calls him Contrary Harry."

"What does contrary mean?" Van asked.

"Sour," Augustus supplied.

"Call me that, Rip," Sundance said, "and I'll kill you right after I kill Warthog."

"Nobody is killing Werthog," Butch said.

"What's your Wild Bunch nickname, Augustus?" Van asked, still playing.

"This is the stupidest conversation I've ever heard," Sundance sighed. Van and Augustus didn't seem to think so.

"I'm No-Fuss Gus. You can call me Gus for short. And what about Maman?"

"Madame Toussaint doesn't need a nickname," Sundance said. "The beautiful women never do. They get full billing."

"Like Ethel," Van said. "We never called her nothin' different, did we? Always just Ethel."

Sundance grimaced like the reminder pained him, but Van was oblivious.

"Noble calls her honey," Gus informed them.

"Augustus Toussaint," Noble sighed. "You don't tell the whole gang our secrets. And if Sundance or my brother call Jane honey, there's going to be more killing going on."

"Such violence," Jane said, making her presence known as she descended the stairs.

The entire kitchen—Emma was temporarily absent—wriggled in discomfort as she reached the landing.

The breakfast spread was truly remarkable, and Augustus was never going to want to leave. His cheeks were fuller than they'd been when they left Paris.

"Mornin', Jane," Van said.

"Mornin', ma'am."

"Hi, honey," Butch said softly, making her blush and Van snicker. Augustus didn't greet her.

She stopped beside his chair and drew him into her arms, though that was becoming harder to do all the time. He was growing so fast; he would soon be as tall as she, and his childhood would be over. She expected the men around the table to excuse themselves and allow her some time with her son. Instead, they kept eating, eyes on their food, ears fully tuned. Perhaps that was best.

"Good morning, darling," she murmured to Augustus.

"Good morning, Maman," he said in a small voice. All his playfulness had fled the moment she entered the room.

"Augustus?"

"Yes, Maman?"

"Do you know how many people dream of singing onstage, all over the world?"

"A lot," he said dully.

"A lot," she agreed. "They want to be famous and rich and admired."

He sighed like the subject bored him.

"But do you know that all I ever wanted was a family? I wanted that more than anything in the whole world. And I didn't have one."

"You were an orphan. Jane Boot."

"Yes. Little Jane Boot with the big voice. And even though I was grateful I could sing, it was not the gift I wanted most."

"And when I was born, you were so happy," he sighed, sounding older than his years.

She'd told him this story before, so many times that he knew his lines, but now he said them woodenly, like he no longer believed them.

"Yes. I was. I looked into your beautiful face, a face that was distinctly and perfectly you, and I loved you so much. The day you were born, I got everything I had ever wanted. I got a family. Me and you."

"And Oliver," he said, throwing his first dart, reminding her of what she'd let him believe.

"No. Oliver was not your father. I did not love him. But he gave us a home. I am grateful for that."

"You gave Oliver a home too, Jane," Noble argued quietly, her loyal defender, but Augustus plunged ahead.

"My father is the Earl of Werthog," he accused.

"Yes. Lord Ashley is your father."

"You didn't love him either."

"No," she choked. "I most definitely did not love him, and he didn't love me. He took something I did not want to give him."

Augustus searched her face, too young to fully understand, and wise enough to understand too much. His anger seemed to slip from his tight shoulders, and he sighed, resting his forehead against her shoulder. Noble stood up abruptly as if he could bear no more, then sat again like he didn't want to leave her alone with the others. He took out his little book of verses instead, distracting himself.

"I'm sorry, Maman. I'm so sorry," Augustus whispered.

"I'm not," she answered at once. "I'm angry. But I'm not sorry."

"Why? He hurt you."

"Life can be wonderfully ironic, my darling. I'm not sorry because I got you."

"But why didn't you tell me before?"

"I think you are smart enough to answer that question for yourself. I had no intention of *ever* telling you. It was information that would only hurt you."

Silence sat heavy on every bowed head in the kitchen, and from the outside, Emma could be heard, scolding her chickens.

Augustus was trying not to cry, and his breaths came out in little pants and puffs.

"I'm going to learn how to shoot . . . just like the Wild Bunch. And then . . . I'm going to find him, and I'm going to kill him," he swore.

"No, Augustus. No, you aren't. Killing him won't change the past," she cautioned him, stroking his hair.

"Yeah . . . but it might change the future," Sundance muttered.

"You kill him, he wins," Noble said gently, looking at Augustus. "And your life will be over. Never, ever talk about killing like it's an option. 'Cause it ain't. Not for Augustus Toussaint."

"Agree to disagree," Sundance grunted, and Noble's fingers grew white around his little pencil.

"I don't want to talk about him anymore, Maman."

"All right."

"I just want you to be okay," he said, and the little boy he'd been peeped out of his big dark eyes. His lip trembled once before he subdued it between his teeth.

"I am better than I have ever been in my whole life. I am happy. I am hopeful. I have you, and we are in America."

He smiled at her, maybe forgiving her a little, and allowed her to embrace him once more before she straightened and released the tension around the table. Augustus reached for the bowl of fried potatoes and helped himself to another serving.

It would take some time, and he wasn't satisfied. Not Augustus Maximilian Toussaint. He would have a lot more questions, and she would do her best to answer them. But it was a start.

Emma bustled back into the kitchen, saw Jane, and immediately grabbed another plate. "There's a big write-up in the paper this morning about your tour, Madame Toussaint," Emma said, filling the plate with enough food to fuel Jane for a week. When she tried to protest the serving size, she received a slate-eyed stare that had her swallowing her words.

"You need your strength, Jane. Now eat," she insisted, pulling rank and demoting Jane in one look. Jane ate and made sure to compliment every bite. The men were finished, but none seemed to be in a big hurry to move.

Van picked up the newspaper Emma had set in front of her and began reading it to himself, his finger moving along the line like a child. A peculiar wave of tenderness washed over her, and when she glanced at Butch, he was watching his brother too, the same conflicted expression on his face.

"You're a big deal, aren't you?" Van asked, not looking up. "Singing for kings and queens and archdukes. How many countries have you been to?"

"I don't know. Europe is much smaller than America."

"It says here you even performed at the Bolshoi in Moscow and met Tsar Nicholas and his wife, Alexandra."

"They have several children now but were just newlyweds when I met them. Very handsome couple."

"In Russia?" Van gasped.

"Yes. St. Petersburg is a very beautiful city."

The men stared at her in wide-eyed wonder. Emma had even ceased stirring, her jaw agape.

"I've met Archduke Ferdinand of Austria. He is a big fan of the opera," Jane added, tapping at her mouth with her napkin and hoping Emma was distracted enough to let her be done.

"Who else?" Emma pressed.

"All the world leaders in the westernized world . . . I think. Though I have not met the current American president. I was supposed to sing for President McKinley, but he was assassinated the day before the scheduled performance."

"You singing for any presidents this go-round? I have an inkling Theodore Roosevelt might recognize Butch." Sundance yawned, insinuating he wasn't as impressed as the rest. Noble just shook his head and winked at her.

"No presidents. But Edward Harriman has invited me to Salt Lake City to sing at Saltair. It might be a good idea for . . . Mr. Cassidy . . . to avoid a meeting with him as well."

It was easier to take the ferry and jump aboard the El train than it was to take the coach across the bridge and up busy streets to Carnegie Hall, but Butch didn't want to put Madame Toussaint on public transit, even if the ride took a bit longer.

"I don't know how long I'll be. It's the full orchestra and will involve several run-throughs. A driver would be waiting all day," Jane fretted. "And I'd rather Harry and Van stayed with Augustus. I know he is safe here, and he will be happier too, even though I don't want him out of my sight."

Butch felt much the same, and they compromised by having Van remain behind and Sundance drop them at the hall and return home. At the end of the evening, they would take a hansom cab back to Emma's.

But when they arrived at the music hall and Sundance jumped down to open the coach doors, he had an odd look on his face.

"They're removing the sign," he said.

Butch stepped out and extended his hand to help Jane, who peered up at the banner being detached from the arches on the front of the building.

Jane Toussaint returns to Carnegie Hall snapped in the breeze as one end of the announcement, and then the other, was released and brought to the ground.

"Hey there. What's that all about?" Sundance asked, approaching the workers, hands in his pockets, one common man to another. "Isn't she going to sing?"

"Heck if I know, mister. I guess not. Mr. Hugo just told us to take it down. He didn't give us a reason."

"No one's here," Jane said. "With an orchestra that size, plus the stage crew and Mr. Hugo's people, this place should be humming. It's not."

Butch wanted to bundle her back in the coach and head for home at a full gallop, but that wouldn't answer the burning question: What the hell was going on?

Sundance was heading for the front door, and Butch almost expected it to be locked, but it came open with a swish, and Sundance stuck his head inside and then took a half step, propping the door with one arm.

"Mr. Hugo?" they heard him yell. "Mr. Hugo. Madame Toussaint is here. We'd like to have a word with you outside if you don't mind."

A pause.

"No. You come out here, Mr. Hugo. They're taking down the sign. Why is that?"

If Hugo was talking back, his responses weren't audible, and Sundance went no farther than the entrance, keeping his exit open and giving them at least one side of the conversation.

"Madame Toussaint will not be coming inside, Mr. Hugo. She'll be waiting out front for a word." He stepped back outside and let the door swing closed, striding back toward them, his long legs eating up the distance, his hand twitching at his side like they were about to stop a train.

"Someone's worked him over," he ground out.

"What do you mean?" Butch asked. "Beat him up?"

"No, not that. But he's fit to be tied. Sweat-stained. Hair a mess. Collar missing. He says the tour has been canceled until further notice."

A minute later, Bailey Hugo stepped out into the sunlight, squinting at the workers rolling the sign and the lone coach parked in front of the famed establishment. It was as Sundance said, though it appeared he'd tried to tidy himself. He ran both palms over his hair, but his curls, ravaged by nervous hands, had been too long without grease, and they bounced back onto his brow the moment he released them.

"Madame Toussaint. Mr. Salt. Hello," he greeted. "Won't you come inside? I've arranged a small tea and we can talk privately."

"What's going on, Hugo?" Jane asked, her voice low and calm. "I don't want tea. I want an explanation."

"I have been instructed not to proceed."

"But the tour has already been financed in great part. At least the first ten shows. The others have been secured with significant deposits. We will lose that money, Hugo."

"Yes . . . well . . . I'm working on that, madame. I will ask for a return of that which is refundable."

"But why?" she asked, aghast.

"The conservatory has withdrawn its . . . permission."

"What permission is that?"

"I have simply been told that I cannot proceed. At this point, I will be doing my best to recoup my own losses and my reputation as a promoter."

He was upset and afraid, and he kept looking behind him as if he suspected someone to sneak up on him and bash him over the head with a billy club.

"But why can we not proceed?" Jane pressed.

"The original agreement was between the Toussaint Conservatory and Hugo Productions, Madame Toussaint. And you are not the signatory. Your late husband was."

"Then make a new contract," Butch suggested. "Between Madame Toussaint and Hugo Productions."

"But . . . sir. A new contract will require new funds. Toussaint Conservatory is demanding that all deposits and donations be returned. I have sent word to both Mrs. Harriman and Mrs. Carnegie this morning and told them the tour is on hold."

"I'll fund the new contract," Butch offered.

Jane gasped.

"You?" Hugo asked, stupefied.

"Yes."

"But . . . sir . . . we are talking about a great deal of money."

"How much?"

"I . . . I don't know," he stammered. "I can't save this tour. To avoid conflicts with the earl, I would have to start over, reissue contracts. I'd have to set new dates, and most venues have their calendars booked months, if not a year, in advance. It is truly a mess. And the earl was quite adamant. If I help you with this tour, he will ruin me. You, Madame Toussaint, are the property of the conservatory, and the conservatory says no tour." His voice dropped to just above a whisper. "The earl claims you are wanted for questioning in Oliver's death, madame. He told me you will be forced to return to France."

"I see," Jane said softly.

Rage, hot and viscous, surged in Butch's chest, and he turned to his old friend, a man he'd loved and hated in equal measure, and met his gaze, letting him see every murderous wish in his heart. Sundance understood, and his flat eyes gleamed with his own bloodthirsty desire. Neither of them said a word.

Jane walked several steps and paused, her hands folded prettily behind her, a lovely woman on a meandering stroll, enjoying the sunshine. The violet feather on her hat caressed her cheek and framed the point of her chin, and they all watched her, three men in her thrall, waiting on her verdict. When she turned back toward them, she was perfectly composed, nary a pink blotch on her slim throat.

"I'm very sorry you've been put in such a terrible situation, Mr. Hugo. Very sorry indeed. You've worked hard and gone to considerable expense. I was looking forward to touring with you, but I can see how impossible this situation has become. You must do everything you can to cut your losses and keep your reputation intact."

Hugo's countenance softened, and his relief that he was not going to face another lambasting was plain. "Oh, madame. You are kind. And gracious. There is no one who compares in talent or beauty. I am certain this is but a bump in the road, and you will be back onstage in no time."

She nodded, accepting his thankful praise with no emotion. Then she climbed back in the coach and called to Butch as if she had not a care in the world.

"Shall we go, Mr. Salt? It appears we have nothing to do today after all."

Butch remained a moment longer, staring up at the edifice that had heralded her name and brought her into his life six years before. It was no longer February. No longer freezing, and he was no longer running away. But damn if he knew what to do. That much hadn't changed.

"Mr. Hugo? I'd like the tour schedule, venue contacts, anything you can give me. I'll keep you out of it, but if Madame Toussaint wants to continue without the conservatory and without you, she will need that information."

"It is here." Hugo held a folder under his arm. "I made copies of everything. Do with it what you will, but . . . you must negotiate without referencing Hugo Productions or the Toussaint Conservatory."

Butch nodded and took the folder, thanking the man. He had no real idea what he was doing, but he couldn't let Jane leave with nothing, without even a possibility of a plan.

"Harry?" he summoned.

Sundance didn't need to have anything explained. He waited for Butch to climb inside, shut the carriage door behind him, and a moment later, they were rattling down the street, heading back the way they'd come only minutes before. When Butch turned, poor Mr. Hugo still stood in front of the hall, his shoulders slumped, his unkempt curls waving goodbye.

21

You make me believe
What my mother used to say
Some folks are just ours

It was summer in New York, Emma's yard was an oasis, Augustus was smiling, and Jane Toussaint was in love for the first time in her life.

She and Noble had ridden away from Carnegie Hall in silence. She'd had nothing to say. She was not surprised. She was not disappointed. She was not even afraid.

Noble didn't reassure her or rant and rave, though his fury had him tugging at his tie and shrugging off his coat. He even rolled his sleeves, as if preparing to fight the injustice she'd just suffered.

But she felt nothing.

She found her thoughts soaring outward, upward, back. To the day she'd arrived at the conservatory. To the day she'd sung for Queen Victoria. She'd sung for many important people. Some had listened with banal appreciation. Some had listened in awe, and she'd never doubted that she could perform, that her voice would carry her, that there would be another performance. And another. Because that was what she did. She sang, and she survived.

She had not ceased singing. Not since the day the real Madame Toussaint, her benefactor, had stopped in front of her as the children obediently sang a song to welcome the noblewoman to their humble circumstances.

"What's your name, little girl?" the woman had asked, interrupting the number.

"Jane Boot, ma'am."

She clapped briskly, bringing the wobbling number to a halt. "Will you sing it alone, dear? I'd like to hear just you."

A flush of pleasure warmed her chest and curled her fingers into her palms. She hadn't waited for the tinny pianoforte to accompany her. She sounded better without it. And she didn't continue to sing the song about saving the king, though she liked it. It did not showcase her voice as well as others, and she recognized that the woman had the power to rescue her if she was good enough.

She sang "Pie Jesu," a song she'd learned by listening to the boys' choir at Westminster. She had no idea what the words meant or even if she was saying them correctly. She'd memorized the sounds and practiced the soaring lines because she recognized their beauty and power and wanted both.

Madame Toussaint had listened, her hands clasped, and when Jane was done, she'd simply moved down the line, saying nothing at all. The piano had started again, the original song resumed, and Jane had been punished for ruining the presentation. But the next day, a man in the employ of the Earl of Werthog had come for her and told her headmaster that she was to gather her things and come with him. She'd been singing ever since.

She'd mastered every score she'd been assigned, every lesson, every exercise. She'd practiced her Latin and her French until she dreamed in both, and she had become . . . great. Renowned. Sought out by dignitaries and dictators. For eighteen years she'd done nothing but study and sing, and she had nothing to show for it.

She had a small reticule filled with jewelry and cash that she'd carefully saved. She had a wardrobe fit for the stage and for the circles she'd learned to move in. But she had no home and no pride in her accomplishments.

And yet . . . she felt nothing.

She'd heard Noble gather Van and Sundance and talk of train tickets and travel and financing a tour himself when the "trouble" passed. They'd argued about it in the kitchen for the better part of an hour. It was a good thing the doctor was gone and Emma and Augustus were busy planting peas and carrots and all manner of vegetables Augustus would never see flourish. Jane had listened from the back porch, rocking on Emma's bright blue chair, her hands in her lap, her mind strangely still.

Van was full of suggestions. "We'll take her and Gus to Browns Park . . . or even better, Robbers Roost. The bastard won't ever find them there."

"I'm not going to hide Jane and Gus in a canyon. In a cave," Noble shot back. "And I don't think Browns Park is an option."

"Ann and Josie Bassett would be glad to see you, I'm sure," Van said, laughter in his voice.

"Yeah, but they wouldn't be glad to see Jane," Sundance exclaimed.

She imagined Butch Cassidy had left plenty of broken hearts behind him, and she experienced another first. Jealousy. Hot and sour and pea green.

"And you aren't coming with me. You and Harry have a good thing here, driving the coach," Noble argued. "Emma likes having you around, helping out, and you're staying out of trouble."

"I'm bored out of my damn mind," Van grumbled. "And Emma has sons that can help out. She doesn't need us as much as she puts up with us. I'm comin' with you. Gonna guard your back."

"No, you're not, Van." She could almost hear Noble shaking his head. "No, you're not. This is my job. An honest one. Just like you've got going here."

"It's not an honest job!" Van shot back. "It's not a job at all. You married the woman, and her kid calls you Dad. You're in so deep, your hair is floating."

He had married her. Her son called him Dad.

The realization washed over her, sudden and warm, and her envy dissolved into wonder.

"He ain't smart, but he ain't wrong, Butch Cassidy." Sundance added his two cents. "I'm comin' too. I hate it here. Soon as I came back, I remembered why I left."

Noble groaned, but he didn't argue, and a few minutes later he was planning again. He said they could leave as early as Friday—she didn't even know what day it was—and Sundance said he'd purchase the fares.

"I'll give you the money," Noble agreed. "Buy the best. A Pullman car, so that Jane has some privacy and some space. We need to stay out of sight as much as we can."

If she let him, Noble would take care of everything, and she loved him for it. But she could muster no enthusiasm for the trip. She couldn't muster enthusiasm for anything.

For three days, she sat in Emma's garden instead and lifted her face to the sun, listening to Augustus compose verses about various plants and shrubs, her little poet botanist. She fell asleep one afternoon on a particularly thick patch of grass, waking only when Butch patted her cheek and told her she was going to burn to a crisp if she didn't come inside.

"Do you think you could teach me how to hold up a bank or rob a train?" she asked drowsily, blinking up at him. "I think I should like blowing things up."

"No, honey. I don't."

"I used to pick pockets. Long ago. I was quite good at it. I never got caught. Just like you. We are more alike than you think."

He picked a bit of grass from her hair, but she continued.

"Then I discovered that singing was more lucrative and a thousand times easier, and I sang on the corners instead of stealing. But the headmaster took my money. Oliver always took my money too. Perhaps I should find a corner in New York City with my tin cup and try again. You wouldn't take my money, would you?"

"I wouldn't. Not a dime of it."

For a moment he simply sat with her, letting her wake.

"I can't pay you, Noble. You realize that, don't you?" she murmured, unwilling to rise. He stayed crouched on his haunches above her, hands clasped between his knees, and she fought the urge to pull him down beside her. Over her. She wanted his weight to press her into the earth, his body to shade her. And she did not want to sing.

"I don't need your money, Jane. I never did. That's not why I agreed to this. I only wanted to go home. Now . . . I just want to be with you."

"How far is home?" she asked, her heart skipping at his sweetness, his courage. His lack of artifice. She had no choice but to believe him.

"Two thousand miles. A little more than that, actually."

"Then that's where you should go."

He nodded. "Will you come with me?"

She struggled to hold his gaze. "I want to. It's the only thing I want. But I did not intend to become a millstone around your neck, Noble Salt."

He smiled, and there was something so sad in his eyes, she caught her breath.

"One man's millstone is another man's dream," he said.

"Which is it for you?"

"I've told you how I feel."

"Yes," she whispered. "You have. But if I never sing again . . . what then? Will you love me still?"

"Well, that would be a damn shame. If you never sing again it would be a tragedy."

"That was not what I asked, Butch Cassidy," she said, sitting up abruptly. She dusted off her skirt and shook out her hair. She'd left it unbound that morning, unable to find the will to coil it up and bind it tight.

"I know you're tired, Jane," he said softly. "But this isn't going to end. Werthog doesn't know where you are, and I'm grateful. It's bought us some time, and it's given you a chance to rest. But he's not going to stop looking for you. Sundance was right about that."

"He has no right," she whispered. "No claim."

"It don't matter, honey. I learned that lesson a long time ago. Powerful men—rich men—do whatever they want." He paused, gathering his thoughts. "I want you far away from here. Two thousand miles isn't far enough, but it's better. It's a start. And I've got enough money that I won't need to teach you to rob trains."

He grinned, and she tried to laugh with him, but her face stayed frozen. She didn't want to take his money, his love, and his care and give him nothing in return. She had absolutely *nothing* to give him.

"You won't have to sing either, if you don't want. I certainly wouldn't recommend it for a while, though the thought makes me so mad I can't breathe. You sing like an angel. The world needs angels. And he's taken that from you and from all of us. It ain't right. And nothing burns me more than injustice. He's going to have to be dealt with, but right now, I just want you and Augustus as far away from him as I can get you. Maybe you can still sing at Saltair. We'll try to coordinate something when we get to Utah, but if not, we'll just keep moving until he tires of traipsing all over the West and goes back to England."

She hadn't seen Sundance all day. Van had left after breakfast wearing the yellow cashmere suit that had been Oliver's favorite. She was guessing Noble hadn't given it to him. He'd been furtive about it, and when he cut through the backyard and saw her watching him, he'd winked and held his finger to his lips. She liked Van, oddly enough, but his presence weighed heavy on Noble.

The whole world weighed heavy on Noble, yet he bore it and asked nothing in return.

She stood, smoothing her skirts, and he rose too, looking down at her, unsure of himself, unsure of her. She still hadn't given him an answer.

"Come with me," she demanded, turning and striding for the house. Her blood surged and her ears rang, a delayed cymbal to the timpani of her heart.

Emma was baking, and Augustus had taken over the room Dr. Laszo had vacated, though at night he still insisted on sleeping on the couch near her and Noble.

She'd been relieved to have him there. She wasn't sure what was expected of her when she and Noble were alone. Augustus had provided an excuse, though Noble had not made an advance. He'd held her hand and kissed her brow, but nothing more. He'd let her heal and brood.

That would end now. She had something she could give him. Something a real wife—and she wanted to be a real wife to him—would give her husband. She just had to be brave.

She rushed up the stairs, determined, and Noble followed after her, slower. Steadier. Still unsure. As soon as he entered the room, she shut it behind him and locked it.

"Jane?"

She stepped into him and slid her arms around his neck, drawing his head to hers like she'd done days before. His mouth was soft amid the prickles, and she was immediately at home, immediately reassured. This was Noble, and she loved Noble.

He kissed her back, following her lead, but when she pressed closer, went deeper, drawing his hands to the swell of her bottom, he froze.

"What are you doing, honey?" His voice had gone soft and his eyes were closed, like he didn't want her to see him. She was immediately on guard, stiff and uncomfortable, and his arms clamped around her, keeping her close. "I'm not asking you to stop. I'm just asking . . . what you're doing."

"I like kissing you."

"I like kissing you too. But this is something else. So I'm asking if you like that too." He ran a hand over her hair and down her back, one long stroke, and put his hands back where she'd placed them.

Ice and heat warred in her veins. She wanted to bolt. And she wanted to bear down.

"Please touch me, Noble," she said, and the heat in her blood became a flood of embarrassment.

He kissed her again, coaxing her sweetly, finally—*thank heaven*— leading the way. When she pressed herself against him, his big hands were gentle on her flesh, kneading and nuzzling, and the coiling in her belly began again, beating back the fear, warring with her shame. She grew desperate, afraid that this new, delicious desire would abandon her and disgust would come crashing down.

She suckled his throat and bit at his lobes, wanting to get closer and wanting to tear him apart. It boiled in her, that dichotomy, and when he offered her his mouth again, she took it, suckling his lips and seeking his tongue. He gave it to her, returning sweetness for venom and tenderness for teeth. She drew blood and he didn't withdraw, but held her face in his hands, stroking her cheeks with his thumbs, and whispering her name.

"Jane. Honey. My sweet Jane."

"I need you to help me," she panted, close to tears. Close to disintegration.

"You take whatever you need," he said, but his body was hard against hers, and it both angered and aroused her.

When she clawed at his belt and tore at his buttons, he loosed them for her, and bared his skin to her hands and his heart to her lips. And still she bruised him, trying to love and needing to mark, not understanding herself or the need that pulsed in her head and in her belly.

"I need you to touch me," she implored again, but she didn't recognize her voice. She was panicked and impassioned, clueless and cruel. And his hands stayed motionless, holding her gently, the weight of his palms like ballast to her fury.

She pressed her face into the crook of his neck, and slid her hands over his hips, needing to face what she most feared, to separate passion from pain and coupling from force. His breath caught, but he remained still, letting her find her way.

Fear and fury bloomed and bore terrible fruit. She pushed him away, pushed herself away, and moaned in shame and disgust, grinding her palms into her eyes. She could smell his loamy flesh and her body burned in a way she couldn't interpret, making her moan again.

"This is not what I want. I told you no. I told you no kisses. And yet here we are, pawing at each other like animals. This is not what I want."

She had stunned him, but he didn't protest.

"All right, honey," he whispered, but when she told him to get out—*Get out!*—his jaw was tight and his blue eyes weren't mild or kind anymore.

She'd finally made him angry.

Without a word, he righted his clothes, buttoning and tucking, and snapped his suspenders into place. Then he turned and walked out of the room, hands shoved in his pockets, leaving her behind like he couldn't get out of the room fast enough. The door swung widely, slamming into the wall and leaving a dent from the door handle. Before it had even closed she was striding after him.

"Come back here, Noble Salt!" she demanded, stamping her foot. "You are in my employ, sir. And I am not finished with you."

"We're finished for today, honey."

She was almost running to keep up with him, and she felt like a fool, but he made her crazy. She was a raving, lust-filled lunatic in his company, a complete stranger to herself.

"What is that supposed to mean?" she cried.

"I don't want to talk to you right now, Jane. You're hurting. And it's hurting me."

"I am not hurting you!" The thought horrified her, mostly because she knew it was true.

"You're on that teeter-totter, up and down, hot and cold. And I understand. At least I think I do. But I can't bear any more right now. So you take your pretty self back upstairs and let me walk it out. Okay?"

He took the stairs with a great deal more speed than he'd climbed them. She was right behind him.

"No. Not okay. I have things to say. And I'm paying you to listen." She was ridiculously close to tears, but she fought them back.

"You're not paying me for a damn thing, and you know it. We've gone way beyond that, Jane Boot. If anything, you hired me to protect you, and that's what I'm doing right now. I'm protecting you *from me*."

She reached out and grasped his hand as they reached the landing, sliding her palm against the weathered skin, and he stopped immediately, tense, though he didn't look down at her or even shift his gaze at all. He was rigid and straight, his hand in hers.

"I am . . . I am sorry," she choked. "Please don't go." She lifted his hand and pressed it to her lips and then rested it above her breasts so his knuckles sat against her heart. The tears had begun to seep from her eyes and dribble down her cheeks.

"Please . . . wait."

He did, his hand against her heart, his eyes trained ahead, and she gathered her courage and searched her soul for sanity.

"I have been beastly to you," she whispered.

He exhaled in a great whoosh, and his chin dropped to his chest. She clung to his hand, pressing it back to her lips, and he let her, though he didn't turn toward her.

After a painful moment, he spoke, his voice so kind she broke anew.

"You haven't been loved hard enough. You haven't been loved well enough. And you're like a little wounded she-wolf, snapping at me and licking your wounds."

"You s-scare me," she babbled.

He sighed again, like the weight of the world was sitting on his chest. "I know."

"I'm afraid I'm going to lose you."

"You're *trying* to lose me."

"No."

"Yes, honey. Yes. You're testing me. And I can take it. But I need a minute."

"I'm afraid . . . you'll grow sick of me . . . or I'll grow sick of you."

"Yeah. I know that too."

"I won't be good at this, Noble." She swallowed, trying to beat back her panic. "I'm afraid I won't be good at it."

"Good at what?"

"At loving you."

"Do you *want* to love me?"

"No," she wailed, and he laughed, breaking the tension that pressed upon them in the narrow stairwell.

"It's not like singing," she explained, desperate. "It does not come naturally. At all. I don't know what to do."

"No," he breathed. "It's not like singing. And it's not like riding. Or running, or thieving. It's not like anything in the world."

"You're going to have to help me. And you're going to have to forgive me for being . . . the way that I am. I d-don't know what to do," she said again, imploring him to understand.

"I don't know what to do either, honey. Never been here before. Never been in love before. But maybe we just . . . stop running . . . and let it happen."

"If you hadn't noticed, I was running after you," she retorted.

He chuckled and turned so he could press his brow to hers.

"That's a start. That's definitely a start."

She stood a full step above him, giving her a height advantage, but he didn't try to embrace her, and his body still thrummed like he expected her to bite.

"I'm so sorry, Noble. I can do better," she said, her tears falling in earnest. "I know I can."

"I don't need better."

"Yes, you do. And I want to give it to you."

"Just let me love you, Jane," he said. "That's all I want."

"Why?" It made absolutely no sense. "Why me?"

He was silent for a moment, thinking. "You make me believe . . . what my mother used to say. Some folks are just ours."

"You're speaking in hokku again," she said, trying to make him smile, but his words had struck a chord, and neither of them laughed.

Some people are just ours.

"Yeah," he murmured. "I guess I am. Bad habit. But it doesn't make it any less true."

"Next time . . . next time will be different," she promised.

"Okay," he said simply, accepting her declaration, but he pulled his hand from her heart and ran it over her tangled hair and across her tearstained face before turning away.

"I'll be back in a bit," he whispered, and she climbed the stairs again. Alone.

22

Time to catch a train
The whistle's getting louder
Telling me to run

The Plaza Hotel was so new that the sharp tang of fresh paint and plaster was even stronger than the pungent cigar he smoked in the lounge in his fancy yellow suit. The color was a nice contrast with his Parker blue eyes, but he wasn't trying to hide them. Not now. He'd been careful in his preparation and wanted to look the part. No sweat. No grime. No hesitation. He planned to bring a whole new level of attention to the grand opening. They should pay him for publicity.

He'd wondered what name he should use when he walked through the doors, but nobody asked. The doorman called him sir. The waiter too. The man who commented on the cigar they were both smoking—"best one I've ever had"—didn't seem to want to chat beyond that.

To live in such a world, where everyone was rich and good-looking— or maybe good-looking because they were rich—was something he could get used to. Everyone had a polish, a sheen that he knew he'd never have, no matter how often he shined his shoes or how much he spent on his clothes. He looked like what he was, a stupid, broad-faced farm boy from the middle of nowhere, and that made him a little nervous. He couldn't get too comfortable.

He only waited an hour, though he'd expected to wait much more. The earl walked into the lounge where he sat, ordered a drink, and conversed briefly with a man who looked like a Pinkerton.

That made him squirm too, and he almost abandoned his plan, but the encounter was brief. The Pinkerton handed the earl a file, and the earl paid him promptly, peeling off a bill like it was beneath him to pay at all. The Pink shook his head, shoved a cigar in his mouth, and walked out of the hotel lounge without a backward glance. Not a man loyal to the earl. Not a servant or a valet. An American, definitely, and not one impressed with British airs. Yep. Probably a Pink. Or maybe just an off-duty deputy picking up extra work.

The earl moved toward the soaring lobby, never stopping to read the file or even glance over his shoulder. Never suspecting a thing. Completely unaware of the shadow behind him on the wide staircase. He didn't check the hall when he opened the big door with 413 stenciled in gold on the pristine surface.

Four thirteen. Butch's birthday. It was destiny.

Parker walked up to the door and knocked. Firm, but not angry. Twice, but no more.

Knock, knock.

The earl didn't even ask, *Who's there?* He just opened the door. He hadn't yet slipped off his shoes or removed his collar. He hadn't poured himself a drink. Maybe he didn't plan on staying. Too bad for him. He wasn't going anywhere now.

The earl's brow lowered and then rose, recognition dawning. "Ahh, Mr. Salt." This time he did look from side to side, down the long corridor and back again, his eyes narrowed. Not a soul was in sight, and still . . . he ushered him in. *Stupid Englishman.*

"You were wise to come, Mr. Salt," he said. "Or did Jane send you? I'm sure she realizes now that I won't be trifled with. I need a bloody heir, and I'll be bringing the boy back to London, with or without her."

The earl turned toward his snifter with the same disdain he'd shown the Pink, expecting information. Expecting a report. Expecting everything except for what he got.

Which was dead.

Bang, bang.

The bang was no louder than the knock on the door—he'd even thought that through—but the Plaza was going to have to change out the brand-new carpet and repaint one of the walls in room 413. After a cursory look in the mirror to make sure he hadn't picked up any red spatters, he did a quick search of the room.

The folder was next to the snifter, along with the room key. Whoever the Pinkerton was, he'd discovered where Jane and Augustus were staying, and he'd written up a report with Emma's address front and center. That wasn't good. Or maybe it was very good. Consider them all warned.

He almost didn't read the rest. He needed to hurry, but his eyes strayed and caught, and he mouthed each word as quickly as he could.

Mrs. Emma Harvey, proprietor of the home listed above, is the sister of Harry Longabaugh, also known as the Sundance Kid. Longabaugh is wanted for grand larceny in several western states, along with Robert Parker, aka Butch Cassidy. Two men matching the description of the two fugitives have been seen at this establishment and are believed to be boarders of Mrs. Harvey. Consider them armed and dangerous.

Whether Mrs. Toussaint and her bodyguard are aware of the identities of the two men is not known. The boarders work at the piers and frequently shuttle passengers from the steamers to their various lodgings. Mrs. Harvey has a constant stream of short-term renters. Madame Toussaint, her security guard, and her son are also in residence.

I have not notified authorities and will wait for your instruction, but recommend that a dispatch be sent to US Marshals and an arrest coordinated before we make any attempt to contact or collect Mrs. Toussaint and her son. Doing so could put them and any other residents at undue risk. Proceed with caution.

A circular from the Pinkerton Detective Agency was included in the file. Butch Cassidy and Harry Longabaugh looked up from the page, half a dozen years younger and nattily dressed, their descriptions and crimes listed in two neat columns. Another photo featured Butch from his arrest in Wyoming, his face puffy, his hair matted from his hat. It didn't look anything like him.

"Well, I'll be damned," he whispered. "I'll be damned. I'm thinking the earl hadn't seen this yet."

Whether the earl had seen the information before he opened the door didn't matter at this point, but he'd have to make sure they weren't followed when they left for the train station in the morning. It would be a nervous night, but the Pink—or whoever the hired man was—would be "waiting for the earl's instructions," and no instructions would be forthcoming.

He considered the earl's collection of cuff links, but he wouldn't wear them. Still, he took them and dropped them into the earl's valise. The bottom was lined with neat stacks of cash.

"Jackpot," he said, grinning. His luck was definitely changing.

The missing valuables might make it look like a robbery, and he'd earned them.

He wasn't going to tell anyone. Not for a while. Even though it would make everyone feel so much better. Especially Gus. The poor kid had wanted to do it himself, but he'd been saved from that. Saved from everything. They all had.

He left the room two minutes after he'd entered it. Maybe less. He passed a couple on the stairs, but they were discussing dinner plans and the "disappointing" reception they'd just been to. They didn't even glance at him.

He whistled "Waly, Waly" all the way home and realized it sounded like a completely different song when the tempo changed. It was almost cheerful the way he did it, like a marching tune instead of a funeral dirge.

The thought gave him a twinge for his mother, and he tipped his hat in her memory.

The ferry ride back was uneventful, the evening walk no more than a pleasant jaunt, and he was sure no one followed.

He was even home in time for dinner.

∽

When night fell and bedtime came, Jane was rigid with dread. Augustus wanted to spend his last night at Emma's house sleeping in a bed, and he'd abandoned her in favor of the spare room.

"Nothing's changed, honey," Noble said, turning down the lamp.

"No?"

"No. You're nervous as a cat. You're thinking you've got to give me something now that we're alone. That's not how this works. I'm not taking anything you aren't ready for."

"You're not taking. I'm giving," she said, trying to figure out what to do with her hands. She set them on his shoulders and then on his waist before folding them over her heart.

"Like the first kiss you gave me?" he asked gently.

"What?"

"You gave me a kiss the night we met. But you didn't do it because you wanted to. You did it because you thought you owed me. I don't ever want another kiss like that."

"I wanted to kiss you. I just got scared."

"I've thought about that kiss a thousand times over the years, and it's always embarrassed me. I got carried away. I shouldn't have done that."

"But . . ."

"But nothing. Go to sleep." He dropped a kiss on her head and turned over, belly to the mattress, pushing his head beneath the pillow.

"But . . ."

"Shh. I'm so tired, honey," he said, voice muffled.

"Okay," she whispered.

"Okay."

She sighed, and all the knots and coils that had been building in her belly the moment he'd lain down beside her dissolved into lovely relief. She wrapped one hand around his upper arm, enjoying the heft and the heat of it. *Oh, how she loved him.* Tears pricked her eyes and sleep crept over her limbs.

"I love you," she murmured, though she'd only intended to thank him.

He was silent, but she heard the small intake of breath and felt the tremor in his arm. He didn't respond, and that too was a relief.

But sometime during the night, the arm she clutched had encircled her, the warm flesh of his palm cradled her face, and she was no longer fearful or afraid, no longer intimidated by her own need or ashamed by her own confusion. And she pressed a kiss to that open palm, holding it to her mouth and breathing in the warmth and flavor of him, the comfort of him, and he curled his fingers around her jaw and lifted her face to his.

He wasn't as careful or as cautious as he'd been before. But neither was she, and one kiss became another and another, until they paused to breathe, wrapped around each other, her lips pressed to his throat, his lips in her hair, and they fell asleep again, almost like they'd dreamed together, taken flight together, and drifted back down, never waking.

But the morning bore witness to the nocturnal nuzzling.

Her lips were raw, her cheeks mottled, and when Augustus stumbled out of his room in search of breakfast, waking them both, Butch stared down at her, his eyes widening in horror.

"Oh, Jane. Oh, honey. I'm sorry."

"Why?"

"Your face . . . it's all red and scratched. Your lips are swollen too. I . . . I kissed you too much."

She jerked up, the covers sliding around her waist, and scampered to the mirror. She looked like she'd run headlong through a mile of brambles. Even her hair was beyond description.

"Oh no." She covered her mouth, horrified, and her shoulders began to shake with quiet mirth.

"Are you crying?" Noble asked, rising from the bed and coming to stand beside her. He was glorious in all his rumpled, half-clad worry. How odd to be so at ease with someone and so completely enamored.

"No, my darling. I am laughing."

His eyes crinkled, and he ran a hand over her wild mane. "I'll be gentle," he whispered, and he leaned in to kiss her again, barely touching his lips to her swollen mouth, but she loved him so much. And the tenderness on her skin only amplified the enormity of her feelings. She *liked* kissing.

Before she knew it, she was wrapped around him again, limbs and long hair, and he walked them back to the bed, where reverence and revelry continued until a door slammed down below and the smells of breakfast wafted up from Emma's kitchen.

He rolled away from her, plummeting them both back to reality. His feet hit the floor and he rose, pulling on his trousers over his drawers and snapping his suspenders into place over his undershirt.

"I'll see to our boy, though Emma has a firm grip on the grub. I'll find a paper too. See what we're dealing with today. Then we got a train to catch."

His mention of a paper knotted her stomach and her skin stung anew. They'd been watching for the articles Hugo had warned were coming, though there'd been no sign of anything yet.

"'Grub'?" she asked.

"Food, my English wife."

She liked the way he called her *wife.* "Noble?"

"Yeah, honey?"

"I do love you," she said in a rush.

"You don't need to tell me that," he said gently. "I told you . . . you don't owe me anything."

"You do not understand what you have done for me, Robert LeRoy Parker."

He shook his head, resisting the name, the way he seemed to do every time she addressed him, as if nothing felt right, as if every name she tried to hang on him was an ill-fitting suit coat that pulled across his shoulders and restricted his arms.

"No. Don't shake your head," she scolded.

He stopped immediately.

"Please look at me."

He did, his eyes so bright she knew he was struggling with his own emotion.

"You have given me something I have never had before."

He ducked his head.

"You love me. I don't know why. I don't know how I got so lucky."

He grimaced again, and she crossed the distance between them and cupped his face in her palms.

"Augustus proved to me—and he keeps proving it every day—that who we are has little to do with the circumstances of our births. I marvel at that constantly. And then there's you."

"Then there's me."

"I've stopped trying to unravel sorrow from joy and pain from happiness. It's impossible to do, because they so often go together. And it doesn't make sense. My love for my son didn't make sense. I loved him before I held him in my arms, even though . . ."

"Even though," he agreed, not making her say what he already understood.

"So love doesn't always make sense."

"No."

"Some people are just ours."

"Some people are just ours," he repeated, his eyes soft.

"You take care of us so well, I hardly know what to do with myself."

"I've always been good at taking care of people. But I've taken care of the wrong people and hurt the people who needed me most. I don't deserve you," he whispered. "I know I don't. But the way I love you . . . I don't even care if you love me back."

She was so stunned, for a moment she had no reply, and he pulled on his clothes and stepped into the washroom, shutting the door behind him to make use of the plumbing and the sink.

She was waiting outside the door when he opened it again.

She stepped into him and wrapped her arms around his middle and pressed her lips to his heart.

"But I do love you back," she said, careful to enunciate each word so he could not misunderstand. Then she stepped around him and slipped into the washroom, ending the conversation.

Noble shaved his beard but left his mustache. Maman said he looked a decade younger, Sundance stared in disgust, and Van promptly went upstairs to shave his beard too. Van wanted to be just like Butch. It drove Noble crazy, but Augustus understood exactly how he felt.

"We're leaving for Utah on a train," Sundance said. "Today. Utah. Where you're still wanted, dead or alive, for armed robbery. And you removed the only disguise you have. Why?"

"I didn't like it. Never have liked it," Noble said, eyes twinkling. Maman was blushing furiously. She was powdered and fixed with rouge and lipstick like she was getting ready to perform, but they were going to Grand Central Station.

From there, they would take the train all the way to Salt Lake City.

He was so excited he couldn't eat. Or he couldn't eat as much. He didn't want to disappoint Emma, who'd made him all his favorites.

"I thought you were the smart brother," Sundance continued to complain. "You're going to get us all caught."

"You don't look any different than you did when we left out, Harry. I think that's even the same hat," Noble responded mildly. "Maybe it's you who'll get us all caught."

"The woman and the boy are all anyone will be looking at anyway," Sundance conceded. "But I wish you'd left well enough alone."

"We're not going to be in Utah long," Noble reassured him.

"We're not?" Augustus asked. Maman seemed surprised by that too.

"No. We're not. There's someone waiting for Sundance in San Francisco."

"Damn you, Butch," Sundance muttered, and rose from the table. "Nobody's waiting for me anywhere."

Noble went on as if Sundance hadn't even spoken. "And nobody knows me in Frisco. Nobody will know any of us . . . I hope." He shot a look at Maman. "We'll spend a week in Utah, maybe two. I want to show you my valley, and I need to see my dad."

When Sundance left to hitch the horses to the coach and Augustus helped Emma clear breakfast away, he could hear Maman and Noble talking. Maman wasn't happy with Noble either. She was worried about him.

"Why did you shave your beard? You're putting yourself at risk."

"I don't want to stop kissing you, and the beard hurts your skin. So the beard had to go. It's that simple, honey."

"Your priorities—"

"My priorities are exactly where they should be," he interrupted. "I spent my whole life waiting for you. And I don't want to miss a single minute of loving you."

"But your jaw is so square, and you look much more like the circular without your beard. And you are so handsome. People will stare. Someone will recognize you."

"I won't smile."

"No, you should. You are very disarming. It is your eyes that I worry about most. You'll have to pull your hat low to shade them a bit . . . and don't make eye contact! I do think the way you dress—you look very fine, very smart—is wise. You look like a businessman, not a cowboy. You are very much a gentleman. But I do wish you'd kept the beard," she fretted.

"Come here, honey. Let me show you why I shaved the beard."

Augustus wrinkled his nose in disgust and gagged aloud.

Emma saw his face and grinned, patting his head.

"They are very much in love, my boy. It's nice. Don't ruin it for them."

"I'm going to miss you, Emma. I wish you could come with us," he said. He loved her cheerful home and her food and her flowers. He loved the poker games and the Wild Bunch gang and the way Noble took such good care of Maman. No one had ever taken care of Maman.

Augustus suddenly wanted to halt time, to stay put, and even told Noble that he had a bad feeling about the trip. It was one thing to read about the Wild West, it was another thing to go there, and he liked everything about New York City.

"We are so happy here. And so safe. Can't we stay for a little longer?" he'd asked as they loaded their trunks in the wagon. Emma's oldest son, Evan, and her grandson, Francis, were going to take them to the station and bring Harry's coach back to the house.

"It wasn't mine to begin with," Harry said, shrugging. "So I don't mind leaving it."

He was eager to go, Van too, and Augustus imagined them shedding their skins as they got closer to Utah. Utah was an Apache Indian word, Noble said. It meant people of the mountains. Maybe Van, Sundance, and Noble were people of the mountains, but Augustus wasn't so sure about him and Maman.

"It's not as safe here as you might think," Van said, shoving at the last trunk. "Too many people. You'll love the West. A man could walk for days and never see another soul."

Noble just straightened his cap and leaned down so they were eye to eye. "I'm not going to let anything happen to you or your mother, Gus."

"But what if something happens to you?" he said to himself, chewing his lip, but he forgot his trepidations when they descended into the belly of Grand Central Station. The light that poured through a wall of windows onto the grimy tunnels and tracks looked like a sign from heaven itself.

Sundance and Van walked on either side of him, his mother and Noble made a wall in front, and nobody stared or even seemed to notice him at all. His spirits continued to lift as they boarded a green Pullman private car so opulent and spacious, it challenged the comfort of the staterooms on the *Adriatic*, and Maman joked that no dolphins would be stealing her hats on this journey.

It was the last car on the Overland Express, and though the train wasn't anywhere near the size of an ocean liner and the lounge and dining cars weren't as big as the ballrooms, the private cars were just as well appointed. In addition to the private car, they had two additional sleep compartments with two bunks apiece. Noble said Maman should have the bedroom in the Pullman car to herself, for privacy, and Gus could share one of the bunkrooms with him.

"How long will we be on the train?" he asked, his nose pressed to the window, watching the people scramble to board other cars. A row of men sat on platformed chairs between the tracks, newspapers open, capped boys shining their shoes.

"It's a day and a half to Chicago. Half a day to St. Louis, and two more to Salt Lake City. This train is fast, and it's smooth," Noble said, reassuring his mother.

"It should be. Fare in a Pullman Palace costs more than a good hand makes in four months," Van said, shaking his head. His face looked odd without the beard. It was pale where he'd shaved, a half-moon dotted with little nicks and sores. He needed a better barber. Maybe Noble, whose cheeks were buttery smooth, could help him next time.

Without their beards, they looked less alike, though their relationship was obvious. Van had a fuller lower lip and his jaw wasn't quite as square. Noble had a divot in his chin that Maman had pressed her thumb into with a little smile. She'd blushed and looked away, like she'd forgotten herself, but Augustus hadn't missed it.

His mother was so changed. It hadn't even been three weeks since they'd set sail from Cherbourg, and he hardly recognized her. She reminded him of a painting. He and Maman had spent many early mornings in the Grande Galerie of the Louvre before the corridors filled with people who would stare at him instead of the walls. His cold, hard vase of a mother had become the *Mona Lisa* with a secret smile and blurred edges.

"What are you grumbling about, Rip?" Sundance murmured, stretched out over a tufted chair. "You didn't pay for it. You never do."

"Did you get a paper, Noble?" Maman asked suddenly, her eyes trained on the shoeshine station. Two more men sat down on the platform, snapped their papers open in sync, and revealed a thick black headline that took up half the page.

Murder at the Plaza

The whistle blew and the train shuddered, drowning out Noble's reply. Augustus cheered, and Van grinned. Even Sundance looked excited.

They were on their way.

23

You opened me up
And took my heart from my chest
Now how will I live?

The sense of well-being Butch had enjoyed on the voyage from Paris to New York was glaringly absent, and were it not for the flush of wonder he felt whenever he looked at Jane Toussaint, four days on a train with Van and Sundance would have driven him to violence.

The first-class dining car made Butch nervous—he'd had a pit in his stomach since they'd boarded—and he mandated that they remain in the private compartment as much as possible. When the porter knocked, Van—the only one without a reason to hide his face—was the one who answered and interacted. The rest of them moved into the bedroom and waited until the porter left.

The opulence of their accommodations didn't make the forced proximity much easier. There were no decks to stroll or rehearsals to attend like on the *Adriatic*, but Jane tolerated the train better than the ship, and Augustus was his normal agreeable self, entertaining them with his conversation and quick wit.

Augustus had won both the outlaws over, and Harry Longabaugh was not a particularly easy or congenial man. Van was. Van was all kinds of nice, but his decision-making was flawed and his vision short-sighted.

Gus had begun to call him Uncle Van, which pleased Butch's brother no end but set Butch's teeth on edge.

Van regaled Augustus with stories about Butch that bore little resemblance to what really happened, and Augustus had listened with wonder and considerable disappointment when Butch adjusted the stories to the truth.

"Has Butch told you about Betty?" Van asked, his gaze jumping between Jane and Augustus.

"Van," Butch warned.

"She wasn't much to look at. Not like Miss Jane," Van teased, shooting Butch a wicked grin. "But she's the only girl my brother has ever loved . . . until now, of course."

"Betty?" Jane asked, a wary look on her face.

"Betty was a horse owned by a friend of mine. A mousy, scrawny mutt of a mare," Butch clarified. "She was half blind too. Could only see out her left eye."

"And that little girl could run," Van supplied.

"I've never seen the like," Sundance joined in. "Where did you first see her race, Butch?"

"Telluride." Butch met Jane's eyes briefly. He'd told her Telluride had not been good for him. Betty was just another reason why.

"She'd been put up against the Mulcahy colt," Van continued. "Everyone bet against her. Even Butch."

"I'd seen the Mulcahy colt run and knew it hadn't ever been beat," Butch said.

"Betty won?" Jane asked.

"Betty won easily," Butch answered. "She wasn't even breathing hard."

Van picked up where he'd left off. "Butch told Matt Warner—the friend that owned the horse—that with him in the saddle, she could go even faster."

"Did she?" Augustus pressed.

"Boy, did she ever," Van hooted. "Butch and Matt raced her from one small town to the next. Everyone laughed at poor Betty and bet against her, making Butch and Matt a lot of money when she smoked the competition. But word of the Betty hustle started to spread, and nobody would race her anymore. Nobody but the Navajo. Right, Butch? You think Betty's still racing? Or do you think she died of a broken heart when you took off outta there without her?"

"I don't know, Van," he said. He hated this story. It filled him with shame, but Van loved it.

"What happened to Betty?" Augustus prodded, his brown eyes big. Butch should have known the little horse that didn't look like a champion would appeal to the boy.

"Butch and Matt and a big, mean son of a gun named Tom McCarty took Betty to race against some Navajo Indians in a place called McElmo Gulch in Colorado. They hadn't heard about Betty, and were conned just like everyone else by her appearance."

"I hadn't heard this part," Sundance said, showing new interest in the story.

Van smiled, enjoying the rapt attention of everyone in the car. Butch rose and poured himself a glass of water, unable to sit down for the rest.

"When Butch and Betty won—handily—the Navajo refused to pay up," Van said. "They said they'd been tricked."

"Van . . . this isn't a good story," Butch muttered. Jane was watching him, her head cocked, a groove between her dark brows.

"McCarty lost his temper. Started shooting, even though he, Warner, and Butch were surrounded by two hundred braves. They were lucky to get out of there alive, and Butch had to leave sweet Betty behind."

"Is that why it's not a good story?" Augustus asked.

"It's not a good story because McCarty killed a brave in cold blood over a horse race," Butch answered. "Leaving Betty was the least I could do."

"He left everything else he had too," Van said, still jovial. "And that was the end of his racing days, right, Butch? He never got over Betty. She's still in McElmo Gulch wondering when he's going to come back for her. Kinda like poor Ethel and Sundance."

Van never knew when to stop. Sundance rose and poured himself a drink too. But it wasn't water.

"Butch was always leaving everything behind." Van was still going strong. "He paid off a widow's mortgage in a little town in Wyoming . . . or was it Colorado . . . and then robbed the bank the next day and got all his money back." He threw his head back and laughed. "That always made me laugh."

"You weren't even there, Van," Butch sighed. "For any of it."

"Sundance was. He told me all about it. There ain't nothing about you I don't know, brother."

"I robbed a bank in Denver, paid the mortgage off in Cortez. Wasn't the same town at all."

"Who was the widow?" Jane asked, and the wary look was back.

"Her husband was a sheriff, from what I remember," Sundance offered, his eyes on his whiskey. "He took the side of some homesteaders over a big cattle outfit, and the outfit took him out, though nobody could ever prove it."

"Nobody ever tried. They never do," Butch said, and remembering made him angry all over again. It'd been fifteen years ago or more, but he still remembered the devastation on the woman's face when her husband, one of the few lawmen Butch respected, had shown up dead, tied to his saddle.

"She had a son, about Gus's age," Butch said. "They didn't just kill her husband. They tried to get the bank to call in her note."

"Butch has a soft spot for the widows and their sons," Van said, winking.

"What was her name?" Jane asked.

Butch shrugged. "Her husband's name was Conrad—Connie—Clark. That's all I know."

"Maybe it was Betty," Van said, straight-faced.

Augustus laughed at him, and Van was off again, this time elaborating on all Butch's near misses and lucky breaks.

"He was shot at, point-blank, gun pressed to his belly. Gun didn't go off. Gun didn't go off again. Butch turned and ran. Deputy fired for the third time, but it was a wild shot and whizzed over his head, taking a tiny bit of scalp with it. Butch still has the scar, don't you, brother?" Van reached over and felt the back of Butch's head, searching for the scar.

Butch sighed, but Augustus wanted to see—Jane did too—and everyone had to feel the nickel-sized bald spot normally covered by his hair.

"Then there was the Montpelier bank job," Van said, never tiring. "Butch and Meeks—Meeks is as gentle an outlaw as you'll ever meet—trained a little sorrel to follow them, even if they got separated. At the bank, they loaded her down with bags of cash, but in the excitement of the getaway, they got way ahead of her. Elzy Lay—you ever told them about Elzy, Butch?—Elzy was moaning and complaining, certain they'd lost their take. But Butch just waited, patient, and told Elzy and Meeks to stay hidden and wait too."

"Noble is very patient," Augustus said, and Jane smiled, her eyes soft, easing some of his discomfort.

"Sure enough, that little mare—Butch has a way with the mares—showed up about two hours later, plodding along, saddlebags full of cash—fifteen thousand dollars—and off they went. That was the money that got Matt Warner out of jail, wasn't it?"

"That was also the money that got you outta jail," Sundance grumbled. "Can we stop now?"

The first night, bedtime came with such relief that Butch fell into his bottom berth—Augustus wanted the top—and wouldn't have awakened had the US Marshals come bursting through the door.

By the second night, just outside St. Louis, Missouri, and halfway through their trip, he missed Jane so much, he wondered if he could sneak into her bedroom and climb in beside her. The nights at Emma's had spoiled him forever, and he just wanted to be close to her, but he refused to make assumptions. Jane needed to go slow, though the three weeks since they'd come together felt like a strange lifetime, a lesson in patience and awakening.

He stayed in his berth and listened to Gus prattle on about Betty the racehorse until his voice faded off and sleep pulled him under. When Butch heard a light tapping on his door, he sat up so fast his head collided with the underside of the upper bunk, and he swallowed a curse and lunged for the door, praying it was her and afraid she'd leave if he didn't answer fast enough.

Her hair was loose, and she wore a nightgown covered by a robe, but her smile was brittle. She stepped inside the compartment and rose up on her toes so she could see that Gus was slumbering.

"You are my husband," she said, her eyes still trained on her son. She drew the little drape around his berth.

Butch didn't want to argue or clarify. She'd married Noble Salt, and he didn't exist. Butch Cassidy had no real claim. He'd been committed—all in—the moment she'd given him the first-class ticket on the Rue Lamartine, but he had no expectations of her. He didn't let himself think about anything but the immediate future.

"You should sleep with me," she continued. "Not Augustus. There are no stops until morning, and he knows where we are."

"Is that what you want?"

"That's what I want."

᳕

He followed her from the compartment and into the private car, but the moment they were alone, he swept her up, hugging her so tight, her feet came off the floor.

"I missed you," he said.

She hugged him back, swamped by her own longing. She tried to tell him she'd missed him too, but the words stuck in her throat. They felt wholly incomplete, a little white flag of surrender to a long and bloody war. She had missed him too. She missed him now, and his arms were locked around her. But then he let her go, pulling back so he could look down into her upturned face.

"I'm going to kiss you now," he said. "Anytime you don't like something. Anytime you're scared or uncomfortable, you tell me. I'll stop."

Her chin hit her chest and she covered her eyes with her hands. She even groaned.

"What? What did I say?"

"You are so kind. Why are you so good to me? I don't deserve it."

He pulled her hands away and held them to his heart. "I love you. Always have. From the moment I saw you, you owned me."

"I wish that were true," she said, trying jest to escape the emotional onslaught his honesty unleashed in her. "I was supposed to be the boss in this arrangement. But somehow . . . you have been in charge since day one."

"You own me, Jane," he repeated. "Heart and soul."

"See? That's what I'm talking about. What kind of man admits that? What kind of man says that?"

"A man who's tired of lies and lying. A man who's never known who the hell he is. A man who doesn't even have a name."

"You have a name."

"I don't. I have a dozen, and not one of them feels like it's mine."

"You are Noble Salt."

"That isn't my name."

"Yes, it is. It's who you are to me and Augustus."

"It's who I *want* to be. I've never wanted anything so much. If I could, I would just be your Noble Salt forever."

"Why can't you be?" she blurted.

He was silent, like he was trying to find the answer. But he didn't give her one.

"I'm forty-one years old. Older than my dad was when I left home. And I thought he was an old man." He laughed, the sound painful and dry. "He *was* an old man. An old man with thirteen kids and nothing but hard work behind him and hard work in front of him. No wonder folks age so fast. Life is too hard to take much more than fifty years. But I'm not old the way my dad is. The way he was. I'm like that Peter Pan character in the play Gus told me about."

"He loved that play. We've seen it multiple times."

"He didn't want to grow up, because he knew what that meant. It meant never being free, never seeing anything but the valley you were born in."

"But Peter Pan wants to be loved."

"Yeah. Augustus explained that part too. The thing with love is . . . we have to take it when it's offered. We don't get to mold it like clay. Peter Pan wanted to love like a man but stay a boy. Doesn't work like that."

"No."

"That's why . . . that's why, no matter how pretty the face or how welcome a kiss, it wasn't enough for me. It wasn't worth the trap. It wasn't worth growing up. I had my own band of lost boys. And hell . . . were we ever lost."

"Van is still a lost boy."

"Yeah. He is."

"But you aren't Peter Pan," she argued. "Not anymore."

Again, he shifted, answering indirectly, circling around a simple response, as if he was thinking out loud.

"I have never loved a woman before. I thought it wasn't in me. All the boys had ladies. Some even had wives."

"But not you?" It was so hard for her to believe.

"Not me. There was never a woman who could compete with Neverland." His smile was wry. "I know some good women, some fine women who I call friends and a handful more who taught me a few things in the bedroom. I was a very good student." His cheeks flushed a little at that. "And then . . . I went to see Jane Toussaint at Carnegie Hall. I saw a woman onstage, a woman whose voice cracked me open, and I loved you on sight. I think . . . that was the night I stopped being Peter Pan."

She held her breath, impossibly moved.

"I stopped being Peter Pan and became Noble Salt," he whispered, but his eyes still wore a faraway look.

"You said you couldn't even look at me. You still can't," she said, and her voice trembled with suppressed emotion. She wanted his gaze, wanted him to promise her all would be well. She didn't like it when he got pensive, and he'd become more and more pensive the closer they got to Utah.

"The American West isn't Neverland, Jane. When the games are over, people die."

"Noble," she begged. "Please look at me."

He did at once and smiled, making her heart gallop and her body long for things it had never wanted before him. For a moment, something bloomed in his face, something wonderful and rosy, as if he felt it too, the possibility of them. The possibility of a future. And then it was gone, chased away by something blue and bruised and doubtful.

"You're not telling me something," she said. "You're worried about something that you haven't told me. What's going on?"

He frowned and swatted at the air, dismissing his apprehension. "I can't be with my brother or Sundance for very long before I start losing my optimism. It's been a long few days."

"They remind you of Butch Cassidy and Peter Pan."

"Yeah. And Robert LeRoy Parker and all the other versions of me that I'd rather forget. I prefer being Noble Salt. Every inch of Noble Salt belongs to you and Augustus."

"I want all the versions of you."

He hesitated and then shook his head. "You don't want Butch Cassidy."

"Yes, I do. I want him too, because if he's not mine . . . he'll take you away."

"Ah, honey." He cupped her cheek and she pressed it into his hand. "You've been listening to too many of Van's stories. He's turned me into something I'm not. Something I never was."

"He tells the stories because they make him feel close to you."

He sighed but didn't deny it, but when she opened her mouth to reinforce her argument, he put a finger on her lips.

"I'm going to kiss you now . . . all right? I need to kiss you."

"All right," she whispered, eyes locked with his, and she backed him up against the wall. She liked that. He couldn't run . . . and she still could. She rose onto her toes and settled her mouth against his with finality.

For a moment, he was careful, kissing her with all the attention he'd shown her from the very first, but she was eager and unafraid, and his tempo quickly matched her own until he pulled his mouth away and curled his hands into her nightgown.

"I don't know if I can go slow, honey. So maybe we better stop for a minute."

"No," she said. "I don't want to go slow, and I don't want to stop."

He caught her hand but she shook it free and let her robe fall down her arms. With her eyes on her trembling fingers, she loosened the strings on her nightgown, and he said *honey* so sweetly. So softly. Infusing her with power. The nightgown pooled around her feet along with her robe, but when she looked up, expecting desire, expecting anticipation, she found him with his head bowed and his eyes on her discarded clothes.

"Thank you, Jane," he whispered.

"For what?" she whispered back, and almost giggled again, standing naked in front of a man who was thanking her before he even lifted his eyes.

"When I look at you, I might forget what I need to say. I might forget my damn name, so I'm thanking you now. You're the best thing, by a desert mile, that's ever happened to me, and don't think, for one minute, that I don't know it."

"You can forget your name, Noble Salt. Just . . . please don't forget mine. If you call me Betty . . . or Ethel . . . or Ann or Josie, you'll have to sleep with Augustus."

He laughed and lifted his eyes, but his smile went the way of her nightgown.

"You're not real," he marveled, and she made herself be still and let him look.

"That's my line," she said, tremulous.

His throat worked and his hands flexed, though he kept them at his side. "You're not real, Jane Toussaint."

She took a step toward him and then another, and he reached for her, watching his hands as he moved them from her hips to her belly to her breasts. Then, for a moment, he closed his eyes again, his lips moving like he prayed.

If I died today
I would die a happy man
But let me have this

She responded in kind, her voice sharp.

If you die today
I will never forgive you
I want forever

He grinned again, swept her up, and followed her down onto the bed, kissing her with all the fervor he'd kept closely controlled in every encounter. His clothes followed in tugs and stages—he was far more interested in her nakedness than his own—but when he finally lay fully against her, nothing between them, he paused, breathing on her skin like he couldn't believe his good fortune.

Then he continued, kissing her eyelids and her nose and the point of her chin before moving to her breasts and her belly and every warm and wanting place that begged for his attention. He slid so gently, so seamlessly, from care to consummation that she had no thought but wonder and no fear but that it would end too soon.

And when they lay quiet, catching their breath and clasping hands, she was already plotting more.

She did not let him rest until the square of sky went from dead of night to predawn, but he did not beg for relief. Her hair made a coverlet over her breasts and he moved it aside for one last look, one last kiss, before he pulled her down atop him and tugged a quilt over them both.

"I just need a nap," he composed in a neat five syllables.

"No more than fifteen minutes," she mumbled.

He finished off the verse. "Ready when you are."

Butch woke three hours later, overjoyed but oddly restless. He didn't trust euphoria and he didn't believe in heaven, though he suspected he was as close now as he would ever get.

He slipped out of bed, relieved himself in the toilet cupboard that wasn't much more than an outhouse—the waste dropped right onto the tracks below—and brushed his teeth and washed his body. He moved around as quietly as he could, but Jane didn't stir. She slept with an abandon that surprised him, considering her anxious ways. She also crowded him, kicked him, pushed her cold toes beneath his thighs, and stole all the blankets, and he woke up smiling, eager to do it all again.

Her hair was spread across both of their pillows, and the sheet hung precariously from one breast and partially exposed the other. He stopped beside the bed so he could drink her in.

She took his breath away. Robbed him of his reason. His good sense. And he could not find it in himself to regret his actions, though he sensed that day was coming.

He should have stayed far away from her and Gus. Or at the very least . . . kept some emotional distance. But they'd crashed right through his defenses, and he'd wrapped his arms around them and declared them his. Now they owned him in every iteration, and looking down at Jane in all her rosy magnificence, he was overcome with love, hope, and despair.

The hope scared him most of all.

Hope was dangerous. Hope made a man attempt the impossible. Hope kept a man coming back when he should have stayed away.

"You opened me up," he whispered to his sleeping wife. "And took my heart from my chest. Now how will I live?"

She didn't even stir, and her deep, contented sleep made him smile in spite of his disquiet. She'd taken his heart, but he didn't want it back. He just hoped it didn't kill them both. Kill them all. He pulled the sheet up, covering her more completely, and left it to her care.

24

Playing for money
Will never be the same as
Playing for our lives

Augustus checked his pocket watch—he never slept without it—and groaned at the time. It was only six o'clock, and he was starving. He poked his head down to see if Noble was still sleeping and saw that his bed was empty. Maman had stolen him, Augustus was almost sure. He had a misty memory of her scent and her voice, and she'd undoubtedly been the one to pull the drape around him like he was an infant in a buggy. Emma's words came back to scold him.

They're very much in love. Don't ruin it for them.

He wouldn't ruin it, but he was a little irritated that he couldn't eat until the adults were awake and he was allowed to explore or move about the train.

Noble was far more nervous than he'd been on the ship, and far more careful, but he'd promised Gus that before they reached Utah, they could stand together on the platform on the rear of the caboose and see the world behind them get smaller and smaller.

Noble said there was nothing Augustus couldn't do, and Augustus believed him wholeheartedly. If Noble said it, it must be true. Just one more day, and they'd be in Utah. Augustus wasn't sure what would happen then.

Maman hadn't pressed for a detailed itinerary, though Augustus would like to know the plan. Mostly, he just wanted Van and Sundance to stay with them, and he didn't see that happening. Sundance had a woman that he pretended not to love, at least that's what Van told him. "She is the sweetest woman, and she loves Harry so much. I think he'll go and see her, and if he's not a damn fool, he'll beg her to take him back. We've all been gone long enough. He'd be safe in Frisco, especially after the earthquake. I heard the place was chaos. He's got enough money to get them a house, have a couple children, and live a quiet life if she'll have him."

"And what about you?" Augustus had asked.

Van shrugged. "Maybe I'll go see my pop and my brothers and sisters. They like my stories too. And maybe after that, Butch will let me come along with you, be security on Miss Jane's tour when that gets ironed out."

"Maman says she might not ever be able to sing again. No tour company will take her if the earl starts threatening them."

"They'll take her." Van winked. "You just wait and see. You're not going to have to worry about that bastard Werthog."

Van was forty years old, but he felt more like a kid, a friend, and Gus liked the way he didn't even attempt to parent or be a good example. He was real, and Augustus valued real above all else. Too many people pretended to be kind while secretly being repulsed. Van just said what he thought, even if it was stupid or offensive. It was irritating . . . and refreshing.

Maybe he and Van could go to breakfast, just the two of them. Van could tell him stories and no one would care or cut him off, and Augustus could listen and stuff his face with ham and eggs.

But Van and Sundance were both in their sleeping compartment, a dark curtain pulled around each berth to give them a breath from each other.

"Van?" he whispered. "Are you awake?"

"No. Where's your daddy?" Van mumbled from the top bunk. Augustus smiled. Somehow he'd known Sundance wouldn't climb a ladder, and Van probably thought he'd got the better deal.

"Butch is with Maman."

"What time is it?"

"Six thirty." Six fifteen, actually, but six thirty sounded better.

"Oh man, kid. Just go eat in the dining car. The food is included in the fare. Nobody's going to be looking for you. Nobody's going to mess with you either. They do, you tell me. You'll be fine, won't you?"

"Of course I'll be fine," Augustus said, and left the men to sleep a little longer. In the private car, the door to the bedroom was closed and locked, and he raised his fist to knock and then put it down again. He was ten years old. He could walk to the dining car by himself, eat to his heart's content, and nobody needed to babysit him.

He chose a seat that put his bad side toward the wall and tipped his face slightly to the side so that the dining car porter had somewhere to rest his eyes that was comfortable for both of them. If the man was bothered by it, he didn't react, and Augustus ordered with happy abandon, telling the porter that maybe his family would join him, and if not he'd bring what was left back to the car.

"Why, Augustus Toussaint. Is that you?" A surprised voice had him looking up from his plate.

Mary Harriman beamed down at him with a welcome smile. He'd seen her briefly at the Plaza, and she'd been just as gracious as she'd been years ago when he'd stayed at her home.

She was a nice lady, and her children had been just as friendly after the first awkward moments. It was the only time in his life he had played with a group of children, and he remembered the visit fondly.

"Where is your mother?" she asked, searching the car.

"She'll be along shortly," he said, hoping desperately that she would not be.

"Are you still going to Saltair?"

He swallowed and nodded, blotting at his lips. "Yes, ma'am. That's right."

"We will be making a visit as well. We go every summer. The children love it, and the Union Pacific is breaking ground on a new depot in the city. You remember Roland and Averall?"

"Yes, ma'am."

"Here they are now." She waved her two sons, who had just entered the dining car, toward them.

"You should join us for breakfast," Mrs. Harriman continued. "Or perhaps we could join you."

She summoned a waiter, who scurried to accommodate the two boys and their mother. Roland was the same age as Augustus, and Averall was sixteen, and both remembered Augustus from the days he, Maman, and Oliver had spent at their home. They stared at his cheek, but their study held more curiosity than distaste—maybe because they'd seen it before—and he tried not to duck his head and lower his eyes.

"Do you still play cricket?" Averall asked. "You were pretty good at it for such a little fellow. I'll bet you're great now."

"I do," Augustus said, "though I haven't had friends to play with for so long. Could I interest you in a game of chess or maybe . . . poker?"

Mrs. Harriman balked. "Poker?"

"Sure. We wouldn't play for money. I've a bag of candy we can split up and play with. Or we can eat the candy and just play for points. It's a lot of fun." He sounded eager, probably too eager, but the lure of friendship was too much to resist.

The boys seemed eager as well and plied him with questions all through breakfast until Maman suddenly appeared, eyes bright and color high on her cheeks. Her hair had been drawn up into a knot but tendrils fell around her cheeks. The buttons at her throat were misaligned too, like she'd dressed in a hurry.

She greeted Mrs. Harriman and her sons with surprise—"I had no idea we were aboard the same train!"—and an apology for interrupting their breakfast. Then she turned to Augustus, who was sheepishly trying to wolf down one more tart even though he was full to bursting.

"Augustus," she scolded, her hand to her heart. "I was worried about you. I didn't know where you were."

"Sorry, Maman. I woke early and didn't want to disturb you."

"Are you finished?" she asked, and he could see that she was not going to retreat without him.

"Yes, I guess so. But maybe we can meet for a game when you're through?" he asked the boys. They darted a look at their mother, who gave a short nod of consent.

"Of course. Meet us in the observation car in ten minutes?" Averall said.

"It'll give them something to do." Mrs. Harriman smiled. "They bickered all day yesterday. I will welcome the peace and quiet."

Maman made to excuse herself, but Mrs. Harriman put a hand on her arm and lowered her voice, though her sons and Augustus could still easily hear.

"Jane, I was shocked and horrified to hear of the happenings at the Plaza. Your family must be devastated. I'm surprised you're still going to the Saltair. I thought the tour had been canceled."

"My family?"

"Well, yes. Wasn't the Earl of Werthog a Toussaint?"

"He is, yes." Maman was rigid.

"Have you not heard the news?"

"What news is that, Mary?" Maman asked. She kept looking toward the door between cars as if she desperately wanted to escape.

"Oh dear, you must sit down. I assumed . . . Run along, boys. You've eaten enough. All of you. Go enjoy your morning. I'll check on you later."

Augustus scrambled after the Harriman brothers with an apologetic look back at his mother. Maman had been persuaded to sit, but she was perched on a chair, her back ramrod straight, signaling she didn't have time for a leisurely chat.

"I'm sorry, Maman," he whispered, flinching, but ran to borrow a set of cards.

Noble, Van, and Sundance were in the private car when he bounded through the door.

"Sundance, I need a set of cards. I'm going to teach my friends how to play poker."

"Your friends?" Noble asked, his voice slightly sharp.

"Yes. Averall and Roland. I just had breakfast with them. We'll be in the observation car."

"Gus . . . ," Noble warned.

"Please, Noble. Please. I want to play. They're nice. Maman is talking to their mother right now. She knows where I'm going to be."

Noble rubbed at his beardless cheeks, and Sundance handed him a deck of cards. "Have fun, kid," he grunted. "You got money?"

"We're not playing for money. Just wins."

"Too bad . . . They rich?"

"Yes. Their father is very rich."

"Who are these kids?" Noble asked. He sounded funny.

"Roland and Averall Harriman," he blurted. "But Mr. Harriman's not with them. So don't worry."

Van, Sundance, and Noble groaned together like he'd run them all through in a single thrust, skewering them to the wall.

Augustus turned and fled, not waiting for further permission or interrogation, and Noble didn't come after him.

Jane was not far behind Augustus, but she walked slowly, her skin was ashen, and she'd missed a button at her throat. She held a newspaper clutched in her right hand.

"Jane?"

"Augustus is . . . playing cards with the Harriman boys," she said. She couldn't meet Butch's eyes. "There is to be a new Union Pacific

Depot in Salt Lake City. The groundbreaking is taking place during the annual July celebration."

"July 24, 1847. When the Mormons entered the valley and decided, 'This is the place.'" Van raised his hand and lowered his voice in a reenactment of the story of Utah's founding. He grinned like he'd put on an entire production.

"Harriman is on this train?" Butch asked. His nerves were shot. He wanted to pull Jane into the other room and kiss her senseless, straighten her clothing, or just pull it off her again, but something was wrong. Something was terribly wrong, and her walls were up so high, he doubted he could get within an arm's length of her.

"I'm not sure."

"You're not sure?" he asked, disbelief making his voice a trifle harsh.

"I only saw Mary and the boys. It hardly matters now. What's done is done. The Harrimans have always been very . . . kind to us."

"Jane?" he pressed. *Had he hurt her?* Had the lovemaking been too much, too soon, too one-sided? He was suddenly drenched in self-doubt.

"Will you all excuse me for a minute? I got ready so quickly . . . I was worried about Augustus. I'm afraid I'm a little disheveled." She smoothed her hand down her front and fiddled with the button she'd missed. She walked into the little bedroom where Butch had spent the best night of his life, shut the door, and turned the lock.

For once, Van had nothing to say, and when the porter brought their breakfast, they sat in silence, eating because it was something to do. When Butch knocked and told Jane to come eat, she didn't answer.

"She's probably just feelin' out of sorts," Van said. "Ethel used to get like that sometimes . . . right, Sundance? Always just better to give 'em a little space."

"I wish you'd quit sayin' her name like it matters to me," Sundance grumbled, but the groove between his brows was deeper, and he kept glancing toward the bedroom door.

By lunchtime, Jane still hadn't exited her room, but Augustus returned, flushed and happy, detailing every word and every card played. "Roland is my age. Wouldn't it be great if I could go to school with him? He was nice to me. And I'm sure he has lots of friends he could introduce me to. It'd sure make school a lot easier. I'm going to talk to Maman about it. If we go back to New York, maybe the Harrimans can put in a good word for me."

"That'd be nice, Gus," Butch said, glad to see the boy so happy.

"Did Maman come back?" he asked, nervous.

"What do you mean 'come back'?"

"She was upset this morning. I just wondered . . . if . . . she was mad at me still. I should have just waited for everyone to wake up, but I was starving, and I didn't want to disturb you." He flushed and tugged at his vest. "I think I scared her, and then I ran off with the Harriman boys. I was just wondering if she's angry with me."

Butch nodded toward her closed door. "Maybe you should go talk to her. She's been pretty quiet all morning."

Again Augustus hesitated. "Did something happen to the earl?"

Butch frowned. "What are you talking about?"

"Just something Mrs. Harriman said. She made us leave the table."

Butch gaped at the boy and then turned to look at Van and Harry. "I don't know anything about that, Gus," he said.

"I'll ask Maman," he blurted, and knocked on the door.

A moment later, Jane opened it and allowed him to enter, but she closed it immediately, never showing her face.

For a moment, Butch simply stared at the closed door, his heart heavy and his hands cold.

"What do you two know about this?" he asked the silent men beside him.

Sundance was the one who answered. "I haven't looked at the papers. Figured ignorance was bliss, at least until we got to Salt Lake. But don't worry. I didn't kill Werthog. I'm too lazy and the timing wasn't good."

"Ring the porter, Van. They should have papers from every stop. If the news is big enough, there'll be information."

Van shifted, started to speak, and then thought better of it. He did as he was asked, and a few minutes later, he had a stack of papers spread out in front of him.

It only took them a few minutes to find the salient details.

Sundance shoved a paper beneath Van's nose.

"Read this. Then tell me what you think."

"I don't read that great, Harry. You read it."

Harry shook it out and began: "'On Thursday, July 18, a murder took place at the newly opened Plaza Hotel on Fifth Avenue. The Earl of Werthog was found dead of a gunshot wound in his hotel room.'"

Van took the paper from his hands and read the rest, his mouth moving over the words. Then he put it down, raised his eyes, and shrugged.

"Good riddance. Guess we won't have to worry about the earl no more."

Butch just stared at his brother, that old helpless feeling settling in his chest.

Van grinned, sheepish and smug, but underneath it all was the need to confess, to air it all out, or maybe he just wanted to brag.

"I knew it needed to be done. Just like you said, Sundance. So I did it. Planned it out. Just like the boss man here woulda done. Made it look like a robbery gone bad. Walked outta there with a thousand pounds. Probably more if I want to trade in the cuff links. They aren't the cheap kind."

Butch rose slowly to his feet, unable to face his horror sitting down.

"Oh, Van," he whispered. "Oh, brother. I can't fix this."

Sundance was stone-faced, but Van looked nervous, and he didn't even wait for Butch to sit back down, though his voice was pitched so low Butch had to hold his breath to hear him.

"You don't gotta fix anything. It wasn't hard. I figured he was staying at the Plaza. That was where Jane was supposed to stay, right? Then

I just watched and waited. If you really want to kill someone, it ain't hard. And I thought we . . . you . . . really wanted to kill him."

"You . . . killed . . . the Earl of Werthog," Butch verified, incredulous.

"Yeah, brother. I did."

Butch had no response, and Van rushed to fill the silence.

"I just followed him up. Then I knocked on his door."

Butch could picture it, and his stomach roiled with dread. He didn't want to hear the rest, but Van wanted to tell it.

"Here's the funny part. He called me Mr. Salt. He thought I was you, brother. He thought she'd sent you. Jane. He let me right in, and I didn't wait. I didn't go all chickenshit. I just pulled out my gun and drilled him. Point-blank. He didn't suffer. Didn't even know what hit him. I wasn't cruel. I know you don't like it when I'm cruel. Then I threw some stuff around. Took as much loot as I could carry in his case, and left. Problem solved."

He tapped the newspaper on the top of the stack.

"They don't have any leads. The paper just said he was killed. They don't know who done it. He's just dead. And now Jane and Augustus can breathe. You can breathe. I did you a favor. I've always had your back, even though you've never had mine."

His announcement had not had the desired reception, and he was starting to stammer, to fall back into old roles and old wounds.

"Didn't you say some people need killing, Sundance?" His voice had grown too loud and a little shrill.

"Quiet," Sundance snapped. "There's a traumatized woman and her son on the other side of a very thin wall."

"I wasn't going to tell you at all," Van whispered. "Just gonna keep it to myself. But everyone's all tense. I wanted to reassure you."

"When did you do it?" Butch interrupted.

"The day before we left. I thought that was best. Not to stick around, you know. And nobody else was doing anything."

"So you took matters into your own hands."

"I did. Sometimes you don't know what's good for you, Butch. Like that time you tried to turn yourself in. I'm just trying to help you. That's all I ever wanted to do."

"Well, shit," Sundance whispered.

"You just went to the Plaza." Butch started back at the beginning. He wanted it all out.

"Yep. Took the ferry. Then the streetcar. I'm a city boy now." He chuckled. "I borrowed one of your fancy suits so I would look like I belonged. That yellow cashmere one. It fit good too. You didn't even notice it was gone."

"That's because they aren't mine."

Van talked right over him. "I had a drink. Read the paper. Had the best cigar of my life. They've got a nice little lounge. Saw Werthog come in with another fella. They talked for a minute. Parted ways. I followed him. Saw which room he was in. Waited some more, just walking down the hall like I belonged. I learned that from you, Butch. You could always make yourself look right at home anywhere."

"Nobody saw you?" Sundance asked.

"Nobody paid any attention to me," he responded, defensive.

"So you killed him . . . and you walked out of there."

"Yep. Right outta that fancy hotel. Nice and slow, the way you always did after a bank job. No hurry. Don't draw any eyes. Just walk away. That's what I did." He shrugged and threw up his hands. "I thought you'd be glad."

Butch buried his face in his hands, needing space and silence so he could come up with a plan. His mind raced, and he couldn't get ahead of the horror and the dawning realization that things had just gotten very bad.

He strode through the car and knocked on the bedroom door. "Jane. We need to talk. Right now, honey."

"Why you gotta tell Jane?" Van whined. "I don't want her to be scared of me. You can't tell Gus."

A moment later, Jane stepped out of the bedroom in a deep blue dress, her hair perfectly coiled, her face serene. Gus walked out behind her and shot a worried look at the three men but swiftly walked through the car, his novels and his journal underneath his arm.

"I'll be on my bunk," he said, as if he worried that he might be forgotten and left there to languish all day while the adults talked.

When the door closed behind him, Jane sat primly but she didn't look at any of them. She didn't look at Butch.

The glass of her skin was the same. The roses in her cheeks, the rise and fall of breasts that he could still see in his thoughts. But it was as if she'd drawn the curtains over her love, pulled a mask over her smile, and a shade over the flame that had burned so brightly between them mere hours before.

She did not weep or rage. He wished she would so that he could do the same. She simply sat, her head bowed in thought, a drooping bud.

"I am glad he's dead. To say anything different would be a lie. He made my life hell for a long time. But I need to know which one of you killed him. And then I need to know how we're going to fix this." She dropped a paper on the table, one they hadn't yet seen.

A picture of Jane, identical to the one that had hung in the ballroom of the *Adriatic*, was centered between a picture of Sundance and a picture of him, the same images that graced Pinkerton circulars all over the country. The headline above their faces was big and bold.

The Curious Case of Madame Toussaint and the Wild Bunch.

25

*I can't hold on to
Anything good, and I can't
Let go of the bad*

"I will read it aloud," Jane said, voice wooden. "Mrs. Harriman gave me this copy. It was published this morning in the *Omaha Daily News*. She thought I should know what is being said . . . and what her husband contributed to the tale, though his statement was one made years ago and not at all in the context the article asserts."

She began:

On July 18, a man matching the description of one Butch Cassidy, a notorious outlaw wanted for bank and train holdups throughout the West, walked into the Plaza Hotel. Two hours and a single gunshot later, he walked out again, leaving Lord Ashley Toussaint, Earl of Werthog, dead in his hotel room.

The same man was seen at the Plaza a week earlier in the company of Madame Jane Toussaint, the famed soprano, who was set to begin an American tour spanning both coasts.

Robert Pinkerton, president of the Pinkerton Detective Agency, said his agency was hired by Lord Ashley Toussaint to investigate Madame Toussaint after she left France amid troubling allegations about her husband's death. Oliver Toussaint, the singer's late husband, was a distant relation of the Earl of Werthog.

Pinkerton believes that Jane Toussaint and Butch Cassidy met years ago on Mrs. Toussaint's previous American tour. Mr. E. H. Harriman, president of the Union Pacific Railroad, reported that while Mrs. Toussaint was a guest in his home, she recounted the meeting, and he observed that she was quite taken with the outlaw. Where and when the two became reunited is still unknown.

Madame Toussaint's tour was canceled abruptly just days before the earl's murder. Mr. Bailey Hugo of Hugo Productions also told Pinkerton agents that Mrs. Toussaint was accompanied to Carnegie Hall for a rehearsal by Butch Cassidy and Harry Longabaugh, aka the Sundance Kid, a known associate of Cassidy's and a man wanted for many of the same crimes.

It is not known whether Mrs. Toussaint is aware of the exploits of the two men in her company or if Butch Cassidy acted alone, but at this time, all three individuals are wanted for questioning in the murder of Ashley Toussaint, Earl of Werthog.

The room was silent for all of three seconds when Jane finished. Then Van began to plead his case.

"Butch didn't kill him, Jane. I did. But I had to," Van said, defensive. "The earl knew where you and Augustus were." He looked at Harry.

"He knew who we were too, Sundance. He had a file—some Pinkerton gave it to him right there in the lounge while I was watching. I took it. If I hadna been there, the earl would have given the word, and we woulda been rounded up by US Marshals before we even got out of town."

"You didn't think the Pink he hired was going to be suspicious with the earl being shot dead right after he talked to him?" Sundance hissed, his voice so cold Van actually shivered. "You thought that Pink was going to keep the information to himself? Whatever he knew, he still knows."

"I want to see that file," Butch insisted.

"I don't have it. I burned it. Didn't want someone getting their hands on it. It didn't say much. Just had the circular and Emma's address. They knew Emma was your sister, Sundance. Knew we were living there. But we're gone now. It's fine. Better than fine. The Pinks aren't looking for me. I'm not on a circular. My name and face aren't plastered everywhere."

"The hell they aren't. You look just like Butch. Whatever you do, they'll just blame on him. Half the time you use his name, asshole," Sundance shot back.

That shut Van up. His grin was gone, and he paced in silence for several minutes.

"Do you hate me, Butch?"

"*I* hate you! I'm about ready to kill you," Sundance snapped.

Van ignored him and stopped in front of his older brother, demanding he look him in the eyes.

"Did I screw up? I thought . . . I thought you'd be . . . you'd be glad." His voice was plaintive and small, and Butch fought the old need to grind his teeth and weep in frustration. But he wasn't that man anymore. Somewhere along the way, he'd changed. Maybe it was Gus. Maybe it was Jane. Maybe it was Noble Salt.

"I don't hate you, Van," Butch said.

The soft words took the strength out of Van's legs, and he collapsed onto the couch.

"It's my fault this happened," Butch said.

Sundance was watching Butch and taking it all in, not offering anything, but not missing anything either.

"I haven't been a good brother. I've always made you feel like you had to be bigger and badder than everyone else just so we'd let you stay."

Van's eyes got bright, and he blinked rapidly. "I just wanted to fix things. You've always been so good at fixing things, making things better."

"You didn't make this better, Van," Sundance said softly. "Butch might love you, but I don't. You can't kill a goddamn English earl and expect for the law to just shrug and move on. It's not like one of us getting killed. We get taken down in cold blood, and it's ignored. But you take down an English nobleman in a fancy hotel, you start an international incident and a manhunt the likes we've never seen before. We shut this down fast, or it's going to swallow all of us whole. All of us."

He held up another article, one Van hadn't bothered to read. "From his office in New York City, Mr. Robert Pinkerton, president of the Pinkerton Detective Agency, has put out an alert across the wires for Butch Cassidy and Harry Longabaugh, and now they've added murder to the list of possible charges against us."

Jane covered her face and bowed her back, but Sundance continued to rail.

"And it ain't just us with targets on our backs, it's Jane too. Jane and Gus can't blend in or hide out in a small town, and she sure as hell won't be singing again. They might even find out her history with the earl and think she *hired* Butch to take him out. I'm guessing they'll have some questions for me too. Mr. Hugo got a good look at me. Wouldn't surprise me if there's already another warrant out for my arrest. In fact, when we get off this train, I'm guessing we're going to have a whole posse waiting to escort us off and string us up."

"They don't know we're on the train." Van's voice was shaking.

"Mrs. Harriman knows that Jane Toussaint and her son are on the train! You think she's just going to keep that quiet? She'll tell her husband the minute she sees him, and he'll call in the US Marshals, the Pinkertons, and every county sheriff in the whole state."

"They won't go after Jane. She didn't do anything wrong."

"According to this article, 'Madame Toussaint is believed to have a connection to Butch Cassidy and the Sundance Kid,'" Harry read, his voice rising with every word. "The only one these papers don't mention is the stupid brother who got them all into this mess."

Sundance threw himself down into a chair and covered his eyes with his hands, and Van sank lower into the couch.

Butch stared at the landscape that rushed by, trying to lose himself in the wide expanse where a man could roam for days without ever seeing another soul. Nebraska was nothing but rolling grass, yellowing in the July heat.

"You have that look in your eye, Noble Salt," Jane said, startling them all.

"What look is that, honey?" he asked, meeting her gaze.

"The tumbleweed," she said, and her voice cracked.

He pushed away from the window and took Jane's hand, pulling her up beside him.

"Go get Gus," he told Van. "He's been alone too long, and he's too smart not to be scared. Order some dinner. Play some cards. The train doesn't stop again until midnight, and I need to think."

"You always did come up with the best plans," Van said, smiling. Hopeful. "It'll work out, right? It always does."

Sundance looked as though he was five seconds from detonation.

"Harry," Butch directed. "Van can take care of Gus. Go get some rest. Some distance. I'll talk to you in a couple hours. Ain't nothing can be done now."

Sundance nodded once and bolted from the drawing room.

"Van . . . I need a moment with Jane. Get the boy, but don't interrupt us unless there's trouble."

"Okay, Butch." He smiled again, relieved he wasn't being knocked unconscious, hog-tied, and left behind again, though the planning was still in its early stages.

Jane followed him from the main car and into the bedroom with a straight back and bristling skin, his little cholla keeping him away, but he ignored the barbs and embraced her, every pointed edge and sharp corner.

She dissolved against him, her hands running over him as though she needed to ascertain that he was still solid and whole.

"I don't know what to feel," she moaned. "I'm relieved and devastated. I've been flung off a cliff and taught to fly. I'm in love, and I'm on fire. I'm afraid, and I've never been more alive."

"I'm going to take care of this, Jane. I'm going to take care of you. I'll get you someplace safe, you and Augustus both, and I'll fix this mess. I promise."

She gripped his face in talon fingers and brought his mouth to hers, kissing him with all the angst and ardor that had marked their romance from the start, and he gave it back, unable to communicate his own devotion and devastation any other way.

They came together like the sky was falling and the waters were rising, and there was no place for timid touches or careful caressing. Clothes were tangled and tossed aside as they fell across the bed with open mouths and open eyes, trying to beat back the unwelcome intruder, time.

"You think you're protecting me again. Protecting me from you," she panted, throwing back her head in pleasure and protest. "You're going to leave."

He could not deny the truth she spoke, even as he buried himself in her body and kissed his fidelity into her skin. Even as he begged her to come for him, he knew there was no way she could come with him.

The wave that swept them up hurtled them back down, ferocious and fleeting, and they lay panting together, dazed and unsatisfied, hungry for more.

"Take us with you," she begged.

"I can't," he moaned against her breasts. "I'm so sorry, honey."

She drew him up and gave him her mouth to silence his doubts, and for a moment he was distracted, lost again in the wonder of her and the pleasure of them, but even Jane's lips and Jane's love could not quiet the reality that pressed down upon them. He found himself confessing once more, speaking his anguish into her throat as he merged his mouth with hers.

"I've felt it coming for a long time, like the rumble of a train when it's still miles off. I don't know how much longer I can outrun it. And now . . . now I've tied you to me. If I stay with you, I'll take you down with me."

"Take me down. Take me up. Take me anywhere you like, just don't leave me," she said. "Don't leave us."

He closed his eyes, trying to steel himself, but he found himself confessing again.

"I've kept my hands clean. Even when everyone around me was back to their old ways. I've been running, trying to stay ahead of the flood, but then I ran right into you. How's a man supposed to keep running when he's got a chance to finally live?"

"We will think of something. Love means you stay," she scolded. "You can't give up so easily."

He shook his head. "The outlaw life was not what I wanted, but it's what I chose. I didn't know I was choosing it. Not until it was too late, and I sure as hell didn't understand the cost. But I'm paying it. I'm paying it now that I want a life with you."

"Where is your outrage?" she challenged, fisting her hands in his hair. "What is this calm acceptance?"

There was nothing he could say. He had no defense. He'd known. He'd always known, and now his only wish, his singular purpose, was to extricate Jane and her son from the trap that was his life, the snare they'd unwittingly stepped in.

She moaned, low and loud, and set her teeth against the skin of his shoulder like she wanted to hurt him or mark him, but she rolled away instead, denying herself and sparing him.

He wasn't ready to let her go, but he did. They dressed in agonized silence, covered their naked longing, and pulled on their well-used composure.

"You warned me . . . right from the first," she whispered.

He halted, his heart in his stomach.

"You said, 'There hasn't been a single person in my life I haven't disappointed.' Do you remember that?"

"Yeah. I remember that. I was giving it to you as straight as I could."

"I fell in love with you in that moment. But now . . . now I'm just . . . angry. With you . . . and with myself. Because I knew it too. I knew you'd break our hearts, right from the beginning. But I didn't see any other way."

Van wasn't particularly good at hokku and pretended disinterest, though Augustus caught him counting syllables when he thought no one was looking.

"You keep counting words, Van," Augustus reminded him. "It's syllables."

"Well, some words don't sound the same when I say 'em as when you say 'em, Frenchie," Van said, which was a fair point.

"Let's play something else, shall we?" Augustus said. He and Van had been killing time together for the better part of two hours, and Maman, Noble, and Sundance had not reappeared. He didn't mind. He liked Van, but the tension that was present earlier still permeated the car.

"I'm better at drawing than I am at word games," Van said. "Maybe I'll use this book you gave me for sketches."

"It's rather small," Augustus said doubtfully.

"Well, I'll draw little things." Van shrugged. "I used to sit real still so I wouldn't scare the birds and the jackrabbits around our place in Circleville. Jackrabbits are extremely skittish."

Sundance let himself into the car and closed the door behind him. He'd been drinking, and his nose was red, but his words weren't slurred.

"What's a jackrabbit?" Augustus thought maybe Van was teasing him.

Sundance shot a warning look toward Van, like he didn't want to hear a solitary word from his mouth, but sat down beside Augustus and answered the question.

"Jackrabbits aren't even rabbits. They're hares," he said.

"They've got longer ears," Van added, beginning his sketch. "The pioneers called them jackass rabbits because they had ears more like a donkey. They're born with hair, with their eyes open, ready to run."

"Rabbits aren't born ready to run?" Augustus asked.

"No. Rabbits are born pink and naked like babies," Sundance grunted.

"They're different species. As different as sheep and goats," Van added.

Sundance kept it going. "As different as Mormons and Baptists."

"Which are you?" Augustus asked.

"I'm neither," Sundance said. "Not a sheep or a goat."

"Sundance is more reptilian," Van quipped, leering at Harry.

"Are you a Mormon, Van?" Augustus asked.

"My family was. Jack Mormons . . . but still . . . Mormons."

Augustus cocked his head. "Are Jack Mormons like jackrabbits?"

Van hooted, surprised and amused, but then he nodded his head. "Yeah. Kinda."

"You have longer ears and hair and you're born ready to run?" Sundance laughed in spite of himself.

"I was definitely born ready to run," Van boasted. "But nah. Jack Mormons are Mormons that aren't all in on the doctrine or the culture, but they aren't hostile to the religion either. My dad was like that. Sometimes you gotta decide what you'll leave and what you'll take."

"But you left it all?"

"You never leave it all. Not something you're raised on. It's part of you. You don't ever get rid of it. Most things aren't all good or all bad."

"Like the Wild Bunch?" Augustus asked.

Van frowned and Sundance sighed wearily.

"Yeah. I guess. Just like us."

26

I can stop a train
Tie myself across the tracks
Just don't say goodbye

"We need to get off this train," Noble said. He was calm, and his big hand rested safe and heavy on Augustus's back.

Dinner was over, bedtime was still hours off, and Augustus just wanted to sleep, but the adults were gathered in the drawing room of Maman's car, and Noble was laying out his plan. Unlike before, Augustus had not been sent away.

"There'll be time for a nap, Gus. I promise. But you need to hear this too. We've got some decisions to make."

"The sooner the better," Sundance said. "I'm about to jump outta my damn skin. I'm guessing Pinkerton has telegraphed every depot on the overland route. I'm surprised we've made it this far."

"It's a whole lot easier to grab us when we step off than to storm a train," Noble said. "And if Mrs. Harriman decided to inform the conductor of Jane's presence, he's sent a message ahead too. They're waiting for us. I guarantee it."

"I don't think she would do that," Maman said softly.

"Jane . . . honey . . . for all you know, she thinks you've been abducted."

Sundance tugged at his mustache. "We'll wait until it starts on an upgrade and slows way down. Then we bail. Find some horses. Long as we got money, that shouldn't be a problem,"

"I'm not throwing Jane or Augustus off the train, at any speed," Noble said.

"Then Augustus and I will get off alone in Evanston, tonight," Maman suggested, back straight, chin high. "That's the next stop. I will plead innocence, cry a great deal, and pretend I have absolutely no clue what they are talking about. I'm a skilled actress, you know." She wouldn't look at Noble, and panic began to bubble in Augustus's belly. He didn't want to leave the Wild Bunch.

"They'll still be waiting for the rest of us in Ogden," Sundance said. "We'll have to get off the train sometime."

"And I'm not feeding you to the wolves for a little cover," Noble added. "We'll get off together."

"Then we need to stop the train," Sundance said. "Engineer a break-down. Middle of nowhere. And just get off."

"You wouldn't happen to have a little dynamite, would you, brother?" Van chortled.

Noble shook his head slowly.

"I've got a different idea. Something a little less explosive and something that doesn't involve stopping the whole train." Noble looked at Maman for a minute, like he was willing her to trust him. Maman pulled at the neckline of her dress. Her throat was red and splotchy, and she hadn't eaten any of her supper.

"What are you cooking up in that head, Butch Cassidy?" Sundance asked.

Noble was silent a second more. "We're in the last car."

"Perks of being richie rich," Van sang.

"We only need to uncouple the last one," Noble said. "A porter isn't going to see it's missing until he opens the door between the cars, which he'll have no reason to do."

"You're going to climb out and uncouple the car?" Sundance said, incredulous. "'Cause I sure as hell won't."

"I'll do it," Van said.

"You wouldn't know the first thing about uncoupling a car," Sundance sneered. "You'll just end up killing yourself and creating another bloody mess for us to clean up."

"I could uncouple a car in my sleep," Noble said quietly. "They don't have locks on the pins. Not on the Pullmans. The express car is the only one with a messenger—a guard—and that's in the first section. All you need is some muscle, some balance—"

"And a death wish. You'll have to do it in the dark," Sundance warned. "Otherwise someone'll see, and they'll try to stop the train. And I'm not keen on walking out of a canyon, which we'll be doing once we cross the Utah border."

"We're scheduled to pull into the depot in Evanston at midnight," Noble said, like he'd already thought it all through. "I'll uncouple when we're half an hour out. We'll be out of the canyon but not so far out of the city that we're walking for miles looking for lodging or a buggy."

"You act as though it's a simple thing," Maman whispered.

"It is, honey."

Augustus gaped, imagining Noble clinging to the side of a speeding train in the dark.

"They won't notice the car's gone until they've pulled into the next station, if they even notice then," Noble added. "The only monitor is the money car. It'll be easy."

"Easy." Maman looked positively green.

"They'll have to send an engine back for it, but that won't be until morning. And we'll be long gone. No harm done."

"It's worth a try," Sundance said, eyes wide.

Van shrugged. "What have we got to lose?"

"What if we lose Noble?" Maman snapped, her eyes like hot coals, but even Augustus could see the decision was made.

Noble started making lists and giving out orders, Maman excused herself, and Sundance was smiling like he'd been handed down a pardon.

"You know why I'm not scared?" Van said to Augustus, squatting down so they were at eye level.

"Why?"

"'Cause I've never seen him fail. Even when things go wrong, he just makes it work. Always has."

"And he's lucky," Augustus said, already feeling much better.

"That's right."

"The luckiest son of a bitch in the whole wide world," they said together.

"Van," Noble warned. "Language."

"It ain't just luck, though, kid," Van added.

"No?"

"No. He's lucky because he treats folks good. Takes care of people. And what goes around comes around. You'll see. Everything's going to be just fine."

"Jane's not going to like the rest of your plan any better than the first part of your plan," Sundance muttered, his eyes on the closed bedroom door. They were ready and waiting, all assembled in the caboose, watching the time tick by. Jane had retreated, and Butch hadn't tried to follow.

"It's the only play I've got. It's like you said. If I don't get ahead of this, and fast, it'll take us all down. The only bargaining chip I have is myself."

"You for her?" Harry asked. "Or you for him?" Van had fallen asleep on the floor, his arms folded over his belly, his feet crossed at the ankles, a cushion from the sofa stuffed under his head.

Augustus had done the same and was curled into Van's side.

"I promised my dad a long time ago that I'd take care of Van. I can't take care of him and take care of Jane and Augustus, not now. And not by myself."

"I know. I've got him." Harry sighed. "He's a pain in the ass . . . but I've had worse." He grinned ruefully at Butch.

"When you two get to San Francisco, go see Ethel, Harry," Butch pleaded softly. "Give her whatever time you have left."

"Is that what you've done? Given Jane whatever time you have left? That's cruel, Butch, 'cause I'd say it's not a whole hell of a lot."

Butch had no defense. He hadn't meant to be cruel; he'd just fallen in love. Sundance sighed and shoved at his shoulder. It was as much affection as he was capable of.

"Van screwed up. He was stupid. But he also killed a bad man, and I have to believe Jane and Gus are better off having known you. Maybe having known all of us. That's something to be proud of."

Butch nodded, trying desperately not to weep. Harry had compassion on him and changed the subject.

"I've hurt Ethel enough. I should let her move on."

Butch cleared his throat and swiped at his eyes. "She did move on, Harry, but that doesn't mean she won't move over the moment you come back."

"I don't know about that."

"I do."

The silence thickened and time swelled with all that had been and all that was still to come. Butch just wanted the night to be over.

"She hasn't returned my letters. I've written so many," Harry confessed.

Butch stared at him, dumbfounded. "You have?"

"I have," Harry whispered. "And I haven't heard a word back. Not in over a year. I can face the fact that she doesn't love me anymore, Butch. But I don't think I can bear it if she's gone. If she's gone . . . I don't want to know."

⌒℘⌒

The couplings on the cargo cars—especially if the car was doubly reinforced to withstand a burglar's blast—required a key that the conductor and the engineer both carried, but the coupling on the Pullman cars was very straightforward, according to Noble.

It was almost comical, really, how the car just gently fell away from the train when it was unattached.

Noble crawled back inside, his hands dirty and his shirt torn, wearing a smile of triumph and reassurance that belied the acrobatics he'd just performed.

"It'll take a minute for it to stop completely," he said, but already they were squeaking and slowing, and the Overland Express, oblivious parent, was completely unaware that it had lost a duckling.

The quiet was almost surreal, no humming, no vibrating, no whistle that sounded the stops and starts. They all sat, even Noble, and waited for the car to clatter to a stop.

Augustus looked on in wonder, Van was all smiles, and even sour Sundance betrayed Jane with his hope-filled assessment of their situation.

"I'm guessing that wasn't as easy as it looked, Cassidy, but damn if it didn't work."

Jane couldn't even look at any of them. Her fury was a blacksmith's bellow, and it kept her moving though her heart had long since stopped.

"I'm going to see where we're at," Noble said, "and we don't know what'll be coming along these tracks. Hopefully, nothing."

They climbed out, surveying the landscape around them. A few lights glimmered through the trees. The valises they could take, but the trunks would have to be left behind unless they secured a wagon, and Jane had chosen one dress and a change of clothes for Augustus, along with the picture of Butch Cassidy she'd stolen a lifetime ago. Even now—especially now—she could not make herself part with it.

"Stay here," Noble demanded. "All of you. I'll go see what I can rustle up. We need a wagon and a willing seller."

"It's somebody's lucky day. Butch pays well," Sundance said, positively cheerful. He had even begun to whistle, the tune disjointed but familiar.

Onward, Christian soldiers. He was whistling "Onward, Christian Soldiers." *Marching as to war.*

Her whole life had been a war. *Her whole life!* She wanted peace. Just peace, and she'd fallen in love with a man who'd never known a day of it.

Noble was back within the hour with a wagon pulled by two horses and an extra pair, saddled and ready to go. Another man, mounted as well, was leading the additional horses.

"Look who I found," Butch crowed. "You remember Ted Wilkins, Van?"

Van stood, his eyes wide, and then clapped his hands and took off his hat. "I should say I do! What'd I tell you, kid?" He looked down at Augustus. "I ain't never seen him fail."

Ted Wilkins had grown up in their valley. A few minutes of merry reminiscing commenced as they loaded the trunks into the wagon and Noble helped her up into the seat.

"Aren't you worried he's going to try to collect on the reward?" Jane asked as Noble settled beside her and gathered the reins.

"No. Ted's a good sort. And I did him a good turn, a long time ago. I also paid him for the wagon and the horses. Wouldn't do him much good to turn me in now, anyway."

"Why is that, Noble Salt?"

He looked at her with his bottomless eyes, but he didn't repeat what they both knew.

"Everything's going to be all right, honey. You'll see."

"Your definition of all right and my definition of all right are very different, I'm afraid," she clipped, and when he reached for her hand, she reacted so violently, she almost toppled over the other side.

"Careful, Maman," Augustus scolded, and Noble shot out an arm and righted her. But he didn't linger.

Everything about the town—Ogden—was pretty. Noble was right. The mountains were like nothing she'd ever seen. The sun rose at their backs as they made their way from the base of the hills, through farmland and orchards, cutting past the center of the city and veering south toward Salt Lake on a road that bustled with buggies and wagons, bicycles, and an occasional car, though most travelers looked on the contraption with annoyance as if unsure of what to make of it. The families were big, and the wagons teeming.

"We've still got another thirty miles to Salt Lake," Noble warned, once Ogden was behind them. "But the drive is pretty, and no one is looking for us on this road."

It was near the end of July, and as the dawn crept into morning, they pulled onto the shoulder of the road, and Jane unearthed two parasols.

"I'm a man, Maman," Augustus had grumbled, but he took the lacy shade and propped it between two of the trunks, and promptly fell asleep beneath it. Jane held the other between Noble and herself, and Noble wasn't too much of a man to refuse it.

Sundance and Van rode a ways ahead; it was safer for them all to not appear as if they were together.

"Nobody will be looking at you, Butch. Not with Jane wearing that fancy hat," Van hooted, but by noon his neck was red where his derby provided no shade, his shirt sweat-soaked, and the yellow cashmere suit coat and vest he'd pilfered and started the day with were slung across his horse.

Noble had changed his shirt after uncoupling the cars, and he wore a straw hat with a red band from Oliver's trunk that matched the suspenders holding up his brown trousers. He wore no suit coat or vest, and his sleeves were rolled to his forearms. She was transfixed by them, the way the muscles and veins looked like hills and streams rising up from the valleys of his palms. His skin seemed to simply soak up the sun, growing deeper in color as the day commenced. So little fazed him, so little slowed him down. He was a wildly capable man, a singular sensation. And she was going to lose him.

She'd been stewing in that horrified realization since Mrs. Harriman had placed the paper in front of her and broken the news.

Sometimes . . . you fall in love with someone. And it doesn't matter if it makes sense. It doesn't matter what they look like or what they've done.

That was what he'd said. And that was what she'd felt, looking down at that terrible article. Mrs. Harriman had asked her if she needed help. She'd immediately rejected the offer. She didn't need help. She needed Noble Salt, and she had no idea how she could keep him.

"I knew nothing of this," she'd stammered, and Mrs. Harriman had seemed to believe her. Perhaps because it was true.

"And Mr. Cassidy?" she'd asked, tapping the picture.

"I know no one by that name," she insisted. "This story is ludicrous."

Mrs. Harriman had tsked and shaken her head. "I can see how upset you are, dear. I'll keep an eye on the boys. And when we reach Salt Lake, you must stay with us. We have plenty of room. Edward's been there since early June, all by himself, poor darling. We call it a summer cottage, but it's more like a château." She'd smiled and winked, so kind and so clueless, and Jane had managed to thank her before scurrying away. She'd been cowering in a dark corner of her mind ever since.

She'd asked very few questions and schooled every expression, though Noble answered the one she asked.

"When we get to Salt Lake . . . what then?"

"I have a friend, a lawyer. A man I trust. We're going to see him."

"And Van and Sundance?" she prodded, wooden.

"They're heading for San Francisco. They'll have to get there in a roundabout way, but they'll be fine. We need to split up."

Van hadn't liked that idea.

"I'm staying with you, Butch."

"No, you ain't. You're coming with me, Rip Van Winkle," Sundance interceded, eyes as flat and hard as the purple mountains that pierced the endless sky everywhere she looked. "We'll ride ahead to find lodging for everyone tonight and circle back. But tomorrow you and I are on our own."

∽

A creek ran past a dozen cabins nestled in the trees, and Sundance rented the two on the far end and came back to ride with them the rest of the way.

The men removed everything but their drawers and sank into the water as soon as the animals were seen to. Jane was not so free, and she walked farther upstream, took off her shoes and stockings, hoisted her skirt, and sat down on a flat rock, not caring if she soaked her dress.

She'd expected Noble to follow her; she knew he was keeping watch from downstream, but it was Sundance, dripping but clothed, who picked his way toward her and sat on a log that jutted out from shore.

"It was Ethel who wanted to go to Carnegie Hall to hear you sing," he said, surprising her. "Ethel that we have to thank for all of this," he grunted. "She was a singer too, though not as good as you. I made sure to tell her that. I was so hard on her. Didn't want her gettin' big ideas."

"Why?"

He was silent for a minute, but he didn't elucidate.

"She looked a lot like you too. You could be sisters. That bothered me. It still bothers me, like God is poking His fingers in my eyes."

"Why?" she asked again, confused and a little annoyed that he'd intruded on her solitude with his disjointed conversation. She was honest enough to admit that Sundance hadn't done anything to contribute to their current situation. None of it was his fault, but irritation was better than devastation.

Sundance kept talking, not addressing her whys, at least not directly, and she stopped asking.

"I always thought she shoulda chosen Butch . . . and I thought, when he was so taken with you at Carnegie Hall, that it was just proof that he really wanted Ethel."

"He told me she always loved you. Right from the start."

"Yeah. I know that now."

He fell silent, and she wished he'd go. She couldn't think about Ethel and unhappy endings when she was so busy drowning in her own.

"I spent a long time being angry. Sour. Contrary Harry. But I'd give anything for one more day with her."

"Perhaps you'll get one. Perhaps you'll get many," she said, softening toward him.

He shook his head, morose. "I don't think so. I've used up all my second chances."

Her panic rose, swift and salty, and she splashed her face and neck, willing it back.

"People like Butch and Ethel . . . they get taken advantage of. Taken for granted too, because they're good and kind, and it'd make more sense if they fell in love with each other . . . but they never do. They fall in love with people like us."

"Like us?"

"Yeah. Like us, Jane Toussaint. All piss and prickles. I'm not saying you don't have a reason. Because, woman, you've got a helluva good reason. More reason than I ever had. From what I can tell, you're as strong as you are beautiful. And you're a good mother, which makes you a good woman, in my book. I had a rotten one, so I'd know."

He studied Noble, who was splashing at Augustus and listening to his brother yammer on about something. Van was incapable of silence.

"Butch loves you the way Ethel loved me." He rose suddenly, like he'd said all he was going to say, but then he stopped, his back partially turned. "You might only get one more day with him, but at least it's one more day. And instead of being angry and scared . . . cherish it. You can be angry and scared when it's over."

27

My love is not fine
Or made of silver and gold
But it's all I have

July 1907

Orlando Powers had some unexpected visitors Tuesday afternoon. He was alone in his office in Salt Lake City, sitting by the window that gave him a view of the Mormon temple at the city center. Weston Woodruff, his earnest clerk, was gone for the day, and Orlando planned to leave too, just as soon as he'd buttoned up his last brief. A fly buzzed around his head, drawn by the sweat on his brow, and he growled in frustration and slapped the air, determined to finish before five. It was for that reason that he bellowed, "Come back tomorrow," when he heard the outer door open and someone call his name.

"Are you alone, Mr. Powers?"

"Except for this damned fly. But I won't be here long."

"I'll make sure you're well compensated for your time," the voice said, stepping across the threshold, and Orlando Powers raised his eyes in aggravation.

Butch Cassidy was older, his hair darker but shot with gray, and he wasn't alone. The woman beside him was well-formed but slight, with a heavy sweep of dark hair covered by a gray hat that matched her pin-striped dress. A boy of ten or eleven hovered behind his mother's back and darted his head to the left, like he wanted to get a look around but didn't want to be seen. He had a huge, purple mark on one side of his face that drew the eye and hurt the heart, and for a moment Orlando Powers was distracted from the outlaw he never thought he'd see again.

"Can we sit down?" Cassidy asked, pointing at the chairs across the desk, and Orlando peeled his eyes from the boy and stammered a sheepish "B-by all means."

Two chairs were arranged across the desk and another two were pushed against the wall. The woman hesitated and moved toward those, and the boy followed. When they were seated, Butch sank into the same seat he'd occupied almost seven years before. His blue eyes were steady and his big hands clasped in his lap as he began to speak.

"Mr. Powers, I want to turn myself in."

The woman flinched, and the boy was immediately on his feet.

"Noble?" he cried. He had an accent, and Orlando wasn't even sure who he was talking to.

Cassidy turned and extended his hand to the child in what appeared to be apology, and the boy threw himself into the man's arms.

"Don't do it, Noble. Maman and I need you." He leaned his poor face into Cassidy's chest and began to weep tears that would soften the heart of any man, and Orlando Powers was not immune.

"Gus, shh, now." Cassidy wrapped his arms around the boy and kissed his brow.

The woman stood abruptly and gently peeled the boy from the arms of the outlaw. Her face was devoid of all emotion, but her breath was short and her hands trembled, and her stoicism moved him even more than the boy's tears.

"It will be easier for everyone if we wait elsewhere," she said, and her voice was as cultured and lovely as her face.

"You're Jane Toussaint," Powers blurted. "We—my wife and I—have been anticipating your performance at Saltair."

She nodded, acknowledging him, but led the boy through the door and out into the street. The temple grounds were open to all, and she headed for the grassy, tree-lined walkways across the thoroughfare. Cassidy watched them until they were out of sight.

"I thought you were gone for good, Butch. I hoped you were."

"I've kept my hands clean for a long time, but some stains don't ever go away. And now . . . I've gotten her in trouble too, and I can't allow that to happen."

"I saw the papers. They don't seem to know much. But your picture, along with the English lord, is making headlines. Mrs. Toussaint is mentioned, although peripherally. She has some family connection to the man?"

"He was related to her late husband."

"And he was murdered at a New York hotel—the Plaza—last week."

"Yes. He was."

"What exactly are you confessing to, Mr. Cassidy? And what is it you expect to accomplish? Your last attempt at turning yourself in didn't go so well."

"This story is long and complicated, Judge, but if you've got time, I believe I can explain it."

As succinctly as possible, Butch told him the story of meeting Jane Toussaint six years earlier and then running into her again on a Paris street. He kept to the truth as closely as he could until he got to the murder itself. Then he lied.

"He found out who I was. Tried to blackmail me. I just wanted to scare him, but things got outta hand. I left outta there and hightailed it here, fast as I could."

"Why did you come here?"

"I didn't want to turn myself in in New York City. I wanted it on my terms. I wanted to make sure I was looking out for her. I think she can salvage her performances at the Saltair. I'm hoping she won't lose everything she's worked for because of him. And because of me."

"You killed him."

"Yessir."

Orlando Powers had represented a lot of bad men in his life. Heard a lot of twisted explanations and poor excuses. Butch Cassidy had always owned up to every one of his sins, but he wasn't a killer, and he wasn't a stupid man. Going to the Plaza to confront the Earl of Werthog was not his style, no matter the circumstances.

"I think you're lying to me, Cassidy, and you haven't lied to me before."

Butch sighed and looked down at the palms of his big hands as if they could help him find the truth. "Whatever I tell you, you can't disclose. And whatever plea I give, you have to allow."

"That's right. But I don't have to defend you."

"I don't need to be defended, Judge. I just need to make sure my wife—and it would probably be better if we didn't refer to her as my wife—and Augustus aren't dragged down with me. I shoulda stayed far away from her. Far away. But I couldn't. I loved that woman on sight, and there isn't anything I wouldn't do to take away her suffering or make her path easier. And I thought I could do it. Instead . . . everything that could go wrong has gone wrong, and she and Augustus are now casualties of my choices. I can bear anything, Judge. I want no concessions. No leniency. No trial. I'll plead guilty to everything—all the charges, outstanding warrants, everything."

"And murder? You're claiming that too?"

"I'm claiming that too. I want the Pinks to leave her the hell alone."

"You'll hang."

"No doubt I will. But she won't get dragged through the dirt in the process. That's my only request. Her name is kept out of it. Bring in the sheriff. Notify Robert Pinkerton himself. Bring in the governor and Edward Harriman if you like. I'll plead to everything I've ever done and everything they want to pin on me. Case closed."

"So why do you need me?"

"Like I said, I want her kept out of it. You keep her in the clear. She's in Utah to sing at the Saltair. No connection to me. After that, she decides."

"I see."

"She'll be free, not just of him, but of Butch Cassidy too. She worried once that she was a millstone around my neck. But I won't be one around hers."

Orlando Powers nodded and sat back in his chair. A suspicion was niggling. Call it a hunch or just plain old experience.

"Where's your brother?"

"Which one?"

"Van. Van Campbell Parker. He wouldn't happen to have anything to do with this mess, would he? This has his stink all over it."

Butch said nothing, but it was enough to make the judge throw down his pencil and let off a stream of blue curses that surprised even Butch, who'd heard the foulest of the foul.

"Tell me this, Mr. Parker. Why doesn't *he* sacrifice himself for a change?"

"His confession doesn't clear *my* record or solve my problems. My cover is blown. I can't be with my wife anymore. Either we run for the rest of our lives—not good for the boy or the woman—or I turn myself in and clear the slate. It all goes away if I go away."

"Where is your brother now?"

"That is not your concern, Judge."

"You're still trying to save him, after all these years."

"I know it doesn't seem that way, but I think he's been trying just as hard to save me."

Orlando Powers snorted. "And Harry Longabaugh. How does he play into it? He was in the papers too."

"He doesn't play into it. Not at all. I got him into this mess, and I'd appreciate if you would leave him out of it."

"It'll be the scoop of the century. Butch Cassidy turns himself in, confesses all."

"I'm thinking you know a reporter at the *Deseret News* who can tell the story just like that."

He sighed. "In the meantime, you'll be hanging from a noose for something you didn't do."

"I may not have pulled the trigger," Butch admitted. "But it was my fault."

"And what about her?" Orlando motioned toward the window and the woman and boy who were so clearly devastated by Butch Cassidy's presence in his office. "What about them?"

"She needs to sing again, Judge. She needs to get on that stage right away, like she has nothing to hide, because she doesn't. You'll go with her, make sure she's got legal backup when she negotiates. After Saltair, she needs to go back east. She has a place to stay in Jersey. Emma Harvey, Harry Longabaugh's sister, will be glad to have them back. Jane's got money. I made sure of that, and she can make more. I hope she'll resume her tour, and maybe Gus can go to school. He wants to. He needs to. They'll be all right. They'll have a good life. A safe life."

"A life without you."

"A life without me."

∽

"Mrs. Harriman said Augustus and I could stay with them," Maman said. She was composed, but she'd been unable to look at Noble since they'd reentered the lawyer's office. "She gave me her address on the train."

The man named Powers with the great, drooping eyes and thinning hair had balked at that. "Harriman?"

"Yes. They have always been kind to us, and it will be a great comfort to Augustus. We will stay there until other arrangements can be made."

Powers folded his arms and paced for all of ten seconds. "It's not a bad strategy if you think you'll be welcome. A friendship with the Harrimans will help you . . . and it might help him." He pointed at Noble.

Maman stared at a spot above Noble's head. "It's decided then."

"I'll . . . hail a hansom cab." Orlando Powers paused. "And if you're not here when I get back, Mr. Cassidy, your secret's safe with me. You left before. You can leave again."

Noble simply shook his head. "I'll be here, Mr. Powers. But allow us a minute."

Mr. Powers nodded. "I'll wait for you outside, Mrs. Toussaint."

Maman did not move, and for a moment Noble hesitated, as if he didn't know what to do. Then he strode across the room and swept her into his arms. Augustus could not bear to watch, and he pressed his hands over his ears and closed his eyes, but he could still hear, and he could still feel, and it was terrible.

"You are going to get back on that stage," Noble demanded. "And you're going to take back the life that was stolen from you."

"I want this life. I want our life. I want you." Maman was crying so hard, Augustus didn't recognize her voice, and he opened his eyes to make sure she had not become someone else.

Noble's arms were bands around her, his face pressed to her neck, praying words into her ears.

"Jane. Honey. Jane. I've got to do this. Help me do this."

"I won't. I won't let you," she cried, and Augustus cried with her.

"Gus told me once that you loved him too well. That some love doesn't make us strong. But it's made you strong. You're going to be just fine, honey. You're Jane Boot, and you've beat all the odds."

"I don't want to be fine. I want to be with you."

"Somehow I found you, Jane, and I got to love you for a little while. I'm the luckiest son of a bitch who ever lived."

"It isn't fair," she gasped, clinging to him, coaxing him to find another solution. "I have never asked for anything of this life. I have simply borne it. I have borne it, Noble Salt, but I will not bear the loss of you. Please don't make me. Please stay with us. We will run together."

"Look at me, honey. Look at me. I've tried that life. Running doesn't work. Life is faster than we are. Always. And you both deserve better. Take Augustus. Hold his hand and smile, the way you do. Give him the spine he's always gotten from you. Don't look back."

"They will kill you."

"They can't kill Noble Salt. He only existed for you. He's yours."

She buried her face in his chest and screamed, muffling the sound in his shirt and the circle of his arms.

"Think about Augustus. Think about Augustus," he said, almost chanting the words. "Just like you've always done. You can do anything if you think about Augustus. Come on, honey. Say his name."

She screamed again, balling her hands into fists.

"Go now," he demanded, and gave her a little push. But she dug her hands into his cheeks, as if she could make a plaster of his face, an imprint of his features.

"Promise me you will come back to us. That you will do everything you can," she ordered. "Give me that. Give me some hope, damn you."

"I'll do everything I can," he promised.

"And promise me you will live."

"I can't."

"Promise me," she ground out, so angry and so heartbroken she could hardly say the words.

"I can promise you one thing, I will spend my last breath saying your name, and my last thoughts will be of you. And if there's a heaven, somewhere, we'll be together again. Nothing could keep me away."

"You're a liar," she panted. "You're a liar. And I wish I'd never met you, Noble Salt."

She wrenched herself free and swiped at her face, and Noble let her go. Then she took Augustus by the hand and squared her shoulders.

Augustus pulled away from her and threw himself into Noble's arms, horrified by his mother's parting words. Noble rubbed his bristly face across Gus's cheek and kissed his brow with tear-streaked lips.

"I love you, Noble."

"I love you too, Gus. So much."

"I want to stay with you," he moaned. "Why can't we stay with you?"

"You've got everything you need. You and your mother are strong. It'll be a fresh start. And the money . . . it's there. Just waiting for you. It's got Jane's name on it and yours too. Jakob will help you."

"What if he doesn't remember me?"

Noble smiled through his tears and clasped Gus's face between palms that felt more like home than anything Augustus had ever known.

"You're unforgettable, kid. Nobody's ever going to forget your face. That's a blessing in disguise. Let it keep you honest. Let it keep you good. Live in a way you can hold your head up high, because people will remember you."

"M-Maman is so mad at you. I'm sorry."

"I know, Gus. It's okay."

"It's all my fault."

"None of this is your fault."

"But Mrs. Harriman saw me on the train. I should have stayed hidden like you told me to."

"I was wrong. I don't ever want you to hide, Augustus Toussaint. Not ever, do you understand? Not like me."

Maman reached for his hand once more. Her fingers were like ice, small and sharp and brittle, and she spoke in French, shutting Noble out in the only way she had left. She was Madame Toussaint again.

"Viens avec moi, Augustus," she said.

He shook her off, and she opened the door, demanding he follow.

"If you come back, she'll forgive you, Noble. I know she will."

"It's okay if she doesn't. It's probably better if she doesn't."

It was exactly what he'd said the day they spent in the city.

"I love your mother."

"I think she loves you too, though it's hard to tell."

"It's okay if she doesn't. It's probably better if she doesn't."

Augustus hadn't understood then. He thought maybe he understood now, considering how angry Maman was. How hurt.

"Noble?"

"You gotta go now, Gus. The hansom cab is here."

"I want you to be with us, Noble," he said in a rush, making one last desperate plea, but he stopped at the almost imperceptible shake of Noble's head.

For as long as he lived, Gus would never forget the look on the outlaw's face. It was a mask of devastation, devotion, and resignation. He was saying goodbye, and there was no hope in his eyes. No faith or fight whatsoever.

And all at once, Augustus understood his mother's rage.

"I want you to be with us," he repeated, and this time his voice didn't shake and he wasn't pleading. He was drawing a line. "I want that more than anything. And I know Maman does too. But . . . but . . . don't come back to us if you can't stay. Don't come back if you . . . won't . . . stay."

The devastation became desolation, and Noble nodded once, accepting his terms.

Augustus turned then, and without looking back, caught up with his mother and took her arm—not like a child, but like a man—and he helped her into the carriage that awaited them.

28

I too have felt the
Captive void of noble rage
Love has set me free

Butch signed everything he was asked to sign, including a confession to the death of Lord Ashley Toussaint, which Orlando Powers carefully edited.

Powers, Sheriff Frank Embrey, a Pinkerton out of the Denver office named Blevins, and the new governor—a man named Cutler—were the only men in attendance, and they all left the hearing a little deflated.

Butch didn't argue. He didn't explain. He let Powers talk, but in the end he was so agreeable there wasn't much to quibble about.

Powers didn't want him to hang, and he kept trying to negotiate life in prison instead of a death sentence, but Butch shut that down too when it prolonged the inquiry.

"I'm happy to hang. I'd prefer it," Butch said, and Orlando Powers threw up his hands.

The only thing Butch insisted on was that Jane Toussaint was absolved of all speculation and involvement.

"She had nothing to do with my actions past or present," he said. "She hired me, not knowing any better, and I just wanted to come home. Unfortunately, my past caught up with me. Werthog found out who I was, I wanted to shut him up, and that's all. She was an innocent bystander. I'd like to leave it at that."

Thankfully, no one seemed intent on bringing her down. An affidavit was sent to British authorities in the matter of Lord Ashley Charles Toussaint, and there was very little outrage on his behalf. His mother was deceased. He had no wife, no children, and no loyal friends. He'd been powerful in life because he was titled and he was rich, but no one seemed to care one cent about his death. Even his allegations that Jane was wanted in France for questioning quietly dissolved the moment he was gone.

Butch was remanded to the Utah State Pen, a castle-like fortress on the eastern bench overlooking the Salt Lake Valley. For the next month, Orlando Powers continued to sue for leniency behind closed doors. The Pinks thought he should hang, Governor Cutler was oddly ambivalent—Harriman had even declined to comment—and Sheriff Embrey was up for reelection in November. He wanted to see how a Butch Cassidy execution would poll.

The guard crouched down beside him, waking him from a dream where Jane rode Betty to victory against a dozen Navajo ponies in McElmo Gulch, but when she tried to collect her winnings, Tom McCarty shot her dead.

"You don't know me, Mr. Cassidy," he said. He hung a lantern by the door.

"Should I?" Butch asked, rubbing the bad sleep from his eyes.

"Nah. I was just a kid when I met you. It's been fifteen years at least."

Butch frowned.

"You paid off my mother's house and the land it was on. Little town called Cortez. I haven't been back for years. I married a Mormon girl. She likes it here."

"A kid from Cortez. And you became a lawman?"

"Just like my dad. Yep."

"Your dad? Did I know him?"

"My dad was Connie Clark. He was the sheriff in Cortez. That's my name too."

"Connie Clark," Butch whispered. "I'll be damned."

The man started to remove the shackles.

"You can't let me go," Butch protested, panicked.

"I'm not letting you go. You're going to escape."

"That's decent of you. And I appreciate it. But I made a deal, and well, I need to keep up my end of it."

"I've heard so many stories about you. You never killed a man, so I'm wondering why you killed the English fella. Wondering if there's a whole lot more to the story than any of us know. I also heard that when they brought you to the pen in Laramie in '94, the deputy said he didn't even have to cuff you. You told him you wouldn't run, and you didn't."

"And I won't now."

"You're worried about your lady. The singer. She was in the papers, and you know there aren't any secrets in the sheriff's office."

Butch didn't answer.

"They're going to hang you. We just got word. What's that going to do to her?"

Butch's chin hit his chest.

"The thing is . . . you confessed. Case closed. Oh, they'll hunt you. Marshals and Pinks both. You'll still be a wanted man. You'll have to leave like you did before. The stories are true, aren't they? You've been in South America all this time? You and the Sundance Kid?"

Butch nodded, but he couldn't keep up. He'd kept a tight rein on his emotions, his eyes on his purpose, but it'd taken a toll on him in the last month. He was locked down so tight, he couldn't process what was happening or even what Connie Clark—Connie Clark Jr.—was saying to him.

"You can't be with her. I'm sorry for that. But if you stay away from her, she'll be just fine, her boy too. Just like my mother and I were fine—because of you—when we lost my dad."

Connie Clark tossed the shackles aside and set a pouch with all of Butch's belongings—clothes, hat, money, watch, and wedding ring—next to him.

"Get dressed. Walk outta here. Turn left when you leave the cell and take every left until you reach the exit door. Then keep walking. Nobody's going to stop you." And without a backward glance, he left the cell unlocked.

⁂

The house in San Francisco where Sundance had last seen Ethel in an upstairs room no longer existed. The entire street of pastel homes all in a pretty row had been reduced to rubble. Sundance and Van dug much of the day, looking for something that had belonged to her. But the wreckage was a year old, and scavengers had picked the area clean.

A man stopped to watch them and after a moment asked him who they were looking for.

"A woman named Ethel Place," Van said. "Lived upstairs there, in this boarding house."

"I remember Ethel. Beautiful girl. Nice voice too. Taught some of the kids music lessons."

"Do you know where she went?" Van pressed. "After the earthquake, I mean. I don't imagine she stayed in the city."

The man rocked back on his feet and shoved his hands into his pockets. "Are you Mr. Place? She always told us you would come back."

Van shook his head and pointed at Harry. "Ethel was waiting for him."

"I'm sorry, Mr. Place," the man said. "Ethel's gone. Most everyone who lived here died."

"Gone where? You mean dead?" Van cried, but Harry just nodded. He'd known, but it was odd how the confirmation made him feel a thousand years old. Any minute he would disintegrate. He thanked the man with dusty lips, and left the rubble and the last of his hope behind.

"What do you want to do now, Harry?" Van asked, walking a few steps behind him. They'd spent a month getting to San Francisco. They'd been in no hurry. When Butch turned himself in, everyone had stopped looking for Sundance. They'd meandered through a few old haunts and even stopped in Circleville to see Max Parker, who'd been overjoyed over the return of one son and devastated by the fate of another.

"Do you think they'd let me see him?" Max had asked. "I want to see him." But then the news broke that Butch had escaped, and Sundance and Van hit the road.

"I want to get a postcard for Gus," Van said. "One of the bridge. I'll send it to Emma. But I won't sign it."

When Sundance didn't respond, Van tried again.

"We could find out where she's buried. Maybe put some flowers on the grave."

"No."

"No?"

"No, Van. I don't want to see her grave. I want out of this city. I don't ever want to see it again. The first ship out of here . . . I'm on it. And I'm not coming back. You can come or you can stay. Don't matter to me."

"But . . . Butch might come here looking for us. Now that he's out."

"Butch isn't going to look for us, Van. He's spent his whole life trying to shake you off. But I guarantee the Pinks and the marshals are looking for him."

"He'll go south again. Don't you think?"

Sundance sighed. "It's the only place he can go."

"Then I'll come with you. I found him before, I can find him again."

᪆

Jane could not leave Salt Lake City. Instead she agreed to sing at the Saltair once a week in their open season—Memorial Day to Labor Day—and give a concert on New Year's Eve.

"I don't want to tour anymore," she told Orlando Powers. "I want peace. I want to raise my son in peace."

When the Harrimans went back to New York City, Mr. Powers helped them find a house not far from his own. It had rosebushes and cottonwood trees and a backyard big enough for a dog. So they got one of those too.

They didn't speak of Noble. Or Butch. Or Robert LeRoy Parker, though it was not anger or fear that kept his names from her lips. It was love, and grief, and longing.

News of his escape had buffeted them both with hope and worn them out with waiting. He did not send word.

He didn't send letters.

Wherever he'd gone, he wasn't coming back. He had honored Augustus's request.

"He is too recognizable now," Jane said. "At least in America. His face has been plastered in every public space. You know he won't come near us."

"He loved us, didn't he, Maman?" Augustus asked, needing to be reassured.

"Yes. He did. He . . . does." Her hurt had given way to grief, and grief was so much kinder. So much softer.

"'Better to have loved and lost than never to have loved at all,'" Augustus quoted. His teacher had read them Tennyson's poem at school, and Jane had been stricken by the line that bore her beloved's name. *The captive void of noble rage. The linnet born within the cage.*

She had felt noble rage. Noble denial. Noble grief and noble forgiveness. She was the linnet born in the cage, and it was time to let herself go.

Augustus received several postcards via Emma, but they weren't from Noble. They had no words on them, only pictures. Drawings of little things. Birds. Tarantulas, lizards, and snakes. The picture of the jackrabbit wearing a derby hat was his favorite. It was Van's way of letting them know they were well, and Augustus hung them on his wall.

The only letter they received was from Robert Pinkerton himself. His agency had been hired to find Mrs. Jane Toussaint and her son, Augustus Maximilian Toussaint. It was an easy job, since they'd monitored her every move since she'd settled in the Salt Lake Valley. She even recognized the lead detective and greeted him by name whenever she saw him.

The letter forwarded from Robert Pinkerton was from the barrister of Oliver's estate. Ashley Charles Toussaint, tenth earl of Werthog, had died without an heir. As the only male relation in the line, Mr. Oliver Toussaint's son, Augustus Maximilian Toussaint, would inherit the title and holdings of the Earl of Werthog.

Orlando Powers made inquiries, and it was decidedly so.

"You are an earl, Augustus," Jane informed him. "The only remaining Toussaint in the line. How is that for poetic justice?"

"I'm an American boy now. I don't want to be an earl," Augustus said, though she suspected the idea intrigued him. "I don't want to be anything like Lord Ashley."

"It is just a title. You choose whether or not it is a blessing. You choose what kind of man you want to be."

"Would we have to live in Lord Ashley's house?"

"He had several houses. Even a house in Paris. I suppose we could live anywhere we like. But there would be responsibilities, I'm sure."

"Would you like to live in London again, Maman?"

She laughed at that. "I have not lived in London since I was your age, and I'm guessing it would feel like a different world. Jane Boot, dowager," she said, scoffing.

"Noble said you beat all the odds."

She smiled at him then, and her eyes grew soft. "I suppose I have."

"I'd rather wait for Noble," he confessed. "And live in Salt Lake City."

"There is time yet to make a decision. I will ask Mr. Powers to represent us in the particulars."

"He will not come back to us here," Augustus worried.

"He will not come back to us there either. But it is love that keeps him away. I am sure of that too."

"But, Maman . . . no one knows Butch Cassidy in London. No one knows us. London is a long way from the Wild West. It's a very long way from here."

"It is not far enough."

⁂

"Van?" Sundance groaned.

"Yeah?"

"You got a bullet left?"

The click of the chamber being checked and closed was too loud in the blood-soaked room. They'd been foolish and desperate and didn't have a good plan. Butch had always been the one to plan. Being the boss was harder than it looked.

"Yeah. I've got one," Van said. "How 'bout you?"

"I've got one too. And I'm not wasting it."

Van wasn't sure what that meant.

"I'm dying, Van. But damn if it ain't too slow."

"I'm not dying," Van whimpered. "I wish I was. Got a hole in my arm as big as my fist."

"I've got a few of 'em."

"Is this how you thought it would end, Harry?"

"Yeah. Pretty much. I'm not sorry, though. Just wish it'd come already. I'm ready."

"My dad said hell is what we make of our lives. What we put ourselves through . . . what we put other people through. Did we put people through hell, Sundance?"

"I did. No doubt about it."

"Yeah. Me too," Van whispered, close to tears.

"We aren't going to make it out of here, Van. Neither of us. You know that . . . don't you?"

"I ain't done yet, Harry. I'm not dying."

"You know all those federales out there think you're Butch Cassidy."

Van laughed, a watery hiccup that sounded more like a sob. "Butch Cassidy never dies."

"It'd be a blessing if he did."

"What are you talking about?" Van shot back, angry. "My brother is the best man I know."

"He's the best man I know too, Van."

"I don't understand you, Harry."

A pained sigh, a grunt, an attempt at repositioning himself on the bench beside the door.

"If you die, Van, they'll think they got him, and they'll stop looking for him."

"Who?"

"Butch Cassidy. They'll think they finally got Butch Cassidy and the Sundance Kid. It'll be over."

"But . . . what about me? What about Van Parker? What about Rip Van Winkle?"

"The world has changed, Van. There isn't a place for us anymore. Maybe there never was."

"I got nothing to show for my life," Van whispered. "Nobody will miss me. Nobody will remember me. Butch was always trying to shake me off. Always leaving me behind. I just wanted to be with him. I just wanted to be like him. And I wasn't. I wasn't brave. And I wasn't good. People didn't like me."

"He was a hard man to live up to."

"Yeah. A big, fat, noble pain in the ass."

Sundance groaned. The pain kept him from drifting off, and Van was glad. God, help him. He was glad. He wasn't ready for Sundance to go. He wasn't ready yet.

"He wasn't trying to shake you off, Van," Harry muttered.

"Yes, he was."

"He was trying to save you from this."

Van sobbed softly. "I don't know if I can do it, Sundance."

Silence was the only answer, and Van cried harder, but he inched along the dirty floor below the beams of sunlight that were clawing at the cracks.

"Harry?"

Harry's eyes were closed and his hands were folded over his middle, but breath still hissed in his throat.

"Harry?"

"You know . . . Ethel told me she'd wait. I'm hoping that's true. I'm ready to see her again."

"Not yet, Harry. Not yet," Van moaned.

"Help me, Van. This shit is taking too long. You'd be doing me a kindness."

"I can't."

"It's easy. You killed Werthog without a thought. Easiest thing in the whole world. But I can't make my hands work anymore. I need you to do it."

"I can't."

"You can. You have to. Help me, Van."

"Please, Sundance. I don't want to be alone."

"Then come with me, Rip Van Winkle. And give your brother a new life. Be the hero for a change."

Van wiped at his eyes and rose until he was seated by his friend. Maybe they'd see his shadow and take him out, and he wouldn't have to do what Sundance was asking. But no shots came.

"That's it," Sundance breathed. "Thank you, Van."

"You ain't afraid?"

"It can't be worse than this. Might even be a whole lot better."

Van unwrapped the gun from Harry's limp hand, and aimed it at his brow. It shook so bad, he put it down again.

"Set it up against my head," Sundance directed. "I don't want you to miss." Van gritted his teeth and did as he was asked.

"Now close your eyes, and pull. I'll be waitin' for you."

"I can't."

"Pull it!" Sundance demanded, his roar almost otherworldly, and Van obeyed, screaming his sorrow and regret.

Van didn't open his eyes again. He couldn't. His ears were ringing and his hands shook with the recoil. Dropping the gun, he turned and crawled away, ramming his head into the adobe walls until he found the opening into the other little room, his pistol dragging from his weary gun belt. He hoped it'd go off and save him from himself. But he'd never been a lucky man.

He crouched in the corner of the other room, his hearing slowly returning. He could hear voices outside. The cavalry had heard the single shot and come to see if it was over.

He knew it was.

"It'll never be over. That shit'll go down in history," he mumbled, wiping at his dripping nose. His hand came away wet, and he gasped at the red streaks on his hand. The blood wasn't his.

"Damn you, Sundance," he moaned. "Look what you made me do."

But he *had* done it. And he could do it again. Easy.

He studied the Colt .45 with the nickel barrel and the black handle, the one just like his brother's. Just one bullet left. One bullet for Butch Cassidy.

He took the little notebook Augustus had given him from inside his shirt and scratched a verse on the front page.

"Well, look at that. I finally did it, Gus," he marveled, counting the syllables. "And I wasn't even trying."

I'm Butch Cassidy
Luckiest son of a bitch
In the whole wide world

He didn't know if the federales would read it. They didn't speak English. But the Pink that'd been trailing them for the last few months would. It would be enough.

"Don't say I never did nothin' for you, brother," he said. For the first time in his life, he felt noble. And he liked how it felt.

Then Van Campbell Parker pulled the trigger, killing two outlaw brothers with a single shot.

29

If I look back now
I'll surely turn to salt, Lord
Keep my gaze forward

Butch had enough money to buy a horse and enough experience to disappear. When Governor William Richards pardoned him on January 19, 1896, he'd been asked to go straight and leave Wyoming forever. He hadn't made that promise—and said point-blank he couldn't—but he'd been let out anyway. He'd been all over the state and knew the Hole-in-the-Wall in Johnson County better than the valley he'd been born in. But he didn't go that far. He had no desire to haunt the outlaw trail or resume his old life.

He'd buried a bag of gold coins in '89 near Horse Creek. It was still there, near a stump seared in two by lightning, and so was the old trapper's cabin that gave him a place to hole up for the rest of the summer while he tried to make a plan.

His old friend Margaret Simpson, she of the tinctures and tonics, lived in the area. He would have liked to know how she fared. She'd been good to him once, and he'd tried to be good to her, but he had no wish to bring trouble to her door. He ended up sleeping in the undulating grass with his bag of gold, certain that any moment a posse would turn up and haul him away.

He wrote verses to Jane and Augustus and dated them in his book, but he never sent them. That would be cruel. Better to let them move on than be bound to a ghost. He posted a letter to Orlando Powers, asking after their welfare. He didn't dare send a letter to Emma. He reckoned her mail had been monitored since he and Sundance had left in '01. He'd signed it Matt Warner, and knew Powers would understand who was asking.

Orlando posted a letter back, care of the General Store in Lander where the whole town sent and received their mail. The letter Butch got back was two pages long and filled to the brim with miracles.

Jane and Gus had stayed in Salt Lake City. They lived in a little house with a big front porch and rosebushes lining the walk. Gus was going to school.

The Harrimans visited when they could and were very protective of Jane and Augustus, even Edward, whose health had slowed him down considerably. Maybe that was why he'd abandoned his obsession with a washed-up outlaw.

Gus had adopted a dog, the ugliest, shaggiest excuse for a canine Orlando had ever seen, but they called her Nana, and she seemed to be well named.

Jane had not resumed her tour, but she'd performed several times at Saltair, drawing crowds from far and wide.

Butch attended one of her performances about a year after his escape. After they'd shaved his head at the pen, his hair had grown in slate gray, and he wore the clothes of an old man, lurking at the back with a cane and a pair of dark spectacles to hide his blue eyes.

He wasn't trying to get caught—he'd promised Jane he would do his best to stay alive—but to hear her sing had pumped life back into his veins.

He couldn't go back to her. Connie Clark was right about that. But he had managed to clear her name and restore her peace, and that was enough for him.

Butch Cassidy sightings frequently made the front page, but after a while the interest faded with no crimes to fuel the search, and life—and a half-hearted manhunt—had gone on.

Last but not least, Augustus Maximilian Toussaint was an earl. Butch had laughed and cried about that for days, but they did not leave Salt Lake for the greener pastures of England. He feared they were waiting for him and didn't know how to tell them to go, without giving them all the more reason to stay.

The papers called Butch Cassidy an old has-been, a relic of another era. One article said he'd gone back to South America with Sundance, and soon that seemed to be the consensus. His picture still hung in train stations and post offices and at the general store, but people stopped looking at those things after a while. He kept to himself, let his hair and his beard grow until he looked like a prospector, and after those first few months in the Wind Rivers, he was always on the move.

His pain was sharp, and it lanced him daily, but it was sweet too, because it was real. The realest thing he'd ever known. He marveled that it had happened at all, that for a brief, blissful window of time, he had loved so completely and been loved in return. Those memories sustained him more than anything else ever had.

November 1908

At half past seven, Butch unfolded the newspaper carefully, just like he did every morning, organizing the sections into most favorite and least favorite. He liked the early-morning crowd in the cafés, though he never went to the same place twice, no matter how much he liked it.

He found a glowing review of Jane's performance at Saltair at the top of the Society section. For a boy who'd grown up where high society was only talked about in books, the page had always fascinated him.

Every article centered around parties, places, and people who seemed to live in a wholly different world.

The Society page didn't talk about crops that were destroyed or matters of church and state. The only horses they mentioned were as highly bred as they were, with lineage extending back to Washington and King Louis. It made him laugh and think about Betty. Maybe there was a hidden nobility somewhere in her ancestry, or maybe the little mare just didn't know she wasn't supposed to win.

The comparisons of his Jane to Jenny Lind were typical, though the writer of this particular article preferred Jane Toussaint and her "less theatrical style."

Butch's favorite paragraph was this: "Having heard Miss Toussaint many years ago at Carnegie Hall, I find her truly remarkable voice has become only more impressive with time, but it was the deep feeling and musical expression in her performance that was the most notable improvement. The little songbird has become a soprano of the first water, and her rendition of 'Waly, Waly' brought this critic to tears."

She had always brought him to tears. From the very first. *O waly, waly.*

He read it several times, so proud his eyes grew wet, and then put the paper down so he could blow his nose and enjoy it again. The paper was a few days old and someone had dropped a dollop of jelly on one of the pages. He carefully tore the article out, using his thumbnail to score the paper. He didn't know what he'd do with it, but he wasn't ready to let it go. He folded it into fourths and slid it between the pages of his notebook.

A few coins were enough to cover his breakfast and the paper, though it'd been perused by more eyes than his, but he left extra for the old-timer who'd brought him his plate and refilled his coffee. Then he stood to leave, eyes scanning the table to make sure he hadn't left anything behind.

The hole he'd made in the paper framed a headline all in caps:

AMERICAN OUTLAWS KILLED IN BOLIVIAN SHOOT-OUT

He flipped the page and sank back down to his seat, reading the words as though he dreamed and floated above himself.

San Vicente—Bolivian authorities near San Vicente are reporting that on November 6, 1908, they engaged in a shoot-out with two men thought to be famed outlaws Butch Cassidy, born Robert LeRoy Parker, and Harry Alonzo Longabaugh, also known as the Sundance Kid.

The fugitives are believed to be responsible for the armed robbery of a mining company's payroll courier and were seen in possession of the courier's mule. Local authorities contacted a small unit of the Bolivian cavalry stationed nearby, who rapidly moved in and surrounded the adobe hut where the two men were staying. Sustained gunfire was exchanged, but after a period of quiet and repeated demands for surrender, authorities moved in and found the two men deceased.

Harry Longabaugh sustained several bullet wounds in his arms and one to his head. Butch Cassidy was found in the adjoining room, dead from a shot to his temple, a revolver still in his hand. The wound was believed to be self-inflicted.

The Pinkerton National Detective Agency had been tracking the two wanted men, charged with a decade's worth of bank holdups and train robberies throughout the West, for many years.

A recent tip convinced Pinkerton agents to distribute

347

the outlaws' photos and criminal histories throughout Bolivia. Officials are convinced they have successfully brought two armed and dangerous men to justice. Pinkerton president Robert Pinkerton issued this statement with the agency's report:

"Cassidy was the shrewdest, most daring outlaw of the present age, and I am relieved to have this era brought to an end. These were not good men. They were not heroes. They plundered, terrorized, and killed, and this country, and every other country, will be better off now that they are gone. They will not be mourned."

Butch stood, crumpling the paper to his chest so he wouldn't have to read it again. His chair clattered behind him, and when he moved away from the table, his vision blurred and swam, making him trip and fall to his knees.

"You okay, mister?"

"He's drunk and it's not even nine o'clock," someone grumbled. "Get him out of here."

He stood, waving off the man behind the counter and the one who rose to help him, and stumbled out into the morning light.

The world would not be
Better now that they were gone
Not better at all

The article made no mention of Van. Maybe his luck had changed, and for once he was the man left standing, slipping away, moving on like he'd complained his brother had always done. For several days Gus nursed the wound, unable to tell his mother what he'd seen. Unable to bear her pain and his own. Then he found her crying, poring over the newspaper the way she'd once pored over the picture she'd stolen from Edward Harriman's collection. She hadn't hung it up again, though he knew she had it with her in the trunk beneath her costumes.

At the beginning of the new year, Orlando Powers came to see them, his hound dog eyes sadder than usual, his gaunt frame a little more stooped, though Augustus didn't think he was an old man.

Mr. Powers and Maman talked over tea that neither of them drank, and Augustus ate all the cakes. Nana stretched out beneath his chair and dutifully cleaned up his crumbs.

"This came from the telegraph office," Mr. Powers said. "It's addressed to me, but I'm quite certain it was intended for you. It's from Mrs. Harvey." He handed Maman a paper with the Western Union Telegraph Company banner across the page and a series of numbers with PAID beside the code.

The message was just a string of words, irregularly spaced and capitalized with no punctuation, typical of the short, clipped style of all telegrams.

RECEIVED
Via Salt Lake City UT
Manhattan NY Jan 5
Atty O Powers
S Temple Street

Rip Harry both dead Passage to London all paid By
Noble Salt Corp

Emma Harvey

Augustus stared at it, his heart quickening at the name Noble Salt. Maman read it aloud and then read it again, her voice breaking on the first four words.

"Rip Harry both dead," she said. "I wonder why Emma said it that way."

"We know what she means. Her brother is gone, may he rest in peace. Butch too. She's learned to be careful after her civil liberties were trampled." Powers sniffed, perpetually outraged by the tactics of the Pinkertons.

"Poor Emma," Maman murmured. "She was so good to us all."

"It's the rest of it that has me befuddled," Powers said, frowning. "Noble Salt Corporation is a Utah company. I'm not sure what she's trying to communicate or what passage they've paid."

"Can I keep this, Mr. Powers?" Maman asked softly.

"Of course. It's yours." He rose, pulled on his coat, and affixed his hat, but he paused at the door. The day was cold and evening was descending quickly, frigid and gray. Gus and Maman faced another Utah winter alone.

"Mrs. Toussaint . . . have you given any more thought to Augustus's inheritance? He should have it. You both should. It is so rare that I get to see true justice in my line of work. Maybe Mrs. Harvey agrees. Maybe she's telling you it's time to go home."

If Maman answered, Gus didn't hear her. Mr. Powers wished him goodbye, calling his name, and Augustus waved his hand and thanked him politely, but he didn't look up from the telegram. Something was niggling, but he hardly dared hope.

Maman came back to the table and began clearing the tea, and Nana stretched and lumbered to the fireplace.

"Maman . . . look," he whispered, reaching for her arm. She set down the saucers and did as he asked.

"It's hokku," he cried. "It's hokku, Maman. Look." He rearranged the lines on the blank space beneath Emma's name, his fingers gripping his pencil so hard the lead snapped, and he had to grab a new one. Maman was already counting syllables.

Rip Harry both dead

Passage to London all paid

By Noble Salt Corp

"Rip? Is he talking about Van?" Maman whispered. "Van and Harry are dead, but Noble is alive?"

"Yes." Gus swallowed, joy and grief warring. *Poor Van. Dear Harry.* "Yes, I think that's it."

"It can't be."

"He promised me, Maman. He promised me he wouldn't come back unless he meant to stay."

"He hasn't come back," she whispered, but her eyes were wet with wonder.

A week later, two first-class steamer tickets to Southampton arrived by post from Mr. Jakob Hurwitz.

It wasn't like the day in Cherbourg more than eighteen months prior. The sun was not shining, and the harbor was filled with chunks of ice that threatened to delay the departure, but he and Maman still stood side by side at the railing, braced against the wind, braced against disappointment, and Maman still wore a massive, impractical hat. Augustus suspected it was so Noble could find them.

"He may not come, darling," Maman said, though hope quivered in her voice and lit her eyes as she scanned every face. "He did not say he would be here. We cannot even be sure it was him. Or that he's alive. He may have simply left instructions for Mr. Hurwitz."

Emma had known nothing of the telegram or the steamship tickets, though she'd welcomed them with open arms and endless tearful questions that they could not answer. They did not dare share their hope with her nor did they discuss it much among themselves. It was too painful—and dangerous—to speculate, but privately they'd allowed themselves to believe.

Maman had let him decide, in the end, and he had chosen London.

"I think I will be a good earl, Maman," he'd announced, but it was not England that called to him or the title of a family he felt no connection to. It was the memory of Noble's face when he'd said goodbye. If there was a chance that the outlaw was alive and could come back to them, Augustus was going to give him every opportunity to do so, even if it meant leaving Nana with Orlando Powers and never seeing Salt Lake City again.

His timepiece sat open in his hand, ticking away the seconds until the big horn blew. He snapped the cover shut and pressed it to his cheek, letting it reassure him before he slid it back into his pocket.

"Augustus," Maman breathed. "Augustus, there he is."

Noble's hair and beard were as gray as the sky, and the derby hat he'd always preferred had been exchanged for the black fur cap of a Cossack, but as they watched, he raised his hand, and even from the full length of the massive deck, they could see his tears.

Augustus, not caring if the whole world stared, waved back with all the exuberance he'd once shown on the deck of the *Adriatic*, but Maman began to run. When Noble swept her up, this time in greeting and not goodbye, Augustus wasn't far behind.

Epilogue

Some say he died young
Many claim he grew quite old
No one really knows

To the world, or at least their little sliver of it, he became Noble Salt, a name chosen on a whim, and one he easily embodied. Augustus called him Dad. The few that knew him called him Mr. Salt.

Jane called him honey.

He kept the beard that just grew whiter with time, and Jane didn't mind. No one in London had ever seen Butch Cassidy before. No one recognized his Parker blue eyes or told stories about the Wild Bunch. No one talked about the outlaw trail. He was simply Mr. Salt, the young Earl of Werthog's reticent stepfather, a capable man who kept to himself.

When he wasn't sitting behind the curtain, listening to Jane perform, or walking behind Augustus as he took on the world, he lived a very quiet life. He spent a good deal of time in the stables, and the horses of Werthog became highly sought after. A Werthog horse called Sundance won the Grand National in 1913, and no one even noticed Jane Toussaint's husband, though a few people commented on her enormous hat.

Augustus grew and learned to keep his eyes steady and his shoulders back, even when people flinched or the world stared. He found that fate rewarded excellence, and he strove to do what Butch Cassidy had once counseled: *Live in a way you can hold your head up high, because people will remember you.*

Jane did not return to the stage in an official capacity. She sang for the joy of it, a few appearances a year, and more often than not, in exotic locales.

Her husband was a tumbleweed, after all.

They traveled to Egypt and Tibet, Pamplona and Rome, and even to a little mining town in Bolivia called San Vicente to say goodbye to old friends. The locals told them that the monument at Huaca Huañusca—basically a towering pile of rocks—had been built not for the gringos buried nearby, but as penance for sin. A big rock, a big sin, a little rock, a little sin.

Noble Salt, in all his inescapable guilt, had lugged two enormous rocks up the hill and placed them on the monument to the condor god whose name literally meant "the heavens."

Noble thought that fitting, and carved his brother's name into one stone and Sundance into another.

It was the only true memorial they would ever have—especially Van, who even in death had claimed his brother's name.

They traveled the world, drew little attention to themselves, and raised their son to be a remarkable man. A nobleman in truth. They rejoiced when he, too, fell in love and had children of his own, a daughter named Ethel Jane, a son named Harry Alonzo, and another named Augustus Van, a nod to the man who'd given them all a second chance. Noble called him Waly, Waly and always let him tag along.

AUTHOR'S NOTE

There was a point in writing *The Outlaw Noble Salt* where I was overcome with grief. I've written some very sad historical novels, novels about war and loss and incredible grit, so to be "struck down" by this novel, in particular, was unexpected. I thought maybe it was me—my life, my career, the crisis of faith I seem to be continually caught in—and not the book at all. Then in the midst of a heart-to-heart conversation with a friend, the thought came loud and clear: *these are Butch Cassidy's feelings, not yours.*

I understood this character in a way that might be surprising. Like Robert LeRoy Parker, I was raised in Utah in an empty valley just north of his. I have Mormon pioneers—immigrants from England just like the Parkers and the Gillieses—on my mom's side. They crossed the plains—some died from the cold before they even started—and made new lives far from home.

I am still a Mormon—sometimes a Jack Mormon, sometimes a firm believer, sometimes an apostate—and I deeply understand Robert LeRoy's restlessness and his disillusionment, even though we were born a hundred years apart. I've felt the same love for the land, the people, and the history, as well as a need to find my own way. And every time I drive through the Beaver River Valley, which is at least once a year on our family's trek to the beach in California, I am overcome. It was the valley, even more than the man, that called to me.

The love story I gave Butch Cassidy isn't true. There was no Jane Toussaint. No Augustus Maximilian. I modeled Gus after my son, Sam, who was born with the same disfigurement Gus is challenged with. It was healing to explore some of the struggles and feelings Gus and Jane dealt with, having lived them myself. I also loved the discoveries both Butch and Gus made about hiding and the burdens that can be blessings.

If Butch didn't die in Bolivia (and there's a lot of evidence he didn't), he certainly didn't die in London, stepfather to an earl. But the Butch Cassidy hunters are still alive and well, following his trail from Circleville to the Andes Mountains, spending *their* lives trying to figure out what happened in *his* life and looking for buried treasure.

Butch Cassidy was the oldest of thirteen—born on Friday the thirteenth—and he did have a younger brother named Daniel who tried to follow in his older brother's outlaw footsteps. Butch took that very seriously and ran poor Dan off a number of times. Unlike Van, Daniel figured things out, straightened up, and lived a long, full life with a family of his own. Some of Butch's siblings insist that Butch came back to his valley, and many folks believe he is buried there, though his siblings took the location to their graves. The cabin where he was raised still stands in the loneliest little spot you've ever seen.

There really was an attempt at amnesty, and many of the stories—Betty the racehorse, paying off the widow's mortgage, the Wyoming pardon, and the way Butch treated people and kept his word—are documented.

Orlando Powers represented many of Butch's outlaw friends (on Butch's behalf), and it is believed that he encouraged Butch to leave it all behind when he wanted to seek amnesty. There was respect between the two men, and Powers's role in my story felt like an honest leap.

Harry Alonzo Longabaugh was a Pennsylvania boy, the youngest of five, and all of his siblings were quite industrious in spite of deadbeat parents. Harry's brother Harvey helped build the boardwalk in Atlantic City, which gave me the idea for a Jersey connection, though Harry's sister Emma never lived there. Emma never married and managed the books for a blacksmith, but I gave her a bed-and-breakfast and borrowed her name for my Emma, who took such good care of Augustus. It was Harry's sister Samana who raised a passel of kids and kept track of all of her siblings. It was her mail that the Pinkertons often (illegally) monitored, in hopes to catch her little brother. I found it interesting that Sundance was the youngest and Butch the oldest in their families. It says interesting things about their personalities.

The Plaza Hotel in New York did not open until October of 1907, but I had it open in the summer of 1907 for the sake of my timeline. I thought it was close enough, and enjoyed including the historical landmark.

Ethel Place, aka Etta Place, is a mystery. I gave her as much true information as existed. No one knows what happened to her after Harry took her to San Francisco, but to have fallen so completely off the map, and to have been so clearly committed to Sundance, I could only imagine one ending. I hope someday we uncover more of her true story.

Robert LeRoy Parker was a fascinating character, full of the contradictions that make humans remarkable and fallible. He was good even though he did bad things. He was honest even though he was a thief. He was foolish even though he was wise. If it's possible to channel characters—and research starts to feel like channeling after a while—the overwhelming feeling I got from Butch was genuine regret. He knew he'd gotten it wrong and chased a false happiness, and like his father says in the book, there are so few second chances. My goal with this novel was to give him one. Everyone deserves a love story, even an outlaw, and I hope he (and you) liked this alternate ending to an American legend.

—*Amy Harmon*

ACKNOWLEDGMENTS

To my agent, Jane Dystel, and the team at Dystel, Goderich & Bourret. To the Lake Union team, namely Adrienne Procaccini and Jenna Free. To Sunshine Kamaloni, writer and dear friend, who checked in with me every day when the going got rough and helped me believe in my story. My continued thanks to my assistant Tamara Debbaut, who has been my right hand for most of my career, and all my gratitude to my family for sharing their wife and mother with an endless stream of literary characters. Robert LeRoy Parker, thank you for the inspiration. I hope you've found peace.

ABOUT THE AUTHOR

Amy Harmon is a *Wall Street Journal, USA Today,* and *New York Times* bestselling author. Her books have been published in more than two dozen languages around the globe. Harmon has written twenty novels, including the *USA Today* bestseller *Making Faces.* Her historical novel *From Sand and Ash* was the Whitney Award–winning Novel of the Year in 2016. Her novel *What the Wind Knows* topped the Amazon charts for thirteen weeks and was on the top 100 bestsellers chart for six months. *A Different Blue* is a *New York Times* bestseller, and her *USA Today* bestselling fantasy *The Bird and the Sword* was a Goodreads Best Book of 2016 finalist. For updates on upcoming book releases, author posts, and more, head to www.authoramyharmon.com.